Shut In

Book One of the Isolation Series

By Nathan Jones

Nathan Jones

ISBN: 9781707893508

Books by Nathan Jones

BEST LAID PLANS

Fuel

Shortage

Invasion

Reclamation

Determination

NUCLEAR WINTER

First Winter

First Spring

Chain Breakers

Going Home

Fallen City

MOUNTAIN MAN

Badlands

Homecoming

Homeland

Mountain War

Final Stand

Lone Valley (upcoming)

Nathan Jones

ISOLATION

Shut In

Going Out (upcoming)

Shut In

Table of Contents

Nathan Jones

Author's Note

The possibility of a pandemic has always been out there as a danger in the world, hovering as a possible disaster to fear, but I never really gave it much thought.

It has a terror all its own, though. Most people have the urge to give sick people, even sick loved ones, a wide berth. The idea that merely touching someone could cause an unseen pathogen to smack you down and make you miserable, even threaten your life, is an uncomfortable one. Confronted by a highly contagious, deadly disease, that sensation is magnified a thousandfold.

I've explored what could happen to our society, and the people in it, during various disasters. The chaos and violence that inevitably comes with societal collapse. I even have something similar to the fear of pandemic in some of my other series, with the fear of nuclear fallout. But terrifying as that is, at least you have some idea of where it is so you can avoid those areas.

How do you avoid an invisible danger that could be anywhere, carried by anyone around you? What do you do when faced by that threat?

Your home becomes your only refuge, and you take your life in your hands every time you step out your door.

As I launch the Isolation Series, I'd like to express my appreciation to my family for all their advice and invaluable help, and to all the readers who've supported me over the years. I made writing my lifelong goal at a young age, and have now spent more years working determinedly at it than not. To be able to support myself doing what I love is a tremendous gift, and I want to offer my sincere gratitude to all those who've made it possible.

From the bottom of my heart, thank you.

Prologue
Grounded

Josh Thurston mopped at his face with the cloth the flight attendant had given him. It was already sopping wet and probably didn't even do anything. That, or he was sweating so much that he felt it beading on his forehead and sliding down again almost immediately after.

He felt utterly humiliated, keenly aware of how the nice young woman seated next to him was leaning away in distaste, practically crawling into her husband's lap. He couldn't blame her; in spite of the deodorant he'd worn, the stink of his sweat was rank in his nostrils, and starting to permeate the rest of the plane's coach section. Not only was he distasteful, but she'd probably suspect he was sick.

If he'd been seated next to a sweaty, stinking, sickly stranger on an airplane he wouldn't have been all that happy about it either. He'd already apologized for it twice, the first time drawing a studious blank expression from the couple, as if they hadn't even been aware of it, and the second drawing mostly sincere reassurances.

Well, at least some young folks were polite enough to respect the elderly, even in a situation like this.

The thing was, Josh didn't *feel* sick. There was no achiness, or nausea, or weakness, or anything else he'd associate with being ill. And after almost seventy years of suffering his fair share of ailments, not to mention the ever-increasing discomforts of old age, he would've recognized anything like that.

No, what he really felt like was the flight attendants had turned the blasted temperature in the cabin way too low. He'd bundled up in preparation for that, of course, but even so he still felt like he was freezing. The only thing the extra layers seemed to do was make him pour sweat.

He should've asked for a blanket, but to be honest he hadn't wanted to get it all filthy like the sweat-soaked cloth. Which was silly, since he was sure the airline's staff would wash it before reusing it anyway.

Josh mopped at his face again, then froze when he saw that the sodden cloth he held was tinged pink. What the blazes?

He dabbed again, carefully, with just one corner, beneath his eyes. When he pulled the cloth away it was tinged a deeper, more ominous red. A sudden surge of soaring dizziness washed over him, one he wasn't sure was due to his shock at the implications of what he was seeing or some aspect of his sickness.

He tried to push to his feet, intending to go to the bathroom and see if they had a mirror he could check. His strength failed him and he sagged back into his seat, worry turning into alarm.

Then he felt his nose begin to run, gradually joined by an unpleasant liquid sensation in his ears. When he dabbed beneath his nose with his cloth it came away definitely bloody. He choked on sudden dread, and flecks of bloody spittle sprayed the chair in front of him.

Josh stared at the crimson dots in blank shock, horrible realization dawning. This wasn't some simple cold or flu, or if it was it was an incredibly serious one. He might even be dying.

He took a breath, fighting the soaring dizziness. "May, was it, dear?" he asked quietly. The nice young woman beside him jumped slightly in surprise and turned to give him a questioning look. He started to ask her to go alert the flight attendant that he needed a doctor, but the moment she saw him she screamed.

It wasn't some simple gasp or yelp, either, but a full on horror movie being murdered by a masked madman sort of scream. What did he look like?

May scrambled backwards into her husband's lap as he also screamed, the two of them collapsing back into the opposite aisle as they stared at him. Other passengers were now staring at him too, many gasping or yelling themselves.

Josh noticed movement to his left, from the other aisle, as a flight attendant hurried up to him, only to freeze a safe distance away and stare at him with an expression of horror and disgust.

"Ma'am," he said as loudly as he could over the commotion around him. "I believe I need a doctor."

The next few minutes were a blur of attendants calling over the intercom for any doctors or nurses aboard, nearby passengers vacating their seats and clogging the aisles to get away from him for a few rows. At Josh's polite insistence someone threw him a hand mirror, allowing him to see what had so frightened May and the others.

In retrospect it might've been a mistake, because the sight terrified him as well.

He appeared to be bleeding from his eyes, nose, ears, and mouth. It was possible he was even bleeding a bit through his pores. His face was a damp, ashen mask of blood and sweat, haggard as death itself, gray hair plastered to his head and tinged pink.

What kind of sickness could do this?

A professionally dressed woman was ushered back from first class. Josh couldn't help but notice she was wearing a face mask and gloves as she hurried over to him. "Mr. Thurston, I'm Dr. Coleson. I'm going to check your vitals and see what we can do to make you more comfortable, okay?"

He nodded uncertainly. "I'm so sorry about all this trouble, Doctor."

Her eyes crinkled at the corners above her face mask, as if she was giving him a reassuring smile. "Don't worry about any of that, Mr. Thurston. Let's just get you well."

Dr. Coleson's checkup turned out to be surprisingly similar to the countless others Josh had been through over a long life. He allowed himself to be poked and prodded, trying not to feel humiliated at having so many eyes on him. At least the young woman was thoroughly professional as she jotted information down on a little notepad, brow furrowed in concentration, and asked him a barrage of questions.

After fifteen or so minutes a flight attendant gave the doctor a headset, and she excused herself to have a conversation, presumably with someone on the ground. After an agonizing few minutes she came back, face beneath her mask deathly pale.

"You're doing great, Mr. Thurston," she said, voice shaking noticeably. She didn't come quite as close as she had been. "Let's shift to where you've been in the last few days, okay?"

Josh stared at her. "Why? How does that help get me better?"

Before she could answer the cabin's intercom blared as the pilot's voice came over it, solemn and possibly frightened, although he tried to hide it. "Good evening, folks. Due to unfolding circumstances our flight has been redirected. We apologize for this inconvenience, and assure you we're doing everything in our power to get you where you're going as swiftly as possible."

Redirected? Josh stared at Dr. Coleson, who was speaking quietly over the headset. "What's happening, Doctor? Does this have something to do with me? What do I have?"

She held her hand up for quiet and took a few steps back, still murmuring into the headset. Josh grabbed his seat's armrests and tried to stand, intending to insist she tell him just what the blazes was going on. But his strength gave out in a way he'd never experienced before, and he flopped back down as limp as a jellyfish.

That scared him more than he liked to admit. "Doctor?" he whispered. "What's wrong with me?"

The doctor was scribbling something on her notepad, and after almost half a minute she abruptly ripped the page free and shoved it at him, careful to make sure he didn't come close to touching her. Josh grabbed it, blinked a red tinge out of his eyes, then focused on the page. In other circumstances it would've been amusing to note that the words were nearly illegible, although that was probably mostly from the haste with which she'd been writing.

Not to mention the panic she had to be feeling, considering what it said:

"Mr. Thurston, please do not read this aloud or speak of it to anyone. We don't want to cause a panic. I regret to inform you that you've contracted a highly virulent disease. We don't know its origin and have not settled on a name as yet, but yours is not the first case we've seen in the last several days. I also regret to inform you that the disease has a high mortality rate, especially for someone of your advanced age.

I'm sorry, but I'm afraid you should prepare for the worst."

If Dr. Coleson didn't want to cause a panic, it was already too late for the couple who'd been sitting next to Josh. May was noisily freaking out about being exposed to something that would make her *bleed out of her eyes*, while her husband held her tight and looked like he wanted to be sick.

The pilot came back on the intercom. "Attention all passengers. I regret to inform you that we've been ordered to confiscate all phones in the interests of public safety. Be advised that anyone who makes a call or refuses to comply will be subject to criminal charges when we land at our destination."

"What destination?" a man somewhere behind Josh shouted. "Where are we going? Is this some kind of quarantine precaution because of the sick guy?" There was no answer, and the man's voice became angry. "What kind of danger are we in? Answer me!"

No one did, which caused a massive stir of panic from the other passengers. The flight attendants began going from passenger to passenger, politely but insistently collecting phones.

Dr. Coleson fidgeted nervously. "You know what, Mr. Thurston?

Let's go ahead and not worry about where you've been. The C-" she cut off sharply, glancing at the other passengers, then haltingly continued, "that is, the professionals at our destination can handle all that."

Without another word the woman retreated to the bathroom. When she emerged she was no longer wearing the gloves or mask and her hands, arms, and face were carefully scrubbed. She refused to meet his eye as she hurried past to return to the first class cabin.

Josh was left to his misery after that.

People avoided him like the plague, which he bitterly supposed wasn't far wrong. Eventually he felt a pain in his lower gut, joined by a seeping wetness in the seat of his pants that informed him that he was now bleeding out of most or all of his orifices. He felt like it should hurt, all that bleeding. But aside from the deep stomach cramp, and the dizziness and weakness, and feeling like he was freezing and burning at the same time, he didn't feel much.

In spite of his fear and discomfort he must've eventually drifted off, because when he next jolted awake it was to the plane jolting as well. At first he thought it was turbulence, but then he saw the flashing lights outside the plane's windows, an expanse of black tarmac covered with all sorts of emergency vehicles.

Normally landing a jet and disembarking took forever, but this time it was only five or so minutes before a swarm of people in full hazmat suits poured down the aisles.

They made a beeline for Josh, politely but firmly packing him up on a narrow stretcher and hauling him towards one of the plane's side doors, where he was carefully maneuvered down one of those stair cars. He was slapped onto a rolling gurney, and they began wheeling him down one of those plastic tunnels you saw in movies for serious quarantine measures as he was hooked up to various monitors and an IV.

"Excuse me," he said, frightened by how weak and quavery his voice was. "Can someone please tell me what I have? Is there a cure?"

There was no response from the hazmat people, although one patted him on the arm. The reassuring gesture was rendered moot by the man hastily jerking his hand back as if burned, then trying to pretend like he hadn't.

Soon after that the tunnel ended in the glass doors of a sterile, modern-looking building. Josh craned to see through the press of suited bodies around him, and as his gurney was ushered through the doors spotted a plaque near the entrance. It featured three large capital letters followed by two lines of smaller words:

CDC

Centers for Disease

Control and Prevention.

* * * * *

Nick Statton set his phone down beside the keyboard, letting the screen go black in sleep mode with the calculator app still up. It would be an unpleasant reminder when he woke it up again, but at the moment he was too tired and dispirited even to do something as simple as exit out of it.

He rubbed his bleary eyes and stared at his laptop's screen, not seeing the various windows of half-finished coding projects and research displayed there. He honestly wondered what was the point in diving back into them.

He'd run the numbers twice now, and it was the same. Endless expenses all piling up on him, chipping away at his current earnings and meager savings. He could work more billable hours, maybe even take on another project or two, but it seemed like the harder he worked the less he got for his effort. And he was already being crushed by the workload, only to see the mountain of expenses looming ever higher, the blasted numbers on the calculator getting smaller and smaller.

Or bigger and bigger in the wrong direction, to be more accurate. When had just living day to day gotten so expensive? When had being one of the most experienced freelance consultants in his field of expertise started paying so little?

His laptop finally fell asleep too, the light from the screen winking out and leaving him with just the light from the hallway, left on all night because Tallie couldn't sleep otherwise. He just sat there bent over his clasped hands, too exhausted to do anything, even put two thoughts together, but well aware that if he went to bed he wouldn't find sleep for hours anyway.

Nick wasn't sure how long he sat like that before the soft padding of tiny feet on the carpet behind him alerted him to the fact that sometimes Tallie woke up even with the light on. Then he heard her soft voice whispering behind him. "Daddy, did you go to sleep again?"

He sucked in a sharp breath and turned, forcing away his troubled thoughts. It wasn't hard to find a smile as he held out his arms and let his daughter climb into his lap. "Guess so," he said, kissing the top of her head. "Did you wake up again?"

"Just to go potty." She yawned hugely, showing small, even white baby teeth. She was a little cherub in her favorite princess pajamas, all dark brown curls and big greenish-brown eyes and pudgy cheeks rosy from sleeping in her room with the door closed, to keep from heating the entire apartment and wasting power on an only uncomfortably chilly early spring night.

She didn't complain, and neither did Ricky. Still, even though Nick endured even less comfortable temperatures in his own room and office, he felt bad about that; he couldn't even afford to give his kids a properly heated apartment at all hours of the day.

And here he was brooding again, while his daughter was up past her bedtime on a school night. Not only that, but lately she'd been staying awake instead of going right back to sleep.

She should be used to this schedule by now, after being in kindergarten all fall and winter. Maybe it was the spring weather, or possibly he needed to crack the door wider to make sure the room wasn't getting too hot. Or maybe she was troubled by her mom not being there, even though she should be used to Ellie being away on business trips.

But Nick supposed divorce was something different than a business trip. It had upset their children's lives more than he and his ex-wife would've wanted, even though they'd done their best to make the transition smooth. Tallie seeing her mom only half the time probably had more to do with having trouble sleeping than recently melted snow or a hot room.

He bit back a sigh and lifted Tallie back down to the ground. "Get going, sweetie girl. If you hurry I'll read you another story."

The five-year-old gave a restrained squeal, just in time remembering how late it was, and darted out of the room. Nick wearily pushed to his feet and stretched, closing the lid on his laptop and picking up his phone to search for one of his daughter's favorite stories.

If he was honest, the answer might be as simple as that Tallie had figured out if she didn't go right back to bed her daddy would read to her. Or maybe some combination of all those factors.

What a mess. Everything was a mess.

It might be tempting to sink into misery about how things were going now. But even if he sometimes had trouble believing his situation would get better in the future, he was determined to make it happen for his kids.

Things *would* improve. He'd work as hard as he needed to for them, find a solution so he could give them the lives they deserved.

Right after he got a good night's sleep. Or at least, as much as he could before he had to get up in the morning to get the kids off to school, touch base with Ellie to make sure she was still on schedule with her business trip to get back in time to take Ricky and Tallie for her turn in their shared custody agreement, and then get in contact with a client living in a time zone that demanded early calls.

Another day done, another day to get through coming all too soon.

Nathan Jones

Ellie Feldman had never been one to complain or demand answers when it wouldn't make a difference. Like in a situation like this, where the flight attendants and pilots were obviously in the same boat they were, trapped on the tarmac outside Honolulu International Airport for no apparent reason.

It wasn't as if they were delaying the process just to irritate everyone.

On the other hand, she'd been on over a dozen flights in the last year for business, and she'd seen it all. Sometimes some mixup with available terminals or delays in other flights left a plane waiting on the tarmac for what felt like forever. The minutes dragging by with the pilot assuring them it was only a brief delay, as the flight attendants made preparations to help everyone disembark with all due haste once they were finally cleared to approach a terminal.

It actually hadn't been as long yet as she'd sometimes had to wait, so she wasn't sure what was raising the hairs on the back of her neck. Maybe the relative silence from the pilots, or how the attendants kept disappearing behind the curtains for unusually long periods of time, and when they showed their faces their expressions revealed signs of strain beneath carefully professional masks.

Something was up, Ellie could feel it. Her mind flashed over a dozen scenarios, everything from bomb threats to terrorists to hijackings to a pregnant woman going into labor. And in spite of her determination to be patient and wait for news rather than making a nuisance of herself, she began to wonder if she shouldn't at least ask what was going on.

Thankfully, if she was hesitant to cause a scene, there were plenty of people on the flight who weren't; she didn't have to wait long before someone finally asked the questions she so badly wanted answers to.

It was a woman a bit older than Ellie, also dressed in professional attire with the air of a traveling businesswoman. Probably facing deadlines and a crushing workload, and very conscious of the value of her time. Or its lack of availability.

Shut In

Ellie could sympathize.

"Excuse me!" the woman called, standing and stepping into the aisle to confront a passing attendant. "What's the delay?"

The airline employee wore the polite grimace of someone who's being paid to put up with this sort of thing. "Ma'am, please return to your seat and buckle back in," she said in a calm, soothing tone. "The pilot will have an announcement shortly."

"Yeah, and my call is important to you and someone will be with me soon," the passenger said sarcastically. "Why did our plane get sent to the limbo zone, while you guys are whispering about being waved away from the terminal?"

Ellie snapped her head around to the window on the other side of the teenager she was seated beside. Sure enough, their plane had driven off the tarmac to a designated waiting area where it wouldn't get in the way of departing or arriving planes. Even more worryingly, there were other planes parked around them. Far more than she'd ever seen grounded before, to the point where they even crowded onto the tarmac itself. Also far more service vehicles than usual, and even what looked like the flashing lights of police and emergency vehicles painting the planes closest to the terminal in lurid red and blue light.

Most worryingly of all, she didn't see a single plane parked at a terminal; they all stretched out into the distance, eerily deserted with their accordion connectors scrunched in tight.

A bomb threat, then? An attack on the airport itself? Ellie did her best to slow her breathing as worry gave way to the beginnings of panic. What was going on? Would it delay her getting home to her children? Was she in danger?

Almost without realizing it, she found herself on her feet addressing the flight attendant. "Why are there emergency vehicles surrounding those planes? Has something happened?"

The woman gave her a pained look, opening her mouth to likely utter more empty reassurances. But before she could the intercom blared with the pilot's voice. "Attention passengers." Even through the distortion of the speaker he sounded worried, which didn't do much for Ellie's nerves. "We've been informed that it is not safe to approach the terminal at this time. Please remain calm and in your seats, and prepare for a lengthy wait."

The young man beside her cursed. "You've got to be kidding me," he muttered, glaring out the window. "It's always something."

The flight attendants had emerged from behind the curtains and were out in force. The one who'd spoken to the businesswoman earlier grabbed the mic for the intercom, speaking in a forced cheery tone. "Attention passengers. We'll be passing out blankets and pillows. A snack will be provided in an hour or so. Please avail yourselves of the in-flight entertainment or try to get some rest . . . we'll get you out of here as soon as we know it's safe."

Blankets and pillows? Sure, maybe back home in Missouri it was late, but it wasn't even nine o'clock here in Hawaii. Did they expect them to be here all night?

"Can we use our phones?" Ellie called. "I need to check in on my children."

The woman was about to answer when she was once again interrupted. This time it was a nondescript man, dressed like a passenger but holding himself with a clear air of authority, who stepped through the curtain behind her. An air marshal? He whispered a few words to the flight attendant, and she gratefully handed him the mic.

He faced them all with a grave expression. "Please pardon this interruption. I'm an air marshal, and I've been instructed to inform you that due to national security concerns, all passengers aboard this flight must immediately turn off their phones and keep them off until given permission to do otherwise. They will not be confiscated at this time, but as of now anyone who is recorded making a call, or witnessed doing so, may face criminal charges upon disembarking the plane."

Shut In

A dismayed murmur rose from the passengers, and Ellie protectively touched the pocket of her purse that held her phone. National security, criminal charges? What was going on?

The air marshal cleared his throat sternly to quiet the chatter, looking around with a severe expression. "Let me make it very clear that, due to the nature of this situation, the legal penalties for noncompliance will be severe. I will be watching closely to ensure national security is upheld, and if at any point you see anyone seeking to use their phone, I urge you to apprise me of the situation."

He motioned curtly. "Please turn off your phones now."

Ellie joined the others in reaching for her phone and turning it off, while the air marshal watched them all like a hawk. The cabin filled with the chimes of so many devices powering down, although a few people didn't immediately move to comply, not so much out of defiance as bewilderment.

"Why can't we call anyone, sir?" a man shouted from near the back. "Can you please tell us what's going on?"

"All I can tell you is that we're not in immediate danger, and are not expected to be," the air marshal replied with convincing sincerity; either he was a good liar or he believed it himself. "This is merely an inconvenience, one we request your patience for as we all wait it out."

Ellie couldn't help but wonder why they weren't allowed to make calls if this was just an inconvenience. But she accepted a pillow and blanket from a flight attendant and settled in to watch an in-flight movie.

About half an hour later she saw the flight attendants once again stirring near the curtain, then their spokeswoman picked up the mic again. "We have more information," she said. Her professional facade was a good one, but Ellie could see cracks a mile wide spreading across it; whatever her news was, it was bad.

The other passengers must've seen the same thing, because there were none of the questions and demands she'd expected. Only silence, expectation mingled with growing dread hanging heavy in the cabin.

Nathan Jones

The woman took a deep breath. "The State of Hawaii has officially declared an emergency lockdown on Honolulu International Airport. No arriving passengers are being allowed to disembark at this time."

Ellie felt a surge of alarm at the news, although she kept quiet to let the airline employee speak, knowing it was the best way to get all available information.

Other passengers weren't so patient. "Lockdown?" the teenager seated beside her demanded. "What for? Is there a terrorist threat, are we under attack by another nation?"

The flight attendant's face went visibly paler, and she had to swallow and clear her throat before she could speak. "We haven't been given specifics, sir," she said quietly, words carried over the speakers to every inch of the hushed cabin. "They assure us that we're all safe, this is simply a precautionary measure."

"A precautionary measure that's forcing us to waste hours of our time?" an older woman a few rows in front of Ellie shouted. "If this airport is closed, are we going to be redirected to another one? Sent back to Tokyo, or on to somewhere else?"

The poor airline employee shook her head. "I don't know, ma'am," she said, voice barely audible in spite of the mic in her hand. "As the air marshal said, we're being told only as much as necessary in the interest of national security." She straightened. "Please prepare to settle in for an extended wait. Get some sleep if you can. We'll inform you the moment we learn anything else."

Ellie didn't like that news, but unlike the other passengers who raised a storm of complaints and questions she merely snuggled into her blanket, put the headphones back on, and got back to watching her movie.

Guess she'd be a bit late getting home to her kids.

Chapter One
Rude Awakening

Nick jolted awake as his ringtone sounded, blearily scrabbling around on his bedside table for his phone.

Unfortunately, if being woken up halfway through his midafternoon nap hadn't left his nerves jangled enough, the moment he answered the call his worry and alarm ratcheted up a few more notches.

"Nick Statton?" A woman's voice demanded before he could even say hello. She was almost drowned out by a cacophony of other voices in the background, most raised in fear and anger while a relative handful tried to speak calmly over them.

"This is Nick Statton," he said cautiously, an ominous feeling settling into his gut.

The woman on the other end sounded so impatient and harried that he would've thought *he* was the one who'd called *her* at a bad time. "Sir, please shut up and listen carefully," she snapped.

Considering he hadn't said a word besides confirming his identity, all very calm and cooperative, that seemed a bit rude. But he shut up, and his irritation at her behavior vanished as she continued.

"This is Middlecrest Elementary School. We have you listed as a shared custody parental guardian for Richard and Natalie Statton, and that they're in your care at this time. Is that correct?"

"That's right," Nick replied, concern ratcheting up a notch. What were all those people in the background shouting about? What was going on?

The woman raised her voice a bit to be heard, tone fraying even more around the edges. "Sir, we're calling to inform you that you need to pick up your children." A jolt of pure panic nearly made him freak out at that, but he clenched his teeth and let her continue. "A general evacuation has been called for the school, and all parents are being advised to immediately pick up their children and bring them home, then place your home under quarantine until further notice."

Quarantine? What the blue blazes?

Nick's panic morphed into pure nausea as the woman continued on with hurried instructions for orderly pickup, whether to use a vehicle or come on foot depending on distance, and how to avoid direct contact with other parents and children during the evacuation.

Tallie! Ricky! What was going on? Had they been exposed? The authorities would've got a hospital and emergency medical personnel involved if that was the case, wouldn't they? Or placed the school under quarantine if there was even the slightest risk of spreading an infection?

No, he was overreacting. They wouldn't have called for parents to come pick up kids exposed to some sickness and take them all over town. That was just stupid. This was just a precaution and he was panicking over nothing.

Just a scare. Which didn't stop him from speaking right over the harried woman. "What's going on?" he demanded. "Is there a real risk here?"

The school employee's voice became even more impatient. "You didn't catch the Mayor's announcement on the crisis at Kansas City International Airport an hour ago, sir? Or the CDC's official release just after noon on what they know about the outbreaks occurring all over the world?"

Her tone suggested he must be living under a rock, and he felt his face heat. Was it possible he'd slept right through the start of an actual global disaster? "I didn't, no."

"Well what's going on at Middlecrest is that the charter buses that brought the fifth graders back from their visit to the Eastfield Science Museum had just come from the airport," she said, sounding too weary to do anything but answer his questions and hope he shut up and cooperated. "The buses didn't come anywhere near a potentially infected terminal or passengers, and the fifth graders were immediately separated out and placed under quarantine the moment we found out about the risk, as were all those they came in contact with that we could reasonably identify. But still, all things considered it's better you pick your children up."

Wait, there was an outbreak at the *airport* now? With actual infected terminals and passengers and scares about buses spreading it to the rest of the city? What the heck was going on?

Now wasn't the time to panic about what might be going on in the city at large, though; all that mattered was making sure his kids were safe. "I'm on my way," Nick said simply, and hung up.

Without wasting a second he grabbed his keys and his jacket, then his wallet in case the school asked for his ID, and barely paused to lock the door behind him before slamming it shut. He headed down the stairs to his apartment, turning towards the school a couple blocks away.

In retrospect he regretted not asking what disease they were possibly dealing with here, and what he should look out for to keep his children safe from it. But for the moment the best thing was to get Ricky and Tallie back home as quickly as possible, then try to figure out what was going on.

As he jogged along the sidewalk he pulled out his phone again and called Ellie. It went straight to voicemail, and even though that meant her phone was probably off, or more likely she was in the air and didn't have a signal, he hung up and tried again.

Voicemail again. "Ellie," he said after the beep. "Just calling to let you know there's some sort of crisis at the school, and I'm picking the kids up. Not sure if you're home from your trip yet, but . . ." he trailed off as the front of the school came into view, staring. "Um, call me back," he finished hastily as he hung up, then shoved his phone back into his pocket and broke into a run.

The school's parking lot was pandemonium, packed with vehicles and people flooding towards the entrances. Buses loomed like beached leviathans surrounded by smaller cars and SUVs, everybody honking to try to get everyone else to leave, while police officers and school administrators tried to clear a path so the buses full of kids and those parents who'd already picked up their kids could get away.

More teachers and administrators were struggling to get huddles of frightened kids loaded into buses, while parents frantically searched through the seething masses for their own children. But in spite of the crowd being bigger than Nick had ever seen before when picking up Ricky and Tallie, everyone seemed to be doing everything in their power to stay at arm's length from everyone else.

Especially parents with kids that weren't theirs, which Nick supposed wasn't too surprising if the calls they'd received to pick up their children had been as alarming as his had been.

He skirted the parking lot, joining the stream of people on foot walking across the grass. They flowed around a smaller stream of parents protectively clutching children who were headed the other way. Nick couldn't help but notice that those people were given space like they had the plague in spite of the crowded conditions, and that they were equally paranoid about even the arriving parents.

To the point where if keeping at arm's length wasn't possible, sparks flew to a shocking extreme.

The first incident he saw looked fairly innocuous, a woman simply passing a bit too close to a father clutching his daughter to his chest, frantically ducking and dodging through the crowd to get away from the school. The close brush was actually mostly the man's fault, but the frantic father reacted as if the woman had lunged at him brandishing a knife.

"Stay away from my girl!" he screamed, with the sort of hysterical desperation you'd use for a large, vicious predator you had no hope of scaring away with anything but noise and bluff.

The woman skittered away as if zapped by a cattle prod, staring at the man with wide, frightened eyes. She kept eyeing him warily as she edged past and hurried on, while the father hugged his crying daughter close and kept ducking through the crowd, barking at others to stay away.

Shouting wasn't the worst of it, unfortunately. Closer to the entrance Nick saw one mom, who was clutching a boy around Tallie's age in her arms, viciously shove a girl who looked to be in fifth or sixth grade away with her foot. As the poor child was knocked sprawling the woman called out an apology that sounded somewhere between sincere and panicked, while at the same time frantically kicking off her shoe as if it was covered with acid.

Then, limping in one sock, she went bolting away along the wall with her son, while a teacher crouched to help the downed child up and shouted angrily after her.

"Slow down and keep calm!" a policeman near the closest door shouted. "Don't enter the school unless you're a parent of a child living within three blocks of here! All children intended to be picked up by their parents in a car have already been led outside to the back parking lot, but don't go back there! Get in touch with a teacher or administrator and tell them your name and the names of your kids, and they'll go get them for you."

Nick prepared his ID as he approached, then realized that the officer wasn't checking anyone else's. In fact, he didn't even seem to be making sure the people streaming through the doors were actually parents who lived nearby.

Normally that would've really worried him, but at the moment he was just relieved at the lack of delay as he followed everyone else into the school, making his way down a side hallway to Tallie's classroom.

To his further relief, not only was his daughter still there waiting for him, but Ricky was there with her, holding her hand and reassuring her in the midst of the chaos.

His children both rushed over to him the moment they saw him, expressions full of relief. Nick pulled Tallie up to hold her with one arm, holding Ricky's hand with his free one, and started towards the back of the school.

"Daddy, are we going to the car?" his daughter asked, squirming insistently and pointing behind them. "The car's that way!"

"No, sweetie, I didn't bring the car today," Nick replied as he gently but firmly held her tight to keep her from sliding down to the ground and running off. "We're going to walk home."

"That's good, because the parking lot and front of the school are all full of buses and cars and stuff," Ricky declared. "It's even worse than when school gets out!"

"I saw. That's why we're going to cut across the playground and climb over the fence." As he spoke Nick sped up a bit, tugging his son along behind him.

Ricky gave him a doubtful look as he jogged to keep up. "We're not supposed to do that."

Nick glanced at the chaos in the hallway around them, the hysterical parents and crying children and teachers and school administrators and a few policemen trying to keep order. "They don't care today because it's so busy. I'm sure lots of people are already doing it."

If they're smart, he added silently to himself.

It turned out plenty were; the playground and neatly trimmed lawn beyond it were crowded with parents leading their kids away from the school. It was an odd sight, since at most social gatherings and even for routine things like picking up or dropping kids off from school, parents who knew each other tended to clump together to chat, while their kids ran circles around them playing their own games.

Not today. Today, every parent was a suspicious island accompanied only by his or her kids, with at least ten feet of empty space surrounding them. Kids' hands were held tight and the smaller children were almost universally being carried, with any attempts to wriggle free to go say hi to friends earning as sharp a rebuke as if they'd been caught standing over a broken computer.

A few kids *had* managed to run free, and the air was full of the shrill screams of moms and dads acting as if their children were on the verge of running out in front of a speeding car.

Nick stepped to the side of the door, along the wall where dozens of other parents with their children were all standing or sitting a safe distance apart. Some looked to be resting, others seemed to be recovering from weaving their way through the chaos inside, or steeling themselves for the trip across the playground. Some even seemed to just be waiting for things to calm down before moving.

He had no intention of doing any of that, he just wanted to spend a few seconds planning out the best route through the crowd of parents fleeing the school.

With how people kept randomly changing directions to avoid other people, there was no real good route to plan. Nick eventually just gave up and made for a clear area halfway across that might or might not still be there when he reached it.

The next couple minutes were a confusing blur of dodging and looking around frantically, while terrified people screamed all around him, sometimes at him. Tallie spent most of the time with her head buried in his neck, while Ricky huddled against his side close enough to nearly trip him a few times.

Nick reached the clear area, which wasn't so clear anymore, forcing him to change directions and make for a different section of fence than he'd been heading for. Tallie was starting to get unmanageably heavy in his arms, a reminder that his desperate efforts to avoid financial ruin lately hadn't involved much in the way of exercise.

He'd have to get her up on his shoulders once they were over the fence. It was more precarious if he had to suddenly run or anything like that, but hopefully after they put the chaos of the school behind them that wouldn't be a problem.

"Back off!" a couple clutching the hands of a girl a bit younger than Ricky shouted at him. They backed away, nearly bumping into a mother herding two children, who shouted at them in turn. Nick ducked his head and kept going.

After a nightmarish few more minutes they reached the fence. Nick lifted Ricky over, then passed him Tallie and climbed himself. The chain link barrier was swaying drunkenly under the weight of holding several people at once, almost on the verge of falling over. It *was* nearly bent down to the ground in one place, where a heavyset man wasn't so much climbing over it as crawling.

Then they were over. Nick hoisted his daughter up onto his shoulders, took his son's hand again, then crossed the street and set off briskly.

"Dad, where are we going?" Ricky abruptly asked.

"Home," he said, glancing over his shoulder to make sure the cluster of people coming down the street behind them hadn't gotten any closer.

His son frowned. "This is like the opposite direction of home."

"It is. We need to go around a bit, take smaller streets and alleys to avoid people."

"Why?" Ricky demanded. "Why was everyone all mad and scared at school? I heard something about a cor-corun teen, but what does that mean?"

"Quarantine," he corrected gently. "It means sick people being separated from everyone so no one else gets sick."

"Are we sick?" Tallie asked anxiously. She'd had a stomach bug a few months ago that had been pure misery for the poor girl.

Nick patted her knee. "No, they're just being careful. Once we get home we'll find out what's going on."

A few blocks away the crowd thinned to the point where you might think it was just a normal day in Kansas City, if a bit busy for this time of the afternoon. He finally set Tallie down and held her hand, having Ricky hold her other, so he could give his aching shoulders a rest.

The first thing he did once he had a hand free was pull out his phone and try to call Ellie again. Again it went straight to voicemail. Had one of her flights been delayed to the point she was still in the air? "Ellie, I got the kids out and I'm headed home," he said after the beep. "It was pretty crazy at the school. Call me."

After Nick hung up he stared at his phone, brow furrowed in concern. He hoped his ex-wife's phone wasn't off because something had happened to her. Normally he would've waved off that worry as just his usual sense of impending doom that never materialized, but he'd just pulled his children out of a school turned into some sort of nightmarish free for all.

He quickened his pace to the fastest Tallie could manage, determined to get home and figure out just what the heck was going on.

* * * * *

Ellie glanced over as the teenager in the seat beside her finally stirred awake.

She'd slept fitfully all night, fretting for her children, worried that circumstances might be more serious than they were telling her, and wondering if she'd be able to make it back to Missouri. So she couldn't help but feel a bit jealous of the young man, since as far as she knew he'd slept like a rock all night in spite of the situation they were in.

It brought back fond memories of being that age herself, around eighteen or nineteen if she was any judge. Those blissful days in her past when she could've slept right through an earthquake, and only woken up long enough to complain about the roof collapsing on top of her before rolling over and drifting off again.

Her seatmate was the sort who would've definitely drawn her attention when she was in her teens, and even more so right now if he'd been her age and still looked like that. He looked to be a good half a head taller than her, at least as far as she could tell with him slouched in an airplane seat. Muscled but not bulky, skin with the sort of deep tan that she had a feeling came from working out in the sun rather than lounging by a pool. He had short, slightly tussled blond hair with just a hint of red in it, and high cheekbones complimenting a strong jaw covered with a few days' growth of fine stubble.

The young man's eyes slowly drifted open, light green and full of confusion and fear. The confusion faded as he seemed to remember where he was, but the fear remained, making him seem younger than his late teens.

Ellie's heart went out to him. "Morning," she said quietly.

He blinked and rubbed at his eyes. "Morning," he mumbled. Squinting, he cracked the shutter on his window enough to glance outside, grimacing. "Still stuck on the tarmac?"

"Yeah."

The teenager cursed, then flushed and glanced at her. "Sorry."

Ellie chuckled grimly. "You didn't say anything I'm not thinking."

He smiled back tentatively. "Any more news while I was asleep?"

"No. They were probably hoping we'd sleep for as long as possible so we didn't raise a fuss." She glanced ahead at the curtains, where no flight attendants were in sight. "Maybe now that just about everyone's awake we'll get something."

"Guess I woke up just in time, then." He offered her his hand. "I'm Hal."

She took it, noting how in spite of his athletic build he held back his grip almost carefully enough to be insulting; maybe it was the business suit she was wearing. "Ellie."

"Good to finally meet you," he said wryly. "Being seatmates on an intercontinental flight is one thing, but I figure if we're going to be trapped on a plane together we might as well get to know each other."

His tone had become far more casual, and Ellie felt a tinge of annoyance. This was the worst possible time for some kid to be hitting on her.

Then she felt bad for that; the young man was as stressed about this situation as she was, trying to make conversation to take his mind off his own fears. And even if he was working his way up to flirting, there was no reason to bite his head off for it.

If nothing else, like Hal had said she was going to be trapped next to him for the foreseeable future, so it was in her own best interest to keep things friendly. Rather than getting angry just because a young man acted like most teenagers with a pulse would.

Assuming she wasn't being massively egotistical to think he was interested in her; she remembered when she was his age and people in their thirties had seemed ancient. Although to be fair, her teenage years *did* feel like an eternity ago.

"Might as well," she agreed. "Were you headed back to the US from Japan?"

Hal nodded. "On my way to Kearney." He paused, then added, "That's in Missouri, near-"

"Kansas City," Ellie cut in with a smile. "Only fifteen minutes or so from where I live, actually. Howdy, neighbor."

He grinned back. "Hey how about that? Small world." He glanced at her professional attire, although thankfully didn't seem to be checking her out. "So you were there for business?"

"That's right. I'm a workplace cohesion consultant." At his blank look she shook her head wryly. "I help businesses improve morale, raise employee sensitivity, and manage conflict resolution. I also give my professional evaluation on any issues they might be dealing with and advise them on a solution."

The teenager gave her an uncertain look, obviously completely unfamiliar with the field. "That sort of work keep you busy?"

"Busy enough to travel at least once a month, including to other countries," Ellie replied dryly. "For example, in Japan I was helping a branch of an American business train their new employees on working within the Japanese business culture."

"So you must do a lot of work in Japan, right?"

She nodded. "Enough to feel comfortable advising others. Although I'm still not confident enough in my grasp of the language to use it in a business setting."

"Yeah, me either. But not, you know, for business." Hal fumbled a bit before rallying. "I don't suppose you've ever met my dad? Ned Westmont, works at SDI."

Ellie shook her head, not recognizing the name or the business. "Sorry."

He shrugged. "Would've been cool, is all."

A slightly uncomfortable silence settled. "Is that what brought you to Japan?" she finally asked. "To visit him?"

The teenager's expression became . . . hard to read. She saw pain there, and sadness, and more than a little bitterness. "Yeah. I don't get many chances to, so . . ." he trailed off and didn't continue.

Another uncomfortable silence settled. Ellie let it hang; she had no idea what the young man's situation was, although she could guess, but she thought it best to give him a chance to work through whatever he was feeling and talk to her about it if he wanted to.

After over a minute he cleared his throat, tone once again carefully casual. "So I heard you mention wanting to talk to your kids. Are they back with your husband?"

Oh boy. What guy ever tossed out something like that who wasn't testing the waters?

It was tempting to nip things in the bud, but even if Ellie wasn't interested in a kid who looked to be about a decade younger than her, she wasn't about to pretend to still be married to avoid being flirted with.

"Ex," she replied, leaving it at that.

Hal raised an eyebrow and said nothing, and she bit back a sigh. Why did people always want the juicy details? After an uncomfortable silence he cleared his throat. "Explains why you're so desperate to get back to them. Want to make sure they're with someone you trust, with *you*, in a crisis."

There was another thing people always did: the moment they heard about the divorce, they began playing the angle like it had been an ugly, vicious ordeal for her and Nick was the bad guy, and they sidled in to offer sympathy and commiseration.

Although to be fair, it seemed like she was the *only* one who didn't have horror stories about going through the courts. It always made her even more glad that she and Nick had done everything they could to avoid letting it be like that for them and the kids.

"They *are* with someone I trust, and I'm sure they're fine," Ellie said firmly. "That doesn't make me feel any better about being away from them in a crisis."

The young man winced slightly. "Sorry, that's what I get for assuming. Or sticking my nose in your business." He gave her a wry smile, some of that earlier bitterness returning. "I guess you were lucky enough to have that rare and magical thing, an amiable divorce?"

She wondered what experience Hal had to make him so jaded about it, when he couldn't be much out of his teens. Then she realized, with a bit of chagrin, that his experience was probably from the other end of it: watching his parents go through an ugly divorce. The same thing Nick had gone through with his own parents when he was young.

Listening to her ex-husband talk about it, the genuine pain he'd endured as his family was torn apart from within, had kept Ellie in the marriage long after she wanted it to end. And it had made her want to go through the divorce process very carefully and find a good solution for all of them, for all their sakes but especially for Ricky and Tallie.

Even so, she often worried that as hard as she and Nick had tried, their children were still suffering from their separation. She saw it when Ricky and Tallie mentioned missing their dad, or tried to convince her to invite him to events where his presence would be awkward. Or when they came home from staying with him and had so obviously missed her. Or had to go from home to home even when the timing wasn't convenient for them.

Ellie abruptly realized Hal had been shifting uncomfortably while she was lost in her ruminations. "It was about as amiable as a divorce can be," she said reluctantly. "My attorney wanted me to go for blood, try to get the best possible deal for myself, but I didn't see how that would be good for any of us. Nick, my ex, also wanted to be fair, so we tried the best we could to arrange for equal custody and child support, and shared out our assets as evenly as we could. And we try to be flexible to each other's situations when stuff comes up."

The young man was quiet for a few seconds. "I don't know what to say without sounding . . . I don't know, out of place. But good for you, I'm glad you managed it."

Again, there was that long pause where he could've said something about his own experiences. But he didn't.

Before the pause could turn unbearable again, the intercom finally crackled and the pilot's voice came over it. "Good morning, passengers. We appreciate your patience with this unprecedented delay, and again apologize for this situation. The good news is we finally have some information for you about what seems to be going on."

Next to her Hal straightened from his slouching position, expression intent. Around them other people were also sitting up attentively, heads craned to look at the speakers above them.

"It appears the reason Hawaii has closed off its airports is because people suffering symptoms of a new and very virulent disease have been found in over thirty airports across the globe. Air travel is obviously spreading the disease at an alarming rate so many places, including Hawaii, are closing themselves off to it."

Shut In

Ellie felt a chill run down her spine. Thirty airports across the globe? That couldn't have happened overnight, so why hadn't she heard a thing about this up til now?

Her thoughts, focused on the big picture, hadn't arrived at a more immediate problem. But Hal's had. "Is someone on *this* plane infected?" he called out. There were shocked gasps from the passengers around them, then calls of agreement and demands for answers.

The pilot had continued talking, starting to list the names of the cities where outbreaks were occurring. But mid-word he paused, either hearing the commotion from the rest of the plane or being informed of it. "Please, folks, stay calm," he said in an easygoing tone. "We have no evidence of the disease being on this plane. In fact, there's no evidence of it being on *any* plane at this airport. This is merely a precaution."

The man went back to listing the names of infected cities, and Ellie found a new and far better reason to panic. There were eight major cities in the US on that list: New York City, Washington D.C., Baltimore, Miami, Dallas, Portland, Chicago . . . and Kansas City.

A soft gasp escaped in spite of Ellie's best efforts, nearly drowning out her seatmate's own sharp intake of breath.

How, out of all the possible cities in the country, was her home one of them? The place where her family was waiting, vulnerable and possibly exposed to this mysterious disease. She had a sudden, almost overwhelming urge to pull out her phone, threats of criminal charges notwithstanding, and call Nick. The fact that so far it seemed like only airports were hotspots of this disease, and her family had no reason to go to an airport themselves, stopped her.

This was just undue panic. Ricky and Tallie were safely in school, and Nick would probably be in the middle of one of his afternoon naps after a late night of working. They'd almost certainly be given plenty of warning by Kansas City officials of any threat, and be able to respond to it.

Although it wasn't just Nick and the kids she had to worry about.

Nathan Jones

Ellie was an only child and her parents had had her late, so her extended family were all older and she didn't know them well, or were younger and she'd never really been in their lives. Of her parents her dad had died of natural causes a few years ago, but her mom was still in Kansas City in a home, being treated for early onset Alzheimer's.

That was a much more likely source of concern, since she had no idea if her mom's caregivers would be exposed to other medical professionals who might be working to treat people sick with this mysterious disease.

The thought filled her with anguish. Caring for her mom in her current state had been difficult to the point of impossible with all her traveling for work, and even more so since her divorce. She already felt guilty enough about not visiting her often enough, even when on half of those visits she might as well have been a stranger.

But the thought of losing her mom to some disease because she'd been stuck in a place where she'd been exposed to it was unbearable. Which just made her all the more desperate to get home.

To Ellie's vast relief, once the pilot finished naming off airports he immediately shifted gears. "The other piece of news is a bit better . . . although we cannot disembark or approach the airport, we've finally been given clearance to refuel and take off again."

The announcement was met with a chorus of cheers, although some people, obviously those who'd been heading to Hawaii as their destination, looked disgruntled. "Where are we going?" a man's voice near the front of the cabin called out, fairly uselessly.

Although it was an obvious question, and the pilot answered it anyway when he continued. "You might be wondering about our destination. First off I regret to inform you that we cannot return to Japan . . . just like Hawaii, it has closed its airports to all but emergency landings. Since we're unable to go back there, and the officials here insist we refuel and depart, we will be traveling to Los Angeles International Airport. We've been given leave to land and disembark there, and assured that as long as none of our passengers present with symptoms by the time we arrive, none of us will be placed under quarantine."

That news was met with an even louder round of cheers, Ellie and Hal joining in enthusiastically since that's where they'd been headed anyway. Although Ellie felt bad about all the Japanese passengers on the plane who were stranded away from home.

"We'll be taking off shortly," the pilot concluded. "And I'm pleased to report that along with fuel, we'll be taking on enough food to see everyone comfortably fed to our destination. Please settle in and enjoy the rest of your flight, and thank you for your patience in these trying circumstances."

Ellie snorted bitterly at that; enjoying her flight would be a trick, considering the state of her family back home. She glanced over at Hal to find him brooding, a worried expression on his face. "I'm sure our loved ones back in Kansas City are fine," she told him, briefly resting a hand on his arm.

The teenager gave a start of surprise and turned to her, forcing a smile. "Yeah, sure," he said unconvincingly. "I just can't believe KCI is one of the affected airports."

"Me either."

He shook his head grimly. "I guess the silver lining on this cloud is that if people are catching this disease in airports, I'd rather be trapped in a plane."

True, although that meant they might be at risk the moment they arrived at the Los Angeles airport. The pilot hadn't mentioned it on his list, but LAX was a major international hub; if the disease was spreading as fast as it sounded, it was highly likely it would spring up there before long.

On top of that, and even more terrifying, was the pilot's casual comment about none of them having symptoms by the time they arrived.

What if someone on the plane *was* sick? In that case they'd been trapped together for over two thirds of a day, and would be trapped together for hours longer. Plenty of time to infect everyone from first class to coach with whatever it was that was making officials panic to the point of closing off entire islands, entire *countries*, to keep it from spreading.

Forget quarantine, Ellie might be infected with something that would kill her before she ever got a chance to see her kids again. Sure, it seemed unlikely, but even the possibility was enough to terrify her.

She settled back to her own brooding, wishing she could use her phone. *Please be okay*, she thought to her loved ones back home. And to Nick, *please, please take care of our children.*

Chapter Two
Falling Apart

The moment they got home the kids immediately rushed to kick off their shoes and toss their jackets and backpacks beneath the hooks for hanging them, then made a beeline for the kitchen to grab a snack.

Almost as if this was a regular day and they'd just got home from school at the usual time.

Well, Nick wasn't about to complain about them settling into that normalcy, considering the panic they'd just escaped. He took a minute making sure they were settled, and weren't so shaken by their experience that they needed him to stay with them. They didn't seem to be, so he let them know he'd be in the den and made his own beeline for the TV there.

In retrospect he probably would've been better off going for his computer in his office, since he spent a minute or so floundering around trying to find a way to look at the news on the TV.

Nick had to admit that he'd never even used it for local broadcasting, the stuff you used to get from rabbit ear antennas or as part of basic cable packages when he was a kid. He wasn't even sure his Smart TV worked for that, and poking around on the various devices he used to stream and record videos didn't turn up what he was looking for.

It turned out to be a case of being too smart to be stupid, though. Or maybe vice-versa. Pretty much all the major news channels put their videos up, and even streamed live footage; all he had to do was hop on everyone's favorite video sharing platform and type in "Kansas City", and he was soon swamped with news.

More news than he wanted, really, considering the subject.

The first stream he hopped into on a local channel showed a horrifying image of an elderly man in a hospital bed, attached to monitors and with an IV in one arm. He had bandages over his ears, plugging his nostrils, and a nurse in a full hazmat suit was currently dabbing at bloody saliva frothing from his mouth as he wheezed weakly. His eyes were open and looking around with a sort of confused fear.

And they were rimmed with crusted blood while more red tears slowly trickled from the corners.

". . . is Josh Thurston," a grave woman's voice was saying. "He was on a flight from Boise to Kansas City, on his way home from a visit with family in Idaho, when he began showing symptoms of this mysterious new illness. He is just one of thousands of reported cases from all over the country, most discovered on airplanes or in airports."

Nick felt his blood chill at the implications of that: it meant this disease was spreading by airplanes to, well, everywhere.

"According to a recently issued CDC statement, this disease, which has been designated Zolos, is a virus which survives for extended periods of time on any surface it's exposed to, and can also be waterborne or airborne. After infection the patient exhibits no noticeable symptoms at all for between two to four days, then swiftly exhibits the symptoms seen by Mr. Thurston, beginning with dizziness, chills, and excessive sweating, then swiftly progressing to bleeding from all orifices, debilitating weakness, severe stomach pains, and ultimately internal bleeding leading to death. The majority of patients live no longer than three days once they begin showing symptoms."

The old man thrashed feebly on the bed, the nurse doing his best to restrain him while he spat out a glob of blood onto the nurse's sleeve. Even though the hazmat suit protected the man, he still shied away from his patient for a moment in clear terror.

The woman's voice had paused, but now continued grimly. "The CDC reports that when compared to other diseases that have caused concern in current years, Zolos is one of the most infectious on record, while simultaneously being one of the most deadly, with a staggeringly high mortality rate. Because of all these factors there is some speculation that it could not have occurred naturally, and has been engineered. At present there is no evidence supporting this idea or pointing to any culprit."

There was another long pause as Josh lay limp and gray on his bed, slowly dying of a horrible disease. Then the woman finished in a quiet voice. "There is as yet no known cure for Zolos, and because governmental efforts to contain its spread have proved fruitless, they are urging everyone to avoid high traffic public spaces. Particularly airports, bus stations, docks, highways, and other places where you might encounter travelers. If at all possible, they recommend remaining at home with family in self-imposed quarantine, and only going out when strictly necessary.

"If you do need to go out, they advise taking precautions to avoid exposure to infection, such as gloves and face masks, or even full-body covering that can be taken off and sanitized once you are back in a safe place. Ideally hazmat suits are recommended, although they acknowledge that those are not practical for day to day activities. They also recommend hand sanitizer and cleaning high-traffic surfaces such as doorknobs with chemical wipes before handling them."

Nick couldn't stand to stare at the poor old man anymore, so he backed out and sought out a different video, finally settling on what looked like a panel of newscasters and experts.

"You'd have to be insane not to find it suspicious," a smartly dressed woman around his age was saying as the livestream loaded, scowling defiantly at the others around the semicircular table she sat at. The header beneath her identified her as "Susanna Barnes, KCNBS Evening Anchor".

"Eleven airports all across the country, and more constantly being discovered," she continued fiercely, "all reporting widespread cases from multiple flights and quickly spreading into the cities at large in the space of just a few hours or days at most, given the nature of Zolos. That looks an awful lot like a coordinated attack to me."

A man across the table from her cut in mildly. "I've always believed we shouldn't attribute to malice what can just as easily be explained by incompetence. The CDC says this bug is shockingly virulent, and takes long enough to show symptoms for it to spread far and fast before it's been identified as a threat."

"So it just appears out of nowhere and spreads across half the globe before anyone's aware of it, like *that*-" Susanna snapped her fingers for emphasis, "and you don't see anything suspicious?"

Her colleague scowled. "You know as well as I do that the government has done everything in its power to try to keep this problem under wraps while it tried to contain the outbreaks, and only publicly acknowledged it within the last few hours. These outbreaks could've been going on for weeks without our knowledge."

An older man, whose header identified him as a guest expert on epidemiology from the UMKC School of Medicine, cleared his throat politely. "I think, given the growing crisis, we should focus less on pointing fingers and more on informing people about the steps they should take to protect themselves from this threat."

To her credit, Susanna took a sharp breath and nodded curtly. "What steps would those be?"

The expert's shoulders sagged slightly. "Well first off, you may have heard a lot of good, commonsense advice about things like wearing gloves and face masks, sanitizing surfaces, and avoiding places like public restrooms. While all very useful, I'm not quite sure they're going to be enough with Zolos."

"Why is that?" an anchorman identified as Gregg Ferdinand asked sharply. It was hard to tell whether he was displeased by the bad news or eager to get a controversial opinion.

"Because what we have here is essentially a super virus. Its ability to propagate as a waterborne and airborne contaminant, and survive extended periods of time outside a host body, means it's going to be fiendishly difficult to avoid being infected by it. To the point that if it is introduced to an area, the most realistic way to protect yourself is to avoid that area entirely." The expert smiled grimly. "I'm afraid we will need to become a nation of shut-ins to avoid this turning into a catastrophe of apocalyptic proportions. If it's not already too late."

A grim silence settled. "Gregg mentioned virulence," Susanna eventually told the epidemiologist, "what about lethality?"

The man's sickly smile became a grimace. "As you might know, there's generally a shifting scale between virulence and lethality. That's because highly virulent, lethal contagions tend to burn out quickly in populations, since they usually incapacitate and kill off people too quickly to spread beyond the initial victims. Slow acting, less virulent contagions with high lethality, up in the eighty or ninety percent range, are what generally cause epidemic panics, because if they *do* spread they're so deadly. Conversely, more virulent but less deadly contagions tend to cause scares, but not generally panic."

The other anchor, Randy Critch, cut in impatiently. "All very pertinent, Doctor, but what about *this* particular contagion?"

The expert shook his head, expression sagging. "I'm afraid it falls in the most dreaded category . . . it's slow to advance to initial symptoms, from two to as much as four days during which time the infected are still highly contagious, it spreads by just about every imaginable medium, and it has a projected lethality rate of up to ninety percent based on initial losses. Add to that the fact that transportation is so prevalent, with people constantly coming and going almost everywhere on the globe, and the spread can be horrifically thorough."

Susanna's expression was grim, voice reserved when she spoke. "For those of us who can't unpack the raw data, Doctor, what does that mean in terms of our viewers?"

"It means," he replied with slow, heavy solemnity, "if this crisis is not adequately contained, assuming it even *can* be at this point, it could potentially lead to the deaths of billions of people." He took a long breath. "And considering the near certainty of societal collapse from losing so many people so quickly, and the inevitable social upheaval, we might even be facing a near or even complete extinction event."

Randy gave him a dubious look. "You mean the extinction of humanity."

"It is certainly possible." The epidemiologist coughed. "Although that's not my field of expertise."

"Then maybe we should avoid speculation that may cause undue alarm," Susanna said sharply. She glanced to the side, off-screen, and her voice abruptly became brisk. "Let's go now to realtime footage from the sickbed of Josh Thurston, the gentleman whose infection led to the grounding and quarantine of Flight 53 early this morning, as we check in on his condition and cover the latest updates from the CDC."

Nick turned off the TV, feeling sick, and pulled out his phone to call Ellie. Voicemail. "Ellie, I'm really getting worried. Please call me as soon as you can. I hope you're okay."

He hung up and headed into the kitchen, where Ricky was drizzling way too much honey on a peanut butter sandwich while Tallie munched on an apple while looking at a picture book.

"You'll have to take your snacks to go, guys," he told his children briskly. "Grab your jackets and put on your shoes."

Tallie was only too happy to rush back to the front door, apple in hand, and get ready to go. Ricky was slower to obey, looking at him curiously; Nick usually had them do their homework first thing when they got home, so this was unusual.

Then again, so was this entire day.

"Where are we going?" his son asked.

"Upstairs." Nick plopped another slice of bread down on the unfinished sandwich and picked up the plate. "Come on, let's go."

Tallie overheard that and squealed with excitement, happy at the chance to see her friend, while Ricky scowled. At home he could watch whatever he wanted on his own tablet, but while being babysat Gen had all three kids vote on what to watch, majority rule.

Shut In

Needless to say, the two youngest kids usually agreed more on what to watch than the eight-year-old. Ricky could sometimes talk Gen's son to go for something he liked, but was usually frustrated that he didn't get his way as the oldest.

Nick nudged his son's back to get him moving. "Come on, this is important."

Playing the aggrieved martyr like only kids that age could, Ricky reluctantly grabbed his jacket and pulled on his shoes. Nick locked up again and led his kids up to the apartment above his.

That was where Imogen Foss and her son Billy, who was a bit older than Tallie and got on well with her and Ricky both, lived. She'd introduced herself when Nick first moved in several months before the divorce, warm and welcoming as she offered to help out with the kids if he needed it. It hadn't been an idle offer, and she'd been a lifesaver pretty much ever since.

Nick was a bit ashamed to admit how heavily he'd leaned on her during those difficult months, when it had been such a blessing to have someone who could watch the kids during emergencies in the couple weeks a month he had custody, especially when Ellie was gone on business trips. There were times he needed to run errands he couldn't take them on, usually for work, or just had to have things quiet in his office during important calls.

He wasn't sure he could've handled it all without her.

To be fair, circumstances hadn't really been all that different from how he'd cared for Ricky and Tallie before he and Ellie split up, since he could work from home while she traveled and he'd usually been the stay at home parent. It was pretty much the same as when he watched the kids while she was gone on business trips.

Aside from the fact that he'd had to do it in an entirely new place, without neighbors to lean on during emergencies and their established network of babysitters. And all the while feeling like his life was crashing down around him, his children confused and scared about the changes in their lives, which had been upended every bit as much as Nick's had been.

Probably even more, and during their formative years to boot. Youthful resiliency might've helped them adjust better to the new situation, but it had also made them feel the painful changes to their lives all the more strongly.

It seemed like such a small thing, but just having someone he could ask to watch the kids when he needed it had probably kept him from falling apart completely during the worst moments. He only hoped he'd been as much help to Gen when she needed him to watch Billy, or move heavy furniture or do basic maintenance around her apartment that she couldn't do herself.

Although he had to admit, with a bit of chagrin, that when she dropped her son off he usually just plopped the kids down in front of a screen and made sure they had healthy snacks to munch on. He tried to reassure himself that the times he took them to the nearby playground to run around, more infrequently than he probably should've, made up for that.

Tallie, bless her heart, ran right up to the door as usual and knocked enthusiastically, calling hello to Gen and Billy. Nick caught up and gently pulled her back, telling her to be polite; Gen insisted she didn't mind, but he still thought his daughter shouldn't be so noisy, especially in consideration of their other neighbors.

Considering the panic at the school, he was half afraid Gen wouldn't be there, or if she was would refuse to open the door. But to his relief it opened within ten seconds, his neighbor puffing and glistening with sweat in the doorway.

Gen was a few years younger than him, and while he felt bad thinking it, it would've been generous to call her pleasantly plump. Although he could admit that he'd gotten more than a bit doughy himself lately, stress and his workload preventing him from proper exercise, rest, or focusing on healthy eating.

Shut In

In any case, the pleasant part certainly fit his friend; cheerful and kindhearted, she was one of the sweetest people he'd ever met. His kids loved her, and the few times they went together to the park he always had enjoyable conversations with her.

There was a lot of truth to that old saying about a friend in need.

Under the circumstances, Nick wouldn't have blamed Gen for keeping her distance. But to his surprise she immediately pulled him into a fierce hug, then leaned down to hug Tallie and Ricky in turn. If he'd thought of it, he might've been worried about whether or not *she* was safe, but he hated to think like that about his friend. Especially when the risk of being infected was pretty much the same for everyone here.

"Glad you made it out of that madhouse at the school," she said. "I can't believe how crazy it was!"

He felt a surge of guilt; he should've called to ask her if she wanted to go with him to pick up their kids, or at least checked she'd made it home safely with her son.

Before he could think of an appropriate apology, she caught his expression and seemed to read his mind, patting the air reassuringly. "We were just fine. Actually, the school was calling the parents up alphabetically to tell them to pick up their kids, so I was closer to the first notified and was able to get Billy out of that mess before things really got hectic."

"Good," he said sincerely. "There was some freaky stuff happening while I was there. Like parents on the point of going medieval on anyone who got within five feet of their kids. I saw some lady shove a girl to the ground with her foot, then kick off her possibly contaminated shoe and run off. I think a few people might've actually attacked each other as I was leaving."

Gen's plump cheeks, already pink from exertion, flushed even more. "That bad? I'm sorry, I should've called you and given you a heads up about what was going on. I was just in such a panic, needing to get the kiddo out of there, that I didn't think of anything else. Speaking of which

. . ."

She bent down to usher Ricky and Tallie, still with their snacks, into her apartment. "Billy's watching right now, guys, how about you go join him?" She glanced up at Nick as the kids ran inside. "I'm guessing you need me to watch them?"

"Yeah." He allowed himself to be ushered inside. "I'm going to head to the store to buy food that'll store a long time, so I can keep the kids home in this self-imposed quarantine like they're advising." He paused. "Unless you want to come with me? You probably need to do some shopping too."

Gen gave him a regretful look. "You know I'd love to, but I probably won't be here by the time you get back. I don't think I can watch the kids this time, either. Sorry."

Nick looked around, seeing the possessions strewn all over the living room and kitchen, the loaded cardboard boxes and bags. Realization dawned; that's why she'd been so out of breath when she answered the door. "You're leaving?"

Gen nodded, expression tight. "To stay with Darryl's folks until this all blows over."

He frowned. From previous conversations he knew her ex's parents lived up in Gentry County, a little house just outside of Stanberry. It was about as out of the way as you got without jumping in the Missouri River and swimming out to the center, far from any real highways or big cities. He even thought it might be in the fork between two smaller rivers, making it that much harder to get to; of course, a lot of towns around here were between rivers, or at least streams.

"Guess you can't go wrong with getting away from the crowds when there's a disease scare," he agreed.

His friend nodded again. "I have a hard time seeing Zolos finding its way there. And if it did, it would be easy enough to keep it contained. Nobody will be bothering us out at Billy's grandparents' house."

Shut In

Nick hoped so. "Need help loading up?"

She paused, obviously wanting to accept his offer, before shaking her head reluctantly. "The store will probably be pure chaos before too long, once this panic gets in full swing. You'd better get there before shoppers start jousting with their carts over the last case of ramen noodles."

In spite of the situation, he couldn't help but smile at the mental image of people ramming each other like they were playing bumper carts. Then he realized that if it actually got bad enough where he saw something like that happening, it wouldn't be funny at all.

He nodded. "I'll hurry, and if you're still around and need help when I get back I'll be right over. Did you want me to get you anything in case you *are* still here?"

Again Gen paused, tempted, before shaking her head. "I'm going to hurry, so I probably will be gone before you get back. Besides, you'll be loaded down enough getting the food you need for yourself and your kids. I'll try to stop at someplace on the way up."

Nick felt a bit bad about being relieved that she was leaving him free to handle the disaster for his own family. Maybe he should've insisted, but he had a feeling she was right on both points. "If I leave the kids home while I go to the store, could you check on them before you leave? Make sure they're okay?"

"Of course." Gen pulled him into another hug, squeezing tight. "Be safe, you guys."

He hugged her back just as tight. "You too," he said, making his tone as jovial as possible. "We'll see you when this is all over."

His friend held the hug longer than was strictly necessary, seeking some comfort in this frightening situation. Nick couldn't complain, since he wasn't in a hurry to break the hug either; the world had just turned upside-down and there were no assurances anymore.

Nick finally pulled back and hurried to gather up his kids, ignoring their complaints (even Ricky's he noticed with some amusement), and ushering them towards the door.

Gen absently gathered her son in her arms as they left, staring after them worriedly. "You should think about leaving too," she called after them. "If this turns into a pandemic even half as bad as they're predicting, the city will be dangerous even if you never catch the virus."

Again, he had a feeling she wasn't wrong. But where could he go? Ellie's house was in a reasonably upscale neighborhood farther down the river, no better than his apartment for getting away, and they were both only children, him estranged from his extended family and hers nearly nonexistent.

His parents weren't an option, even if he could find his dad or get his mom to agree to help. And Ellie's parents had been older, her dad passed away years ago and her mom in a home suffering from Alzheimer's.

If anything, he'd need to worry about helping *her*, rather than the alternative.

He supposed if worse came to worst, he could head out into the countryside and hope to find a place to stay. But that seemed like an extremely risky prospect when anyone they met could be carrying Zolos and pass it on to them, and for that matter would fear the same of *them* and refuse to offer help, and might even attack them on sight.

Better to hole up in the apartment with plenty of food and wait this out.

"Wasn't Gen going to watch us?" Ricky asked as Nick led them back down to their apartment.

Nick shook his head, cursing inwardly as he struggled to get the key in the lock. There was no immediate danger, he shouldn't be panicking. "Richard," he said solemnly, and his son perked up warily; the only time they used his full name was if he was in trouble or the situation was serious. "I need to go to the store and buy food, and I can't take you."

"Because the store will be like the school?" his son asked.

Shut In

"Maybe." He led his children inside and headed to the TV. "You guys can watch after school today, until I get back. We'll worry about your homework later."

"I didn't get homework, Daddy!" Tallie announced as she hopped up onto the couch and grabbed one of the blankets to snuggle up in.

"Yeah, neither did I," Ricky agreed. "Miss Terrence usually gives it out at the end of the day, and we left early."

"Fine, okay." Nick handed his son the remote and crouched to meet him eye to eye, lowering his voice. "I'm going to leave you here in the apartment while I'm gone. I know I don't usually do that," actually he never did, unless it was just to take out the trash or something like that, "but this is an emergency. I need you to keep a very close eye on your sister, make sure she stays inside and watches TV, and you need to stay inside too."

"I will," his son promised in a solemn voice.

"Good. Keep the door locked, and don't open it for anyone but Gen if she comes by to check on you. If you need anything, and it's a real emergency, see if Gen's still here, or go to Mr. Bennison in the next apartment and ask him to call me. You remember my number?"

The eight-year-old nodded uncertainly, staring up at him with wide eyes and obviously overwhelmed by the flow of instructions. "How long will you be gone?"

"Not long." Nick straightened. "You guys can take treats from the junk food cabinet while I'm gone, and if you're good then when I get back you can have an ice cream bar."

Tallie cheered at that, while Ricky gave him a sickly smile. He hoped he hadn't worried the boy more than necessary for a simple errand.

Nick made sure his daughter had something she wanted to watch on the TV, and Ricky had his own show on his tablet, then left and carefully locked the door behind him.

45

Nathan Jones

Then he hurried to his car.

Chapter Three
Shopping

Traffic was unusually light, even for this time of day, as Nick made the short drive to the nearest store. It probably meant people were already putting themselves in quarantine, and he hoped he wasn't making a mistake by risking being around other people at the store.

He felt even less confident in his decision when he parked in the lot and noticed half the shoppers heading to or from their cars wearing face masks or at least gloves. It made him want to slap himself in the forehead for not thinking to grab any gloves or a mask himself, although he wasn't sure he had either at home.

Aside from winter gloves, although he supposed that would've been better than nothing.

Still, the Zolos virus was supposedly mostly centered around the airport; maybe if he hurried and tried not to touch anyone or anything suspicious, he could get out without any trouble. He'd have to hope so, since he needed food or his family's self-imposed quarantine wouldn't last a week.

Even with those flimsy reassurances and considering the necessity of it, it took Nick a few minutes to work up the nerve to leave the car. He'd never considered just how terrifying being infected by a deadly disease could be: a threat he couldn't see, had no way of knowing was there until suddenly he discovered he was dying of it.

Only the incredible rarity of those sorts of diseases kept them from being scary enough to fear leaving the house every day. If this Zolos was as contagious as it sounded, and spreading as quickly as reports indicated, then the outside world had suddenly become a truly terrifying place.

It gave him an inkling of what agoraphobes must feel. And the threat was all the more terrifying with the knowledge that if he was careless or unlucky, it wouldn't just be himself who suffered but also his kids.

Nick finally forced himself to climb out of the driver's seat, wasting no time locking his car behind him and hurrying to one of the outdoor cart racks. Once there he went to the front of the line of carts, to the one that had probably been sitting there for hours or even days, and manhandled it free and over the barrier.

Even with that precaution, he still grabbed the push bar through the sleeves of his jacket, just to be safe. Although he had a feeling it wasn't doing anything for him other than to make him look like an idiot.

At least he *felt* safer.

Automatic doors had never been a more welcome sight, as was the fact that everyone around him was carefully keeping their distance from everyone else. Even more so than was usual for residents of a densely populated and mostly lower income part of the city.

It was obvious he wasn't the only one who'd had the idea of shopping for food to survive a lengthy quarantine. In fact, if it had been hours since the government openly admitted to the presence of Zolos then that explained why half the shelves were looking pretty bare, and shoppers were moving more frantically to snatch up what remained.

Nick was a bit surprised to see that in spite of the disaster, a lot of people didn't seem to be changing their buying habits; he saw shoppers with carts full of fruits, vegetables, and other perishables that wouldn't last more than a week, and others with carts loaded down with cereal, junk food, and frozen dinners.

In fact, aside from the quantity, what had to be ludicrously more than these people usually picked up during a trip to the store, they could've all just been doing some regular afternoon shopping.

Going on a hunch, he made a beeline for the aisle that displayed things like canned foods, rice and dried beans, oatmeal, and spices. He was almost surprised to find the shelves mostly still full, since this seemed like just the type of food he'd want to have for a long term situation: cheap, easy to store, reasonably healthy, and above all else long-lasting.

Well, Nick wasn't one to look a gift horse in the mouth.

He practically walked down the aisle with his arm held out, scooping things into his cart. Mostly he focused on things his kids would be willing to eat like canned fruit, chicken noodle soup, stew, chili, spaghetti noodles and sauce, tuna, and oatmeal. The rest of the cart's basket, and the rack underneath, he loaded down with whatever he could get his hands on, especially bags of rice and flour and beans and unopened boxes of cans, since they took less time to grab than individual cans and would be easier to move.

Nick was no expert, and was in too much of a hurry to do the math, but he was reasonably confident all this food would last him and the kids at least a month. Also Ellie, when she got back and if she decided to live with them during the emergency. In fact, even with her there it could possibly last them as long as two months, although they'd be forced to ration.

Which was, fingers crossed, as long as it would take for the Zolos scare to pass and everything to get back to normal.

It only took him about ten minutes to load his cart down to the point it took physical effort to move it, and the wheels screeched alarmingly under the weight. By that time people were starting to flood into the aisle, either coming to the same realization he had or because there was no other food and they were desperate.

Heck, people might be fighting over bags of dog food by the end, if things got bad enough. Kind of like the news stories he remembered about the panic before hurricanes.

He dodged around the people crowding into the aisle, surprised to see that in just the short time he'd been in the store the crowd of shoppers had doubled in size. Every checkout station was open, harried-looking store employees rushing to run purchases as the lines of customers got longer and longer, clogging the front of the store and even stretching back into the aisles.

The problem was only exacerbated by the fact that everyone was keeping a cautious bubble of open space around them for fear of infection. Although on the plus side even though there was plenty of shouting, including swearing and shockingly vicious threats, nobody so much as jostled anyone else.

It was the politest panic Nick had ever seen.

He joined the shortest line he could reach, then settled in to wait as the store grew louder and more chaotic by the minute. Of which, going by his phone, there'd been almost 30 when he checked it near the front of the line; it was like the shopping rush the Friday after Thanksgiving, except now people were leaving electronics and toys on the shelves and stripping the store bare of anything edible, wearable, or that had the slightest emergency use.

The man behind him had a cart half full of donuts and other baked sweets, of all things, and the other half was filled with curtains and sheets in the largest sizes possible. To use as blankets? Bandages? Partitions? Just to feel like he was buying something that might help?

Most shoppers were purchasing too many products to ring up efficiently, not to mention the confusion caused by people knocking things off the little escalator things to put their own stuff on, or refusing to use them at all for fear someone infected might've touched them at some point. So most employees were simply having customers bring their carts right up to the register, then scanning the items through, bagging them, and crowding as many as possible into the tiny space beyond the register before loading bags up into the carts again.

The employees were wearing gloves and masks, unsurprisingly, but even so seemed very unhappy and grudging about having to let so many products handled by possibly infected shoppers pass through their hands. A few, Nick noted, were actually having customers bring their carts around to scan and bag items themselves, while supervising from a cautious distance.

Shut In

A thief probably could've walked stuff right out the front door in full view, and he had a feeling nobody would've tried to stop them. Or at least lay a hand on them. Surprisingly, though, there didn't seem to be anyone trying it; maybe they were afraid if they did, other panicked customers might view their stuff as fair game and steal it from them in turn.

The illusion of order was often all it took to maintain it in truth. Although given the increasingly frantic mood, Nick didn't want to stick around any longer than he had to. He'd already seen a furious customer throwing potatoes at everyone around him in some spate of fury or panic, and while it might have looked funny on the surface those things could hurt.

From the sounds of it some of those hit *had* been hurt, in fact; he didn't want to still be here when more people realized that chucking hard objects was something they could do without risking touching infected people, causing a downward spiral of escalating violence.

Like the world's most vicious food fight.

Partly out of boredom, and partly to feel like he was doing something, Nick tried calling Ellie every five minutes or so. Although he eventually stopped leaving voicemails when he realized how frantic he was starting to sound.

He couldn't help it. His ex-wife made a point of always being close to her phone, especially when it was his turn to watch the kids, in case there was some emergency with them. In a situation like this he couldn't think of much besides her phone being smashed to smithereens or confiscated that would keep her from answering his calls, let alone calling herself.

The thought of why she hadn't yet was pointing him to some grim possibilities he didn't want to contemplate.

Nick also called Gen, and was relieved to hear that she'd checked on the kids not long ago and they were doing fine. His friend also reported that she and Billy were out the door on their way north, and wished him and the kids the best.

"I can't really invite you guys up to visit, considering I'll be crashing with my ex's parents," she said in a wry tone, a subtle indication that she wasn't thrilled about the prospect. "But if you do decide to leave KC and head my way, let me know and I'll do whatever I can to help you."

"Thanks," he said, "but I'm buying tons of food here, and me and the kids will be fine holed up in the apartment until all this blows over."

"I hope so. Take care of yourselves, Nick." She hung up.

He contemplated checking in on his mom, then decided that not even the end of the world could make that call tolerable. Besides, she should be okay with Mack and his kids. As for Nick's dad, he wouldn't even know how to go about contacting him, so that was out.

With his thoughts on Ellie, he also called the nursing home where her mom was staying. The receptionist who answered his call sounded harried, informing him that he wasn't the only one checking in on parents or grandparents with this Zolos scare, and their phones were ringing off the hook. She assured him that she wasn't aware of any issues with Mrs. Feldman, but that she'd have someone check on her and call him back to let him know how she was doing.

To his relief, the woman also assured him that the nursing home had almost no contact with the nearby hospitals and emergency rooms, and they were being extra cautious about turning away visitors and keeping the place closed down to make sure nobody was exposed to the dreaded virus.

That was more weight off his shoulders than he'd expected, after seeing the pitiable state of poor Mr. Thurston on the TV; in spite of the divorce, Nick had always thought Ellie's mom was a sweet woman, even when Alzheimer's began taking its toll. Considering she was the only grandparent the kids really had, he'd even taken them to visit her a few times when Ellie was gone on business.

He hoped the home was able to keep out the sickness; the kids were sad enough about their grandma not always recognizing them, but to lose her entirely would be devastating. Especially with their emotional states already so fragile with the divorce.

Of course with this current crisis, especially with their mom not answering her phone, they might be facing even worse tragedies. Nick tried to force himself not to think like that, but stranded in a checkout line in the middle of a store full of paranoid, panicking people wasn't the best place for thinking happy thoughts.

An eternity or almost exactly forty minutes after entering the store, Nick finally reached the register. His cashier was one of those who was still personally running items, although the poor guy acted as if he was handling radioactive waste, and sharply ordered him to leave things on the end of the escalator and he'd pick them up from there and ring them.

For all the good that would do, although Nick didn't bother pointing that out.

In fact, he wished he hadn't thought of it so carefully when he realized that while the gloves might've protected the employee, the outside of them had touched items touched by every single person who'd gone through that line. Meaning if anyone in it had been infected, Nick might soon be too.

And far worse, so would his kids; maybe he should've insisted on ringing up his items himself after all.

Although that probably would've made this trip to the store take minutes longer. It was a laborious enough process to slowly empty the cart across the scanner with the employee's help, then bag everything up and load it all back on. The young man at least seemed grateful that so many of his cans were in unopened boxes, or big sacks of grain, beans, or flour.

Finally it was time to pay. Nick glanced at the little monitor that told the final tally as he pulled out his credit card, then froze when he saw the numbers. "What is this?" he demanded.

The cashier had the resigned look of someone who'd been through this way too many times. "Just got word a half hour or so ago to double prices. Employees are still putting up notices, but the change in policy was effective immediately."

Seriously?

If there was one thing Nick had really, really, *really* learned in his life, it was that throwing money at problems didn't always make them go away. And throwing *lots* of money made them not go away even worse.

On the other hand, when the problem was not starving to death while under quarantine as a virulent disease ravaged his city, throwing money at it seemed like a better alternative to, well, starving to death.

So he barely hesitated in swiping his card, thinking bitterly that if he'd gone to the store immediately instead of watching the news first he'd be paying half as much. And even more bitterly that only hours ago the idea of putting his card over the limit just to buy food would've filled him with despair.

He supposed there'd be plenty of time for that if the world ever got back to normal, and he found himself once again crushed under a mountain of debt. "Never let the suffering of others stand in the way of making a quick buck, huh?" he said caustically as he put his card back in his wallet.

"I'm just an employee, sir," the young man replied in a weary tone. There wasn't even much of a "screw you" behind his tone; how long had he been putting up with this from customers, when the decision had been made far above his head? Probably up at the corporate level.

Nick felt a bit guilty. "Sorry, that wasn't cool."

The cashier shrugged. "I'm just living for the end of my shift, dude."

He couldn't help but glance at the teenager's mask and gloves. "I'm a bit impressed you stayed, considering this Zolos scare."

The store employee obviously wasn't in the mood for chitchat; he just motioned to Nick's bags as the card reader confirmed the purchase and a receipt printed out for him to take. By far the longest receipt he'd ever run up. "Thank you for shopping with us, sir. Have a nice day."

Shut In

"Yeah, you too." Nick struggled to get his cart squeaking its way to the door, waiting nervously through a minor bottleneck as people slowly poured through. Then he was in the parking lot and headed briskly for his car.

There were abandoned carts all over the place, people in too much of a rush or too paranoid to risk taking them to the cart return areas. Many clogged parking spaces, and Nick shook his head as he saw the drivers of newly arrived cars risking scratching their paint by pushing the carts away with their bumpers as they parked, or even scraping along beside them and wedging the carts between their vehicle and the one next to them.

He wasn't pleased at all to find that the truck next to him had done that as well, half crumpling a cart against the passenger side of his car and denting the door.

He cursed up a blue streak as he unloaded as much of his cart into the trunk as it could fit, and the rest into the backseat through the driver's side. He had the strong urge to throw a can at the truck's windshield, but valiantly resisted it. Although more to avoid wasting precious food than out of any desire to be reasonable.

In spite of his anger, though, Nick ended up leaving his own cart where it was. And instead of trying to disentangle the cart crushed against his car he just backed out. The squealing of metal on metal as his paint job took damage he couldn't afford to repair set his teeth on edge, but he at least had the minor satisfaction of seeing the cart's push bar smash the truck's tail lights on that side.

Hopefully it hadn't also smashed his.

Another car was waiting to take the space he'd just vacated, the woman driving it staring at him like he was a lunatic as he drove off. Nick ignored her as best he could and wove through the parking lot maze of abandoned carts, cars searching for parking spaces, and shoppers pushing absurdly overloaded carts, breathing a sigh of relief once he reached the road.

Which, in a chilling contrast, was just as eerily abandoned as before. As if everyone who was out and about at the moment had all gathered at the store. Which maybe they had.

At least he didn't run into any problems on the way home.

* * * * *

Tallie was waiting to throw her arms around him the moment he opened the door. Her eyes and nose were red and she'd obviously been crying, and even now that he was home she looked like a little lost fawn caught in the headlights, bewildered at this strange change to her peaceful world.

"Daddy, are things okay now?" she asked.

Nick thought of the mangled side of his car, the panic he'd seen at the store. He still had the rest of the groceries to unload, another few minutes outside at least where he could come in contact with someone, possibly picking up this infection from them.

But the sight of his little girl so obviously distressed overshadowed all other considerations. He hastily set the bags he was holding down, then stepped forward and swept her up in a hug. Her arms and legs locked around him with every ounce of strength in her tiny body, and from the way she shuddered he had a feeling she'd started crying again.

He hugged her back fiercely, kissing the top of her head. "Of course things are okay, sweetie girl," he murmured. "This is just like that flu scare last year . . . it'll be over in a few weeks."

Ricky, standing nearby looking as if he wanted to rush forward and throw his arms around his dad too but was trying to act mature, spoke up diffidently. "We never had to evacuate from school last year. And you never went to the store and bought a bunch of food."

Nick felt Tallie hug him even tighter in sudden fear, and had to resist the urge to shoot his son a sharp look; Ricky was just as scared as his sister, even if he was being brave about it. So brave Nick couldn't help but feel a fierce surge of pride for his son.

56

Shut In

He stepped forward and crouched to wrap an arm around Ricky's shoulders. "It's a bit different," he admitted. "But it won't affect us at all. I mostly work at home anyway, and I can do must of the things I usually have to travel for in conference calls if I really need to. You guys will probably like it more anyway, since you won't have to go to school."

Ricky thought that over solemnly, then looked at the bags he'd brought in. "You need help with the groceries?"

Nick paused, weighing his desire to unload the car quickly with his need to protect his son. It wasn't a hard choice. "No, I've got it." He gently set Tallie down. "How about you and your sister take the stuff I bring in to the kitchen and start unloading things?"

Fifteen minutes later, Nick locked the car and carried the last few bags into his apartment. He paused in the doorway, staring out at a deceptively peaceful world.

One he no longer felt safe venturing out into.

So this was it. They had what they needed, fingers crossed, and there were no more reasons to go outside. That meant it was time to lock the door and hope against hope their little apartment stayed a protected bubble against the dangers of Zolos.

He threw the bolt with an almost ceremonial feeling, wondering if he should find a way to keep the kids from opening it. He fully intended to make sure they both, especially Tallie, knew very well that they shouldn't go outside, and exactly why; the consequences for disobeying could literally be death in this situation. Nick didn't want to scare them, but they needed to understand the danger.

But no matter how well he explained things, that might not guarantee two young children wouldn't try to go outside anyway while throwing a tantrum, or if they were going stir crazy.

In the end, though, he decided it was better not to make it harder to open the door than was strictly necessary, in case there was an emergency and they needed to leave quickly. It would be a bit ironic if he nailed the thing shut to protect his family from Zolos, only to be unable to flee if there was a fire.

Although there was the fire escape connecting to his office.

Nick turned his back on the door and made his way to the kitchen to begin helping put away all the food. Now that they were safely inside, he didn't have to worry about potential exposure to the virus. He hoped. Although what he *did* have to worry about was any exposure they might've already had today, or possibly even previous days without realizing it.

He resolved to watch his children closely over the next few days for Zolos symptoms, and teach them to Ricky and even Tallie so they could tell him immediately if they noticed anything wrong.

If the unthinkable happened and they *did* get sick, he wasn't sure what he'd do. The hospitals would probably be overloaded to the point of uselessness within days if the outbreak got out of control, if they weren't already, but even so they might be able to offer care, medicine and whatever, that he simply couldn't offer if he tried to help his kids at home.

Well, he'd have to keep an eye on the news, make the decision if the unthinkable happened and they were infected with Zolos.

Although fingers crossed, the next few weeks would be nothing more than a boring wait in the apartment for things to blow over.

Chapter Four
LAX

Ellie was tense as their plane bumped down onto the tarmac at LAX. It wasn't the landing, of course . . . it was everything else that could go wrong afterwards.

"Think we'll finally get to leave the plane?" Hal asked, staring intently out the window at the distant airport.

"I'd be happy if they finally let us use our phones so I can call my kids," she replied.

He turned from the window just long enough to give her a sincere, reassuring smile. "Hey, I'm sure they're just fine. Probably sitting at home fretting for *you*, and already left a dozen messages to your voicemail asking where you are."

"Probably." Ellie appreciated the reassurance. Hal had turned out to be a kindhearted young man, an unexpected friend during this long confinement on the plane.

He went back to looking out the window. Or maybe brooding about the people he cared about. "I'm sure all our loved ones are fine," she said, patting his hand. He just grunted in reply.

They weren't the only ones fretting. The entire cabin hung heavy with tense silence as the plane inched closer to the airport, and Ellie wasn't the only one who jumped when the pilot's voice abruptly crackled over the speakers.

"Hey, folks," he said, sounding tense. Which was understandable; how much sleep had the poor man had during all this? "Got some news from LAX, mostly good, some bad."

Nathan Jones

No bad news would've sounded better when a deadly virus was sweeping across the globe. Especially when the man continued and it turned out the news was more than "some" bad.

"During the time we were in the air, an outbreak of Zolos was discovered in the luggage retrieval area of the airport. It has now been contained, the remainder of the airport scrubbed as well as possible, so we're going to risk disembarking at a terminal. Your luggage will be manually unloaded and distributed to you there. Once you have it we would advise you to hurry through the airport, ignoring the quarantined area if possible, and leave as quickly as you can."

"Why go into the airport at all?" a woman near the back of the plane yelled in a mixture of panic and anger. "Why not just drop us off on the tarmac, and we can leave the airport without going near anyone?"

There was no reply from the pilot, of course, although a flight attendant appeared to look around worriedly.

"You want to have a bunch of idiots running around where airplanes and ground vehicles are driving?" a man called back. "They'd never let us do that."

"You calling me an idiot for being cautious? Why can't the plane drive to somewhere they *can* drop us off?" the woman insisted. "Why risk taking us into a place where we can get sick and potentially spread this disease? That doesn't make any sense."

"What part of *contained* did you not understand?" the man shouted.

The cabin filled with the babble of arguing people. Ellie watched it all, not sure where she fell on the issue. She certainly didn't want to risk being exposed to Zolos, but she could also understand that efficiency wouldn't allow for ideal solutions.

She just hoped the officials containing the outbreak knew what they were doing.

None of the airplane's crew had any answers for them, or at least any they were saying. The plane continued on to a terminal as if this was any ordinary flight, the tense silence returning as it carefully moved into place and the accordion connector extended.

The flight attendants, seeming eager to have some semblance of the usual routine to keep to, made sure everyone retrieved their possessions from the overhead compartments and departed the plane in an orderly fashion. Ellie noticed a few people holding their breaths as they stepped into the airport, although she wondered what the point was. They couldn't exactly keep that up the entire time until they were able to leave.

Although it was hard to pay attention to much besides the maddeningly calm, soothing woman's voice speaking almost constantly over the airport's loudspeakers. "YOUR ATTENTION PLEASE. A NATIONWIDE STATE OF EMERGENCY IS NOW IN EFFECT. PLEASE REMAIN CALM. ALL ARRIVING AIRPLANES ARE GROUNDED UNTIL FURTHER NOTICE. PLEASE AVOID PHYSICAL CONTACT WITH OTHER PEOPLE. PLEASE REMAIN CALM. PLEASE EVACUATE THE AIRPORT IN A SWIFT AND ORDERLY FASHION. AVOID CROWDED AND PUBLIC PLACES.

"PLEASE REMAIN CALM. IF YOU HAVE HAND SANITIZER, GLOVES, OR SURGICAL MASKS IN YOUR POSSESSION, PLEASE MAKE USE OF THEM. THOSE ITEMS ARE SOLD OUT AT THE LAX GIFT SHOPS, PLEASE DO NOT GO THERE SEEKING THEM. PLEASE AVOID BATHROOMS AND FACILITIES UNLESS ABSOLUTELY NECESSARY, AND USE THE AVAILABLE TOILET SEAT COVERS. PLEASE REMAIN CALM.

"YOUR ATTENTION PLEASE . . ."

Ellie wasn't sure how anyone was supposed to remain calm while being shouted at in a soothing voice about a nationwide state of emergency. Especially concerning an invisible peril that could kill them all, one they had no way of knowing about until it was too late. And even more so when the message was frequently interrupted by things like, "Security to Terminal 3a," and "emergency services required on the concourse."

Since it would be a while before their luggage could be offloaded, she took the opportunity to step off to one side and turn her phone back on. Since the calm, soothing airport voice lady was screaming about this being a nationwide state of emergency at the top of her lungs, it was reasonable to assume that the government no longer cared whether she called anyone and told them what was going on.

Also she saw a bunch of people wandering around talking on their phones, and there were no grim suited men with earpieces tackling them and confiscating the devices. In fact, it kind of annoyed her that nobody had bothered to inform her that it was now okay to use her phone, considering she'd spent the better part of a day desperate to get in contact with her loved ones.

Although she supposed it was an understandable oversight, all things considered.

As Hal had predicted, she had indeed received dozens of calls and there were 31 new messages on her voicemail. Most of the calls were from Nick, one was from the nursing home where her mom was staying, a couple were from friends, and a half dozen or so were work related.

Ellie fully intended to listen to the messages, but at the moment she wasted no time calling Nick's phone. It only rang once before his familiar, wonderful voice sounded in her ear, desperate with relief. "Ellie! Are you okay?"

"Nick?" she said, fighting back tears. "I'm fine. Are you guys safe?"

"We're fine," he practically babbled. "Me and the kids are all safe. We're okay."

"Oh thank God," she said, sagging back against the wall. "I was so worried."

"*You* were worried?" he shot back with a ragged laugh. "I've been trying to call you all day!"

As evidenced by the dozens of missed calls. "I know. They made us turn off our phones for national security reasons, probably to avoid sparking a panic."

Her ex-husband grunted sourly. "No escaping that now that the word is out. Had a bit of a panic getting the kids home from school, but we're all home safe."

Wait, *what*? "What do you mean?" she demanded.

Nick quickly explained his day, getting the kids safely home from school and buying enough food for them to wait out this Zolos panic, then locking themselves into his apartment. "We've got plenty for you when you get here," he finished, then paused uncertainly. "That is, if that's how you want to arrange things."

"I don't care, as long as I'm with my kids and they're safe." Ellie noticed the people around her shifting, turning towards the far side of the terminal, and followed their gazes to where airport employees were starting to bring in luggage. She continued hastily. "I don't have too much time and I want to talk to the kids. But first, I have to know if you're going to be okay until I get there."

She heard him draw a breath to reply, but before he could she continued firmly. "I don't want you to just say what I want to hear, either. I need to know if you're going to be able to handle this."

Her ex-husband was slow to answer. Long enough that she wondered if he was going to do exactly what she'd just told him not to. And to be fair, rationally speaking she knew if there actually had been a problem then of course she didn't really want to hear it. What good would it do other than to make her worry?

But he took the question seriously. "You know," he said in a low voice, as if worried the kids might overhear him, "for most of my life I've lived with a sense of doom hanging over my head. Like something terrible was about to happen, or already had but I just didn't know it yet."

Ellie stared at the phone for a few long seconds. "What are you talking about, Nick?" she demanded, half exasperated, half bewildered. "I've never seen the slightest hint of that sort of anxiousness in you."

"Of course not. The feeling was irrational, so what good would it have done to show signs of that sort of dread bubbling in me?"

Even considering she'd asked him to be honest, this really wasn't what she'd had in mind. "If you're trying to make me feel better by telling me this . . ."

"I'm just saying, Ells, since I first heard about this possible pandemic that sense of doom has disappeared. Entirely."

Ellie again stared at the phone. Okay, now this was getting weird. "Are you saying . . . you somehow knew this was coming?"

"No, of course not, I just said the feeling was irrational!" he snapped, then moderated his tone with a hint of embarrassment. "I'm saying that when there was nothing to worry about, I worried. But now that we're in the middle of a real disaster, I'm calm and focused."

She heard him take a deep breath before he continued in a tone of pure conviction. "Nothing is going to happen to our kids, Ellie. If there's one thing you can be sure of, even if the country falls apart around us, it's that when you make it home they'll be waiting for you, safe and sound."

Ellie felt tears come to her eyes. She didn't know if it was because of his reassurances, or from her desperate need to be there for her children when she was half the country away. She sniffled and did her best to fight back the surge of emotions. "I'd like to talk to them now," she said in a thick voice.

Nick's tone became lighter. "Well you're in luck, because they're practically climbing up my legs in their eagerness to talk to you."

She could freely admit she cried openly when she heard Tallie's and Ricky's sweet voices. Just her luck that the stress and worry of her situation picked that exact moment to smack her in the tear ducts. She kept it together enough to talk to her children, listening to them describe their frightening experiences at the school during the evacuation, and then about staying in the house alone for the first time ever while their dad went to get food for them.

Shut In

Ellie wasn't sure she approved of that, although when they told her that Gen and Billy had left she grudgingly admitted that he might not have had much choice.

She turned as the airline employees called over the terminal's speakers that the luggage had been brought in and was ready to be passed out. "I need to go," she told her children reluctantly. "I love you two so, so much, and I promise I'll be with you soon. Until I am be safe and stay indoors with your dad, okay?"

"Okay," Tallie said, with Ricky solemnly echoing her.

Ellie reluctantly said her goodbyes, promising Nick she'd call again when she had more time, then hung up. For a few seconds she just stood there composing herself, then she tucked her phone back into her purse, wiped at her eyes, and put on her best business face as she prepared to tackle the challenge of getting home.

Although she was in a hurry to leave, not just because of the danger of Zolos but to get back to her children, she at least wanted to say goodbye to Hal before she left. He was standing not far away, also on his phone and seemingly coming to the end of his call as well so he could get his luggage.

"Okay, let me know when you find out anything," he was telling whoever he was talking to as she approached. There was a pause, then he said. "Yeah, absolutely." Another pause. "I know. Love you too."

The teenager lowered his phone, then looked up and saw Ellie standing nearby. He gave her a weak smile. "My dad," he said to her questioning look. "He says there's talk that the Japanese government is going to load all foreign nationals onto planes and send them back to their country of origin, or at least any country that will harbor them. Which probably means the US, he hopes."

"Is he going to try to come to LA to meet you?" she asked.

Hal shook his head. "KC, if it comes to it. I need to get back and check on my family, and he said he'd try to meet me there if he could." He shifted uncomfortably. "Speaking of which, would you mind if I asked how you plan to get there from here?" He hesitated, pride obviously warring with desperation, before taking a breath and continuing. "I'm, uh, kind of at a loss."

Ellie could imagine; at his age he wouldn't have had much experience responding when life threw him curveballs. And he almost certainly didn't have the money to change plans on a whim; having his flight home grounded, without the slightest mention of reimbursement from the airline, was probably a huge problem for him.

"I was thinking I'd rent a car," she replied. "I was actually going to head to the rental place right after grabbing my suitcase, hopefully before they run out."

The young man once again shuffled his feet. "Would you mind carpooling? I can help pay for gas, maybe chip in for the rent. We're headed to the same place anyway."

That gave her pause. She liked Hal well enough and he seemed like a nice person, but at the same time he was still practically a stranger. Then again he was also just a kid, and her neighbor, and he needed help.

And it wasn't as if she hadn't jumped onto the carpooling board in college once or twice to get places, traveling with complete strangers. Those had all mostly turned out very well, and she'd made some good friends on the way.

Still, she wasn't the type to make rash decisions. "How about you tag along with me to the car rental place while I think it over?"

"I really appreciate even that." The teenager nodded towards the pile of luggage. "Should we grab our stuff?"

Ellie nodded back and walked beside him across the terminal. If she was being honest with herself, she'd pretty much already decided to let Hal come with her. If nothing else, it meant she wouldn't have to travel alone. Especially if the threat of Zolos led to any sort of civil unrest; safety in numbers and all that.

Especially numbers that were built like a quarterback.

Shut In

The baggage was being handed out first come, first served, passengers pointing out their suitcases and other items as airport employees, wearing masks and gloves, slid them across the floor towards their owners.

It took Hal five minutes to get his suitcase, then they had to wait a few more minutes while Ellie shouted among the crowd to get hers. As they did, the teenager pulled out his phone and made another call. Ellie tried not to eavesdrop on her tentative traveling companion, although it was hard not to since he was standing right next to her and speaking loud enough to be heard over the background babble.

"Hey, Mom. Sorry I've been out of contact, they wouldn't let us use our phones." A pause. "Yeah, just checking in to see how you and the kids are doing." His tone was surprisingly neutral, especially considering he'd been out of contact with his mom for a day or so during a pandemic scare.

Ellie's heart broke at the thought of Ricky ever talking to her like that, and had to remind herself that she didn't know Hal's situation, or why things might be strained between him and his mom.

"Good, keep doing that . . . yeah, I'm on my way home now," he continued. "I'll try to get back as quick as I can, but it might be tough." Ellie didn't miss the quick glance he shot her way, and resisted the urge to shake her head wryly as he continued. "Yeah, you can use my place if you need to. Yeah, it's in the same place." He looked annoyed for a second as he listened. "I guess, sure, take whatever you need to feed the kids."

He stressed that last slightly, and as he listened for the next ten or so seconds his face became stony. "Okay fine, whatever. I don't have time for this right now. Yeah . . . yeah. Um look, I need to go. I'll call again when I can. Yes, I *will*."

The teenager hung up with no further preamble, stared at his phone for a second with his jaw clenched, then pocketed it and glanced at Ellie. "Sorry about that."

She wasn't sure whether he meant making a call in front of her, or what had sounded like a tense conversation with his mom. She decided to go for the less awkward option. "No problem, I'll probably need to make more calls myself when I can."

Hal nodded and faced forward, and they waited in slightly uncomfortable silence until an employee slid Ellie's suitcase to her. The young man made to carry it for her, but she shook her head and retrieved it herself.

It wasn't a trust thing, she just had no problem carrying her own suitcase. "I've got it."

"Okay." He gave her a smile, his previous easygoing mood making a tentative return. "Just figured playing pack mule might butter you up about letting me carpool with you."

Ellie laughed and shook her head. "If it had anything in it besides clothes and toiletries and weighed more than ten pounds I might take you up on that."

Now that they had their luggage they wasted no time exiting the terminal, following the signs pointing them to the car rental place. The airport around them was the least crowded she'd ever seen it, which she supposed wasn't surprising since anyone who didn't have to be there had probably left.

Although she *did* notice a fairly large crowd around a bank of TVs, those ones airports had to show departure and arrival times. Only these ones showed no departures and only a single monitor for arrivals; the rest had been changed to what looked like a news channel, which is what had drawn the crowd.

Not that Ellie blamed them, considering she'd been in a news void for almost a day with no idea what was going on.

"What are you doing?" Hal asked, nervously glancing at the crowd around them as she drifted towards the bank of monitors. She waved him to silence and kept going, eyes glued to one of the screens as she got close enough to hear the audio.

Shut In

". . . must once again strongly repeat, for the sake of all viewers currently tuning in," a distinguished looking older newscaster was saying in the gravest tones, "that this is NOT a case of isolated incidents that we are reporting as a point of interest, but a severe emergency situation. From what we've been told from official sources, there are already outbreaks outside of airports in several major cities across the United States. Including in our own fair city. And more are being discovered by the hour."

Ellie drifted to a stop a cautious distance behind the loosely gathered crowd also intent on the news. Hal slowed to a stop beside her, expression troubled as they listened.

"All knowledge of this situation had previously been suppressed in an attempt to avoid a panic. However, at this point the Federal government, State of California, and City of Los Angeles are in agreement that the outbreaks cannot be contained. They are turning to the citizens to take all precautions, starting immediately, to help with containment efforts and for your own safety. At this point the President is seriously considering taking measures to lock down infected cities, in a last ditch effort to contain what is looking to be a widespread pandemic."

Hal swore softly. He wasn't the only one reacting to the news, and several people were shushing loudly as the noise volume of the crowd drowned out the newscaster's voice.

Ellie, leaning forward in an attempt to hear better, jumped and gave a frightened squeak as someone touched her elbow. With Hal beside her it could only be him, which was a relief in spite of the glare she shot him for scaring her like that.

He didn't seem to notice as he leaned close to her ear to be heard. "The car's radio will have the news too." He looked around uneasily. "Something tells me we should try to get out of here as quickly as possible. Out of LA, I mean."

She didn't recall ever agreeing to let the young man ride along with her, only to let him walk with her to the rental place while she considered it. But she supposed he might've meant that in a more general sense, as in both of them should be in a rush to get out whether or not they traveled together.

Besides, under the circumstances she couldn't blame him for making assumptions since she'd been leaning towards letting him tag along anyway. Not to mention she also agreed with him; the quicker they got out of here and on their way home, the better.

Still, as they hurried on their way Ellie caught a last snippet from the newscaster. "-confirmed that as yet travel to and from cities where outbreaks are reported has not been restricted, however officials are strongly urging all citizens to remain in your homes under self-imposed quarantine if at all possible. In the meantime all flights are grounded for the foreseeable future, and all trains and long distance buses are halted. Beyond that, our sources with local law enforcement tell us they are drawing up plans to put barricades in place across all roads into the city as early as tomorrow morning, working in conjunction with emergency services to test all . . . ."

She wanted to hang back to listen to the rest of that, but it looked as if there was even more need for haste than she'd realized. The news simultaneously filled her with relief and made ice crawl down her spine: relief, because it meant she wouldn't be kept from going home to her children. And terror, because if infected cities weren't already being closed off then it was almost guaranteed the disease would spread.

If it hadn't already.

The government really *had* failed to contain this disaster. And if Zolos had managed to escape the airport in Kansas City, her family was in the path of it.

* * * * *

"I'm sorry, ma'am, there are simply no cars available at the moment." the woman behind the counter at the car rental agency said, with the forced polite tone universally adopted by service industry workers who were currently wishing they could be anywhere else. Including possibly the bottom of the ocean or the surface of the sun.

Ellie could sympathize with her, since she'd certainly been in that position before. Which was why she usually tried her best to avoid causing those sorts of headaches when she was on the other side of the encounter. "Is it a matter of waiting until one becomes available?" she asked.

The car rental employee shook her head emphatically. "They've all been commandeered by Federal relief services to ferry people to the quarantine camp north of Los Angeles, just outside city limits." She hesitated. "Since you can't rent a car, you might consider making use of one anyway, to ride to the camp. It's probably the best situation you can be in under the circumstances."

"We're not infected!" Hal protested heatedly.

"I sure hope not," the woman replied, deadly serious. "But the quarantine camp is for everyone left stranded in Los Angeles from the airports, harbors, bus stations, and anywhere else. The actual infected are in their own containment areas, with zero contact with anyone else until they're no longer contagious."

"People can stop being contagious?" Ellie asked eagerly. That offered a glimmer of hope that this nightmare might one day end.

The car rental employee grimaced. "Assuming they don't die, which apparently nine out of ten do. The survivors need to wait at least three weeks for the virus to clear from their system, then go through decontamination to make sure they're not carrying any on their clothes or skin, and then they're safe to rejoin the general population."

"You sure about that?" Hal asked. "Have we even known about Zolos for three weeks?"

"I don't know, sir, I sell cars for a living." The woman's grimace deepened. "Or at least I did. I've heard it's the quarantine period for some other viral infections, that's all I know." She straightened tiredly. "Go to the camp or don't, but if that's all then I need to help the next customer."

71

Ellie shook her head morosely, backing away from the counter so the next person in line could move forward to try to rent cars that weren't available.

There was no way she was going to any quarantine camp. Her children needed her, were probably scared to death in a crisis like this, and she wasn't about to be trapped more than half the country away for weeks. Even more than her own safety, she'd move heaven and earth to be there for Tallie and Ricky.

Although she had no intention of ignoring her own safety either, which was an equally important reason to avoid this camp like, well, the plague. She had no doubt the officials in charge of it would very carefully section off everyone who came in, isolating groups to reduce the risk of infection, and quickly remove anyone discovered with the virus to a more secure location. They probably had carefully crafted plans for just this sort of situation.

And the plans, no matter how ingenious and thoughtfully prepared, were pretty much a waste of time.

In her line of work, Ellie had had enough experience with large corporations managing hundreds or even thousands of employees to know how they operated. There were always errors, everything from minor mistakes to catastrophic oversights to real nightmarish boondoggles caused by greed and shady activity at the mid or high levels.

A quarantine camp in the middle of an epidemic, or more likely a pandemic, was like an egg in the middle of a herd of stampeding elephants: it would just take one misstep for it to all fall apart, and there were countless opportunities for that one thing to go wrong. Practically every person in the camp would present such an opportunity.

The emergency relief personnel would have to be absolutely flawless in order to prevent just that one tiny slip up that could spell catastrophe for countless vulnerable people. Even if they were absolute professionals, it wasn't realistic to expect that kind of perfection from them. Especially for any length of time.

Shut In

So no, a quarantine camp was the last place she wanted to be. In fact, if she couldn't get out of the city, quickly and without coming into contact with anyone or anything a contagious person might have touched, she might not live past the next few days, let alone long enough to get back to her children.

She needed a car, and it was obvious finding one at the airport was going to be as difficult as it was dangerous. Best to get away entirely, since this place was a hotspot for spreading Zolos in spite of the authorities' best efforts.

Hal had been intent on his phone while she was stewing on the problem, and he abruptly grunted. "Got it."

Ellie turned to look at him with a frown. "Got what?"

He pointed the screen towards her and tapped it. "These are all people within ten blocks who are putting themselves in voluntary quarantine in their house or apartment until the crisis is over, and are willing to sell their car for the right price since they won't have any use for it and might need money."

She arched an eyebrow. Buying a vehicle from people in that situation was an option she hadn't even considered, although it seemed logical. Those families likely wouldn't have any objections to selling a car they wouldn't be using any time soon, especially if they had two as many households did. Particularly in the wealthier neighborhoods.

Although she had to wonder how people in voluntary quarantine went about selling to complete strangers who might be infected. Ellie looked at the list of cars displayed on the teenager's phone, complete with pictures, pertinent details, and contact info. "How is there already a website for that?"

He scrunched his forehead. "There's an existing platform where people are responding to current events. This crisis has been public for what, seven or eight hours? That's practically an eternity on the internet." He leaned forward eagerly, clicking on one of the listings. "See, you take care of payment online, then they leave the keys in the car along with the title signed over to you and give you the location. That way you can come pick it up without needing to have any direct physical contact with anyone."

Ellie motioned for him to take his phone back. "Well I think I could probably buy a car if it's not too expensive." It would probably eat up most of her savings, but maybe she could resell it when she got home. Maybe even on the same site Hal was using. "Can you find one that'll get us to KC?"

Hal stared at her. "You want me to shop for a car for you?"

"Well, I'll want to look at what you find before actually buying it."

He opened his mouth to reply, but before he could a woman spoke up from behind them. "Excuse me!"

They both spun warily, relieved to find that the person who'd spoken was a cautious distance away, standing with a man who had a protective arm around her waist. Her husband, judging by the rings on their fingers. Ellie thought the voice was familiar, and after a moment recognized it as the woman from their flight who'd wanted to disembark onto the tarmac.

She was a bit taller than Ellie, although she stood with a nervous stoop to her shoulders that made her seem smaller and more vulnerable. Her hair was dark brown, worn long in a tight braid that made her features seem more pinched. Although that might've just been her fearful expression. The man with her was tall and slightly overweight, lighter brown hair beginning to recede in spite of the fact that the couple looked to be in their early to mid twenties. Both wore latex gloves and masks.

"Can I help you?" Ellie asked politely.

The woman looked at the man expectantly until he cleared his throat and stepped forward. "Hi. Um, I'm Brock Nowak, and this is my wife Hannah." Hannah beamed around her mask when he said that, practically bouncing excitedly. That led Ellie to guess they were newlyweds.

Very new newlyweds, as it turned out when Brock continued. "We were on our way home from our honeymoon when this all happened, and overheard you talking about buying a car to get to Kansas City. We live in St. Louis, so we're wondering if we could carpool."

Well, this was turning into quite the crowd. And Ellie didn't even have a car yet. Still, safety in numbers and all that. "I think that would be fine," she said cautiously. "You can contribute to buying the car and paying for gas."

Hannah stared at her blankly, as if she'd just asked for something unreasonable. "Why wouldn't you help us get home?" she demanded. "It doesn't cost you any extra to let us tag along."

That wasn't strictly true, although the added weight wouldn't really add too much to gas costs. Still, it was as if the two had no idea how carpooling worked; even Hal, who'd admitted he couldn't contribute much, was giving the couple an odd look.

Brock seemed to sense they weren't making a good impression because he hastily spoke up. "We could probably chip in." He motioned to a plastic bag his wife held. "Also, we were able to get our hands on gloves and masks and hand sanitizer and things like that. We'll be happy to share them with you."

"Actually, we insist on it," Hannah cut in hastily. "If we're going to be traveling together we need to make sure none of us get infected with this Zolos virus."

That seemed reasonable enough, and actually useful. Besides, it would be cruel to refuse to help newlyweds who'd just come from their honeymoon, just because they didn't know carpool etiquette of all things. "All right," Ellie said. "We're looking for a car now."

"Actually, it's mostly just a matter of picking one," Hal said. He'd been busy on his phone during the conversation, and now offered it to her again. "I've found a few cheap options that aren't far from the airport."

She began going over the shortened list, while Brock and Hannah cautiously approached to also take a look. The cars all looked reasonable enough, about the same price, mileage, and appearance. Older vehicles, but ones that looked as if they'd make it a few thousand miles to get them to Missouri.

After half a minute Ellie picked one that seemed fine, a red sedan with faded paint that was chipped around the wheel wells, and pointed to it. "This one will work. Let's go."

No one sccmcd to have a problem with that, so they left the car rental place behind and headed for the exit.

Chapter Five
Getting Out

Hannah passed out more gloves and masks for Ellie and Hal as they walked. Ellie wasn't sure how much good those would do against an airborne virus that stayed alive on surfaces, but she had to admit that if nothing else, the psychological effect of having even that protection was enormously comforting.

She'd just need to make sure it didn't cause her to let down her guard.

They finally found crowds in the mostly deserted airport once they reached the entrances; everyone seemed to have converged there in their desperation to get out. Ellie realized why when she saw a police cordon, complete with officers in hazmat suits, blocking off half the airport's exits over by the luggage claim area, and a wall of plastic that stretched across the vast open space to seal off the area, guarded by more officers.

The people who'd been trapped on the other side of the plastic when it was sealed off obviously weren't happy about their situation; they pressed against it and crowded the blocked off entrances, shouting that they weren't sick and desperate to get out before they were infected themselves.

The police weren't risking the slightest chance of the crowd getting out, shoving back against the stretched plastic with plexiglass shields and making liberal use of pepper spray and air horns wherever the barrier had been torn. All the while shouting for the frantic crowd to stay back and remain calm until they could be safely evacuated to the quarantine camp.

A few were even bringing out their batons when the crowd became too unruly.

In any other situation the sight of such treatment would've horrified

Ellie. At the moment, though, the prospect of those people getting through and possibly infecting her filled her with dread, and she silently rooted for the hazmat suited men and women.

She unconsciously broke into a jog towards the bottleneck at the entrance farthest from the cordoned off area, the fastest she could go while lugging her suitcase, laptop bag, and carryon bag. Hal was right there with her, and Hannah actually bolted ahead, eyes terrified above her face mask, as her husband struggled to keep up while managing all their luggage.

Their haste brought them to the bottleneck a few seconds sooner, at which point they had to wait anxiously for the people ahead of them to stream through the doors. A process that took far longer than it otherwise would've since people were reluctant to get within three feet of each other.

Across the room, the frantic crowd in the quarantine area surged harder and harder against the police cordon, the situation looking on the verge of breaking out into real violence at any moment. Canisters of tear gas flew, sending the people crowding through an increasing number of rips in the plastic reeling away coughing and gagging. But that just made those who remained even more desperate to break through.

As Ellie watched in growing alarm, she was startled to realize that amidst all the screams and shouted warnings echoing across the cavernous room, Brock was humming the final part of "In the Hall of the Mountain King" beside her as he watched the crowd get closer and closer to breaking through.

Hannah heard him and made an outraged noise. "That's not at all appropriate."

Her husband flushed scarlet, looking unduly devastated at the rebuke, and jerked his gaze away from the panicking mob. "Sorry," he blurted. "It's keeping me from seriously freaking out."

Ellie certainly didn't approve herself, although from her experience in conflict resolution she knew that some people, especially younger people, could sometimes experience an uncontrollable urge to smile or even giggle in high stress situations where doing so was viewed as highly inappropriate. A purely human response that was often misunderstood and even served to escalate tense confrontations.

"Never mind," she said firmly before an argument could break out with the couple. "Let's just get out before things really fall apart."

Her little group of four actually had a minor advantage in the crowd, since they were willing to clump together practically rubbing shoulders; aside from the parents clutching children and a few couples, not many others were doing that. On top of that Ellie was slightly emboldened by the mask and gloves Hannah had given her, and more so by the fear of the people in the infected part of the airport breaking through before she could get safely away.

So while everyone else was shying away from each other, she led her group forward like a wedge through bubbles. She tried not to actually touch anyone, of course, she wasn't crazy, but to get outside she was willing to nudge aside rolling luggage and take advantage of the fact that the people around her would make a space for her if she got too close, as long as they had space to move away into.

At the doors themselves not even people's fear of infection could keep them from pressing together in a squirming mass, which sort of made all their previous caution kind of pointless. Ellie struggled through the press, jostled so hard she nearly lost her suitcase, and only Hal at her side kept her from being pushed to the ground at one point.

With every body that pressed against her, every hand that shoved her away, she felt an irrational fear that Zolos was crawling all over them and now over her. Hannah was huddled against her back, practically sobbing as she shoved her forward with greater haste. It got to the point where Ellie was nearly tripping over her own feet, getting uncomfortably friendly with the backs of the people in front of her as her traveling companion nearly tackled her forward.

She didn't know why the woman was using her as a human shield instead of her husband; in fact, Brock didn't seem to be helping them get through the press much at all. Aside from snarling surprisingly dire threats at the people around them, who couldn't have complied with his demands even if they'd wanted to.

After what seemed like an eternity, the press of bodies ahead thinned enough that she could go back into her own bubble with her little group, grateful to no longer be getting jostled and shoved. A thrown elbow had connected with her right breast hard enough to potentially leave a bruise, and she would probably have more on her lower thighs from flying knees.

The crowd around them dispersed rapidly as everyone fled in different directions, giving Ellie an opening to rush into as she led the way forward. "You okay?" Hal asked, speeding up to walk beside her.

She wasn't sure she was; that entire ordeal had left her shaken more than she liked to admit. But now wasn't the time to fall apart. "I think so. That could've been worse than it was." She glanced at him, eyes widening when she saw a small bruise forming on his cheek. "Are *you*?"

He grimaced. "Meh. I shoved away some guy who was about to trample you flat, and the nutjob clocked me. It's nothing."

She felt oddly gratified at knowing he'd had her back. The only one of her companions who had, truth be told. "Thanks." She grimaced and glanced back at the doors. "Next time I'm heading into a mosh pit, I'll be sure to bring you along."

The teenager laughed. "Deal." He glanced around to make sure they were out of immediate danger, then juggled his luggage into one hand so he could pull out his phone. He fiddled with it for half a minute as they continued across the oddly deserted airport parking lot, then pointed with it. "We need to head that way."

Hal helped her finalize the arrangements for buying the car as they walked the five or six blocks to its owners' house. Ellie usually would've spent a while double checking details and verifying everything was on the up and up, but in this situation she just wanted it to be done by the time they got there, so they could hop in and be on their way.

Shut In

To where her kids were waiting, needing their mom.

Los Angeles looked eerily deserted as they made their way along streets that should've been busy. Even the homeless were mysteriously absent, either fled to shelters or maybe to this quarantine camp. Or maybe the city had arranged for emergency aid for them, recognizing that a Zolos outbreak among that population would spread like wildfire.

Ellie probably should've been grateful that there was no one around to potentially infect her. But the idea of so many people hiding indoors from an invisible peril, while she was out walking through the world they were so afraid of stepping into, unnerved her more than she'd expected.

It was a relief when Hal finally veered them towards a red car parked out on the street, in front of a house with a small yard and a closed garage that the vehicle was likely usually parked in. The teenager looked between the car and his phone, frowning.

"Yeah, definitely looks like it," he finally said. He sped up to reach it, squinting. "I think that's the title sitting on the passenger seat. Let's see if they left the keys, too." He started to reach for the driver's side door handle as he closed the remaining distance.

"Wait!" Hannah screeched, with such an alarmed tone that the teenager stumbled while coming to a swift halt. He turned to the woman with a questioning look as she fumbled inside the bag Brock was holding. "We have no idea who had this car before us," she continued, taking out a container of chemical wipes.

As the rest of them watched blankly, Hannah briskly stepped up to Hal and yanked him back a few steps, gesturing with the container. "We need to wipe this thing down, inside and out, to make sure it's safe. We shouldn't even touch it before that."

Hal wore an expression of pure consternation as their traveling companion opened the wipes and shoved a few into his hands. "The entire outside? That's a bit much, isn't it?"

"Right up until the moment you accidentally lean against it and infect us all with Zolos," Hannah shot back. She got to work handing out the wipes.

"She's right," Brock said, reaching into his bag to grab another container of wipes.

Ellie wasn't sure about that, but she supposed it would only take a few minutes. She just hoped the people they'd bought the car from didn't think they were nuts, going to such excessive lengths cleaning the car they used to own. Hopefully it wouldn't insult them.

Then again, not being infected with a deadly virus was more important than worrying about being polite.

Sure enough, as they got to work a few subtle glances confirmed that the family inside the house was peeking through the blinds and from behind curtains, watching them. Probably hoping they'd just go away already, taking any threat of infection with them.

What Ellie was wrong about, it turned out, was how long it would take. Hannah insisted on a thorough job, starting with the entire outside before moving to the inside of the doors, then carefully going over every square inch of the vehicle's interior within reach through them. She made sure they didn't clean deeper into the car until there wasn't the slightest chance of them brushing any surface that hadn't already been cleaned, and if their chemical wipes came even close to drying out, she insisted they throw them away and get a new one.

It took over a half hour, even with all four of them working together. A half hour while Tallie and Ricky were half the country away in who knew what danger, frightened and needing their mother. At least during that time Ellie was able to confirm the keys were in the ignition, and that the car started and the engine seemed to run smoothly. Also, as soon as she could get to it without Hannah blowing a gasket she was able to grab the title and confirm it had been signed over to her.

After her traveling companion made her wipe it down thoroughly, of course, leaving damp stains across the important document and slightly smudging the ink.

Shut In

Finally, though, even Hannah admitted they'd done all they could. "We should take our gloves and masks off before getting in," she said as they all groaned with relief and knuckled their backs. She suited her words by peeling the thin latex off her hands, tossing them aside on the sidewalk without a second thought about littering as she prepared to enter the car.

The normally laborious process of removing the gloves had been surprisingly easy for the woman, and at a closer look Ellie realized it was because her hands were covered with a thin coating of what looked like soap. She gave her new traveling companion a baffled look. "Why are your hands all soapy?"

Hannah gave her a blank one in return. "To kill any Zolos that got underneath the gloves." Her tone had a definite "duh" in it.

"That's not how soap works," Ellie said, doing her best to hide her amusement. "It doesn't kill anything, it just makes the stuff on your skin slippery so it can wash off, including dangerous microbes. Leaving a clean surface."

The younger woman's expression turned suspicious. "That's not true," she snapped. "You're making that up, trying to make me look stupid."

"I'm not," Ellie said as gently as possible. "It's an easy mistake to make, because nobody ever bothers to teach people how soap works."

"I think she's right," Hal said. "Otherwise there wouldn't be any difference between regular soap and antibacterial soap."

Hannah abruptly brightened, scrabbling in her bag of precautionary items until she found and withdrew the bottle of soap she must've used. "This *is* antibacterial, though!" she said, brandishing it triumphantly until it nearly slipped out of her soapy fingers. "Look!"

"Zolos is a virus," Ellie pointed out. Hal snickered.

The other woman floundered, face reddening as she hurriedly began reading the label on the back of the bottle. "It probably works for those, too."

"I'm pretty sure they'd be advertising that if it did," Hal said, grinning.

Whatever their traveling companion found on the bottle either confirmed that, or at least didn't refute it. She scowled. "You *are* trying to make me look stupid," she snapped.

Brock put a supportive hand on his wife's shoulder. "It's good to know, so we don't make a mistake that could get us killed," he said. She turned her scowl at him and sullenly shook free of his hand, acting betrayed, and he looked disproportionately devastated as he continued in a wheedling tone. "Hey, it's fine, honey, I didn't know either." He reached for her shoulder again. "Let's go ahead and get that soap wiped off. We need to get going."

That, at last, Hannah couldn't seem to refute. She allowed her husband to help her get her hands cleaned up as Ellie and Hal loaded all the luggage into the trunk, making it fit, and prepared to go.

Finally, finally, Ellie climbed behind the wheel, with Hal settling into the passenger seat and the newlyweds climbing into the back. The chemical reek of the cleaning wipes made her eyes burn, but the moment they were inside Hannah insisted they close the windows to prevent the chance of airborne Zolos coming in.

That was a ludicrous demand considering they'd just been outside for over an hour, but apparently now that they'd taken off their masks the woman wasn't taking any chances. "You know, the masks are intended more to help prevent people from infecting others with sneezes and coughs and things like that, or getting germs on their hands by touching their mouth and nose, than they are to keep you completely safe from airborne pathogens," Ellie pointed out.

Hannah gave her an exasperated look. "Oh, so now those don't work like that either?"

She shrugged. "It's not like they form a tight seal around the mouth and nose and have a filter rated for stopping microbes. They help, but stuff can still get through."

The younger woman crossed her arms stubbornly. "Close the window, or we're not coming." Brock made an alarmed noise of protest at that, although he quickly subsided when his wife glared at him.

Ellie was tempted to take her less-than-delightful traveling companion up on the offer. But aggravating as this couple could be, she didn't want to leave them stranded in the middle of LA with a dangerous virus potentially breaking free of containment a mile or so away.

So she grudgingly nodded her agreement, and they all rolled up their windows and immediately began stewing in the stink of drying chemicals.

That seemed to be the last objection to finally leaving, so she started up the car and pulled out onto the street.

* * * * *

The drive through the city went smoothly, the streets mostly only filled with emergency vehicles.

Ellie wondered if many people had even gone to work, let alone were out running errands. She did see lots of cars in the lots of the stores they passed, people snapping up supplies while they were available, and gas stations and places like that were similarly crowded.

Speaking of gas, looking at the gauge the people she'd bought this car from had left it with a quarter tank at best. She was going to need to fill up, probably several times over the trip, but decided it would be a good idea to get out of the city before looking for a place.

That decision was reinforced as they followed I-10 east towards I-15, planning to take it up into Utah to I-70 which ran all the way to Kansas City, because not far outside Las Angeles proper traffic slowed to a crawl.

Craning to look ahead around the vehicles blocking her view, Ellie could see a roadblock set up a mile or so up the road. Along with police vehicles she saw ambulances and buses. More concerning than that, however, was the fact that rather than being allowed to continue along the Interstate, cars were being redirected north.

Towards the quarantine camp? There did seem to be a few patrol cars scattered along that road to keep vehicles moving in the desired direction.

Whatever the purpose of the roadblock, even if it was just to redirect traffic to another road, Ellie wasn't about to risk being trapped in LA with her movement directed, or even restricted, by officials with their own goals. Luckily, if she could get off 10 she was fairly confident she'd be able to take smaller streets all the way to I-15. And since it was impossible for the city to block off every single street between here and there, she was confident that being stuck in this traffic jam was the only obstacle between her and continuing on home to her waiting children.

So she immediately began searching for a way off the highway, even if it meant driving off the road for a bit.

If she really wanted to just go, she could drive on the shoulder. Several cars were already doing that, although it seemed kind of pointless since that would just take them right to the roadblock, and probably tick off the law enforcement there for the fact that they'd cut in line.

On the other hand . . . the roadblock was redirecting traffic from both directions, which meant across the median the Interstate was incongruously empty, considering the major traffic jam on this side.

Was Ellie desperate enough to cross the median and head back the way she'd come?

In normal circumstances, especially with patrol cars in view, that was the last thing she'd ever consider doing. But with public services completely bogged down managing the Zolos crisis, she'd be incredibly surprised if the police even bothered to chase her down. In fact, she was kind of surprised no one else had thought of it first.

Maybe they were still adjusting to the scope of this disaster, studiously following the traffic laws as if a citation or even arrest was still the worst thing that could happen to them. Ellie had no intention of resorting to undue lawlessness, but if it was a question of making choices like this so she could be with her kids, well . . .

"Hang on," she said, putting the car in reverse.

As her traveling companions stared at her in bafflement, she backed the car until she was nearly hitting the bumper of the car behind her, turning the wheel as she did so. "Um, Ellie?" Hal asked nervously as she shifted into drive again.

Ellie ignored him and wedged her car into the narrow space between the car to her left and the one in front of it, just as it opened up as the other car began pulling forward. She heard outraged honking and felt a shuddering lurch as the sides of her new car scraped against bumpers, while Hannah began screaming practically in her ear and Brock shouted in alarm.

At least Hal was keeping quiet, although he had a white-knuckled grip on the dashboard.

Concentrating in the face all the noise was tough, but luckily adrenaline was surging through Ellie's veins. She was able to keep control of the car as she forced it through the gap, across the left shoulder, and onto the median.

Behind her more cars began honking, and she heard the whooping siren of what could've been a firetruck or ambulance start up. But as she skittered her car onto the other side of the Interstate and stepped on the gas, taking her away from the roadblock, a glance at the rearview mirror reassured her that no patrol cars were hot on her tail.

In fact, it looked as if other cars were following her lead, crunching across the median themselves to head the opposite direction.

Ellie took the first off ramp she reached, then turned onto the bridge leading back across to the other side and began searching for a smaller road to take her in the direction she wanted to go. With the tense moment over she felt her thundering heartbeat begin to slow, and thankfully her passengers in the backseat had finally quieted down.

She glanced back to ask how they were doing, then noticed Hal staring at her. "What?"

He didn't look away, although she saw his cheeks start to redden. "Nothing. It's just I think that was the sexiest thing I've ever seen."

In the backseat Brock and Hannah let out twin heartfelt groans. Ellie, still coming off the rush of what they'd just escaped, couldn't help but roll her eyes and laugh as she turned her attention back to the road. "Seriously?"

"Seriously!" the teenager said, voice perfectly fervent. "You just pulled some seriously awesome driving moves and yanked all our bacon out of the fire. Haven't met many girls that gutsy."

"Hey, thanks," Hannah said sarcastically.

Ellie felt her face flushing at the praise, then felt silly for it. "Driving through KC's rush hour traffic while kids scream in your ear is good practice." She wryly gave her passengers in the backseat a pointed look in the rearview mirror. "Not all that different, really." Hal snickered and she saw the couple begin to stiffen in affront, especially Hannah, and Ellie decided to kill two birds with one stone. "Although in this case the kid's in the front seat."

The couple in back looked mollified, and Hannah even laughed at the teenager's expense.

Ellie's eyes were back on the road, but even so she thought she saw Hal's blush deepen as he gave her a hurt look. She felt bad for that, but honestly . . . what did the kid think was going to happen here?

Still, her jibe was a bit unfair, and she couldn't help but feel even more guilty when Brock spoke up, his amused tone on the verge of mocking. "You know you asked for that. Seriously, dude, dream on."

To the teenager's credit, he did his best to laugh it off. "Yeah, I know. Can you blame me, though . . . cute, gutsy, and a heck of a driver? I'd kick myself for not at least trying." He slouched in his seat and lowered the back a bit, as if drawing attention to his sudden nonchalance. "Not to mention, you know, you being the only girl I can be sure won't potentially give me a horrible disease that'll get me killed."

Ellie couldn't help but laugh at that, mostly because she was still riding the rush of what they'd just survived.

She found a good road and continued on, encountering no more roadblocks as they left LA behind and continued on to I-15.

Chapter Six
Carpool

Nick was shocked at how quickly things went downhill.

The government's efforts to quarantine the outbreak in Kansas City had proven too little, too late. He would've said laughably so, if there was anything funny about this situation. It had been less than twelve hours since the announcement of the Zolos outbreak at the airport, and since then hundreds more cases had been reported in the city, alarmingly scattered across both sides of the Missouri River.

Experts predicted the number of cases would skyrocket to a thousand by morning, at which point the number would rise exponentially.

At least emergency services had finally got their act together and begun closing off affected areas, isolating the infected as much as they could. The word was also getting out to people on their phones with emergency alerts, on TV, all over the internet, and even by patrol cars driving down streets blaring messages on their loudspeakers.

There was a lot of excitement going on out there, although Nick had seen barely any of it personally. Aside from glimpsing emergency vehicles blazing by through the apartment's windows. He'd spent most of the day browsing the news on his computer in his office, while the kids watched movies or played in the den.

Since he'd recently put them to bed, at the usual hour in spite of their protests that this was a special occasion, he'd moved into the living room himself to watch on the TV, wrapped in a blanket and half dozing.

He felt an odd sense of lassitude in spite of the dire situation. None of the companies he was consulting for had called him to announce a change of plans, and he still had that workload and a mountain of debt hanging over his head. But he had no desire to dive into work at the moment, and had a feeling if he tried he'd just end up going in circles.

So Nick lounged on the futon and watched things spiral out of control, helpless to do anything and feeling like a spectator to the end of the world.

At the moment he was watching a press conference featuring an administrator for the Federal Emergency Task Force named Henry Pohler, who was reporting on national efforts to contain the burgeoning pandemic and administer aid to those already infected.

He used a lot of flowery language, dense, poorly explained statistics, unnecessary big words, and highly technical terms, interspersed with feel-good soundbites about how they were doing everything they could and the situation was well in hand.

Nick was no expert on that sort of obfuscating political lingo, or even the similar business lingo since he mostly operated on the technical side of things; that had always been Ellie's strength. Still, it didn't take a genius to see how nervous Pohler looked and sounded, or how he rushed his speech and stumbled over words.

And for that matter, Nick *did* have a head for statistics, even deliberately muddy and misrepresented ones, and what he was hearing from this guy was making the hair on the back of his neck stand on end.

Pohler finally wound down his speech and fell silent for a moment. Then, with the look of a man standing in front of a firing squad, he took a deep breath and said. "This concludes FETF's statement. Any questions?"

Oh boy, were there. The dozens of reporters packing the room surged to their feet and raised a tide of fearful and angry voices, nearly bowling the administrator off his feet.

Finally a reporter about Nick's age, more casually dressed than the others in the room, jumped out of the crowd and raised her voice above the clamor until the man behind the podium nodded to her. "Sir, that was a very artfully worded statement, if a bit hard to unwrap. To be absolutely crystal clear, are you saying that Federal emergency services do *not* have the resources to handle this catastrophe?"

The official shifted uncomfortably, giving her a sickly smile. "We are currently collaborating with state and local services, as well as private sources, to make up the shortfall. Rest assured, we're doing everything in our pow-"

"Sir!" the woman cut in sharply. "That sounds an awful lot like a no. Where did all the tax dollars your organization has vacuumed up over the years gone? Hundred thousand dollar toilet seats?"

Pohler looked visibly irked, although he fought to keep his voice smooth. "There are somewhere in the area of 327 million people in the United States. The Federal Emergency Task Force was created to manage localized emergencies like hurricanes, grid outages, and terrorist attacks. We've made inroads into preparations for more large scale disasters, but you have to understand that supporting the entire population of this country even short term is a logistical impossibility."

"Then you admit you dropped the ball," the reporter called, sounding almost triumphant. As if the important thing here was scoring points and making FETF look bad, right when everyone was depending on the task force to keep them all alive.

And, for that matter, just when FETF needed the public's confidence and support to do their jobs.

The administrator seemed to be thinking the same thing. "Everyo-" he began in a furious voice, then took a sharp breath and once again moderated his tone. "We have given the citizens of this country detailed guidelines on preparing for disasters. We have made extensive efforts to encourage people to prepare themselves. Yet in spite of this, barely a fraction of our population has more than a few days' worth of food and water stored away, and almost no other emergency supplies or preparations. In a power outage few even have ready access to light sources, and fewer still to sources of heating."

Another reporter, a tall man with perfect hair, cut in incredulously. "So wait, you're blaming the *citizens of this nation* for the fact that you dropped the ball? How do you think that plays out for you in the next elections?"

Nick shook his head in amused disbelief. The government was outright telling them they weren't equipped to manage a crisis that could spell the end of their society, and this guy was talking about *elections*?

Pohler seemed equally incredulous. "Sir, blame is the last thing on our minds," he said quietly. "We're focused on the reality of the situation. And the situation is that a pandemic of this scale was too big for the government to realistically prepare for, and the citizens of this country did not adequately take responsibility for preparing for their own needs." He held out his hands, genuinely helpless. "So here we are, all doing the best we can."

A short, terrible silence filled the room. Then an older reporter, serious and troubled, spoke quietly. "Sir, you've spoken of FETF's efforts to respond to this disaster. You haven't mentioned how bad it will be. What can we expect to happen, say, over the next week?"

The administrator looked away, studiously examining the podium. "It would be rash to speculate until we have concrete conclusions. And even then, you know that information would likely remain classified for national security reasons."

"Zolos is in twenty major cities and who knows how many minor ones!" the serious reporter declared. "What is the death toll going to be, even if the spread of the disease is stopped in its tracks? How many innocent people are going to die?"

Nick felt a leaden weight in his gut. He was sure the man wouldn't answer a question like that, but he desperately wanted to know.

Pohler coughed. "As I said, it would be rash to speculate. Next que-"

"Thirty million."

Heads in the room whipped towards a man standing near the back, dressed in a slightly rumpled cheap suit. Nick noticed that at the sides of the room security were already starting to push towards him.

"I beg your pardon?" the man behind the podium demanded, glaring at the reporter with narrowed eyes.

The rumpled man continued in a firm voice. "Based on every reliable bit of information the government has been willing to release, or that I've managed to get my hands on from other sources, the spread has been exponential at every single outbreak point. And considering those points are all international airports, ie heavy traffic hubs, this pandemic was already running wild before we were even aware of the threat."

He paused solemnly. "But even if the disease is miraculously contained solely to those currently infected, the mortality rate of Zolos points to just over thirty million deaths in the United States alone."

That announcement was greeted by a deafening clamor from the other reporters. Demanding to know if the rumpled man's estimation was correct, or just generally freaking out at what they'd just heard. The weight in Nick's gut became a churning pain that forced him to swallow bile; if that reporter was correct, that meant almost ten percent of the population was already doomed.

And the pandemic was just getting started.

Whether or not the man was right, security reached him soon after that and quickly ushered him towards the door. "That number is a complete fabrication!" Pohler shouted angrily over the babble, creating a burst of feedback from the mic. "I don't know what absurd massaging of statistics or outright guesswork went into it, but let me state very clearly that it is *not* accurate!"

The woman who'd asked the first question managed to once again speak over the clamor of her fellow reporters. "It's the only number we have at the moment! Unless you want to set us straight?"

The FETF administrator threw up his hands in disgust. "Any more questions?" There was another deafening wave of voices, mostly still focused on the death toll. By some miracle Pohler managed to pick something out of that. "You, sir!" he called, pointing. "You have a question about the source of the outbreak?"

Shut In

A rather dazed looking man, obviously surprised that he'd managed to get his question through, stammered slightly as he raised his voice above the tumult. "Have we discovered where Zolos originated? Was it manufactured? Did some country or organization deliberately release it as a biological attack?"

The administrator looked like he regretted picking that particular question out of the babble. "As yet we know little about where it came from. The first recorded outbreak took place in Heathrow Airport in London, the patient a passenger who'd come on a flight from JFK in New York City. We cannot determine at this time if either airport was the point of origin, or if the patient was infected by another passenger from elsewhere."

Pohler glanced off to the side, and a look of relief swept across his face. "This concludes the question/answer portion of this meeting! Thank you for your time." Without another word he turned and darted for the exit behind the stage.

The video ended there, although Nick couldn't help but wonder if he was the only one who'd reached the obvious conclusion from Pohler's response about the death toll: if the number had been lower than that reporter's guess of thirty million, wouldn't the administrator have offered it up to help offset a panic?

How bad was this situation, really?

"Dad?"

Nick turned to see Ricky standing in the doorway, wrapped in his blanket. "Couldn't sleep?"

His son nodded. Normally Nick would've sent him straight back to bed if he was up wandering at this hour, but this situation wasn't normal, and Ricky had been through a frightening situation at school. So he patted the futon next to him in silent invitation.

His son came over and curled up against the other raised armrest. "I heard shouting outside," he said as he stared at the TV, which currently showed the video's ending screen and the countdown to load the next video.

Nick had been about to back out and look for something else to watch, or maybe hop on the KCNBS livestream that had been his go-to for news for most of the day. But at that announcement he stood and stepped over to the window, peering cautiously outside and listening.

He didn't hear anything. "Was it close by?" His son shook his head, and he relaxed a bit. "Wouldn't be the first time people have shouted at night. Just part of living in this part of the city." A worrying part, admittedly.

"I guess." Ricky burrowed deeper into his blanket, voice coming out tiny. "There was a lot of people shouting at the school."

"Yeah, people act different when they're scared or angry. That's another reason it's good we're shut up in the apartment . . . nobody will bother us here." Nick settled back down on the futon and opened the KCNBS livestream.

Unfortunately, the news there was just more cause to worry.

"-Mayor has ordered the closing of all high-traffic locations," Susanna was saying grimly as it loaded. "All public spaces, including stores, restaurants, parks, and entertainment venues, are to be closed until further notice. All citizens are strongly encouraged to remain in their homes, and to not admit any visitors. If you must go outside, avoid contact and even close proximity with other people and living animals who might be carriers of the Zolos virus."

"They're closing stores?" Ricky demanded incredulously. "How are people going to get food?"

Nick thought that was a surprisingly mature and astute observation from his eight-year-old son, until he remembered how super disappointed Ricky had been that he hadn't bothered to pick up much in the way of candy or other treats while buying emergency food supplies. His son had been begging him ever since making that awful discovery to go back to the store and buy more stuff, and had even gone so far as to write up a list.

Shut In

On the bright side, after looking at what the boy had written down the silver lining to this situation was that at least they'd be eating more healthy than that for the time being.

He left Ricky curled up on the couch and went into his office, calling Ellie on his phone. To his vast relief she answered almost immediately. "Nick? Is everything okay?"

"Just checking in," he replied. "Things are getting crazy here, but we're settled in at the apartment, ready for the long haul."

"Great." She sounded distracted. "This isn't the best time to talk. I'm doing some inventive driving, looking for a gas station at the moment."

"You found a car, then?" That was a huge relief.

"Only cost me my whole savings. Hopefully I can get it reimbursed." He could imagine her shaking her head wryly as she continued. "Anyway, fingers crossed we'll be back in KC in a day or so. I'll call in the morning to check in."

"Okay." Nick paused. "Be careful, Ells, okay?"

"Yeah." The call ended abruptly; she hated to drive and talk even at the best of times.

Nick pocketed his phone and headed to his office's window, the one that opened out onto the fire escape. The city looked normal for this time of night, the windows of all the visible houses and apartments lit, the streetlights creating pools of light, and headlights passing on the streets. Although fewer of those than usual.

He'd thought things were bad when his financial troubles started, when he'd had to work longer and longer hours. Impatient when Ellie or the kids had no qualms about interrupting him because he was literally working in the next room and they wanted to see him. Guilty about having to send them away, trapped in his office like some kind of cave troll trying to make ends meet.

He'd thought things were bad when Ellie had started pulling away, started wanting to spend more and more of his limited time talking about the troubles in their relationship instead of using those precious moments to enjoy the time they had together. Then when she finally told him things weren't working and it was time to end it.

He'd thought things were bad when he went through the divorce, gentle as it was compared to some horror stories he'd heard. When he had to adjust to seeing his kids only half the time, being alone for the rest of it. No time or money to date, even if his heart or spirit had been up to putting himself out there again.

He'd thought it was bad when his debts became unmanageable, trying to juggle finances to pay for Ellie's house and his apartment and their student loans and the kids and all their expenses with their combined incomes and dwindling savings. As he got deeper and deeper into the red until he was crushed under the weight and couldn't see a way out.

But even as bad as things had been then, even though he couldn't imagine them getting any worse, he'd been wrong. Terribly, terribly wrong.

This was a nightmare.

Nick had known it was a nightmare the moment he pulled Tallie and Ricky from the madhouse their school had turned into, of course. When some shameful part of him had hesitated for just an instant in hugging them in relief when he finally found them, because he wondered if they'd been exposed to a deadly disease and he might catch it himself.

He'd known it was a nightmare when he had to print out copies of that quarantine warning notice and plaster them on the door and windows of his apartment, then lock the place up for the foreseeable future. And his motivation had been more to keep this dread Zolos virus away from his kids than the slight chance that they'd somehow picked it up.

At least they were safe at home; he couldn't even imagine what Ellie must be going through, struggling to get back to them through the chaos of a nation reeling from a spreading pandemic. He just hoped that now that she was in a car and on the road there'd be no more problems, and he and the kids would see her soon.

With a sigh, he turned from the window and headed back into the den to watch the news.

* * * * *

"I've got the gas," Hal offered, cracking his door as Ellie pulled in at the pump; she just hoped she'd picked the right side, since she hadn't bothered to check where the tank was.

Kind of embarrassing, since she'd had plenty of time while wiping the car down inside and out to notice that detail.

The teenager was leaning out to stand when Hannah reached forward from the backseat and caught his arm. He glanced back with a curious look, just in time to fumble as she passed him a pair of latex surgical gloves and a bottle of hand sanitizer.

His expression became bemused. "I'm just going two feet to pump gas. I won't be running into anyone."

Their traveling companion once again proffered the items, expression firm. "Wear the gloves at all times while outside the car, then when you're finished and ready to come back in take them off and throw them away, *without* touching the outside of them, then clean your hands and your credit card with the hand sanitizer. I don't have to tell you not to touch *anything* without the gloves, do I?"

Hal shook his head wryly, but offered no protest as he accepted the items and laboriously put the gloves on, tugging his fingers into the correct openings one by one. "You realize this adds an extra few minutes to this stop, which increases the chances of some wackadoo running up to the car and trying to cause problems?"

"Then hurry it up!" Brock snapped.

Ellie saw an opportunity and pounced. "If it's going to take that long, I really need to use the bathroom."

She wasn't particularly surprised to find that Hannah immediately fumbled to give her gloves and a bottle of sanitizer as well. She could understand the woman having a box of the thin, light gloves, but where was she getting all this sanitizer from?

"Right," she said ruefully. "Toss the gloves, clean my hands."

"Not just your hands," her traveling companion said sharply. "Clean the seat before using it, then your bum and the backs of your legs afterwards, as well as any other part of you that touches *anything* in there. A bathroom's got to be the worst place for catching this thing."

Ellie suddenly had serious second thoughts in spite of the pressure in her bladder. "Maybe we should just find a secluded place to stop somewhere and take turns behind a bush."

"Maybe we should," Brock agreed. "If you lend me a card and tell me the PIN, or some cash, I can go in and buy toilet paper. And maybe camping gear and other necessities if they have them. Especially food and water . . . with luck, we might be able to get all the way to Missouri without having to go anywhere other people have been, aside from brief stops at the gas pump."

She had to admit she liked that idea, and Hannah seemed to as well. Although the fact that the couple was expecting her to pay for it was a bit irritating; she sure as heck wasn't telling some stranger she didn't exactly like her PIN. Still, at the younger woman's insistence she dug into her wallet and handed over a few hundred bucks from the emergency reserve she always carried while traveling, along with the gloves and hand sanitizer she'd been given. Brock took the money and headed into the convenience store to see what he could find.

Ellie had a feeling she'd be as crushed by worries about debt as Nick by the end of this trip. But that was a problem for later, when she was back with her children holding them safe in her arms.

Hal rapped on her window, then called through it. "Want to swap for a bit?"

In the rearview mirror she saw Hannah scowling at the teenager, maybe for touching the car. She ignored the fussy woman and shook her head at Hal. "We just got started. I'm good for five or six hours at least."

He shrugged and leaned back against the car to wait for the gas to pump, drawing a sound of mingled worry and frustration from Hannah. Ellie wasn't sure whether to be amused or annoyed herself; on the one hand she didn't like the other woman dictating everything they did with obnoxious, time wasting precautions. But there was no reason to needlessly antagonize her, either.

Besides, Zolos was a real threat; the fewer things the young man touched outside the car, the better.

Hal eventually finished with the gas and peeled off his gloves, carelessly splashing some sanitizer on his palm and then halfheartedly spreading it around his hands and his card. Then he dropped back onto the passenger's seat, shooting Ellie a look that invited commiseration. She gave him a reassuring pat on the arm, and they settled in to wait for Brock.

The man emerged a few minutes later, hauling a case of bottled water under one arm and lugging several plastic bags in the other, with a few tents and sleeping bags awkwardly slung on his back. He seemed to be struggling with it all, and Hal climbed back out to help him while Ellie popped the trunk.

"Here," Brock said as he slipped into the backseat, handing out bottles of water. "The convenience store was looking a little bare, but I grabbed a bunch of jerky, cans of roasted nuts, and trail mix along with the camping stuff. We should be set for the trip."

He handed her up a receipt and her change, all of which was damp from hand sanitizer. Ellie would've expected Hannah to blow a gasket even so, since money changed hands so often, but the woman either didn't notice or wasn't in the mood to chew out her husband.

Ellie might've been more worried about who'd last been touching these soggy bills herself, but she was too busy noticing how few of them she'd gotten back . . . even gas station food and camping gear shouldn't have cost this much. The receipt confirmed her traveling companion hadn't tried to pocket some of the change, just that either gas station prices had really gotten out of control lately, or the opportunistic owners had decided to take advantage of the crisis to jack up their prices.

Okay, fine. They had what they needed, and she really needed to *go*. So she started the car and got them moving again.

The next ten or so minutes were agonizing. Ellie deliberately drove on less used roads that would still connect to I-15, not just to avoid more potential roadblocks but in the hope of finding a nice, secluded place for a pit stop.

She finally found one where the road was in a low depression, with an earth berm along one side to keep noise from passing vehicles from disturbing the private homes on the other side. Since the houses all had fences as well, most of them completely obscuring view, that left a nice strip of mostly secluded ground.

Well, beggars couldn't be choosers.

Ellie pulled over and started to open the door to climb out of the car, then paused with annoyance when a pair of latex gloves and bottle of hand sanitizer were shoved in her face. "You're kidding," she told Hannah. The woman's expression suggested she wasn't. At all. "We're in the middle of nowhere, and I'm peeing on a strip of dirt on the side of the Interstate! There's zero chance of me touching anything someone infected with Zolos touched."

"We can't know that," her traveling companion insisted. "This virus is no joke, El, and we can't take any chances."

They *definitely* weren't friendly enough for this lady to be giving her a nickname.

"At this rate we're going to use up all the gloves and hand sanitizer on BS," Hal pointed out. "We won't have them when we really need them if we ever *do* have to do something around other people."

"This trip won't last that long," Brock said. "And *at this rate* we'll be home tomorrow, glad we were careful every step of the way."

Ellie thought it was a bit optimistic to assume they'd get all the way from Los Angeles to Kansas City in a bit more than a day. They'd have to drive practically nonstop, without running into any obstacles and likely speeding the whole way.

Still, she wasn't sure it was worth a fight. They were Hannah's gloves and hand sanitizer, after all, and if the woman wanted to waste them all taking unnecessary precautions that was her business. "Fine," she said, snatching the items and starting to open the door again.

She nearly lost her temper when Hannah once again held her back. "The gloves. Before you go outside."

Ellie was seconds from losing control of her bladder and making a mess everywhere, but she grit her teeth and tugged on the gloves, not bothering with the right fingers. Then she bolted over the berm to the other side.

Less than a minute later she was back, peeling off the gloves and tossing them aside. She squeezed some sanitizer on her hands and smeared it around, then threw open the driver's side door and tossed the bottle back to Hannah. "Happy?"

"No need to be snippy about it," the woman said. "I'm doing this for your benefit."

She held her breath to avoid snapping back, putting the car in gear and getting them moving again.

An awkward silence filled the car as they continued on. Ellie thought Hannah might be embarrassed about the confrontation and wanting to give some time for things to settle down, and she was sure Brock and Hal were keeping quiet to stay out of it.

She was wrong about the other woman's reasons, however, as she quickly realized the moment Hannah opened her mouth five or so minutes later. "Ellen-"

"Eleanor, actually," Ellie interrupted as gently as she could.

The woman breathed in sharply through her nose as if she'd just been flipped off. "Eleanor, we need to talk about your reckless disregard for everyone's safety."

Ellie glanced in the rearview mirror at her traveling companion. "Are you serious?"

"We're very serious," Brock chimed in, although he had the grace to at least sound a bit apologetic.

Hannah kept going with fussy determination. "It's not just your own life on the line. If you want to run around on your own licking toilet seats and sucking off random truckers-"

Ellie nearly jerked the wheel in surprise. "*Excuse me?*" she said, voice coming out louder and higher pitched than she'd intended. Where had *that* come from?

"Hey, let's not exaggerate things here," Hal cut in.

"Exaggerate?" Ellie shouted. "She just called me a slut because I don't want to do a full body decontamination every time I set foot outside this car! What's *wrong* with you, Nowak?"

Brock also cut in, obviously not wanting this to turn into a screaming fight in this enclosed space. "That might've been a bit harsh, Ellie, but we *are* concerned that you might not be taking the proper precautions. And as my wife said, it's not just your life you risk when you don't."

"Why are you even jumping on me about this?" Ellie demanded. "I put on the stupid gloves and did all the other paranoid stuff you wanted, didn't I?"

"Well yes, but it's your *attitude*," Hannah replied primly. "Like the fact that you call me paranoid for taking sensible precautions. I can't be on your case twenty-four seven, and if you don't take this seriously it could lead to disaster for me and my husband. I'm not about to let that happen."

Ellie breathed through her nose for several seconds, struggling to control her temper. "Hannah, I'm not a child. I'm almost a decade older than you. I'm not stupid, either. Nor am I careless. I want to get home safely to my children just as much as you want to get home safely to your family. Just because we disagree on what measures are necessary doesn't mean it has to be an issue. Like I said, I'm willing to do things your way if it'll make you happy."

There was a long pause. "I'm not sure that's good enough," Hannah finally said.

Ellie couldn't help it, she exploded again. "What else can I do? You want to tie me up and toss me in the trunk until we get home? Literally *what else can I do*? At what point will you just accept you got what you wanted and shut up? Do you just want to fight, is that it?"

The woman took several shuddering breaths, and in the rearview mirror Ellie saw tears begin streaming from her eyes. "I don't want to fight at all. I *hate* fighting. Why are you making me have to do this?"

Brock put his arms around his wife and held her protectively, shooting Ellie a glare. "That's enough, Eleanor."

Ellie liked to think she was reasonable and understanding, but at that moment she genuinely despised the couple in the backseat.

Still, what good would it do to say anything? They obviously weren't even going to try to be reasonable, and there really was literally nothing else she could do to fix this situation. Aside from kick them out of the car *she* paid for.

But she wasn't about to condemn two people to possible death just because they were jerks. They were just scared and in a difficult situation, same as her. It was only for a day or two, and then she'd be home and she'd never have to see either of them again.

Ellie focused on the road and turned on the radio, hoping that would distract everyone and prevent any more arguments. Although what she heard over the airwaves wasn't any better.

"-infected rioters at LAX have completely broken containment," a man was saying in a worried tone. "Law enforcement was too slow to set up a secondary cordon around the airport, and caution that any number of people potentially exposed to Zolos might have made it out into the city. We strongly urge all residents within ten blocks of the airport to remain indoors and avoid all contact with unfamiliar people."

Looked as if they'd got out just in time.

The next half hour or so of the drive was mostly quiet, everyone listening to the radio. Ellie even allowed herself to hope that the grim news they'd heard would remind everyone that there were more serious things at stake than petty squabbles. She certainly hoped so.

When Hannah said she needed to take a pit stop, Ellie didn't argue, pulling off I-15 and finding a secluded side road where the woman would feel more comfortable. If that was even possible for her. Brock left the car with his wife, either needing to go himself or out of a desire to protect her from danger. Although the dark glances they kept turning back towards Ellie made her wonder where they thought the danger lay.

She watched the couple walk away from the car, trying to remind herself that it was better to think the best of people, if she could.

"That wasn't cool," Hal said abruptly, making her jump and jerk her head towards him. "What they said to you, I mean," he added hastily.

Ellie couldn't help but be bitterly amused at the fact that the teenager had waited until *after* the others were gone to jump to her defense. Well, she was a big girl and could fight her own battles. "No reason we can't get along until we get back to Missouri," she said, as reasonably as she could.

He shrugged and idly tapped on the window, in the direction the couple had gone. "Or, you know, you could put the car in gear and keep driving until they're an unpleasant memory. Back where I'm from we believe in a little thing called guests being respectful to their host."

She could appreciate the wry humor of the comment, since they were all from there. She shook her head. "Ditching them in the middle of nowhere, and taking their stuff with us, is kind of an extreme response. Even if they *are* acting like jerks."

Shut In

Hal leaned back in his seat, a bit sullenly she thought. After half a minute or so he cleared his throat, forcing lightness into his tone. "So . . . Eleanor, huh?"

Ellie snorted. "I know, right? Kind of a granny name."

"Hottest granny I've seen," he teased.

She felt her face flushing and looked out the window. Holy cow, he was immature.

It took a full ten minutes before the newlyweds returned, climbing into the backseat without a word and wearing stony expressions. Ellie didn't say anything either, just turned the car around and started them back towards the Interstate.

At least Hal was decent company. Even so, the next day or two were going to be the longest of her life.

Chapter Seven
Southern Utah Badlands

After enduring such a stressful, exhausting, terrifying day, Ellie was relieved to find that the next several hours of the drive were fairly uneventful.

Hannah and Brock even settled down, not starting any arguments on the drive. Although that might've been because they were all too busy listening to things fall apart on the radio, with the pandemic apparently spreading like wildfire through Southern California and Las Vegas.

Needless to say, they were all glad they were putting the area behind them.

They crossed the Utah border a bit after midnight, and not long after that encountered a roadblock preventing them from even approaching St. George. The police were redirecting traffic around the city on smaller roads, which slowed Ellie's group down a bit but didn't present any issues otherwise.

St. George was a peaceful little place, nestled in landscape that was breathtakingly rugged even in the darkness, the lights spread out below seeming a reflection of the vast expanse of stars above. It didn't look as if it existed in a world where a deadly virus was threatening to kill everyone.

Then again, that was what the roadblock had been for.

Not long after getting back on I-15, Brock cleared his throat in a way that suggested he wanted to talk. Ellie immediately tensed at hearing it. "Ellie, Hal," he said. His tone was nervous, almost wheedling, as if he was also afraid this might turn unpleasant. "I've found a nice secluded campsite on my phone that's not too far ahead. I think we should stop for the night."

Shut In

"No," Ellie immediately said. "I need to get home as soon as possible."

Hannah jumped in. "You're getting tired, Eleanor. We all are. I think we could do with a bit of rest."

"I'm doing just fine," Hal said with complete confidence. "I can go for the rest of the night."

"I'm not sure you can, and if you nod off it's our lives too," Hannah snapped. "You mean to kill us all just because you want to get home a few hours earlier? We have a say in this, too."

Ellie felt her heart sinking as she saw this conversation heading in the same direction the last one had. She breathed in sharply through her nose, taking several seconds to compose herself.

She'd dealt with more than a few stressful situations in her job. She knew that people had a hard time in those moments, and she'd learned to remind herself that it was the situation, not the people, that was the problem. They were all trying the best they could.

That resolution had helped her remain an island of calm at times when everyone else had devolved into shouting matches, and in many cases had allowed her to diffuse the tension and get the group back on track.

Now, when she needed it most, was the worst time to ignore everything she'd learned.

So she kept her voice mild as she replied. "It's good to be cautious. But I have two young children at home who need me, and I want to get back to them as quickly as I can. I also want to get home and out of danger before things really get out of hand. Now, we've got four people who can drive, which means we can take turns sleeping."

"Car sleep isn't good sleep," Brock said. "If we don't stop to rest we'll all be zombies by noon tomorrow, with half a day of driving ahead of us and not a single one of us not nodding off at the wheel. I want to get back to my family too, not die in a fiery freeway accident."

That was, surprisingly, a good point. Although Hal didn't think so. "Come on, man," he cajoled. "I've done fifteen hour marathon road trips before with no problem. I could drive most of the distance myself, if someone is able to spell me for a half hour or an hour at a time. Even zombies can go that long without nodding off."

There was quiet from the darkness of the backseat. "Just a few hours," Brock finally insisted. "Enough to let us all recharge. Then we can start the big push to get home at dawn."

Dawn was more than a few hours away. Still, maybe it wasn't completely unreasonable to take a few hours to rest. Especially if it prevented another argument.

"We can give it three hours," Ellie finally said. "That'll give Hal a chance to sleep before taking over for me."

Hal shot her a look, but to her relief raised no protest; she was too exhausted right now for another argument.

Brock guided her to an exit a half hour or so past St. George, down a two-lane road for another mile or so, then onto a gravel road for a few hundred more yards. "This place isn't frequently used, I checked," he assured them as they approached a few widely separated dirt tracks, leading to simple camping spots among the flat expanse of barren rock and dirt.

The open, empty space around them was actually a bit of a relief, since true to the man's word Ellie spotted no sign of other campers. She still pulled up to one of the farther away tracks, which led to a simple rock circle for fires. Someone must've taken the effort to drag several larger stones over to surround the campfire, making serviceable if uncomfortable seats.

She parked in a position where the headlights shone on the campsite, since they didn't have wood for a fire. Then everyone gratefully piled out, groaning as they straightened weary muscles.

"I was only able to get two one-man tents and two sleeping bags," Brock said as they all stretched. "I was thinking you and Hal should use them, Ellie, since you paid for them anyway. Me and Hannah can endure the discomfort of sleeping in the car."

She suspected this unexpected generosity from the couple had more to do with Hannah's desire to stay in the car, which seemed to be her magical bubble of protection from germs, than out of selflessness. And to be honest, even scrunching up on uncomfortable car seats was probably preferable to lying on rock or at best dirt, without so much as a sleeping pad.

Still, she and Hal were probably going to be doing most of the driving, so she might as well take the chance at a slightly more comfortable rest. "That sounds good, thank you."

Brock shrugged and turned away to begin pulling things out of the trunk.

It turned out he'd, or more accurately *she'd*, purchased two flashlights along with the other gear, and he handed one to her and kept one for himself as Hal got to work pulling cans of food out of one of the bags. "If we crack the hood we can heat these on the engine," the teenager suggested. "Not sure how well it'll work, but it beats eating cold stew."

Surprisingly, even Hannah seemed to agree that was a good idea. Hal cracked the pop-top lids enough to allow venting in case the heat would've made the cans explode, then they found flat-ish spots on the engine to perch them on.

Once that was done the young man helped Ellie set up her tent, since she hadn't used one since the camping trip she'd gone on with her family for Ricky's third birthday years ago, when she'd still been pregnant with Tallie. And even then Nick had been the one who set it up.

Embarrassed about her lack of knowledge, she insisted on at least helping him set up his, although she wasn't sure how useful she actually was.

While they were working on that, the newlyweds got to work preparing the car for sleeping. Which pretty much amounted to lowering the passenger seat as flat as possible for Brock, while Hannah scrunched up to lay across the backseat.

It didn't look terribly comfortable, and Ellie felt a bit bad about assuming the couple had selfish motives for letting her have a tent and sleeping bag. Especially when she realized they didn't have blankets and this early spring desert air had a brutal bite to it; even after bundling up in sweaters and an extra pair of sweatpants, the couple were forced to resort to taking out extra clothes to lay across themselves as makeshift blankets.

Ellie approached Hannah, wanting to offer some olive branch, and handed her the keys to the car. "For the heater," she explained. "We don't have enough gas to run it all night, but if it gets too cold you can run it for long enough to heat the interior. With the windows up the heat should last for a while." She grimaced. "Just be sure to turn off the headlights before you start it."

The other woman looked unusually delighted by the offer. She even pulled Ellie into a hug and kissed her cheek. "Thank you."

She shifted uncomfortably as she returned the hug. Was a small gesture all that had been necessary to get on Hannah's good side? Why hadn't she tried that to begin with?

Unfortunately, whatever goodwill she'd just earned was squandered soon afterwards.

Hal had finally announced the stew was probably as hot as it was going to get, and they all gathered around the hood to retrieve their cans. The metal was warm to the touch but not quite too hot to hold in their bare hands, so everyone juggled their humble meal as they started to head over to the rocks to sit and eat.

Which was when Hannah cut them off, container of chemical wipes in hand. Her intent was clear.

"You want to wipe down the rocks," Ellie said flatly, more bemused than surprised or annoyed.

Shut In

Hannah's flush was visible, even in the light of the headlights. "Just to be safe. And to be honest, I'm getting pretty sick of you second-guessing every precaution I take."

Ellie exchanged glances with Hal, and the teenager shrugged. "By all means, then," he said with only the slightest trace of sarcasm. "Nothing like having a clean seat while out camping. Should we use the wipes on the ground, too? The tents and the sleeping bags?"

Their traveling companion either missed his tone or chose to ignore it, shaking her head forlornly. "I don't think we have enough wipes. We'll just have to be careful to only touch the ground with our shoes, and wipe them down thoroughly before taking them into the car or our tents when we go to bed."

This woman was unbelievable.

Ellie was too worn down by the constant debates all day to raise a fuss, though. She simply accepted a wipe and got to work on her rock, hoping handling these things for such an extended period of time wasn't going to give her some kind of chemical poisoning. At least the task didn't take long, and she was soon able to settle down and shovel lukewarm stew into her mouth with a plastic spoon from the small box Brock had thought to purchase.

Lukewarm or not, from a can or not, under the circumstances that was one of the best meals she'd had ever had. That alone almost made it worth the unnecessary delay, and she had to admit that even with how desperate she was to get home, she was looking forward to finally having some privacy and peace and quiet to lie down properly flat, even on hard ground in a sleeping bag, and get some real sleep.

So after she'd scraped the last bits of stew out of the can, she wished everyone goodnight and retreated to her tent. After carefully wiping off her shoes and taking them inside with her, of course; she wondered if she'd ever get the chemical stink out of her nostrils.

It was a genuine pain to change into her pajamas within the confines of the one-man tent, and even though Ellie wanted to get out of the

113

uncomfortable business clothes she'd worn for days, she wasn't sure it was worth it. Although given the frigid air, the thick sweatpants and long-sleeved shirt sounded like heaven. Especially if she dressed in layers and wore her yoga pants and top underneath them.

Getting all of that on was an even bigger pain, and involved a lot of squirming and squashing the tent's walls. It probably looked ridiculous from outside.

Still, it was all worth it as Ellie wriggled into the sleeping bag and cinched it closed around her face, swiftly growing warm and comfy enough to let her eyes droop closed.

In less than a minute she was out like a light.

* * * * *

Ellie was jolted awake by the sound of a car engine starting.

For a moment she stared up in alarm through the darkness at the low roof of her tent, only half aware of where she was. Then she remembered that she'd told Hannah to start the engine for the heater if she got too cold, and her panic faded. She sighed and closed her eyes to settle back down to sleep, resolving not to wake up the next time the car started.

That newfound peace was once again shattered as the engine abruptly roared as if somebody had put the pedal to the metal, and the sound of crunching tires and flying gravel joined it.

Cursing in shock and growing panic, Ellie wormed out of her sleeping bag and scrambled to unzip her tent's door just enough to get through, throwing herself at the too-small opening. She got stuck halfway out, practically collapsing the tent and dragging it along a few feet as she squirmed to escape its confines.

She managed to stand gingerly, bare feet painfully cold on frigid desert dirt, in time to see her new car tearing away towards the Interstate, headlights flicking on and carving a brilliant path through the night as it went.

Shut In

A short distance away Hal was tearing his way out of his own tent, cursing furiously as he half ran, half hopped a dozen feet after the departing car. It was a futile chase since the vehicle was already tearing away into the distance, headlights and taillights eventually disappearing. The roar of the engine remained audible for a while longer, slowly fading until it was drowned out by the young man's furious shouting.

Ellie looked between the spot she'd last seen taillights and Hal's dark silhouette, thoughts still muddled from sleep and the surreal nature of what had just happened. So much so, in fact, that her first thought was that someone had snuck into the camp and kidnapped Hannah and Brock.

Hal came to the more obvious conclusion. "Those SOBs!" he snarled, limping back towards their tents. "They ditched us!"

She was still staring after the vanished car, not quite able to grasp that this was actually happening. As if some part of her still believed this was a joke, and the Nowaks would come driving back and they'd all have a good laugh over it. Or maybe the couple had gone out on some errand and would be back soon.

But they wouldn't. They'd actually taken her car, after she'd been willing to drive them back to Missouri and even pay for their food; she was completely unable to comprehend their reasoning for such an act, so much so that it hadn't even occurred to her that they might do it.

She'd even given Hannah the keys!

Why? Why ditch her and Hal and drive off on their own? What did they gain out of it? Was it because she hadn't planned to drive all the way to St. Louis, and they'd decided to steal her car now while they had the chance so they could get all the way home? Or was it possible Hannah had been so paranoid about them being careless about the dangers of Zolos that she was willing to leave them stranded in the middle of a desert in Utah?

Well, stranded was an outdated concept in this day and age.

Ellie reached for her phone, wondering if the St. George police had enough manpower to spare to chase down a grand theft auto case. She could also ask about sending someone to pick them up while she was at it.

She dialed 911, brought the phone to her ear, and waited. Only for nothing to happen; it took her a few seconds to realize that her phone had no signal.

No way. No freaking way.

Unable to believe her awful luck, Ellie walked around with her phone high in the air, trying to get something, anything. It was small surprise that the signal wouldn't be great out here in the middle of nowhere, although they were just off the Interstate and she'd thought those all had decent signal even in places like this. Besides, they weren't *that* far from a decent sized city, so she should have *something*.

Had Brock planned this, too? Not only stranding them but making sure it was somewhere with no signal? That went beyond theft and strayed dangerously close to leaving them to die.

Hal noticed what she was doing and scrambled for his own phone, similarly waving it around. "Nothing." He swore and kicked a rock skittering out into the night. "How could they do this?" he raged. "How? Were they really petty enough to leave us to die over a stupid argument?"

Ellie stared helplessly after the vanished car again. "Maybe they figured us not being willing to wear full hazmat suits out here in the middle of a Utah desert was too dangerous for them, so their best chance of survival was to leave us behind."

Off in the darkness she heard Hal spit. "Or they're just real pieces of work. I hope they get stranded in a ditch somewhere, with hordes of infected pounding at their doors and windows to get in."

Bemused, Ellie tore her gaze from the empty horizon and watched the young man make his way to his tent and stoop to grab his shoes. "What, like zombies?"

Shut In

He paused, and even in the dark his posture looked sheepish. "Well no, duh. I mean, like desperate people I guess."

"Zolos doesn't make people act like zombies, you know. It actually leaves them too weak to move."

Hal abandoned tugging on a shoe for long enough to throw up his hands. "Okay fine, then I hope they drive off a cliff in the dark and explode!"

"Just for stealing a car?" she chided gently. "It's not like they robbed us at gunpoint. And they didn't hurt us, either."

She saw him sag to the ground, shoulders slumped. "They might have," he whispered. "They might've killed us, leaving us stranded in the middle of nowhere with no signal. What are we going to do now?"

He sounded so young right then, so scared and uncertain; it was a reminder that he was still barely more than a kid. And way out of his depth, just like Ellie was.

She turned to look desolately out across the landscape of Southern Utah. It wasn't exactly the most hospitable place; Hal was right, they really could die out here. Without being prepared for what could be a long hike, and without the skills or tools needed to hunt or forage or even find water and make it safe for drinking, death could come for them as early as a few days from now. Maybe less.

Ellie remembered one Christmas, almost a decade ago now, when her car had broken down on the way home from a party. She hadn't had blankets in the vehicle, and considering she'd come from a heated building to her heated car hadn't bothered to bring any coat heavier than the cardigan she was wearing.

So she'd been left in the swiftly cooling car interior with below freezing temperatures outside, stranded on a highway miles from anywhere, hugging herself for warmth while she waited for her roommate to make the half hour drive to come pick her up.

It hadn't exactly been a life or death situation, but she'd gotten so cold she'd had to come to terms with the fact that if her friend had lived any farther away, and there'd been no other source of help in a true emergency, she could've easily frozen to death on some small Missouri highway in the middle of nowhere.

From then on, she'd always kept a few blankets in the car, as well as some of those hand warmers. She'd never needed them again, but just knowing they were there was a comfort. As well as a nagging worry, as she wondered what other preparations she should be making in case of some disaster she hadn't even thought of.

Although she might be about to find out what she'd failed to consider soon, as a sudden trek across the desert with no help coming slammed home the reality of just how sheltered she'd been all her life.

Ellie slumped down in front of her tent, angrily blinking away the stinging in her eyes. Over by Hal's tent she thought she heard him sniffling, although that might've been from a runny nose in the unexpectedly chilly night air.

Still, she gingerly picked her way across the loose rocks and pebbles to sit by him. "We'll figure it out," she said as confidently as she could. "Having a car stolen isn't the end of the world."

He laughed, although with more bitterness than humor. "No, that would be Zolos."

She snorted, although she didn't find that all that funny, then straightened her shoulders purposefully. "We should turn off our phones, check them after every few hours of walking tomorrow to see if we can get a signal. No sense wasting battery life we'll need later."

The teenager nodded dully, following her in pulling out her phone and turning it off. That sense of isolation as her main connection to the world was severed was more unnerving than she'd expected, and she felt herself shivering slightly.

She noticed Hal was doing the same, probably feeling the same sense of despair and desolation she felt, and briefly rested a comforting hand on his shoulder. "Let's get some rest. Things will look better in the morning."

"Yeah." He took a ragged breath. "Yeah, they usually do."

* * * * *

Things didn't look better in the morning.

Ellie woke up feeling like she'd been beaten with padded bats all night, every muscle screaming from sleeping on the hard ground. It actually irritated her how wimpy she was, after living most of her life used to comfortable beds in temperature controlled rooms.

Heck, she'd thought sleeping on the plane had been unbearable.

Well, lying around in this tiny tent wasn't making things any better. She bit back a groan and hauled herself out of her sleeping bag, fumbling to put on her shoes before climbing out into the chilly dawn air.

On the bright side, the view was breathtaking. The landscape stretched out in all directions, all stark lines and desolate angles from the mountains visible on every horizon, dimly distinguishable from the sky by the faint glow of the approaching sun. On the eastern horizon the sky was already lit in rosy pinks and pale blues and whites, promising a truly spectacular sunrise.

Not that she was in the mood to stand around watching it. Neither, it seemed, was her remaining traveling companion.

Hal had dumped out his suitcase and carryon bag, and at the moment was sorting through them for things like changes of socks and underwear, his few long-sleeved shirts, and a light jacket that looked more useful for keeping out rain than keeping him warm.

Of course, the clothes in Ellie's own suitcase weren't much better in that regard.

It didn't take a genius to figure out what the teenager was doing. They were in the middle of nowhere, with no guarantee they'd be able to hitchhike for a ride. With that in mind getting back to civilization with all her clothes, even though many had been expensive, didn't seem all that important.

In fact, the sweatpants and long-sleeved shirt she'd worn to sleep were far more suitable for this harsh environment than a business suit and nylon stockings. She was just grateful she'd packed her yoga pants and top for exercising, as well as a pair of jeans for walking around during her free time. And even more so that the shoes she wore, while looking nice, were also practical for walking.

She hoped; hiking long distances across a desert in Southern Utah was a far cry from ambling around tourist spots in Japan. Definitely not how she'd ever intended to test them out.

She wondered if the designers even had.

Although a far more important consideration than clothes, than anything, was water. Ellie looked around anxiously, fearing the worst, but to her vast relief the bags of gas station jerky and other snacks and the case of water were still there by the fire.

She breathed a sigh of relief, making her way over to inspect them. "Well, at least Hannah and Brock aren't complete monsters," she said, counting the plastic bottles still in the case. "This water should last us several days."

Hal had abandoned his sorting to come join her, staring grimly down at their meager store of supplies. "A few, maybe, in this arid heat and with us walking all day. We'll have to ration carefully, so prepare to be thirsty all the time."

Ellie nodded, not liking to hear that but acknowledging it was probably all too true. At this time of year she wouldn't have thought the days would be all that unpleasant, but that was back in Missouri where it was nice and humid, even in early spring. In the badlands of the Southwest, who knew how miserable it would get?

She was going to find out all too soon, unfortunately. "What about the food?"

Shut In

He shrugged dismissively. "Long term, it's a worry. At the moment it's the least of our problems . . . what we have could last us over a week without getting too hungry. Enough to get back to civilization where we can find more, hopefully."

"Which just leaves where to go." She looked around at the barren majesty of Southern Utah and felt a sort of leaden dismay at the dreary sight.

"Back to St. George," Hal stated firmly.

Ellie stared at him. "That's over thirty miles." With the heat and dry air sapping their strength they'd have trouble making it far each day. Ellie prided herself on being in fairly good shape, but she wasn't used to brutal long distance treks in harsh conditions, and wasn't sure if she could confidently say she'd be able to make it more than ten or at most fifteen miles.

The teenager looked grimly resolved. "At least it should be mostly downhill. Water will be a concern, but hopefully we might find more on the way."

"Why not go forward, hope to find a town in the direction we're trying to go anyway?"

He snorted. "I checked, our buddies the Nowaks didn't leave us a map, and our phones don't have a signal. No way of telling how far it is to the next place, but in Southern Utah it could be a hundred miles."

"There are road signs," Ellie pointed out.

Hal paused, then nodded his agreement. "Okay. What do you say we head back towards St. George while searching for a road sign?" That seemed reasonable enough, so she nodded back. With a grunt the young man stepped over to his things and continued packing. "All right, then. Let's try to get some distance behind us while the day is cool."

She certainly had no argument with that, either.

They ended up leaving most of their clothes and toiletries behind. The dubious silver lining to leaving her laptop in the car was that she didn't have to haul its weight; she didn't think she could've brought herself to leave it behind, even in a desperate situation like this. Of the things they'd agreed were absolute necessities, or at least important enough to justify the weight and space, they packed as much as they could into Ellie's rolling suitcase, and the rest into the school backpack Hal had used as his carryon bag.

"I'd prefer to be lugging sixty or so pounds of essential survival equipment in a proper camping backpack to this," he said wryly, easily hefting the pack. "But at least we won't be slowed by added weight."

Well, that's looking at the best of the situation, she thought as she looked morosely at the hundreds of dollars worth of business attire she was leaving to the elements.

They set off with their meager gear and made their way along the dirt road to the gravel road, then followed it back to the two-lane highway and finally to the Interstate. The distance that had taken one or two minutes in the car took over an hour on foot, and she was already sure that going the entire day like this would be brutal.

At the Interstate traffic was sparse. Hoping for the best even so, as they walked south Hal and Ellie held out their thumbs to every single vehicle that passed, even crossing over to the median to try catching traffic from both directions. But nobody so much as slowed down, and more than a few sped up or even changed lanes, as if wanting to avoid letting even the air around them come in contact with their vehicle.

Ellie went so far as to try to get in front of one car that had slowed down going around a bend, to try to get it to stop so she could at least talk to the driver. Hal looked like he was going to have a heart attack when she did it, and the swerving car barely missed turning her into a smear on the road, horn honking furiously as it sped up rather than slowed down. She had a feeling it wasn't out of concern for her safety, but because the driver was terrified of coming anywhere near her.

Zolos. Even in the middle of nowhere, where it certainly wasn't anywhere to be found, it was still causing them problems.

Shut In

They had to walk for almost another hour before they finally found a road sign for the northbound lanes. The morning sun was already heating the air uncomfortably, and Ellie found herself seriously wishing she'd packed some sort of hat. At least she had sunglasses to block out the blinding glare of sun on pale sand and rock.

They hurried the final hundred or so yards to the sign, circling around to see what it said. To Ellie's delight, there was another town only 10 miles to the north. Far closer than St. George, which was currently 29 miles away going by the last southbound sign.

That seemed like an excellent reason to immediately turn around and head the other way, but her traveling companion didn't seem to agree. "Kanarraville?" he demanded, glaring at the sign in disgust. "Are you kidding me?"

Ellie stared at him. "Don't tell me you actually know the place." That seemed like an impossible coincidence.

Hal snorted, giving her an incredulous look. "Of course not. But just look at that name! It screams "Population: One.""

Unfortunately, he probably had a point. She had a hard time seeing what the problem was, though; they didn't need the Buckingham Palace, they just needed food and water and transportation. "So?"

"So how exactly are we going to find a car in a place like that? Even if it had the other things we need, we'd still end up stranded there."

That was also hard to argue against, since going by the sign the next place past Kanarraville was far enough away to make it an impossible walk several times over. She knew some of the smallest towns weren't always shown on signs until you were practically right on top of them, but those sorts of towns wouldn't be any help to them, either.

Still, it was a lot closer. "You sure you still want to go to St. George, even though it's three times the distance?"

The teenager seriously thought that through for a short time. "We've already gone around two miles closer to it," he finally said, "and it's a place we actually want to go to. I think it's worth the extra time and effort, rather than taking a big risk on the easier option."

Considering they'd only gone a few miles so far, during the coolest time of the day as well, she wasn't sure how well she could handle that much time and effort. But she didn't want to be stranded in some podunk town while her children were trapped in a city where Zolos was running rampant, either.

"St. George it is," she agreed resolutely. "We'll have to keep our eyes open for water along the way."

Hal nodded, and they continued on down the road.

Chapter Eight
Unanticipated

Ellie was pretty sure this parched desert air was literally killing her.

With all the traveling she'd done, to many different parts of the world, even, she'd managed to fool herself into believing she was actually somewhat adjusted to other climates. And even in Missouri, which felt like breathing soup on its muggiest days, there were times of year where the air was pleasantly dry.

Like right about now in early spring, actually.

But there was dry and then there was *dry*. Ellie's eyelids felt like sandpaper if she didn't constantly blink to keep her eyes from drying out, her mouth was so parched that breathing hurt and she had to work to swallow, and her skin poured sweat that did nothing to cool her before it immediately disappeared, leaving her feeling half mummified. Although not until after it had made sure the grit blown by the constant breeze stuck to every inch of her skin and clothes, making her feel grimy and gross.

To add insult to injury, that breeze didn't cool her, either. It felt like it came straight from an oven, heated by the baked earth and baking her in turn.

Although if there was one good thing about the dust caking her from head to foot, at least it protected the exposed skin on her face, neck, and hands from the unrelenting sun. Even so, she was pretty sure she'd have a farmer's tan to match Hal's by the time they finished this trek. After she got over the excruciating sunburn, that is.

To replace the water she constantly sweated out, every few minutes Ellie took tiny sips from the bottle she held. Which seemed like a terrible idea if she was trying to ration, but she didn't think she'd be able to stumble on if she didn't. Even so, it worried her how swiftly empty water bottles were accumulating in her suitcase, ready to be refilled as soon as they found water.

Her muscles were probably suffering most of all, though; her legs felt like rubber, barely holding her weight with every step. She'd predicted this climate would sap her strength, but knowing it intellectually did little to prepare her for how *drained* she felt after a morning of hiking.

Ellie couldn't think of many times she'd felt this wrung out, and the day still stretched on ahead of her.

So physically, she was shot. Unfortunately she wasn't doing so great mentally, either; moving in the opposite direction of home was a serious blow to her morale. She knew it wasn't rational to think like that, since when talking distances of over a thousand miles it made little difference which direction she walked. It would take weeks or even months to go that distance on foot, and seemed close to impossible when faced with barren, unpopulated regions like Southern Utah.

They needed a car. Once they had one again, the thirty miles they'd walked away from home could be recovered in no time at all.

Mentally, Ellie knew all that. But it didn't do anything for the part of her that was exhausted and furious at herself for trusting Hannah and Brock, and desperate to get home to her children. Every mile marker they passed that symbolized moving farther away from that goal felt like a knife to the heart.

What was equally crushing to her spirits were the infrequent vehicles that passed, all of which continued to speed by in the farthest lane, or even on the shoulder. She would've thought a vehicle with a trailer might've been willing to let them hop aboard and ride far from the cab, but apparently the fear of disease overpowered any feelings of sympathy for hitchhikers stumbling through a wasteland.

Ellie wondered if cars would drive on even if the driver saw them collapsed and dying of thirst. Her cynical side guessed they'd probably go even faster, mistaking their condition for Zolos.

At noon they stopped in the shade of an overhang by the side of I-15, relishing an escape from the relentless sun. It even felt marginally cooler, and the breeze became slightly refreshing. Now that they were stopped Hal insisted they check each other for signs of heat exhaustion, or even worse heatstroke, which Ellie agreed was a necessary precaution.

They checked each other's foreheads, and went through a checklist of possible symptoms like confusion, dizziness, headache, cramps, nausea, or fatigue. Some of those signs were hard to distinguish from how they'd usually expect to feel after a morning of walking, but she had a feeling the ones they saw in each other were severe enough for concern.

"Let's rest for an hour in the shade, give ourselves a chance to recover and hopefully for the day to cool down a bit," Hal suggested. He dug two water bottles out of his pack and handed one over to her. "And we should take the opportunity to drink a full bottle each."

Ellie hesitated accepting it. "Can we spare that much?"

"Given our condition, I'm not sure we have a choice." He opened his bottle and took a long, slow sip, then settled back against the rock wall with a sigh, shifting around a bit to get more comfortable.

She joined him, taking a long sip from her own bottle and luxuriating in the feeling of not being completely parched, even for just a moment. They sat like that for a few minutes, resting. Ellie even started to doze.

At least until Hal spoke up abruptly. "You're holding up really well."

Ellie cracked open an eye and squinted at him. "For an old woman?" she teased.

He flushed. "You're not old at all!" She arched an eyebrow, and he fidgeted. "You're just in good shape, you know?"

Well, she'd take a compliment when it came, awkward as it was. "I hope so. I jog every morning when I can, and do yoga a few times a week."

The teenager perked up. "Oh yeah? I'm a yoga enthusiast myself."

Ellie couldn't help but be a bit surprised, taking in his more muscular build. "You do it too?"

"Not so much." He grinned. "But I'm a huge fan of girls who do."

She rolled her eyes. Of course.

Hal noticed, expression becoming irked for a second before he looked away. His tone was almost diffident when he finally cleared his throat. "Hey, listen. Can we clear the air about something?"

Ellie tensed, afraid he was about to talk about his interest in her and press for whether she was interested in him. That was the last thing she needed at the moment, but if it was a conversation that needed happening then she supposed now was the time. "I suppose."

"Thanks." He paused as if collecting his thoughts, then spoke calmly and quietly. "I've seen you looking at me like I'm barely old enough to have finished potty training, like just now. But I'm not a kid . . . I'm 23, only a few months away from my 24th birthday."

Ellie blinked, reexamining his youthful features and the assumption she'd held all this time that he was a teenager. Maybe she was just embarrassingly bad at reading ages, although she'd only been off by a few years and at that age it could be hard to judge.

"Old enough to drink, huh?" she said lightly.

The young man flushed, remaining perfectly earnest. "Old enough to have my own place and a truck. Old enough to work a decent living doing roofing during the summer, and construction jobs for a company that handles disaster damage to homes the rest of the year. Old enough to be out of debt, send help home for my brothers and sister, and even have some savings."

"Oh," Ellie said, feeling a bit stupid. She knew people older than her

Shut In

who still lived with their parents and were searching for a job, so Hal having his life together like that was really impressive. Enough so that she felt a bit guilty for dismissing him so readily because of his age.

He raised his voice slightly, passionate rather than angry. "I know people call my generation the most lazy, immature, and entitled that's ever existed, but I grew up through one of the worst divorces you could imagine. Definitely worse than any I've ever heard anyone else talk about. I didn't have the luxury of being entitled or immature, and definitely not lazy. I had to grow up fast, and make tough choices about whether I was going to work hard to succeed in spite of everything life threw at me, or go down a bad road like a lot of my friends did. I decided to work my a-" he cut off, flushing, "my butt off, and I have."

That sounded a lot like what Nick had gone through, and how he'd chosen to shape his life in response; that sense of diligence and personal responsibility, so different from most of Ellie's friends, were what had originally drawn her to her ex-husband in the first place.

And if she was being honest with herself, the calm and determination with which Hal was handling their current situation, the way he'd stepped up and pushed hard to make sure they survived the most trying experience of her life, certainly pointed to his maturity.

She lost her smile and made her tone serious as well. "I know, Hal. I've met men decades older than you with a fraction of your maturity."

The teen-the young man gave her a lopsided grin. "I dunno, my friends all say I'm pretty immature. Those stupid poopyheads."

In spite of herself Ellie burst out laughing, and Hal joined her. But as their laughter petered out he became solemn, turning to look at her intently. "You really think I'm more mature than guys your own age?"

Oh boy. She'd had a feeling that's where he was going with all this. "Some, yes," she said carefully. "But maturity isn't always a replacement for experience and wisdom."

Maybe her hint had been sufficient to make the young man realize pursuing her was unrealistic, especially under the circumstances. Or maybe he was simply sensitive enough to know that now was a bad time to press the issue.

Either way, he nodded and leaned back against the rock wall again. "Experience and wisdom come best from hard work and personal sacrifice. Don't count me out just yet."

Surprisingly, Ellie didn't. Romantically she did, of course; that was a given considering their age difference, even if it wasn't quite as great as she'd assumed. Although she couldn't help but regret with a bit of wistfulness that she wasn't a decade younger, or he wasn't a decade older, since the more she got to know him the more impressed she became. Beyond just her initial impression of his good looks, of course.

In any case, when it came to surviving in a desert she had a feeling she could've done far worse than to have Hal Westmont with her. And selfish as it was, she was glad he hadn't ditched her with the Nowaks.

* * * * *

Going by the mile markers they made it a bit more than twelve miles that day, after a bit less than fourteen hours of walking.

Their progress absolutely disgusted Ellie. It wasn't a challenge for even out of shape people to walk three miles in an hour, and she'd routinely jogged five miles in a bit over half that and called it a good day. On top of that Hal had been right, and they were going at least a little downhill for most of the time.

It couldn't be helped, though. Exhausted from days of poor sleep and high stress, sapped by the sun and heat, hungry, and above all thirsty, they had to stop for rest more and more often, and when they did move they struggled to put one foot in front of another.

On top of that the water she'd thought would last several days, and Hal predicted would last a few, was mostly gone by the first day. Which meant they had to have guzzled almost a gallon and a half each, easily twice what she'd assumed they'd need.

And she was still desperately thirsty.

Shut In

How much did you actually need to drink in conditions like this? Should she try breathing through her nose, maybe even through a cloth? Travel even slower so they weren't sweating as hard? She'd already taken an extra shirt and tied it around her head to protect it from the sun, but she wondered if there was anything else she should be doing.

"Be prepared for tomorrow to be even worse," Hal warned her during a rest break in the late afternoon, their fifth stop in under an hour. "Conditions will be the same and we'll be even more sore, tired, and weakened."

Fantastic.

They could've gone farther that day, and in fact the sun was still hours from setting when they stopped. But neither of them raised an argument about the decision, because it was unanimously reached the second they came around a bend in the road to be treated to the glorious sight of a river below, meandering into view to run alongside I-15.

The river wasn't wide, and probably wasn't more than a few inches deep. Even so, it looked heavenly. Enough to give Ellie a final burst of strength to totter the remaining distance so she could drop into it, groaning in relief as the water splashed over her.

It was tepid at best, but she still did her best to submerge every inch of her overheated, sunburned skin. And she didn't even mind that it didn't cover her entire body, since in the day's heat it was still so incredibly soothing it might as well have been a cold bath.

She was about to dunk her head down and begin gulping down the life-giving substance, grateful for an alternative to the warm, plastic-tasting water in the bottles. Or at least what little was left of it. That was why she intended to drink until her stomach exploded to quench her overpowering thirst.

Before she could, though, a firm hand caught her shoulder, stopping her. "We should boil it first," Hal said quietly.

Ellie glared up at him, noting the longing in his own expression as he stared down at the water. Tempting as it was to ignore him, to pull free and drink in spite of his warning, her common sense won over.

She wasn't getting back to her kids if she was squirting from both ends from giardia or dysentery or whatever. Heck, she'd be lucky if she survived that under the current circumstances. In fact, instead of fighting her companion she retreated out of the water, spitting out the droplets that had touched her lips, as a horrible thought struck her.

Zolos could be carried in water. Had she just exposed herself? It seemed unlikely, out here in the middle of nowhere far from any population center, but unlikely wasn't impossible and the authorities *had* warned that it could live for extended periods of time in water, air, or on surfaces.

"Yeah," she said in a shaky voice. "We should boil it."

Hal frowned, looking around. "You'd think there'd be something growing anywhere water flows . . . I can't believe how barren it is here."

Ellie also looked around. "We need to find a place where the water's traveling through soil instead of rock. Downstream, maybe in a gulch or ravine."

He sighed, glancing at the gently downward sloping road. "Guess that means we'll be going a bit farther today." He patted his pack, which held a lot of the camping supplies. "Good thing Brock bought a camping pot. It'll be slow boiling water in it and refilling our water bottles, but we can manage it."

After the refreshing dunk in the water, Ellie actually felt like she could go for hours longer. At least until she'd walked for a while in wet, heavy jeans, the cloth painfully chafing her already chafed thighs and hips. She was almost tempted to change into her sweatpants or yoga pants, but preferred to have them clean for when they stopped for the night.

Besides, it would've been embarrassing to bring it up to Hal, even though she was sure he would've been understanding about it.

Thankfully, it didn't take much more than ten minutes to find a patch of ground beside the river with a few bushes and some sparse grass. One of the bushes even looked dead, the wood dry and good for burning. Hal immediately got to work breaking off sticks and preparing a fire circle.

Before joining in to help out, Ellie paused for a moment to pull her phone out of her suitcase's front pocket and turn it on. She'd kept to her resolution to check for signal every few hours, and each time had been frustrated to find there was none.

She shouldn't have been surprised to find it was the same now, but even so it was disheartening; just how little coverage was there in this area?

The time it took to get a fire started with sticks gathered from the sparse bushes, then fill their cooking pot with water and get it hung over the small flickering flames on a crude tripod, *then* wait for that water to boil while Ellie felt like she was literally dying of thirst, well . . .

She couldn't recall many events in her life more agonizing than that.

And to top it all off, once the water was finally boiling neither of them wanted to wait for it to cool down. So they washed last night's empty stew cans in the river and filled them with the boiling water. Then, carefully using spare clothes as hot pads, they retreated to the shade of a nearby rock wall, slumping down in the sparse grass sipping at the scalding water while suffering the unbearable temperatures even this late in the afternoon.

Discomfort didn't begin to describe it; she felt like she'd be physically sick with every sip, the unpleasant heat of the water churning in her gut. She wondered if it was actually worse for her to drink the water hot than it was to wait ten minutes or so for it to cool down when she was so thirsty.

"I just realized why my uncle always brought tea or coffee packets along when we went camping," Hal said wryly, grimacing around a cautious sip.

"You think that would make this any less unbearable?" Ellie snapped. This miserable experience hadn't put her in the mood for banter.

Rather than answering he started to take another sip, then swallowed as his face paled, sweat streaming down it in rivers. Hunching slightly around his stomach, he carefully set his cup down. "I think I'll wait until the water's at least room temperature."

Ellie couldn't help but think that room temperature out here was still practically hot enough to make coffee with, but even thirsty as she was she couldn't bear to drink any more of the scalding liquid. So she set her cup down, too, then went to take the pot off the fire so that water could also cool, at least enough to pour into the water bottles without melting them.

While she was doing that Hal dug out Brock's and Hannah's stew cans, heading to the stream to fill them with water for boiling while the pot cooled.

She could appreciate that he thought ahead like that. Even if without his cautious nature she'd be sprawled in the shade, blissfully curled around a belly bloated with cool stream water she'd thoughtlessly drunk.

Imagining it made her want to cry from sheer misery. Although she knew that a few hours or days from now, when she wasn't squatting behind some bush spewing from both ends and wishing she was dead, she'd be thanking him for keeping her from giving in to the temptation of that temporary relief.

"Think we'll reach St. George tomorrow?" she asked as he worked.

The young man shook his head grimly. "Probably late the day after, at this rate. I just hope we can keep up this speed as our strength gives out."

"Well, I plan on getting a proper night's sleep tonight."

He paused in punching holes in the can he held, which he'd string wire through to hang on his makeshift tripod, and gave her a crooked grin. "Considering what we've been through since Japan, that'll be a first."

Shut In

Wasn't that the truth. Ellie knew she should probably be doing something productive, setting up her tent or something, but there was no rush before dark. So she settled down beside him, looking around. "Well, miserable as this place feels, it sure does look majestic. You don't see anything like this in Missouri."

"I dunno, I kind of like the rolling green hills."

"Well yeah." She gestured idly at the mountains around them. "Can't say I would mind having these in my backyard, though."

"Not if the heat and gritty dust and bone dry air came with them." Hal finished hanging the cans and leaned back, staring at the small flames licking at the pile of sticks. "You get out into the countryside in Missouri very often?"

"Barely at all, these days." She leaned back as well, groaning slightly as she took pressure off her aching back. "You?"

"Go hunting with my buddies every year," he replied. "Nothing like fresh venison jerky, let me tell you."

Ellie groaned. "Let's not talk about delicious food right now."

The young man grimaced. "Yeah."

With plenty of time waiting for water to boil, then cool so they could drink and refill their bottles, then boil more, they settled into a relaxed conversation about their lives, what they did for work and in their spare time, their interests and the shows they'd been watching before this disaster started.

It was surprisingly relaxing, and it certainly helped that Hal was a good conversationalist, a dying art in today's world. Although she noticed he avoided talking about his family, aside from occasional mentions of his brothers and sister.

Then again, aside from talking about her kids Ellie didn't have much to say about her family, either; the divorce was still too raw, and while she had fond memories of her parents growing up she was sensitive to her companion's feelings about the topic and avoided it for his sake.

If he ever wanted to talk about it, she was happy to listen. But she knew from spending so long with Nick that there were some things he just hadn't wanted to dredge up, even if there was a supportive ear to hear them, and guessed Hal probably felt the same.

If anything, the mistakes she'd made pressing her ex-husband when he didn't feel like opening up had taught her that patience was the best idea when it came to people's pasts.

Considering the trying few days they'd had, they set up their tents and turned in early. Ellie was afraid that in spite of her exhaustion her worry for her family would keep her awake, as well as aching muscles, sunburn, and the discomfort of hunger and thirst. But to her surprise she drifted off almost as soon as she climbed into her warm sleeping bag.

* * * * *

"Daddy, there's a sick man outside."

Nick popped his eyes open and squinted through the dim early morning light to see Tallie standing beside his bed, small face scrunched up in worry. "Huh?" he mumbled.

"I saw him out the window." She pointed urgently towards the front of the apartment. "He's on the sidewalk across the street. He crawled out of his apartment building, but then he fell down the stairs and now he's not moving. I think he needs to go to the doctor."

Speaking of which . . . first things first. He forced himself awake, noticing Ricky hovering in the doorway also looking worried. "Okay, come here you two," he said, putting a hand on Tallie's forehead and beginning his routine search for symptoms of Zolos. He'd been checking every few hours since he locked them all into the apartment.

His daughter impatiently put up with his poking and prodding. "But the man-"

"I'm sure someone's already called for an ambulance," Nick said gently, waving Ricky over. "But I'll check once I'm sure we're all safe."

It didn't take more than a minute or two to reassure himself that he and his kids were all still healthy two days after the scare at the school. Which meant that, fingers crossed, they'd remain that way for the next two days, until he could be sure they were past the time they'd be showing symptoms and were really safe.

Nick hadn't really thought his kids had picked up Zolos. Sure, it had filled his nightmares for the last couple nights, but he'd never actually believed it was possible they could be sick. It just couldn't happen, not in his peaceful world.

"Dad, the sick man," Ricky said, grabbing his hand.

He allowed himself to be pulled out of his room, picking up his phone from the bedside table as he went. As he'd done dozens of times since that call with Ellie the night she left LA, he tried her number and it went straight to voicemail.

What was going on? Her constantly disappearing like this was wracking his nerves, and considering she'd been out of contact far longer this time he was seriously freaking out. In fact, she should've been back by now, even if she'd stopped for a full night's rest on the drive. For that matter, she'd be back soon even if she'd stopped for *two* full nights for some reason, in spite of her desperation to get home to the kids.

What if something had really happened to her this time? Ricky and Tallie were constantly asking him if he had any news about her, and it was getting harder and harder to put them off and he refused to lie to them. But he dreaded what he might do if Ellie's phone stayed impossible to reach for all the weeks they were in quarantine. Having to come to terms with the fact that she would do anything in her power to get through to them, so if she hadn't been able to then he should fear the worst.

When did he tell the kids? How? How did he comfort them as their lives were shattered by the loss of their mom?

And what about him? Nick could admit he still loved Ellie, even if since the divorce it had become less romantic and more like a close relative. His only close relative, really, since he was estranged from his parents.

What would he do if he lost her?

No. He was getting way, *way* ahead of himself. There were any number of reasons his ex-wife wasn't back yet. She could've been delayed going around infected cities. She could've been delayed at a roadblock. She could've been detained at a quarantine camp. Or her car could've simply broken down, and she was having trouble getting it towed with emergency services all tied up dealing with the Zolos crisis.

And there could be just as many valid reasons her phone was off. It might've been damaged in some scuffle. It might've been confiscated at some roadblock, or stolen. It could just be out of juice, and she was so occupied with driving back to him that she hadn't bothered to charge it. Although that didn't explain why she hadn't found another way to contact him.

He shook his head and let his children lead him to one of the windows in the den.

Sure enough, there was a man outside showing obvious symptoms of the Zolos virus. He looked as if he could barely move, and in desperation had dragged himself out of his apartment building and fallen down the stairs in front. He was now hunched around himself in obvious pain and misery, not moving aside from the occasional feeble twitch.

Nick didn't recognize the man, which wasn't surprising since he hadn't lived here long and it wasn't as if he'd gone around introducing himself to all the neighbors. It was still a horrible sight, all the more so because it was the first sign he'd seen outside the internet that the Zolos threat actually existed. That it wasn't just some overblown panic or an epic national hoax or something.

The disease was real, and there was a man dying from it not fifty feet away from him. Just one of many.

And it could just as easily be him and his children.

Nick immediately sent Ricky and Tallie away from the windows so they wouldn't have to see a sight that might scar them for life, ignoring their complaints. Every fiber of decency in him wanted to go and give the poor man a hand, help him get to where he was going and offer him whatever help he could.

But he stayed right where he was.

Maybe it made him an awful human being, but he wasn't about to take any chances where his children's safety was concerned. Even if he had to watch a man slowly die right outside his front door.

It looked as if everyone else felt the same, because although Nick saw more than a few faces peeking out of their windows at the poor man, nobody came to his aid. In fact, over the next hour the few people entering and leaving that apartment building took one look at the guy and immediately sought another entrance, refusing to use the stairs he was crumpled at the bottom of.

Nick tried calling emergency services, but while the last news report he'd watched had stated they were busy, at this point it looked as if they were completely down, the call being immediately rejected with an automated message. He tried a few other numbers for hospitals, police stations, fire stations, and other public services that he looked up online, but couldn't get through to any of them, either.

That was hardly reassuring, if some disaster struck his own family and he needed their help.

He also tried a few local websites and forums, hoping to get word of the man's plight out, but from what he could see his attempt was drowned out by thousands, even tens of thousands, of other people facing similar circumstances. He even saw a post that he was almost certain was asking for help for the very same man he'd posted about.

And all the while, the sick man remained huddled on the sidewalk. He made one or two feeble attempts to keep going in search of help, and even raised a ragged voice to call weakly for help every fifteen minutes or so, but his fate seemed sealed.

The mood around the house was even grimmer with his children barred from looking out the window. Nick tried to avoid looking himself, but found himself checking regularly in spite of his resolution. Every time he looked, the situation was the same; it seemed surreal that another human being, probably a decent person with friends and family who loved him, could find himself in dying in the middle of the street in Kansas City, Missouri, USA.

And he wasn't alone in that.

In spite of the city's best efforts the numbers of those suffering Zolos continued to rise, until according to the news that morning a staggering fifth of the city's population was estimated to be infected. Experts warned that the number would continue to go up, no matter how hard people tried to avoid going out and getting in close contact with other people or traveling through known infected areas.

It was just inevitable. As infectious as the virus was, and with how closely packed together people were, infected people could've passed the disease on to others in their everyday interactions like paying for things, or even from touching doorknobs, before the government revealed the existence of Zolos and anyone even knew there was any danger.

Sure, for those who'd been spared infection and managed to lock themselves into their houses or apartments, the situation was better. But there were any number of reasons people might need to leave the safety of their homes, especially if they hadn't managed to stock up on food the way Nick had.

This was all absolutely insane. Like no catastrophe Nick could've ever imagined.

Normally, as things started to fall apart he would've expected civil unrest, skyrocketing crime, maybe even mass waves of refugees fleeing population centers. But instead crime had actually *plummeted* in the most affected cities, public protests were almost nonexistent, and everyone was staying huddled up in their homes.

It didn't seem to matter that the economy was in the toilet with nobody showing up for work. Or that most shipping had ground to a halt and people were avoiding stores and restaurants as possible infected areas, and only local, state, and federal emergency services were bringing in and distributing food. Or that police were completely tied up with disaster relief and couldn't do their jobs.

Nobody was going out, and the few people who did still walk the streets, usually because they had no other option, avoided everyone else like, well, like they had the plague. The sorts of scum who'd usually took advantage of a situation like this to indulge their darkest nature were nowhere to be seen, since only an insane person would try to burgle from any house or business that might have infected people in it.

As for muggings, rape, and other crime of that sort, not even the most desperate criminals wanted to get that up close and personal with someone who might be carrying Zolos.

Among other news Nick had watched that morning, he'd seen a story from Washington D.C. about an armored truck driver who'd begun showing symptoms of the dreaded virus while making a run, and in his panic had actually driven the vehicle right to the hospital and left it there, keys still in the ignition. Nobody would come within a hundred feet of it, even though there was probably millions of dollars worth of cash and valuables inside.

"Can we go to the playground, Daddy?" Tallie asked, ambling into his office. She was carrying her tablet, which squawked obnoxiously with some kid's show, but it was obvious she was bored of it and needed a change.

A change Nick couldn't give her, if it meant going outside. He grimaced. "Remember how we talked about what a quarantine means?" he said gently.

"That we have to stay home, and we can't go around other people. And now we can't even look out the window." His daughter pouted, the expression she knew melted his heart and usually made it impossible for him to say no. "How long do we have to do it for?"

Nick shook his head. "For a long time, sweetie. Weeks."

She stubbornly persisted. "Why don't we go to the walking trail? We never see anyone there, so we won't get sick."

"It's still too dangerous, Tals." Her pout became absolutely heartbreaking, and he sighed and patted his lap, inviting her to come cuddle. Eyebrows drawn together and face a little thunderhead, Tallie climbed up and sat with her arms crossed sternly.

It was hard not to smile at that, even though her disgruntlement was completely sincere.

Nick hugged her and kissed the top of her head. "I know it's a pain but it won't last forever. And I promise you, the moment it's safe to go outside we'll go camping and do all sorts of other fun stuff."

"What do we do until then?" she whined. "I don't want to watch shows anymore."

"How about we play a game?" he offered.

His daughter perked up, coming partway out of her pout. "Hide and seek? Maybe Ricky will play, too!"

"Sure." He lifted her down to the ground. "How about you go ask him while I make one last call."

She nodded and ran off, while Nick grabbed his phone and called the nursing home where Ellie's mom was staying. They'd been curt with him when he called yesterday, but had at least confirmed that Lois was healthy and safe.

This time the call went straight to voicemail, and the voicemail box was full. He got the same result the next two times he tried, even though from what he'd seen the nursing home had multiple lines, and up til now their staff had been reliable about answering calls.

Great, another thing to worry about. Nick spent ten minutes searching for alternative ways to contact the home, and tried getting in touch with emergency services to see if they had news. No luck with any of it.

Shut In

Well, he'd try again in a bit. Pocketing his phone, he left his office to find his kids and try to keep them occupied so they forgot about this disaster for a while.

Too bad he he couldn't seem do the same.

Chapter Nine
Connecting

True to Hal's prediction, the second day of hiking was even more brutal than the first.

In spite of the dunking she'd taken the previous night, Ellie's jeans and shirt were stiff as cardboard and scratchy as sandpaper in the morning. She tried to give them a more thorough washing while her traveling companion took down the tents, but it was obvious she wouldn't be wearing them until they dried.

Since she'd left all her business clothes behind, that left her the option of hiking in her yoga outfit or in her pajamas. Since the sweatpants and long-sleeved shirt were warmer and the nights were chilly, and she didn't want to get them filthy from a day of hiking then try to sleep in them, she opted for the yoga outfit.

Besides, when her clothes dried she could put them on over it without much hassle.

She'd worn the outfit to and from sessions before without much self-consciousness, although usually she tossed on a pair of gym shorts and wore a jacket so random guys wouldn't hit on her; it got old explaining she was happily married with children. At least until the divorce, although even then in her emotional state she still hadn't wanted that attention, in spite of prodding from friends about putting herself back out there.

Still, it wasn't as if she wasn't used to being around a mixed group of people in the outfit, and usually she didn't give it a second thought.

In this situation, though, she felt a bit more awkward about ducking out of her tent in the form-fitting leggings and shirt. Hal had already shown interest in her, and she didn't want him getting the wrong idea here.

To her relief he played it cool. Sure, his eyes widened when he saw her, and he definitely didn't seem to mind her choice of clothes. But he kept his gaze on her face and talked about the upcoming day's hike without any awkwardness.

Ellie was probably just being vain, anyway. She wouldn't pretend at false modesty and say she didn't know men found her attractive, but Hal was the sort of guy who'd have girls his own age, even the hot ones, throwing themselves at him.

Although a treacherous part of her mind couldn't help but tease the idea that she returned more than a bit of his interest, especially now that she knew he was older than she'd thought. Or that she'd actually secretly been looking forward to seeing his reaction to her in this outfit, and if anything was a bit disappointed the sight hadn't left his jaw on the ground and him stammering over his words.

She ruthlessly squashed the thought; she was giving this nonsense too much attention when her focus should be on survival. Survival and getting back home to her family.

Priorities back where they should be, Ellie got to work helping break camp. Once that was done she slung her wet clothes over her shoulders to dry, grabbed the handle of her suitcase, and started off down the road.

Hal fell into step beside her, toting his pack with all the refilled water bottles. He'd taken the time to properly wash himself and his clothes last evening, and she silently envied him the fact that he appeared dry and comfortable.

As much as was possible in their current situation, that is.

The air felt drier this morning than yesterday, if that was even possible, and the day promised to be even hotter. Not to mention empty and desolate; if it wasn't for the road they were on, Ellie could've easily imagined them in some bleak alien landscape, or an ancient primordial desert long before humans ever set foot on the Earth. She once again felt selfishly grateful that Hal was with her, since without him the stark solitude would've been truly intimidating.

A dazed part of her mind even wondered if civilization still existed out there, or if it had all gone away while she was out here. Then the cynical part of her tossed out the reminder that, judging by what she'd heard about the pandemic before being cut off from the world, civilization might actually *stop* existing before she managed to get back to it.

That was an unpleasant thought, but she forced it aside to focus on one thing: her complete conviction that her family was there waiting for her, and would still be there when she finally got back to them.

After an hour or so she decided her clothes were dry enough to put on, so she didn't have to keep lugging them around on her shoulders like some sort of walking clothesline. "Hold on a second, these are finally dry," she told Hal, tossing her shirt onto her suitcase and kicking off her shoes so she could step into her jeans.

To her amusement he politely turned away, which struck her as a bit ridiculous since she was just putting an extra layer of clothes on, not doing a full change or anything. Still, she appreciated the gesture and the respect it showed for her privacy; that sort of thing was especially important when two relative strangers had been put into a position where they were suddenly spending a lot of time alone together.

That was the reason she'd studiously busied herself with boiling water last night when he walked out of view to wash up, and why they'd both been extra accommodating about needing to relieve themselves on the hike. Thus far Hal had proved to be a perfect gentleman, with the genuine effort of someone who actually cared and wasn't just doing what he thought was expected of him.

Ellie had always been of the opinion that most people were decent once you got to know them, although some could be real jerks to strangers if they thought they'd never see them again, and a relative few were just jerks in general. As her current predicament courtesy of the Nowaks bore out.

Shut In

But while there were certainly genuinely disagreeable people out there, on the other side of the coin there were those who stood out for their kindness; she always treasured relationships with anyone she met like that. Which was why, truth be told, she'd begun thinking of Hal as a friend, not just a traveling companion. Hopefully one that she could still keep in contact with even when they were home and this was all over.

Assuming they ever got there.

There were fewer cars passing by today than yesterday. A lot fewer; she supposed that wasn't a surprise, since she would've far preferred being safe at home herself if she had the choice. Or even safe in Nick's ratty little apartment. Needless to say, none of the cars so much as slowed for them.

A bit after noon a military convoy of over a dozen vehicles roared past heading south. Ellie and Hal both waved wildly from the side of the road, hoping for a ride or at least some help. Even a promise that they'd alert the authorities in St. George of their plight would've been appreciated.

But the trucks and APCs all rolled right past without so much as slowing. In fact, like every other car Ellie had tried to flag down they even shifted over to the far lane. From the wary glares of the soldiers in the vehicles, she had a feeling they wouldn't have taken it well if she'd tried to get any closer than the side of the road.

Discouraged, they watched the convoy roll out of sight in the direction they were going, moving at a speed that would let it reach St. George in less than a half hour, instead of the day and a half or so of brutal hiking they faced.

"I'm sure wherever they're going, they'll be saving lives in this disaster," Hal offered, although he was obviously frustrated and discouraged.

Well, he wasn't alone in that. "Orders of magnitude more than if they took the risk to stop and help two hitchhikers," Ellie agreed glumly. "Good thing we're not in any serious trouble."

With no other real option, they kept trudging on down the road.

Around noon they once again stopped to find shade during the heat of the day. The river still ran alongside the road, so they took the time to wash up in the tepid water and boil a bit more water to refill their bottles and get a good long drink.

It frankly shocked Ellie how much water she'd found herself drinking ever since being stranded in this wasteland. She made it a point to stay hydrated in her everyday activities, well aware of how vital it was, but here it felt like she was guzzling down twice or even three times as much as usual.

And it wasn't even all that hot! She hated to think what it would be like to be stuck out here in the high summer. Heck, for all she knew this little river would be completely dried up at that time of year. Compared to Missouri, where it felt like you couldn't go a mile without seeing a pond on somebody's property, and streams and lakes were all over the place, it felt like a miracle that they'd even found this river at all.

In spite of pushing on for longer than they had yesterday, they only made it eleven miles that day. It was still an hour or so before sunset, but they'd reached the point where the river once again wound away from the Interstate, taking their reliable source of water with it. So they agreed to stop and refill their water bottles one last time, then make sure they got a good drink in the morning before leaving.

The good news was that they only had seven or so miles left to go to reach St. George, and fingers crossed they easily had enough water to get them there. Hal assured her they'd make it to the city sometime in the afternoon tomorrow.

To Ellie, that felt like an impossible length of time as she collapsed on the ground in a greener area they'd picked for their camping spot, not caring if she got her clothes dirty or if the asphalt beneath her was uncomfortably warm. "Fingers crossed we'll find a car there, and this is the last walking I'll have do for the rest of my life," she groaned.

Her friend gave her a crooked grin. "I don't know, I think this has been an invigorating few days of hiking."

Ellie mock glared at him. "That's because you've got the indestructible body of a young adult. Have some pity for someone who gets joint pains on a regular basis."

He just laughed as he dropped his pack and slumped down nearby. "Come on, you're running me into the ground." He shook his head ruefully. "And here I thought I was in good shape."

She glanced at his toned, athletic frame, in spite of herself thinking that he thought correctly. "Well, I won't speak for you, but I for one am glad I've kept the weight down. I'd hate to think what this trip would've been like if I was packing around fifty extra pounds."

"Well, you could go longer without starving," Hal quipped. "On the other hand, the extra time it would've taken to make the hike would've offset that a bit."

She just groaned in response.

After half a minute of resting in silence, her friend wearily hauled himself back to his feet, heading over to the scrawny bushes growing beside the water to begin gathering sticks for a fire. Ellie would've been happy to just pass out right there on the road, but instead she wearily shuffled over to help him.

The laborious process of boiling water was starting to become a routine by this point. Although since they'd refilled some of their bottles at noon, Ellie had no argument when Hal suggested they take a break and heat up the last of their stew so they could have a hot meal. It was good timing, too, since with the sun approaching the horizon the air was already starting to cool.

They settled down beside the fire to watch the food heat up, Ellie seated on her suitcase and Hal sprawled on the ground using his backpack as a pillow, occasionally shifting enough to stir the pot with a camp spoon to keep it from burning.

While she waited she checked her phone and confirmed that there was *still* no signal. Her friend was doing the same, and cursed quietly when he reached the same conclusion she had. "I don't know why I even bother worrying about her," he growled, turning off his phone in disgust. "She hasn't earned it."

That was . . . an unexpected outburst. "What about your brothers and sister?" Ellie asked gently.

Hal glanced away, looking ashamed. "Of course," he said. "They can't help it that-" he cut off abruptly, grimacing.

An awkward silence settled, and she sank into fretting about her own loved ones. She was so deep in her worries that it came as a surprise when her friend abruptly spoke up. "Can I ask you something?" he asked, eyes still on the campfire.

Ellie bit back a groan. After the day they'd had, the last thing she wanted was to answer a question that started with that, especially considering the previous direction some of their discussions had taken. She made a noncommittal noise, hoping he'd get the hint.

Unfortunately, he didn't. "I've heard you talk about your ex, your kids," he began slowly, careful tone suggesting he was hiding deep pain. "How did you get through your divorce without tearing your family apart?"

She felt a sharp surge of her own pain, thinking back to the last several months. The resentment and bitterness, the hurt and loneliness. Seeing the confusion and hurt her kids showed at suddenly only having one parent at a time, and having to move to the other house every couple weeks. "Who says I did?" she asked, more curtly than she'd meant to.

Hal snorted, not trying to hide his bitterness. "If you don't mind my saying, I do. You're the only person I've ever met who's been in one who can talk about it as if it wasn't unending torture. Who talks about your ex as if you don't hate his guts."

He finally looked up, eyes haunted. "I know divorce," he said quietly. "I've seen more of it, seen the wors-" he cut off, grimacing, then looked back down at the fire. "I know divorce. So why was yours different? I guess I just want to understand."

He almost seemed to be asking that to the night, looking back at whatever memories so pained him and wondering why he'd had to suffer. He fell silent after that, waiting patiently for Ellie to open up.

Who knew, maybe it would be good to have a sympathetic ear to listen to her story. And maybe it could help him with his own issues with his past. "I got married to Nick when I was about your age," she began quietly. "We'd been together for a while already, and it was more of a "seems like the right time" than any sort of whirlwind romance."

Hal grunted sourly at that, then when she paused and glanced at him flushed slightly. "Sorry."

Ellie waited another moment before continuing. "It was a good marriage, comfortable. We loved each other, loved our kids, and Nick working at home let him babysit while I finished my MBA and dove into my career."

She paused again, although this time it was because she was sunk into her own bitter memories. "It . . . wasn't the easiest time for us. Nick's consulting wasn't bringing in as much as it had been, and I was mostly contributing bills, and to boot being away a lot of the time, so he had to deal with the kids and everything else on his own. We were both aware it was only a temporary thing, and when my career got started our financial situation would ease up and I'd be able to take the pressure off him.

"Except . . . after I graduated and started in my first position, the financial pressure was still there and he didn't ease up. If anything, he buckled down until he was working practically all the time." She swallowed a sudden surge of emotion, then continued in a hollow voice. "Twelve, thirteen hours a day, even longer. Shut up in his office, even eating his meals in there. He barely spent any time with me, with the kids.

"And even when he wasn't working, he spent what little time we had slumped in front of the TV, vegging out to some show or playing a mindless video game. He'd go out on walks on his own, even though before then he'd usually taken the kids with him, and me when I was home. Up until then it had been one of his favorite things to do with us."

Ellie thought back to that time, the loneliness and confusion, the hurt of feeling like he didn't want to be with her. He even seemed too tired for lovemaking, although not too tired to watch some idiot show. At least he was willing to cuddle with her when she joined him, although he never seemed to be watching anything she was interested in and refused to change to something they might both enjoy.

"I tried to talk to him," she whispered, barely even aware she was still talking to someone. "I was seriously worried about what was happening in our marriage. He tried to tell me it was just temporary, that once we got past this financial crisis he wouldn't have to work so hard, he'd be more relaxed and less stressed about money and he'd have plenty of time to spend with us. But the way things were going, I saw serious cracks forming that might still be there even when we were in a better place financially. And if things went on for too much longer the way they were, it might destroy our family completely.

"I kept pushing, and he started to shut down. Like completely distance himself the moment I opened my mouth. The harder I'd push, the less he'd say, until he started finally snapping at me and then storming out, no word of where he was going or when he'd be back. Sometimes I wondered if he'd even come back at all. I didn't know what to do."

To Ellie's annoyance, she felt tears pricking her eyes. She really hadn't wanted to talk about this, but it was too late to stop now. "It got to the point where I dreaded seeing him. It was always sullen silences, or him getting defensive the moment I said anything. I kept trying to talk to him anyway, since I felt like the only other option was just to give up on the marriage entirely.

"It finally came to a head about seven months ago. He told me if I was so worried about him spending time with me and the kids, maybe we should just be doing that instead of me wasting all this time badgering him in a way both of us hated. I told him that was *exactly the problem in the first place . . .*"

She trailed off, flushing slightly at the heat that had crept into her voice, and after a deep breath continued in a milder tone. "At that point he snapped like usual. But instead of leaving after some harsh words to the theme of getting off his back, he really jumped into the argument. He asked me what I wanted him to do, that he was already working himself to death just to keep ahead of the bills, and I was making what little free time he did have a nightmare.

"I yelled back that I just wanted to save our marriage, and maybe he should just cut down to a more reasonable work schedule and have a little faith that our finances would sort themselves out. That way he could actually try helping to save our marriage, too. He burst out laughing, not the pleasant kind, and asked if we should flood the house and hope that that would sort itself out, too."

Ellie paused, scowling as the fury of that night returned. "Things got less reasonable after that, just more yelling. It finally ended up with him shouting that since I had all the answers and only wanted to listen to myself anyway, I was free to continue this discussion on my own and let him know how it went. He locked himself into his office, shouted through the door that maybe he'd finally get more than four hours of sleep for once if by some miracle I could leave him alone for that long, and that was the last I heard from him that night."

She stared dully into the fire, remembering how she hadn't gotten any sleep herself that awful night. The kids had been hiding in their room during all the shouting, and once it finally ended they'd wanted to cuddle with her in bed and be reassured that the world wasn't ending. Then after they'd finally fallen asleep, she'd stayed up until morning crying her eyes out because to her it felt like it was.

"The next day, I asked for a divorce," she said quietly.

After half a minute of silence Hal swore softly. "I'm sorry," he whispered. She wasn't sure if he meant for bringing this painful subject up, or for what she'd been through, or if he was just acknowledging her obvious pain.

"I don't know what your own experience with divorce was, but now you know mine wasn't exactly a fairytale," Ellie said wearily. Hal didn't respond, brooding over the fire, and she suddenly just wanted to be alone; the scent of the heating stew was no longer as tantalizing, and sleep seemed like the best thing in the world at the moment.

Sniffling and scrubbing at her eyes with the back of her hand, she stood and grabbed her tent, walking away to find a good spot to set it up as she spoke over her shoulder. "Good night."

* * * * *

Things were awkward the next morning when Ellie emerged from her tent. Especially when she nearly tripped over the pot with her portion of the stew just outside the door, crusted and inedible after sitting outside all night.

That actually kind of pissed her off. She could've eaten that, and Hal *should* have since she'd chosen not to. But at the same time she could see how it was an awkward position for him, since she'd headed to bed and left him the option of either chowing down her portion without her even telling him it was okay, or bothering her when she clearly wanted to be alone.

So there it was, a mess that made her empty gut growl even louder. Cursing bitterly to herself, she grabbed the pot and took it over to the river, with effort scraping it clean and filling it with water to boil.

Hal already had the fire started again when she stomped back to the camp. He looked studiously at the small flames licking the kindling with a flush to his cheeks as she settled down across from him. "Sorry," he said.

It's the thought that counts, she didn't say. Instead she silently handed him the pot, then dug in her suitcase for one of the packs of jerky and began gnawing on one.

More than waking up on the wrong side of bed, she felt a bit awkward about how completely she'd opened up to the young man last night. More than she'd intended to, truth be told; in fact, more than she had to pretty much anyone else when it came to the divorce, even her closest friends.

Ellie supposed being out here alone with him, with the world ending around them, provided the foundations for a stronger bond than you usually saw in day to day life.

It deserved to be acknowledged, if for no other reason than to clear the tension in the air. "Thanks," she mumbled around a mouthful of jerky. At his surprised look she continued hastily. "For letting me dump on you last night."

"No, I . . ." he trailed off, considering his answer. "It was good to hear how it was for you. I'm just sorry you had to relive that pain. I didn't mean to put you through that."

Ellie wasn't sure how she could've answered his question without reliving the entire miserable experience, but she believed he meant that.

The silence settled again, more comfortably this time. She let it hang for a while, but finally curiosity got the best of her. "How about your family? Are they in a good situation until you can get home to them?"

Hal grimaced. "I hope. Although "good" is always a bit of a stretch."

She frowned at that, waiting for him to elaborate. When he didn't she cleared her throat. "I couldn't help but overhear a bit of your conversation with your mom, back at the airport. And then what you said last night . . . you don't get along with her?"

His grimace became a brooding scowl, although it wasn't directed at her. "As well as is realistic, all things considered."

He once again fell silent. Ellie waited patiently for a minute before speaking quietly. "If you want to talk about it, I'm here," she finally said.

"I don't, really. It's not something I like to think of now that I'm out of it, aside from to worry for my brothers and sister." The young man glanced at her and sighed. "But I guess you told me your story last night, so it's not really fair not to do the same."

She shook her head. "You don't have to if-"

Hal waved that off. "I don't know, maybe it would be good to have someone to talk to about it. I haven't really . . . most people are either caught in the middle of it and don't want to talk about it themselves, or I don't know or trust them enough to feel comfortable opening up about it."

That was oddly flattering.

He sighed, staring ahead at the starkly picturesque horizon. "You might've picked up on it by now, but my parents are divorced. Only theirs wasn't quite as . . . amicable as yours." Bitterness flashed across his features, swiftly suppressed. "Actually as far from it as possible."

"I'm sorry," Ellie said softly.

The young man waved that away as well. "It happened when I was really young, so I don't remember much besides a lot of shouting and screaming and crying and slammed doors. I still don't know the whole story of what happened between them. I mostly only got my mom's side of it, and the older I've gotten, the more I've learned that she likes to . . . paint situations to put her in the best light."

"We all do that to some extent, even without realizing it," she said, tone gentle. She'd probably done it herself when talking about her divorce last night, even though she'd done her best to be open and honest.

He snorted, bitterness returning. "Yeah, well most of us don't do it by trashing the reputations of everyone else involved. She got full custody of me, my dad even waived visitation to get out of the ugly situation, and she made sure to paint him as a monster who didn't love his son because of it."

Ellie winced. Whatever her feelings about what her marriage to Nick had become before she decided it was time to end it, she knew he loved their children and they loved him. She could even admit that he loved her, even if circumstances and their own actions had ultimately torn a rift between them.

She couldn't imagine ever wanting to take Tallie's and Ricky's father away from them by making him seem like the bad guy; what would that do to two young children who were already struggling to deal with such drastic changes to their lives?

Poor Hal, to have suffered that sort of pain.

He noticed her sympathetic look and shrugged uncomfortably as he continued. "And yeah, he sucked for just walking away, and he's never tried to pretend he wasn't just as much at fault for the divorce. But even though it's hard to forgive him for leaving without a word, I can at least sort of understand why. My mom spent over a decade poisoning me against him when he wasn't there to defend himself, and I never even thought to wonder if there wasn't more to the story."

Her friend got back to staring off into the distance. "Maybe she thought she was doing the right thing. I guess with him out of the picture she might've decided it was less painful for both of us to put it all on him, so we could move on."

"It doesn't sound like it was less painful," Ellie said, briefly resting a hand on his arm.

"Yeah, I don't see how it could've been any more painful, actually," he agreed, gritting his teeth. "Although I guess if I'm being fair, once I realized how she'd lied to me all this time I might've overcorrected, shifting all the blame completely on her instead."

He shrugged again. "Anyway, seven or so years ago my mom started going through a rough patch with my stepdad, and she began saying the same sort of things about him to me and my siblings. Only he was still there, and I was old enough see more clearly what was going on. It made me wonder if things were really so cut and dried with my dad, so I sought him out."

Hal took a ragged breath and glanced at her. "Well, to make a long story short that put my relationship with my mom on the rocks. She couldn't forgive me for "betraying" her by wanting to at least talk to my dad. Started insisting more and more that I was just like him, which I suppose is kind of true since I look a lot like him, and the resemblance got more noticeable as I got older. Maybe that's why she began acting almost like she wanted to punish me in his place."

Ellie couldn't help but think of her sweet little Ricky. Hal was sounding a lot like some awful Ghost of Christmas Yet To Come, if she ever let her relationship with Nick affect how she acted towards her son. Something she hadn't even considered before now, and resolved to never, ever let happen.

"So anyway, it got bad enough that the moment I turned eighteen, I was gone. I already had a job, so I was able to get my own place and put it all behind me." He shook his head. "I feel bad about walking away from my brothers and sister, and I try to see them when I can. But I just couldn't stay in that situation a second longer."

The young man's lips quirked upward bitterly. "I guess that also helped me have a better understanding of what my dad had done in leaving. We started talking more, even visiting each other when we could, although it wasn't easy with him in Japan. Didn't talk about the past much, which was fine by me. Mostly we just made up for lost time."

"It's good to hear you're patching things up, in spite of everything." Ellie leaned forward and briefly rested a hand on his knee. "Thank you for sharing this with me."

"Well, I hadn't expected to find a friend out here I could open up to. Thanks." He cleared his throat, forcing a laugh. "Anyway, we're on the final stretch to St. George. Should we get going?"

Ellie had no arguments there. She got busy taking down her tent, gnawing on jerky whenever she had a spare moment. As she worked she fantasized about making a beeline for the first restaurant she saw the moment they reached civilization. A hamburger, or a taco, or a pizza. Each thing she imagined made her stomach growl that much more loudly, and energized her to push the final distance.

Shut In

At least until she remembered Zolos; restaurants would either be closed down, or too dangerous to visit. The realization completely took the wind out of her sails.

They got started, walking through the cool morning along the smooth road. Every indication suggested they should reach St. George within a few hours, but hard experience the last few days had taught her otherwise. Exhaustion and deprivation had taken their toll, and she was at the end of her strength.

Which was why she stopped for a break a bit earlier than usual to check her phone. Only to discover, to her delight, that when the device turned on she immediately began getting notifications for missed calls and messages.

Ellie laughed and threw her arms around Hal, ignoring his surprised look. "You hear that? We finally have a signal!"

Chapter Ten
Contact

Nick was pretty sure the man outside had died overnight.

He hadn't so much as twitched all morning. He just lay there, curled up in a posture of pure misery, with no sign of anyone coming to offer help or take his body for burial. Nick had had to shoo a curious Ricky away from the window all day yesterday and a few times this morning, and Tallie had clung to him ever since yesterday morning in fear.

When his daughter wasn't clinging to him, he'd noticed her creeping around as if she expected a monster to jump out of hiding and lunge at her at any moment. When he finally asked her why, she confessed that she was terrified of Zolos germs, which she described like tiny little green buggies.

She was convinced some had come in through the window from the dying man and were lurking in the apartment, waiting to sneak up on her when she wasn't looking. Apparently she'd misunderstood the reason Nick was keeping her from the window, so she wouldn't have to see the awful sight of a someone dying, and thought the virus was coming through the glass and would hit her if she was anywhere in sight of the man outside.

Now that he knew what Tallie had been thinking, he felt terrible for not sitting his children down and explaining even more carefully what the Zolos virus was and how it was transmitted, so they wouldn't get any mistaken ideas about the danger. The knowledge that his little girl had been driving herself sick with worry made him feel sick himself.

It was good she realized the danger, and he wanted her to be careful, but he didn't want her to be constantly terrified of tiny green bugs seeping in through the windows and killing her in her sleep, either.

Shut In

Nick had quickly rectified that misconception last night, gathering his children close to try to get them to understand about Zolos and what was happening in the outside world. Although he wasn't sure how much it helped, since his daughter continued to cling to him afterwards and even Ricky stayed close. They'd both insisted on sleeping on his bed, and Tallie had woken up once from a nightmare and spent almost ten minutes crying before he was able to coax her back to sleep.

Then again, part of that was almost certainly that they were sensing the distress Nick tried to hide, the way children did so well. He wasn't sure what he could do about that, either, since no matter how he tried to reassure his kids, he couldn't lie and pretend the world wasn't going crazy outside their apartment.

Because it was.

All efforts by top microbiologists, immunologists, and epidemiologists to develop a vaccine had thus far proven fruitless: Zolos was simply so hardy that attempts to culture it in a weakened state were hitting one roadblock after another. Although the eminently qualified people overseeing the project offered the good news that at least this strain of the virus seemed stable and slow to mutate, so once a vaccine *was* developed it would likely be effective for it, and any new strains would similarly be easy to develop vaccines for.

Although such assurances rang hollow, since the pandemic was spreading so rapidly that there was some question about whether anyone would be left by the time a vaccine was developed.

Even though it had only been a few days since the government publicly acknowledged the Zolos threat, the virus had already spread like wildfire. To the point that as more and more outbreaks spread across the globe, people began talking less and less about where the pandemic was and more and more about where it *wasn't*.

For a while Hawaii had seemed like it might remain unscathed, with its quick response closing itself off to the outside. Something Nick was intimately familiar with, considering Ellie had gotten caught up in that mess.

161

But after a couple days of all seeming well on the islands, a single breakout occurred at Honolulu Harbor. Even then, the swift quarantine response seemed like it had caught and contained the outbreak in time.

Then a dozen more outbreaks had occurred in swift succession, all over the island. Too many to contain, especially when that number became a hundred after just a few hours. Zolos, with its deceptively slow to present symptoms, had snuck past their best efforts.

Japan was another place that seemed like it would scrape by, to the point where Nick had almost found himself wishing Ellie had stayed there. Especially now that she'd disappeared without warning, and he couldn't get ahold of her or find out anything about what might've happened to her.

Everyone expected the caution the Japanese showed when it came to infection to make the difference, especially since it had led them to close the country off almost as quickly as Hawaii, and arguably far more efficiently.

Then yesterday an outbreak had flared up in Kyoto. They'd actually gone so far as to seal the city off, not even allowing aid workers in unless they planned to stay. Then another outbreak had hit Tokyo hard in the evening, and when the government moved to seal off their capitol, including most of Japan's leadership, the entire country had begun to unravel. Even that hadn't been enough to prevent the infection from spreading beyond the two cities.

There were countless other islands across the world, and most that didn't have airports or regularly used docks remained pockets of health. The deeper areas of Africa, largely untouched by the rest of the world, also stayed untouched for the moment. As did farther north territories in Canada and Russia, places that were simply too sparsely populated for an outbreak to really spread.

The problem was, whenever people heard of a place that had been spared Zolos, they immediately rushed there so they'd be safe, too. And, people being people, at least some of those refugees were carrying the deadly virus without realizing it.

Shut In

Or, if someone was really monstrous, perhaps they were even spreading it on purpose; who could say, there had to be at least a few nutjobs out there doing that sort of thing. That might even be the explanation for how the infection had already spread to places that should've remained safe.

Unless of course the people with more chilling speculations were correct, and there was some group out there deliberately spreading Zolos as far and as fast as possible. That didn't seem likely, since if it was any specific country or organization there would've been at least some place in the world spared the outbreak. Unless of course whoever was doing it were complete zealots, willing to infect themselves along with their victims.

That, or as some real headcases online suggested, aliens were the source of the disease. Some extraterrestrials' way of wiping out humanity so they could take a fertile world like Earth intact. Some even went so far as to suggest that if it really did look as if humans might go extinct, they should blanket the planet with every nuclear warhead in existence to render it uninhabitable as a last "screw you" to the beings that had done this.

Nick had to wonder what was going through the heads of people like that, to concoct those sorts of ridiculous flights of fancy. He just hoped the world leaders with their hands on the nuclear launch codes weren't that irrational.

Although when it came to irrationality, the response by the vast majority of people came as a pleasant surprise.

Many had predicted that humanity would tear itself apart in the face of a disaster like Zolos. Maybe not literally, since nobody wanted to get close enough to possibly infected people for physical violence, at least aside from isolated incidents. But at least philosophically; during the days after the outbreak, experts had predicted that when it came to interpersonal interactions, even at a distance, everyone would become much more paranoid and hostile.

But surprisingly, that hadn't happened.

163

Instead, people had cooperated and worked overtime to create alternative ways to report and track outbreaks, so those who couldn't get the information they needed from overburdened public sources could find pertinent news online. Groups of volunteers risked their own safety to acquire hazmat suits so they could drive the sick to hospitals, transport the deceased to designated burial areas, and even care for the sick themselves in makeshift clinics.

Although unfortunately for suffering mankind, the numbers of those volunteers were far too few to make much more than a token effort in the crisis; for the same reasons that people couldn't tear each other apart physically during the panic, they also mostly only came together in spirit. People might've been filled with supportive sentiments and calls for sending aid where it was needed, but just about everyone who could had locked themselves into their homes with their families in voluntary quarantine.

It was taking its toll in many ways, not just where the economy was concerned. Humans were a social species, and enforced isolation wasn't good for mental or even physical health. Those who had no family or friends to fall back on became a source of concern for experts, who warned the world would see increasingly disturbing and erratic activity from those individuals as the weeks passed.

Which led many to conclude that if Zolos hadn't been forcing isolation, humanity *would* be tearing itself apart.

Closer to home things were just as bad, if not worse. Estimates had jumped up to forty percent exposed to Zolos in Kansas City. Garbagemen had collected the trash that morning in full hazmat suits, and even so it had taken most of the day because apparently half the staff hadn't shown up to work.

There were talks about a full citywide strike of all sanitation and maintenance crews until the crisis had passed, since dealing with human waste or highly trafficked areas had become a perilous job, and there'd been no corresponding increase in pay to make it worth the risk. Especially since many city workers insisted they wouldn't put themselves in that kind of danger for any amount of pay.

As for Ellie's mom, Nick's attempts to reach the nursing home all day yesterday and this morning had failed. There was no news of any incident there, although in the chaos that might not mean anything. Either way, he was getting more and more worried about the situation, concerned for Lois's welfare.

Adding that to his concern for Ellie, and the worry he stubbornly refused to acknowledge about his mom and her family, he was an emotional wreck. Especially since his kids were going stir crazy cooped up indoors; he never thought he'd see the day when they got tired of watching shows, but they'd been pestering him more and more to play with them, or at least sit with them watching something.

So he did.

After all, what else did he have to do? Watch the news for more and more terrible information about the Zolos pandemic? His consulting projects had all gone belly up, and his feelers with his regular contacts confirmed that absolutely nobody in the market was doing anything right now. Most of them had openly shut their businesses down to the bare minimum operations, handling only the most bare-bones necessary tasks.

It didn't seem to matter that those businesses were in the tech industry, and they could easily do all their work through commuting without any of the employees needing to be in the same city, let alone the same room. The economy had taken a nosedive as huge chunks of the population refused to go to work, and nobody was worrying about anything more than keeping the lights on until things settled down.

If they ever did.

Nick was still trying to figure out how to tell Tallie and Ricky that something might have happened to their grandma, if the fact that he couldn't get in touch with the nursing home meant a disaster and he wasn't just panicking. He hadn't told them yet, since there was no need to worry them until he knew one way or another. They were already worried enough about their mom, constantly demanding he call her, even as often as every five minutes, and leaving voicemails for her until her mailbox was full.

Which was why they both rushed to him when his phone rang a few hours before noon, jumping at his legs as he scrambled to pull it out and answer it. He actually shouted in relief when he saw Ellie's name, and rushed so much answering it that he missed the first swipe.

"Ellie!" he called over Tallie's and Ricky's own shouted greetings, switching to speakerphone so the kids could hear. "Are you okay? What happened?"

His ex-wife sounded like she was crying as she answered. "Oh Nick, thank God! Are you and the children all right? Are they showing any symptoms of Zolos from that scare at the school?"

"They're fine, we all are," he babbled. "We've still got a bit more than a day when symptoms might show, but I'm feeling better and better about us being in the clear."

"Mom, are you okay?" Tallie shouted directly into the phone. "We were so scared!"

"There's a dead guy outside!" Ricky added.

The next few minutes were chaos as Nick let the kids talk to their mom. Then he pried the phone away and shifted back to his own questions. "Where are you, Ells? What happened?"

Ellie was slow to answer. "In Southern Utah, a few miles from St. George. I let a couple carpool with me back to Missouri, and when we stopped to sleep they stole the car and left us stranded. We didn't have cell phone coverage, so we've been walking for the last couple days to get back to St. George. We'll try to get another car there, or find some other way home."

"No cell phone coverage?" Nick frowned. "I'm pretty sure just about every mile of Interstate highways gets coverage."

"Yeah, that's what I thought, too. Maybe not in the middle of nowhere in Southern Utah?"

"You'd think even there . . ." He switched to the internet on his phone, quickly typing in a search. "Ah, there you go. A few signal towers along I-15 north of St. George went down due to severe weather. With the Zolos scare telecommunications companies are having manpower issues, focusing on keeping coverage active in populated areas. So yeah, I guess the middle of nowhere in Southern Utah would be the place to lose it."

There was an even longer pause, and when Ellie finally spoke she had that tone that suggested she was seriously ticked off but trying to be reasonable about it. "So you're saying we would've been able to call except for freak bad luck?"

"Pretty much," Nick replied. Then he paused. "Hold up, we?"

His ex-wife's reply was impatient. "I was traveling with a young man on my flight who lives near KC, as well as the couple who stole my car. They left him stranded with me."

He wasn't sure he liked the sound of that. "Is he a threat? You should be-"

"Nick, he's a good kid. Don't worry, I'm fine."

Well, not worrying was pretty much impossible. And this unexpected bit of news was the last push needed to cement his resolve. "Give me a bit to get me and the kids packed, and we'll be in the car and on our way to you in no time flat."

There was a long pause before Ellie answered. When she did her tone was more serious than he'd ever heard it, even when she'd announced she wanted a divorce. "Nicholas Statton, under no circumstances are you to take our children out of that apartment."

He stared at his phone incredulously for a second, then took it off speakerphone and brought it to his ear, lowering his voice. "Ells, you're stranded in the middle of a freaking desert with no car! That's not a joke, it's life and death. We could be to you in around twenty hours, then bring you home with no more fuss."

His ex-wife's tone showed no hint of budging. "No, Nick. If the rest of the world is as crazy as Los Angeles was, it won't be just a simple trip. You are *not* going to risk exposing Tallie and Ricky to Zolos."

"I could have someone watch them while I come get you. Gen would probably be happy to do it." He'd have to drive them up to Stanberry first, but that shouldn't take too much longer.

"What part of "under no circumstances" was confusing you? The entire country is falling to pieces and tens of millions of people are infected with an invisible, deadly disease. Your job, your *only* job, is to keep our children in your apartment until Zolos is just a distant memory."

"But-" he began helplessly.

Ellie again interrupted, tone gentler but no less resolute. "We're almost to St. George. We should be able to get a car there, even if I have to use my emergency credit card."

Nick grudgingly accepted that. "Okay, but call me if you reach St. George and can't find a car. Or if you run into *any* real disaster. We can figure something out to get help to you and still keep the kids safe."

"Okay." There was a short pause. "I need to worry about battery life, so if that's all . . ."

He abruptly remembered one of his main sources of concern over the last day or so, before her call had completely driven it from his head. Taking a deep breath, he said, "Hold on, Ells. I'm sorry, I hate to have to tell you this, but I haven't been able to contact your mom's nursing home for over a day."

* * * * *

Ellie stared at her phone with a sort of numb blankness.

Not content to take Nick's word for it, she'd tried calling the nursing home herself. The phone had rang and then gone to a full voicemail box three times in a row before she gave up. Then she'd looked up the numbers of some of the nursing home's staff and tried calling them, to similar results.

As a last desperate measure, she'd even tried to contact emergency services in KC to ask them what they knew. Only to find them, of course, so bogged down with other people calling in their own emergencies that she'd be waiting on the line until long after her phone's battery life ran out.

Something had happened, something bad.

Maybe the place had been hit with Zolos and evacuated to the nearest hospital, with no time to inform loved ones of the move. Or maybe the staff had all refused to come in to work, and her mom and dozens of other elderly people in need of special care were all helpless and suffering. Or maybe the local government had created a quarantine camp, like LA had, and her mom had been moved there as a precautionary measure.

The worst thing was that she had no way of knowing. Whether she should grieve or try to take action or simply fret helplessly.

Ellie had already done her best to resign herself to the fact that she might lose her mom, back when she'd been diagnosed with early onset Alzheimer's. That even if her mom lived for a long time to come, before long she'd practically be a stranger. It was a heartbreaking reality that she'd struggled with for a long time, and still struggled with.

But this, this was something she couldn't have prepared herself for.

Nick had offered to go check the nursing home. The fact that he hadn't already done so, even after knowing for over a day that something was up, suggested that he knew the extreme risk it represented. A risk he couldn't take when the kids were depending on him.

The fact that he'd asked had placed an added burden on Ellie's shoulders, forced her to make the terrible choice to put the welfare of her kids above her mom's. She couldn't resent him for it, since the offer had been sincere and he'd been willing to put himself in danger if that's what she'd wanted.

But it still devastated her.

Ellie didn't know how long she sat there slumped on the roadside, staring at her phone and only vaguely aware that she'd forgotten to turn it off yet to conserve battery, before she realized how quiet it was.

She looked over to find Hal on his knees not far away, hunched over with his head in his hands and his phone discarded a few feet away. The sight sent a surge of pity and dread through her, as she realized she wasn't the only one who'd received terrible news now that they finally had access to their phones.

"Hal?" she asked gently. She finally turned off her phone, then pushed to her feet and shuffled over to him.

He didn't stir, although he answered in a dull voice. "There was a Zolos case at my mom's apartment building before she could head up to my place. They shut down central air and warned everyone to stay inside, and were blocking the entrances when my mom called. But she's afraid the virus has already spread through the building."

The young man finally looked up, eyes haunted. "The last time I called her I couldn't wait to get off the phone. I told her my food is only for my siblings, like some sort of selfish, petty brat. I just painted her to you as a monster, after she'd done her best to raise me on her own. And now . . ."

He trailed off, letting his head hang and staring at the road in pure misery.

Ellie dropped down beside him and put an arm around his shoulders. That seemed to be all that was needed for the dam to burst, and he dissolved into silent, shuddering sobs. She let her own tears flow as her grief resurged. "My ex couldn't get ahold of my mom's nursing home," she mumbled. "Neither can I . . . I don't know what's happened with her."

Hal reached up and grasped her hand on his shoulder, holding it in solid reassurance.

She wasn't sure how long they stayed like that, both sunk into their private grief, finally allowing themselves to vent all the fear, anger, frustration, and sadness of what they'd been through the last few days. And taking solace in each other's presence, in spite of the fact that they barely knew one another. Although with this shared experience, she confirmed that she'd found in him a good friend.

Ellie wasn't sure about her companion, but even though she was technically sitting down and resting the emotional tsunami sapped what remained of her strength, leaving her drained and bringing to the fore all the aches and pains of the last couple days of walking.

So she was genuinely impressed when Hal somehow found the strength to stand, reaching down to help her to her feet as well. "We need to keep going," he said, tone unexpectedly gentle.

I don't know if I can, she thought to herself. But putting voice to that thought might make it reality, and he was right that they needed to. For themselves, for their loved ones. For her children.

Ellie took a last shuddering breath, carefully dabbed at her eyes with a dust-caked sleeve, then took his hand and let him help her up.

Chapter Eleven
St. George

The jewel of a city that Ellie had seen as she drove past at midnight . . . was it three days ago now?, looked a bit less spectacular in the daylight. Neatly planned out, and greener than the desolation around it, it still had the yellowing-around-the-edges look of a place in a constant battle to look green and fertile in the middle of a desert.

Although to her exhausted, hungry, and above all *thirsty* eyes, it might as well have been a luxurious oasis.

Unfortunately, that view was still a few miles away. Hal took one look at it, glanced at the sun sinking steadily towards the western horizon, and frowned. "Even at the pace we managed today, we can get still there before dark. The question is . . . should we?"

Ellie glanced at him. "You want to camp out one last time, then head in tomorrow morning?"

He nodded. "I'm not sure I want to stumble around a potentially infected city in the dark, looking for help or someone to sell us a car." He patted the pocket where he held his phone. "Besides, maybe we can use the same app we used to buy your other car to find someone selling down there."

She felt a surprising amount of relief at the suggestion; in spite of her urgency to get home, she was emotionally exhausted by the news about her mom, her agony about not knowing more or being able to do anything to help it. That piled on top of sheer physical exhaustion, to the point where the thought of trying to hike into St. George and search for a car tonight made her want to slump to the ground and just lay there comatose.

And she wasn't the only one. Hal's news about his own family had similarly discouraged him, and they'd moved at a snail's pace all day, forcing themselves to go the remaining distance in what should've easily been half a day's walk at most.

Maybe camping out one last time wasn't the worst idea.

"Let's get to the city limits, at least," she suggested. "Maybe we can find some place with an outdoor faucet we can drink from. Maybe even a socket so we can charge our phones."

"As long as it doesn't look like there's a cloud of Zolos hanging around it," her friend said. He wearily hefted his pack, much lightened from their water being nearly gone, and trudged on down the road.

As they walked Ellie examined the city below, a bit concerned by something she *wasn't* seeing: the roadblocks that had turned them off the Interstate onto smaller roads to keep traffic out when they'd last been through here.

Did that mean Zolos had hit the city, and they weren't bothering to try to keep it out anymore? Or had the local law enforcement who'd been manning the roadblocks all failed to show up for work, staying in their homes and focusing on protecting their families?

She and Hal both agreed to stop at the first house they reached, a rambler far removed from I-15 with a high earth berm blocking the view, and more importantly the noise of passing cars. At least when there'd been those; it seemed like a lifetime ago Ellie had seen one, instead of yesterday.

They stood on top of the berm for almost ten minutes, debating whether to take the risk of knocking on the door to ask for aid, or even to buy the truck or the car sitting in the driveway. It was impossible to tell whether the residents had been coming and going in the last few days, or if the place had remained safely isolated. Such a remote location seemed like an ideal candidate for being well protected from Zolos infection, but still . . .

What if it wasn't?

Nathan Jones

In the end, neither of them wanted to expose themselves to that danger. However, there was a spigot near the edge of the property that looked as if it was meant to water a nearby field, although the stretch of fenced-in ground was currently nothing but patches of parched grass and fine dirt, obviously untended for a long time. They warily drank deep of the cold, clean water, eyes on the house the entire time in case the angry residents charged out to chase them off.

No one seemed in the mood to, probably in self-imposed quarantine and not willing to risk setting foot outside, especially with two strangers lurking around who might be carrying Zolos. Even so, in spite of the luxury of not needing to boil what they drank, and the pure deliciousness of the clean water, Ellie and Hal wasted no time refilling their bottles and moving on.

Instead, they found a stand of rugged trees running along an irrigation ditch farther down the Interstate and found a place to spend the night there.

Their camp that night was quiet, both of them sunk deep in their worry for their loved ones as they set up their tents, then sat around a small fire and ate jerky and mixed nuts.

Ellie didn't know about Hal, but she was doing her best to reconcile hoping for the best when it came to her mom with preparing for the worst. She risked a few minutes of battery life to once again search for any hint about the fate of the nursing home, only to once again be frustrated by her fruitless efforts.

As consolation, she used the opportunity to call her kids to wish them goodnight.

Nick had to wake them up for it, which she felt bad about since she hadn't considered the time zone difference, but it was a relief to hear their voices and tell them she loved them. As she'd agreed with her ex-husband earlier, they avoided mentioning to their children that they hadn't been able to get any news about Grandma, deciding that it was better not to say anything until they knew for sure.

Shut In

Besides, the children, especially Tallie, were already anxious about some man who'd died of Zolos just across the street from the apartment. Nick had tried to keep them from seeing it, and he tried to steer the conversation away now to keep from further distressing them, but the kids wanted to talk about it.

So they had a brief conversation, necessarily so because of her phone's limited remaining battery life, about the reality of death. Perhaps it was a good time for it, with so many people dying and things looking so grim, although it broke her heart to have to take away that bit of her children's innocence about the world.

Especially when the discussion ended with her daughter breaking down crying. "Can you come home tomorrow, Mommy?" she begged.

"I'll try, honey," Ellie replied, blinking away tears of her own. "I'll try as hard as I can."

After they said their goodbyes and she turned off her phone again, she sat for several minutes staring at it, struggling with the bleak sense of hopelessness that washed over her as everything she'd been through, everything that was going on, all came crashing down on her.

Hal had sat in silence across the fire, giving her space. But finally he stood and stepped closer, putting a comforting hand on her shoulder. "Let's get some rest," he said quietly. "We can get an early start tomorrow, find a car and get home."

She nodded and patted his hand in acknowledgment, but stayed sitting a bit longer as he disappeared inside his tent, staring at the dying flames.

* * * * *

Hal hadn't been able to find anyone in St. George willing to sell their cars by looking online, which left the option of either checking around at the city's car dealerships or going house to house.

Dealerships were public areas, and while it was likely many of the cars there had remained untouched by anyone since before the Zolos

175

crisis, it remained enough of a risk to make that an option of last resort. By that same token, they couldn't be confident that the people in the houses they passed wouldn't also have been traveling and possibly infected.

There was one thing they had going for them, though; quarantine notices.

Right from the first, the Federal Emergency Task Force as well as local and state emergency services had put the notices up on their websites. Anyone intending to go into self-quarantine could download and print the notice to put on their doors and windows.

Of course, there was always the risk that the people with the quarantine notices had them up because there was actually Zolos in the residence. But there were good odds the telltale sheets of paper meant the family had closed themselves into their home on time, and they were safe to approach.

Which was just what Ellie and Hal planned to do.

To that purpose, they'd taken a bit of extra time heading back to the pump they'd used the previous night, giving each other some privacy to thoroughly wash up, clean their clothes, and make use of deodorant and other perks of civilization to make themselves as presentable as possible. Hal even shaved the stubble he'd accumulated over the past few days, putting the boyish back into his good looks.

Ellie did her best, particularly with brushing her newly shampooed hair before tying it back in a ponytail again. But even without the use of a mirror, she was keenly aware that under normal circumstances she wouldn't even have wanted to visit the corner store looking like this, let alone engage in a business venture like trying to buy a car from wary strangers. She once again lamented leaving behind her expensive business clothes.

"You look great," Hal told her when she returned to their camp. He'd taken the opportunity during the not inconsiderable length of time she'd been gone to clean his backpack, her suitcase, and their other gear to make it look clean and respectable. She hadn't even considered that, and was grateful he had.

"Thanks," she replied wryly; he seemed completely sincere in the compliment, but given her previous moping about her appearance it was hard to take it seriously.

They made their way into St. George a bit after sunrise, leaving I-15 and making their way into the residential area of the city, where they soon found themselves in a modestly prosperous neighborhood.

It was eerie and unsettling to walk along a street bracketed by neatly painted houses, well-tended yards strewn with toys, and vehicles parked in driveways or along the curbs, and have it be utterly deserted of people. There were no children out playing with the toys, no early morning joggers along the side of the road. No residents in pajamas stepping outside to pick up the newspaper or take out the trash, no harried parents packing kids into vehicles to drive to school. No buses trundling down the streets picking up waiting kids, no crossing guards or kids burdened by backpacks converging on the schools.

It was all deserted, as if everyone had disappeared overnight. The only evidence Ellie saw that people were still around was the flickers of residents peering out through blinds or behind curtains, faces glowering out windows at her as if she'd come to burn down their houses, instead of simply walking along the sidewalk with all the menace of a tail-wagging puppy.

Hal motioned to a driveway with two cars parked one behind the other, in front of a house prominently displaying the quarantine notices. "Well, should we get started?"

She grimaced in response. "You have much experience with cold approaches to potentially hostile business prospects?" The face he made was answer enough, and she shook her head ruefully. "All right, how about I take lead then?"

"I defer to your expertise." He motioned formally, and together they set off towards the front door.

Not that they got anywhere near it, of course. Instead, they stopped twenty feet away and Ellie cupped her hands around her mouth, calling the remaining distance towards the still house. "Excuse me! Can we talk to you about purchasing one of your cars, please?"

There was no response. She hadn't seen any sign of faces peering out windows, either, not so much as a flickering curtain. Still, she gave it half a minute before calling again, even going so far as to shout the house's address so the residents would know she was talking to them specifically.

Still nothing. Ellie couldn't say she was surprised, although she was definitely disappointed. She could tell Hal was as well. "Hey, closing a deal is tough at the best of times, let alone when everyone's jumping at an invisible deadly virus," she reassured him. "We're going to have to resign ourselves to the possibility it might take a while to find someone willing to even talk to us, let alone sell us their car."

He smiled gamely. "As long as we don't get shot by someone who's Hannah levels of paranoid because we're on their property potentially carrying Zolos."

Well, that wasn't a possibility she enjoyed contemplating. "On the plus side, I think we've gone long enough without showing symptoms that we're probably not infected."

Hal opened his mouth, then paused and shut it again, shrugging easily. "That's a pretty big plus."

What had he been about to say? Something along the lines of them possibly having it, but being immune and carrying it everywhere? Ellie wanted to contemplate *that* even less, especially when she was trying to get home to her kids. She did *not* want to go through all this to be reunited with her loved ones, only to expose them to this dreaded virus.

Well, she could consider quarantine when she got to Nick's apartment. "On to the next one."

There was no response at the next place, either, although they saw eyes peeking out through the blinds, confirming that someone was home. At the place after *that* a dude cracked open his window just enough to hurl threats and obscenities at them until they fled the premises.

But the third place was by far the worst: the front door flew open inwards the moment they stepped off the sidewalk, and although they couldn't see into the darkened interior of the house, they heard the distinctive *click-clack* of a shotgun chambering a shell echoing out through the screen door.

Hal moved protectively between her and the house as they fled without waiting for the resident to say anything.

For a dozen steps Ellie fully expected to hear the roar of the gun at least firing a warning shot, and more likely peppering her and her friend with buckshot. To her vast relief, instead she heard the door slam shut again; unless the unseen gunman was planning on firing through a window or something, that probably meant they were safe.

That didn't stop them from passing up several potential houses and going until the menacing house was out of sight. Only then did they get back to work, shaken and far more cautious, but unable to think of anything else they could do other than keep trying.

The morning passed in a miserable blur of silent houses, frightened and angry shouting, and even small, heavy household items thrown at them to chase them away. Thankfully nobody else tried to point a gun at them; Ellie wasn't sure she could've handled that again.

After stopping to gnaw on a few handfuls of nuts and drink some water, they grudgingly agreed to check a nearby car dealership.

That turned out to be a depressing failure, the entire place cordoned off by police tape and warning signs about it being a potential outbreak site. There were even a couple men, either soldiers or SWAT, wearing hazmat suits and holding serious looking rifles, watching the place to make sure nobody tried to go inside.

For their own safety, no doubt, but that didn't change the fact that it meant dozens of cars Ellie could've used to get home were now off-limits.

"Think that's just a fluke?" Hal asked as they walked away. "Or are all the dealerships going to be cordoned off like that?"

At the moment they were passing a big chain grocery store that looked as if it had been abandoned for years: the lights were off, the parking lot was empty save for a single lonely car with its windshield smashed, and even more shockingly some of the big plate glass windows along the front of the store had been shattered.

She shuddered and looked away from the sight, not wanting to imagine what sort of chaos had taken place there. "Even if they're not quarantined, you really think we'll find employees there to sell us a car?"

He shook his head grimly. "We might find the locker where they keep the keys, leave some money on a desk and drive a car off the lot."

Ellie was ashamed to discover she was so desperate she actually didn't find the idea as appalling as she should've. "Let's save that for a last resort."

"So, like, in a few more hours of having guns pulled on us?" her friend muttered. But he reluctantly turned towards another residential neighborhood.

Unfortunately, Hal's prediction of more hours of fruitless searching proved to be all too accurate. On the plus side they weren't menaced by any more guns, at least as far as Ellie knew, but even so the afternoon passed towards evening with nothing to show for their efforts but sore feet and ears ringing from a day of verbal abuse.

They did find some sign that St. George wasn't a ghost town, although it was the last thing she wanted to see. They passed a hospital, not a bigger facility but one that looked to be an emergency room with maybe some of the more necessary equipment for basic medical tests. Ellie was no expert when it came to Zolos pandemics, but it seemed like mostly a place where patients could be processed and sent on to a bigger hospital for more specialized treatment.

Shut In

Maybe those hospitals were all overcrowded, or maybe they would've required too much travel. Either way, the place was literally overflowing with sick people; large tents complete with attached heating units had been set up on a nearby lawn, closed off by double layers of fencing and closely guarded by soldiers in hazmat suits.

Ellie had a feeling they'd found part of the military convoy that had blown past them on the hike here. Looking at them now, she almost couldn't begrudge them leaving her and Hal to fend for themselves in a desert, since they obviously had their work cut out for them.

Beyond guarding the quarantine area, they were occupied shuttling in personnel carriers full of new patients, then carrying them into the tents. Dozens of people just in the few minutes Ellie and Hal watched, as they skirted the hospital at a cautious distance; at this rate the relief workers would soon have to set up more tents, even if the existing ones were currently mostly empty.

Even more troubling than that, soldiers were occupied carrying body bags out of the emergency room to a pile of over a hundred similarly covered bodies, all waiting for humane disposal at one end of the parking lot. And from the suspicious looking tarp-covered mounds near the pile, there might've been hundreds more.

Ellie wasn't sure what troubled her most, the sight of human suffering on such a large scale or the fact that the soldiers moved with the plodding listlessness of men simply doing an unpleasant task, rather than a horrific one. As if they'd been at it long enough to have distanced themselves from the awful reality that it was dead human beings, by the size many of them children, that they carried to an ignoble resting place.

How many people in St. George were grieving lost loved ones now? Were some, like Ellie, unable to contact close friends and family, with no way of knowing whether or not they were still alive?

Was her mother in some pile of bodies in Kansas City? The thought made Ellie want to throw up.

That human need to know seemed to overcome fear, at least for some. She spotted over a hundred people scattered beyond the perimeter set up by the soldiers, looking helplessly in at the hospital and tents as if searching for some glimpse of loved ones. They'd taken obvious precautions to protect themselves from Zolos, or perhaps to protect others if they feared they were carrying the infection. But in spite of the danger of being so close to a place with hundreds or even thousands of infected people, still they were there.

Ellie jumped slightly when Hal put a hand on her arm, expression grim but determined. "Let's get out of here," he said quietly.

She nodded and joined him hurrying away from the hospital, more determined than ever to continue their fruitless search until they found success.

Her friend seemed to feel that same resolve, which might've explained why he finally lost patience when they tried a more upscale house a few blocks away, with two cars in the driveway and one parked on the street in front.

It started out depressingly familiar, with a resident cracking a window just enough to talk to them. "Get off my driveway!" he shouted, voice shrill with anger and fear. "Go away!"

Ellie held up her hands placatingly. The guy might have a gun, after all, even if she thought he'd sound more confident if he did. "We don't want trouble, sir. I just want to talk about maybe renting one of your cars."

A woman's voice swore at them through the curtains, sounding more angry than scared. "Are you crazy, lady?"

"Completely serious!" She fumbled in her pocket and pulled out her wallet, riffling through it. "I've got, um, two hundred and thirty-six dollars." She held it out lamely, as if expecting someone to come take it.

The woman laughed again. "You want to give us money all covered in Zolos? You *are* crazy!"

"We're not infected, I swear!" Ellie fought down an unexpected wave of frustration, tossing the assorted bills towards the door. They went a few feet before fluttering pathetically across the lawn. "Listen! If you give me your info I can send you more, and I swear I'll do everything I can to get your car back to you. Please."

"Ma'am, we're not giving you a car!" the man shouted. "Just go away!"

"You seriously saying you can't spare a single car when you've got three, man?" Hal demanded. "What're you even going to do with these things while you're hiding in your house?" There was no answer, and the young man flushed angrily. "Hey, you know what? We'll leave your cars alone. After we rub our filthy, sweaty bodies all over them!"

As her friend shouted the threat he shrugged off his backpack and peeled off his shirt, revealing a surprisingly muscular chest and washboard abs that must've been much admired by the girls in Kearney. Then he suited his words by rubbing himself on the driver's side door of the forest green sedan parked in the driveway. "There, it's all yours!"

"Hal, you're not helping!" Ellie snapped, looking away from him with her cheeks flushing.

Holy cow, he was built. Fond as she'd been of Nick, her ex-husband had always been more of a runner and swimmer. When he was able to tear himself from his work, that was, and wasn't stressed to his limits and gorging on junk food in the middle of a project; he'd been more dad bod than stud in the last few years.

In the house the couple were both swearing a blue streak at the young man. "What's wrong with you?" the woman demanded. "Why are you doing this? What did we ever do to you?"

"We need the car!" Hal shouted back. He took a threatening step towards the house. "Maybe I'll rub myself all over your doorknobs next."

Ellie put a hand on his arm, gently pulling him back, then stepped forward to face the window. She could see two pairs of eyes peeking at her through the blinds, wide with fear and anger. "Please," she said as quietly as she could and still be heard. Hopefully. "I've got two children at home. They're trapped in the middle of an infected city, and they need their mother. I'll pay you back and return your car, I promise. Just please, help us."

There was no reply.

Hal, panting angrily, retrieved his shirt and dragged it back on, then picked up his pack and came to stand beside her staring at the house. "This is pointless," he said quietly out of the side of his mouth. "Let's just leave these guys alone, keep searching."

"Maybe next time without the threats of biological warfare," she agreed, tone not completely joking. His cheeks flushed, obviously ashamed of his behavior, and with a sigh Ellie prepared to crouch to pick up her money, useless as it seemed at the moment.

Before she could, a click sounded from the front door as it was unlocked. It abruptly opened a crack and a man's arm emerged, holding something that glittered. He hurled it awkwardly onto the lawn with a merry jingling noise.

Car keys.

Ellie stared at them, feeling her eyes fill with tears. "Thank you," she said as the door slammed shut, the lock clicking again. "I promise, as soon as I can-"

"Just get out of here!" the man shouted through the door. "I don't care about any promises of payment, just go!"

Fair enough. She stepped forward to grab the keys, but it was Hal's turn to grab her arm. "Wait!" he hissed. "These guys were so scared of us having Zolos, did we ever stop to wonder if *they* might?"

She gave him a confused look. "If they did, why would they be so scared about us having it?"

"I dunno, maybe they have it and don't know it."

"While they've been closed up in their house?" Ellie shook her head and stooped, grabbing the keys before she could think better of it. "We need the car, so we'll just have to chance it."

Hal stared at her in consternation. "We could've at least used gloves. Maybe tried to find wet wipes or something to clean them with. Hannah wasn't completely insane."

She felt her face flush; in the moment she hadn't considered either of those options. "Well, too late now."

Keys in hand, Ellie made her way over to the driver's side door of the sedan, while Hal hurried to gather their stuff and waited by the back passenger side door for her to unlock it. She felt like a thief as she did so, even though the owner had technically given her the keys willingly.

But she couldn't let that stop her from using this chance to get home to her babies that much faster.

"Thank you!" she called. There was no response, so she slipped behind the wheel and turned the ignition. She wanted to cry when it started immediately; even though the car looked new and it couldn't have been idle for more than a few days, she'd half expected it to not work.

Hal tossed their stuff onto the backseat and threw himself into the passenger seat, almost as if he expected the owners to come bursting out of the house to chase them down. Maybe Ellie subconsciously feared the same, because she wasted no time putting the car in reverse and backing out of the driveway.

Then she put it in drive and they were once again on their way.

Hopefully all the way home to Kansas City, where their families waited for them.

* * * * *

The thirty or so miles that had taken them the better part of three grueling days of hiking took around a half hour in the car. Ellie wasn't sure whether to be depressed about all that wasted time, or elated that they were finally in a vehicle again and could laugh at such a paltry distance.

During that time she called Nick to let him know she had wheels and was once again zooming towards him at a responsible speed. It warmed her heart to hear her kids cheering in the background, Ricky yelling for her to be home soon and Tallie promising to draw a picture as a welcome home present.

She hadn't been planning to stop for anything until she had her children in her arms, but that was an extra motivation.

Which was why after some internal debate and agonizing, she decided not to waste the five or so minutes it would take to pick up their things at the campsite and come back. Maybe part of that was an almost superstitious fear that their car might be stolen again, but at that moment she valued getting home that little bit sooner over the expensive clothes and personal items she'd left behind.

Hal seemed to agree; when Ellie brought up stopping he insisted they drive on and not tempt fate. "It's just stuff," he said. "Aside from getting gas, I say we go nonstop."

It was good to know they were both on the same page.

On the subject of gas, the car they'd, ah, rented only held a bit more than half a tank. So around sundown, well after they'd moved from I-15 onto I-70 headed east, they began searching for a gas station in a small town called Salina. The first they passed was empty and abandoned, but to her relief the second had a sign out in front that said in large bold letters:

"CASHIER IS ARMED

PAY AT THE PUMP OR

KEEP DRIVING!"

It didn't seem to be an idle threat, either. The front window of the gas station that looked out from behind the cash register was shattered, and not far from the front doors a suspicious patch of dried crimson stained the pavement, fading to a trail of spatters moving away towards one of the pumps.

"I, um, think the dude in there shot someone who was trying to come inside," Hal said nervously, staring at the older man perched on a stool behind the register glaring out the window at them. "Looks like he just injured whoever it was, and they were able to drive off."

"I was planning on paying at the pump anyway," Ellie replied, picking one that didn't have a trail of blood leading to it. And not just because of the risk of Zolos.

She paid with her emergency credit card, handling the pump through one of the plastic grocery bags the food from the convenience store near LA had come in, then throwing it away. For once she found herself missing Hannah, if only for the woman's seemingly endless supply of latex gloves and wet wipes.

Then they switched drivers and were on their way again, fully intending to drive nonstop until they reached Kansas City.

On the way out of Salina Hal grunted, staring at a squat building near the on-ramp onto I-15. The wall facing the road had been crudely painted with the words:

"U.S. POPULATION

293 MILLION

AND COUNTING"

Ellie didn't know when the announcement had been slapped on there, but at some point the number had been crossed out and now "277" was scrawled above it. Her friend swore softly.

If the sign was correct, that meant tens of millions of people had already died. Ellie's thoughts immediately turned to her mom, wondering if she was one of them. From Hal's expression he was obviously thinking the same about his mom and siblings stuck in their infected apartment complex.

"Your family still doing okay?" she asked him. He'd been making his own calls as she drove, with them trading off using the car charger for their phones, and while she'd overheard a bit of his conversation with his mom she hadn't gotten the whole picture.

Her friend nodded distractedly, thoughts obviously torn between his driving and his worries for his loved ones. "No signs of Zolos so far. The family in the apartment next to theirs is sick, though. Mom's talking about trying to sneak past the cordon and get to my place anyway."

That didn't seem like a great idea, although she didn't feel like it was her place to say so. Besides, from what she'd overheard Hal had seemed to have been arguing against it as well. "Any word from your dad?" she asked instead.

He shook his head. "Just a text he sent before his flight took off for the States. Hopefully no news is good news."

There wasn't much to say to that. Ellie rested a supportive hand on his shoulder for a moment, and noticed when they got back on the Interstate that he drove faster than she had been, blowing past the speed limit with no apparent worry for highway patrolmen.

Which was probably a safe bet, since they'd barely seen half a dozen cars coming the other way since leaving St. George, and only one on their side of the highway, which had passed them at reckless speeds an hour or so earlier. She resisted the temptation to urge her friend to go even faster; they'd be home soon enough, no sense taking foolish risks.

Around one in the morning, they crossed through Eisenhower Tunnel in Colorado and began the long descent out of the mountains towards Denver.

They'd made good time, although their gas tank was starting to get uncomfortably low. Hal was looking tired as well, so they agreed that they'd stop at the first open, safe-looking gas station they found and switch drivers after they refueled. Preferably some place in the suburbs of Denver, or better yet some small place well outside it where there wouldn't be many people.

When they got closer, however, after battling through over an hour of bumper to bumper traffic, they realized they wouldn't have to worry about the danger of a gas station in Colorado's capitol because it wasn't even an option. In fact, the heavy traffic was due to the fact that like St. George, travelers along I-70 had been redirected around the city.

They had the option between circling north around Denver, or south. Ellie didn't care either way, although she and Hal both agreed that out of the diverging streams of taillights up ahead more seemed to be heading north, so they might have better luck going south.

She had her first hint of what might've motivated the people headed north when, looking at the gauge quickly dropping to empty, they began searching for a place to fuel up.

She wasn't sure if the people going the other way knew something she didn't, or if it was just pure bad luck, or maybe north didn't have any good prospects for buying gas either. Either way, their redirected stream of traffic's slow, meandering route south around Denver showed no good options.

"Should we try leaving the road?" Hal asked, glancing worriedly at the gauge. "This close to a population center there has to be something."

"There's no guarantee of that," Ellie argued. "Let's keep going until we're back on I-70. There *has* to be a gas station along there."

He didn't disagree, although his furrowed brow suggested he had his concerns about that.

It turned out that being in a global pandemic didn't make traffic jams any better. It took twice as long as it should've to circle around Denver and get back on the Interstate, and this late at night with both of them tense and exhausted it was hard not to snap irritably at each other as the gauge finally settled on empty.

"Finally," Ellie said as they approached an off ramp that led to a town called Watkins, which a couple of cars up ahead had turned onto, their taillights splitting away from the line.

Hal frowned and looked to either side of the Interstate, which appeared to be completely dark in the night, no sign of anyone living nearby. "You can go another thirty to fifty miles when the gauge hits empty in most cars," he offered. "This looks iffy, and there's still time to find something farther on."

Ellie shook her head. "It's still worth a shot, to get gas before our situation becomes dire. Let's at least check our options."

"Fair enough."

Her friend followed the taillights disappearing off the Interstate, which led them to a main street that in the dark looked identical to what you could find in dozens of little towns all over the country. Aside from the fact that all the lights in the businesses were off, including the places that should've been open 24/7.

In fact, Ellie was pretty sure that even the closed businesses should've had lights on all night; she had to look far down the street to find a streetlight that still worked, as if the nearby ones had been shattered by some punk and nobody had bothered to repair them. That left her more disquieted than she'd expected, and she wondered how wise it had really been to insist on checking this place out.

Hal turned the car into a gas station lot that was as dark and deserted as the rest. "We can at least try the pump," he said, not sounding very confident.

And for good reason. The convenience store looming on the far side of the lot looked more than just empty and abandoned: even in the darkness it was obvious looters had been through, breaking the windows and cleaning the place out. She had a feeling that every single edible thing in there, and most items that could be considered valuable or useful, had already been carried off.

"Well, at least this place doesn't look highly frequented enough to have had some infected person using the pump," Hal said as he climbed out and stepped up to the pump, pulling his card out of his wallet.

Ellie looked between him and the unpowered screen he was staring at. "The pump's dead, swiping a card's not going to do anything."

"So you want to go back to walking?" he demanded. "I'm going to at least try it." She shook her head, but kept her peace as her friend ran his card.

It did nothing, of course. Hal pulled a pump off its holder and fiddled with it, trying to see if he could make any gas come out. It didn't take long to confirm that the idea, an obvious long shot, wasn't going to happen.

Ellie stared doubtfully through the shattered glass doors into the convenience store. "What if we could turn the pumps on in there?" she said. "The employees have a bunch of switches to control them, right?"

Her friend looked silently at the pitch black interior, expression unreadable in the darkness. She wondered if he was picturing Zolos virus drifting around inside, ready to kill anyone who approached. Then he sighed and leaned into the car. "All right, hand me a flashlight."

She gave him one of the ones Brock had bought and Hal flicked it on. It was still bright even after a few nights of use, revealing the trashed interior of the convenience store as he cautiously approached.

Cheap shelves had been tipped over, displays of keychains and toys and souvenirs smashed and scattered everywhere. As she'd guessed, there was no food to be seen anywhere; even the drink and slushee machines looked to have been torn open, the packs of syrup inside taken.

Hal stepped gingerly through the broken glass of one of the doors, picked his way across a floor strewn with nicknacks and more broken glass, and edged behind the counter. He was there for several minutes, flashlight beam bobbing this way and that as he fiddled with things. Then he disappeared deeper into the store, through a door that had been kicked open.

A minute later the lights in the store flickered on, so abruptly that Ellie jumped in spite of herself. Hal emerged and hurried back behind the counter, either nervous about breaking into the place now that the lights were on to show what he was doing, or that having the lights on would draw more looters.

After another minute or two of fiddling he called out the broken windows. "Anything?"

She glanced at the dark screen of the pump. "Nope!"

Her friend let out a blistering stream of curses, picked his way into the back room to shut off the power again, then made his way outside. "That's it, then," he said as he slumped into the passenger's seat. "If there's a way to turn the pumps on, I can't figure it out."

They both stared hopelessly at the gas gauge, hovering on empty. "What now?" Ellie finally asked. "Look for other gas stations?"

"No guarantee they'd be any better than this one," Hal said, shaking his head. "There's an alternative, though. I saw hoses and gas cans in the store . . . we could find vehicles to siphon gas from."

Ellie immediately hated the idea. She wasn't a thief, and the thought of skulking around stealing from people made her feel sick.

But that was technically how she'd got this car in the first place, wasn't it? Not even theft, but arguably extortion. Besides, her children were waiting for her. "Maybe we can find people willing to sell us the gas in their vehicles," she said heavily. "Or even another person willing to rent us their car."

He snorted, as if also thinking of the lengths they'd gone to get the green sedan, and sagged back in the seat. "We're not convincing anyone of anything if we wake them up in the middle of the night. I know the plan was to drive until we got home, but I'll admit I wouldn't mind a few hours of sleep. Should we get some rest, see what we can do in the morning?"

That was a more than reasonable suggestion. Ellie chafed at the constant, frustrating delays, but whining about them wouldn't change anything. "You want the backseat?" she asked. With his longer legs he'd be more comfortable if he had room to stretch out.

Her friend shook his head and lowered the passenger seat. "I'm already settled in here, you go ahead."

Ellie nodded and climbed back behind the wheel long enough to drive them over to the side of the gas station's lot, in the shadow of an overhanging tree. Then she pulled their sleeping bags out of the trunk, tossed Hal his, and squirmed into hers on the backseat.

Maybe tomorrow would be better than today. Although given how things had been going lately, she didn't hold out much hope.

Chapter Twelve
Notice

Nick jolted awake at a loud thump that came from somewhere outside his room.

As a parent his first inclination was to check his kids, see if one of them was up and wandering around way past their bedtime. And possibly, judging by the racket, having broken something or even hurt themselves. At least he hadn't heard any screams or cries for help, so it couldn't be too bad.

He crawled out of bed and padded out into the hallway, looking around. He was about to open his mouth to call to his kids, quietly in case one was still asleep, but before he could the loud sound of glass shattering came from his office.

Ricky and Tallie knew not to go in there unless they were looking for him, and they especially knew not to go crashing around breaking things in there. So unless one of them was really acting out of character, that wasn't them.

Which left a far more alarming possibility.

Nick threw open the door, flipping the light on at the same time, and was both shocked and unsurprised to find a scrawny kid in his late teens crouched near the window leading out to the fire escape. The glass had been broken inwards, shards scattered all over the carpet, probably by the bigger thug outside on the metal stairs holding a crowbar. Both wore black, outfits that practically screamed "I'm out committing crimes".

"Are you crazy? This house is quarantined!" Nick shouted at the intruder crouched frozen in the corner, blinking in the sudden light. Jeez, cowering like that the teenager looked closer in age to Ricky than to an adult.

Shut In

But young or not, the thug seemed to hear the fear Nick tried to hide beneath his anger. He straightened, looking more confident as he glanced at his buddy hanging back on the fire escape, although the second guy wasn't trying to climb through the window while it was blocked.

The punk out there was older, probably just out of his teens, voice full of cocky contempt when he replied. "Yeah, we saw from the signs you put up. Thanks for the heads up, by the way." At Nick's blank look he laughed mockingly. "Haven't you figured it out yet, dude? The quarantined houses are the only place you're guaranteed to *not* find sick people. They're the ones who were smart enough to lock up and hunker down before things really started getting crazy, and they're the ones with the food and other goodies."

Nick hadn't bothered to think of it before, but now that he did it made a sort of horrible sense. The very act of quarantining his apartment from the deadly disease had made it an ideal target for criminals looking for isolated, helpless, *safe* victims.

And with the government fully occupied dealing with Zolos, and his neighbors all too scared to so much as peek their heads outside for fear of infection, there'd be no help coming if he called for help.

He was on his own. He'd never been in a real fight in his life, was probably in the worst shape of his life, and was outnumbered by younger, physically fit criminals who'd likely been involved in their share of violence. Who wouldn't blink at leaving Nick bleeding to death on the floor to get what they wanted.

On the other hand, just down the hall from the office his two children were sleeping peacefully. Or more likely after all the noise, cowering in their beds trying to figure out what was going on. Even assuming these thugs wouldn't hurt them, that they were all bark and no bite, if they'd been exposed to Zolos they could infect this entire apartment without meaning to and kill his family.

Which left only one option.

Nathan Jones

Nick lunged across the room to where Ricky kept some of his sports gear, including a kid's version of a baseball bat. In spite of its size it was made of solid wood, heavy enough to knock a baseball out of the park if swung correctly. He snatched it up and held it ready to swing, moving to stand protectively in front of the door.

If he was hoping to intimidate the intruders he was disappointed; they seemed to find the little bat hilarious, to the point where the guy on the fire escape actually fell over onto the stairs laughing.

Well, they might think this was all a joke, but Nick didn't. He was willing to die, or kill, to protect his children. And if they didn't realize that they were in for a rude awakening. He stared at the intruder in the corner, making his voice as low and hard as he could. "I've got children in the other room."

The thug smirked. "You trying to appeal to my better nature when half the people in this city are dying of Zolos, and the other half are starving to death? Nice try, dude."

"No." He hefted his bat. "I'm telling you that if you don't get out of my apartment, I'm going to bash your head in to protect them."

"Hardcore!" the teenager said through a peal of raucous laughter. "Too bad it's coming from a fat computer nerd who probably gets his wife to squash roaches for him." He waved contemptuously at the laptop on the desk. "If you really want to prote-"

Nick almost missed the kid's other hand moving, yanked out of the pocket of his black hoodie with a fancy little flick that caused a blurring flash of metal. Just that suddenly the punk was holding an open butterfly knife, held low in preparation to stab.

The intruder was still speaking casually as he lunged forward, driving his knife towards Nick's gut.

Surprise should've frozen him like a deer in the headlights, but somehow Nick found himself slamming the bat down onto the punk's hand. It hit with an audible *crack* of breaking bone, sending the knife skittering away under the desk as his attacker fell backwards with a scream of shock and pain.

He wasn't laughing anymore.

There was a clatter from the fire escape as the other thug began to climb through the window, snarling a stream of blistering curses. Nick threw himself towards the window and swung the bat down at the thug's head. He missed, hitting the guy's shoulder instead, but the force of the solid impact shivered up his arm and nearly made him drop the bat, and the punk's curses ended with a strangled grunt.

Showing far more agility going the other way, the older intruder threw himself back out onto the fire escape and out of sight. Nick heard a series of shockingly loud clangs and rattles as the would-be burglar clumsily fled or even fell down the metal stairs, and for the moment dismissed him, turning back to the remaining thug.

Not soon enough. He grunted as the intruder slammed into him, ramming a shoulder into his gut with enough force to drive the breath whooshing out of him. They both went down hard, the bat flying out of Nick's hand as he hit his head on the bottom shelf of the bookshelf along one wall.

Through the stars exploding in his vision he saw the teenager scrambling for his dropped knife, moving on two legs and his uninjured hand. With a curse Nick lunged after him, getting back to his feet as the intruder's head and shoulders disappeared beneath the desk.

He desperately sought for a weapon, decided the bat was too far away to go for before his attacker retrieved his knife and got back out from underneath the desk, and scrambled for anything closer. His office chair was too heavy and unwieldy, the mug Ricky had given him last year was probably too small, his laptop too light.

The thug snarled triumphantly and started to back out from beneath the desk with a violent lurch, none of his weight on his arms with one broken and the other now holding his knife.

Time was up.

Nick leapt forward and grabbed his spare monitor with both hands, yanking cables with it as he raised it high and slammed it down on the intruder's emerging head. His attacker went down with a strangled grunt in an explosion of glass, then started to rise again with his knife flashing toward's Nick's lower stomach.

Somehow Nick let go of the destroyed monitor in time to catch his attacker's hand, pushing back with all his strength. Then the thug's shoulder hit his legs and he found himself falling.

He'd spend a long time afterwards trying to figure out exactly what happened in the blur of the next few moments. Whether in the desperation of wrestling for the knife and rolling on top of his attacker, he meant to put all his weight behind his arms until he'd sunk the blade to the hilt in the guy's chest.

When his attacker finally stopped moving Nick almost couldn't bring himself to acknowledge that the danger was past. He kept him pinned for who knew how long, before a tiny, terrified voice in the doorway made him jump.

"D-dad?"

"Shut the door, Ricky!" he snapped, voice harsher than he'd meant it to be. Out of the corner of his eye he saw his son flinch, but he didn't obey. Taking a shuddering breath, he calmed his tone. "Please, shut the door and go check on your sister. Calm her down if you can."

Ricky continued to stare at the body with huge eyes, and somewhere in the hall Nick heard Tallie sniffling. He forced himself to his feet and crossed to the door, closing it firmly in his son's face before speaking through it. "It's going to be okay. Take Tallie back to bed and stay with her until she calms down, okay?"

To his relief, after a few seconds he heard his children's voices move away on the other side of the door, then the sound of a door shutting.

Nick turned back to the body, forcing himself to look at it, to see it in all its horrifying reality. It was only then that he felt the trickles of wetness on his face, soaking through his shirt, and abruptly staggered to the window and emptied his stomach onto the fire escape.

It wasn't just the horror of having to take a life, although he was sure the memory of it, the guilt, would haunt his nightmares for as long as he lived. But more importantly to himself, to his *kids*, he'd just got exposed to a bunch of blood from some stranger off the street, when half the city was infected with Zolos.

Even worse, a stranger who'd openly bragged about raiding quarantined houses before trying to stick a knife in his chest. The cooling blood on his skin, dampening his clothes, burned like acid and left him so sick with fear he wanted to curl up into a ball.

Instead he stripped off his shirt and scrubbed his face and hands clean on the back of it, then flung it out the window. His pants were next. Then he grabbed the curtain and scrubbed at his skin some more, his breath coming in frantic gasps that sounded unhinged to his own ears.

Nick was just about to bolt for the bathroom and shower off, with plenty of soap and maybe even rubbing alcohol, when his eyes snagged on the body of the intruder. He froze with a violent shudder, realizing he'd wasted his time cleaning himself off.

He couldn't leave the body there, a possible source of infection for his children. In fact, *he* couldn't go into the rest of the apartment until he knew whether he'd been infected himself. Which meant he was going to have to trust Ricky to take care of himself and Tallie, while Nick stayed isolated in this room and ideally did his best to disinfect it all.

Had he thought watching Kansas City fall apart on the TV was a nightmare? *This* was his worst dream come to life, and if he turned out to be sick . . .

His stomach churned, his strength leaving his legs so he collapsed onto the carpet, rolling himself weakly into a sitting position against the wall as the horrific possibility loomed. If he was carrying Zolos and died from it, Tallie and Ricky would be all alone until Ellie got back. Which he hoped now more than ever was soon.

But if she was delayed again, or something happened to her as well, his only option would be to try to find a neighbor willing to care for their children. And who'd want to risk letting in two kids whose dad was dying from a deadly disease?

If the unthinkable happened to him and his ex-wife both, their kids would be left alone in a world going insane, death and violence and hardship on all sides. It would only be a matter of time before starvation forced them outside and they were exposed to the pandemic too, or some hoodlum like the body by his desk came after them and they were helpless to defend themselves.

He snarled at the horrific possibilities, then forced himself to his feet. He wouldn't let that happen! Even if he had to claw his way to surviving a disease that killed nine out of ten people, he wouldn't leave his children alone and defenseless.

He stared down at the body of the man who'd tried to kill him, revulsion surging through him for more than just the possibility of infection. He'd never even imagined he might have to kill someone, let alone in the safety of his own home to protect his family.

In the surge of emotions following the attack Nick would've thought that what would affect him most was how close he'd come to death. And maybe it would, after he'd gotten over the shock and adrenaline and had time to process what had happened.

But what he felt even more than that at the moment was his sense of the peace and safety of his home being violated. Logically he knew that his apartment wasn't all that secure, with a flimsy door, thin walls, lots of windows, and even a fire escape giving easy access. But it still shattered some feeling of security he hadn't even been aware of to know that someone could just break into his home and threaten him and his loved ones.

What if they'd broken into Tallie's room instead of his office?

What if the other intruder came back with more of his buddies? How would Nick feel safe in this apartment now? How could he feel like he'd be able to protect his kids?

What choice did he have?

It was hard to understand what sort of people would force a man, a father with young children, to this extreme, just for some food and any valuables in the apartment. Who'd make simple robbery a matter of life and death.

Nick had always believed that people in general were pretty decent. After all, in spite of the sad events of his own life he could readily admit that the majority of people he met were friendly and kindhearted. Selfish sometimes, shortsighted sometimes, quick to assume the worst of others in some cases, but usually pretty decent.

But this criminal had been willing to destroy innocent lives, threaten *children* even! And he'd been laughing as he tried to do it. Meeting someone like that shook Nick's faith in humanity, just a bit.

That realization helped him fight off the surge of guilt about having to kill the man in self-defense, although he didn't think he'd ever fully get over the horror of it. It also, if he had to admit, made it easier to not feel guilty about just dumping the body off the fire escape and leaving it to rot on the ground below. He couldn't think of anything else he could safely do.

Nick supposed he should contact the authorities about the incident, although they were probably so busy dealing with the Zolos crisis that they'd tell him they couldn't do anything about it. Heck, they were probably flooded with so many similar calls that he wouldn't even be able to get through to anyone to report the crime.

What a mess.

The intruder's body turned out to be surprisingly heavy. So heavy, in fact, that it took all his strength to wrap it in a blanket and then drag it to the window, prop it up and tip it onto the fire escape, then manhandle it over the railing to drop to the ground below. All the while watching cautiously for the return of the other thug, and barely aware of being outside in just his boxers.

Nathan Jones

He tried not to hear the sickening thud the body made as it landed.

Nick swallowed bile and climbed back through the window, panting and dripping with sweat from the exertion and feeling barely human after the grisly task. He needed to get clean, but more importantly he needed to clean and sterilize his office.

Then quarantine himself inside it for as long as he needed to be sure he wasn't sick and wouldn't infect his kids.

Although first things first, before he got to work he had to consider what that SOB had said about the quarantine notices. If criminals out there were looking for places where people had been in self-imposed isolation from the moment they found out about the Zolos threat, that meant that instead of protecting his family those notices were actually putting them in danger.

So they had to go. Nick hated the idea of going outside and maybe coming in contact to the virus, but considering he'd just been covered in the blood of some stranger who was going around robbing people who might be infected, that seemed like a secondary concern.

He climbed back out the window, inched down the fire escape past the body, and made his way back around to his front door. He thought he saw a few eyes peeking out windows through blinds or behind curtains, and finally began to feel self-conscious about being out in his boxers, something he'd never do under normal circumstances.

With that in mind, he wasted no time tearing down the notice he'd taped to his door before locking himself inside the presumed safety of his home. He crumpled it and tossed it out onto the street, then trotted back to the fire escape and climbed back into his office.

"Dad?" he heard Ricky shouting frantically through the door. "Are you okay?"

"I'm fine, Ricky!" he called, although he'd never felt less fine in his life. "I need you to get me a few changes of clothes, and a roll of paper towels and a container of wet wipes. Just toss them through the door without coming inside. Then I want you to go take down all the quarantine notices taped to the windows in every room."

There was a long pause. "Why?" his son asked nervously. "Zolos is still a danger, isn't it?"

So are those signs, he thought grimly to himself. "Just do it, son. Then get your sister and come back . . . we need to talk about me staying quarantined in the office."

"What?" the eight-year-old demanded in panic. "How will you eat? Who will take care of Tallie?"

Nick sighed and sagged against the wall. "That's what we're going to have to talk about," he said quietly. "You're going to have your work cut out for you for a day or so, taking care of yourself and your sister until your mom gets here. You'll have to be more responsible than you've ever been before, but I know you can do it. She should be here sometime today, probably earlier rather than later."

And none too soon; Nick was just glad she'd found a car, or he'd really be worrying right now.

His son took several minutes to gather up the requested items, but Nick didn't wait for him before getting started cleaning up his office. Starting with digging out the box cutter from his toolbox to hack out the large section of carpet soaked with the blood of his attacker.

His office would never be the same, and for that matter neither would he.

He just hoped he was alive to not be the same for a very long time, so he could be there for his kids.

* * * * *

Ellie jolted awake to the sound of her phone ringing, hearing Hal's soft snores in the passenger seat end with a snort as he also came awake. In the early dawn glow she saw him twist enough to look back at her blearily.

"Sorry!" she hissed, scrambling for her phone. Then she forgot her chagrin with a surge of alarm when she saw Nick's name, rushing to answer. "Nick? Are the kids okay?"

Her ex-husband's reply was worryingly slow. "The kids are okay," he said quietly. He sounded deeply shaken, implying *he* wasn't. "Ells, some punks attacked the apartment."

"What?" she nearly yelled, making Hal jump and twist around to look at her in concern. "Are you hurt? Did they expose the kids to Zolos?"

"I'm fine," he hastened to assure her. "The intruders were only in the office, and I've kept the kids out. I also had Ricky take down the quarantine notices in the windows and I pulled down the one on the door, since that's how they knew the place was safe to attack. I'll stay in the office away from the kids until you can get back and pick them up."

She nodded. "Okay, I'll take them to my house as soon as I get there. Hold tight."

"Right, we'll be fine until you get here." In spite of that reassurance Nick didn't sound fine, at all.

Ellie twisted to face the backrest in the backseat and lowered her voice, holding her phone close. "Nick, are you okay?"

He was slow to answer. "The guy pulled a knife on me," he finally said in a haunted voice. "I-I had to defend myself. Defend the kids."

The implication was clear, and she felt a upwelling of horror mingled with pity for her ex-husband. "You did what you had to do, Nicholas," she said gently. There was no response. "You want to talk about it?"

She heard Nick suck in a sharp breath. "No. No, I still need to finish cleaning the office, and talk Ricky through making breakfast for Tallie. Hurry and get here, okay?"

"Sure." The call ended with a click, and Ellie spent a few seconds staring at her phone.

Shut In

Nick's apartment, attacked. Sure, she knew big cities could be dangerous, and even as a lifelong resident of Kansas City who loved her home, she had to admit it didn't look great when it came to crime. But she'd lived there most of her life, and had never experienced worse than a stolen bike or the occasional car break-in. Usually resulting in nothing more than some small items stolen or slashed seats.

No one had ever tried to attack her or burgle her home. Admittedly, she took the necessary precautions to protect herself and her family, including avoiding dangerous areas and not being out at dangerous times. She'd even taken self-defense classes offered by her college and a couple companies she'd worked with.

She also always carried pepper spray in her purse, and at her dad's insistence when she first moved out had accepted his gift of a .22 pistol and a box of hollow point bullets. Both of which Ellie kept safely separated and securely locked away where the kids couldn't get at them. Although that also made it harder for *her* to get at them, which probably didn't matter since she'd only gone shooting once or twice in her life; she'd have trouble using the gun to defend herself anyway.

It just hadn't seemed like a priority before now, especially when they'd moved into her current house in a safe neighborhood a few years ago.

Only now Nick's apartment had been attacked. Even more than that her normally gentle, unimposing ex-husband had actually been forced to kill someone to protect their children. Had the entire world gone crazy?

Either way, she resolved to dig out her dad's gun and always carry it with her the moment she got home.

"Everything okay?" Hal asked quietly.

No. She sat up briskly, rubbing at her eyes. "We've got light. Should we check the other gas stations, then if necessary try to find a car to siphon gas from?"

He nodded, awkwardly starting to climb over to the driver's seat. "Let's get going."

As her friend got the car moving Ellie climbed out of her sleeping bag and pulled on her shoes, scrubbing a hand through her hair and wishing she could take a shower, or at least had a comb. Maybe at some point this morning she could take a minute to brush and floss her teeth, but that was probably the best she could hope for when it came to freshening up until she got home.

She climbed across the lowered back of the passenger seat and raised it, grabbing her water bottle and swishing water in her mouth before taking a long drink. "Get enough sleep?" she asked around a yawn.

Hal grunted. "Never thought I'd prefer the ground over a padded seat, but meh." He glanced her way. "Someone attacked your ex's place?"

"Yeah." Ellie wasn't up to discussing it at the moment, so she went with something Nick had mentioned that might be pertinent to them. "Apparently criminals are using the quarantine notices to figure out which places have been isolated from the beginning and are probably safe."

He swore quietly. "Takes a special sort to prey on families while hundreds of millions of people across the world are dying."

"That sort's always been there. It's just easy to ignore that fact when society's ticking along smoothly, since we almost never run into them in our day to day lives."

"I've had one or two run-ins with people like that, even when society was "ticking along smoothly," her friend replied with a snort. "Believe me, I know."

Ellie felt her face flush. The "I probably know it better than you" wasn't implied in his tone, but it was evident; from what he'd told her of his life, her own had been easy and secure in comparison. Trying to school him on the darker side of humanity was arrogant on her part.

They pulled into another abandoned station, as smashed up as the one they'd just left. Hal once again picked his way behind the counter and tried to get a pump working, again with no success. This time, however, when he left the convenience store he was wearing gloves he must've scavenged, and carried a plastic bag full of supplies in one hand and a rolled up hose, hand siphon pump, and 3-gallon gas can in the other.

Ellie accepted the pair of gloves her friend tossed her as he deposited the grocery bag on the backseat. But rather than putting away the hand pump and gas can, then climbing back behind the wheel, he leaned into the car to talk to her. "I'm thinking the gas we have left in the tank might be all we have to get us to the next potential place on the highway where we can refuel. We should save it if we can."

She grimaced as she realized what he meant. "Back to searching on foot?"

He nodded. "We'll run the tank empty if we try driving from one car to the next looking for gas to siphon. If it doesn't pan out we've wasted fuel that could've gotten us twenty to fifty miles farther."

"Hey, not arguing." With a sigh Ellie pulled on her new gloves and climbed out of the car, grabbing her wallet but leaving everything else behind. Hal locked the car behind them, and together they set out along the street.

"This shouldn't take as long as St. George, at least," Hal said, glancing around at the nearby houses.

True enough, although that wasn't because they'd have success any quicker here. It was just that Watkins was a small town, a few hundred residents if she was any judge. That would cut down the time they spent searching, but also their chances of finding what they were searching for.

At least they had plenty of experience with this from St. George. At the first house they fell back into their routine of calling to the people inside. Ellie also noticed Hal checking the car in the driveway, although before she could disapprove he shook his head grimly. "Locked, no way to get at the tank without a crowbar unless we can convince them to give us the keys."

"Let's see if we can convince someone to sell us gas before we head back to the gas station looking for a crowbar for looting," she replied wryly. She wondered if she should be worried how quickly her perspective had changed from being an honest, upright citizen to one who pressured fearful people into giving her cars, was an unprotesting accessory to looting, and didn't bat an eye at theft.

Maybe she should be, but with Nick quarantined off from Ricky and Tallie nothing mattered more than getting home to be there for her children. Although she'd avoid telling them about this particular part of her adventures, and if possible in the future she'd try to make restitution for what she'd taken.

That would be the measure of her character, she supposed: whether or not her good intentions were forgotten the moment her recent actions slipped from her mind.

The first house was a bust, unsurprisingly. From their experience in St. George they got no response at all at roughly three-quarters of the houses they visited, and of the remaining quarter ninety percent of the responses had mostly been threats and shouted pleas for them to leave. Only a few people had been willing to have a civil conversation, and only that last family had "helped" them.

The next house proved equally fruitless. Halfway to the next one after that Hal abruptly paused, holding up a hand. His expression was tense, almost fearful, as he glanced back the way they'd come in the direction of I-70. "You hear that?" he whispered.

Ellie listened. She heard it, of course, the sound of approaching engines. Her mind was just so used to the noise that it took her a couple seconds to pick it out as something to pay attention to.

Engines, *plural*, and from the sound of it over a dozen. When everyone was holed up in their houses avoiding Zolos and the roads were nearly abandoned, so many vehicles driving through a small town like Watkins, whether together or separate, was enough to take notice of.

What was more, while she heard the distinctive throaty roar of motorcycles, she also heard the lower rumble of trucks. Although it wasn't until the noise of engines was joined by the screeching of tires that she felt the hairs on the back of her neck stand on end as red flags began to wave wildly in her subconscious.

Hal grabbed her arm and yanked her towards the nearest hiding spot, some bushes growing against a chain-link fence running along the sidewalk. They barely managed to squeeze themselves into the confined space behind one before the first of the vehicles came into view down the street.

Nathan Jones

Chapter Thirteen
Watkins

Ellie's first glimpse of the motorcycles reinforced their decision to hide.

It wasn't so much the way the bikers were dressed, since you'd expect to see them wearing leathers and sporting a certain look. She actually had a couple college friends who'd recently purchased hogs and enjoyed going on road trips in the summer. They'd even half-jokingly tried to convince Nick to get one and join them.

These men, however, had *guns*, rifles or shotguns she wasn't sure, slung on their backs with the ends sticking over their shoulders. And under one leather coat she saw what looked like body armor. As they got closer she also saw many sporting knives or pistols on their hips.

Farther back, a sturdy truck carried half a dozen more men. Along with guns, these men were carrying sledgehammers, crowbars, and even what looked like one of those things law enforcement used to knock down doors.

Hal had a hand on her arm, as if afraid she was about to run out and wave cheerfully at these terrifying men. Or maybe it was to reassure her, since she realized at some point since they found this hiding spot she'd caught his knee in a white-knuckled grip.

“Whatever they're here for, I doubt it's anything good,” he whispered, breath tickling her ear. “We should forget the gas and try to get out of here as soon as it's safe.”

Ellie had no problems with that. Unfortunately they were going to have a bit of trouble with carrying out his suggestion, since the fleet of vehicles split up at the first gas station they'd visited, half roaring into that parking lot while the remaining truck and motorcycles filled the lot of the station where their green sedan was still parked at the pump.

"You've got to be kidding me," she moaned.

Men poured out of the vehicles, giving the abandoned car a wide berth and gathering on the sidewalk by the street. One last man stood on the back of the truck, older and heavyset but with the solid mean streak look of someone who relished whipping young upstarts into line.

"All right, boys, remember what we're looking for," he called. "Vehicles with dirty windshields, meaning they haven't been used since at least the last rain, probably longer . . . take any worth taking and siphon the gas and strip any useful parts from the rest. Quarantine notices on doors and windows, and other signs the residents are serious about turning people away. That means they've held to the quarantine from the beginning and never been exposed to Zolos, so it's perfectly safe to bust in and manhandle them if they put up a fight."

"Or if they don't!" someone in the crowd called, drawing a storm of harsh, hungry laughter. The sound of it, and the implication, sent ice down Ellie's spine.

"Right, right," their leader said easily. "But try to save the fun until we're back safe at our headquarters, huh? Folks around here still have phones, and the law won't stay distracted corralling sick people forever. The faster we take whatever, and whoever, is worth taking, the less risk of some police force or Armed Forces unit on a relief mission interrupting the party."

The implication of *that* was even more sickening. Ellie sincerely hoped hers and Hal's feeble hiding place held out against these robbers and their search; she didn't want to contemplate what might happen if she was found.

Who were these men? Where had they come from? Were they inmates escaped from some nearby prison, or a gang out to cause mayhem now that law and order had collapsed?

Was it possible they were even just normal people, driven to this extreme by the disaster?

Ellie wasn't naive enough to think that there weren't those who'd turn to lawlessness if they thought they could get away with it. The sort of people who only lived upright lives out of the fear of getting caught. Even in the business settings she worked in, she'd seen more than a few individuals and even spiteful little cabals who'd happily cause any trouble they could get away with. Usually out of a desire to get ahead, but some seemingly just because they could; maybe they got some sick thrill out of having the petty power to complicate or even destroy someone else's life, with a minimum of effort and personal risk.

If there were people who would do so much damage within the organized framework of a corporate environment, she hated to think what they'd do if they had free rein out in the world.

Although she supposed she didn't have to think it, since she was seeing it before her very eyes. It just shocked her beyond belief that it had happened so quickly. Did it really take less than a week for law and order to completely break down during a crisis? To the point where roving bands of robbers were running around straight up kidnapping people, presumably women they planned to do unspeakable things to?

How was this happening in the United States of America?

The robbers got ready to head out, some on foot and others on their choppers. "Remember, boys!" the leader called as they dispersed. "There's over fifty million dead or dying in this country, and that number's just going up! That's a lot of swag sitting there for the taking, waiting for some enterprising souls to make use of it." He paused theatrically. "As for the "guests" we drag back to our headquarters, well, we're doing them a favor taking them somewhere they'll be safe from Zolos!"

Ellie wondered if anyone could be so self-deluded that they actually believed that. Did these animals cling to such justifications so they could sleep at night?

Hal's grip on her arm briefly tightened as a small group of men trooped towards the first house they'd visited, trying to pull her down to the ground and closer to the bush. Her first impulse was to freeze like a deer in the headlights, but she realized why he was doing that when she noticed that the bushes would offer them no cover once the robbers got into the front yards of any house on this side of the street; they'd be clearly visible through the chain-link fence.

Sitting ducks.

So she thought quiet thoughts, not even daring to breathe as she sunk flat to the ground and squirmed deeper into the bush's thick branches. Beside her Hal did the same, pressing close enough her face was practically in his armpit.

Under normal circumstances she wouldn't have been thrilled about that, especially considering how long it had been since the young man had showered. Not that he smelled terrible in spite of the slight BO, she had to admit. As it was, though, she found his solid presence comforting.

That didn't stop her from moving her head, of course, although that was motivated more by wanting to be able to see what was going on through the chain links.

They lay frozen, breathing slowly and quietly, as they waited to find out if the robbers had noticed them moving. After a couple seconds Ellie judged they were safe, and she relaxed slightly and craned her head even more for a better look.

While hers and Hal's attempts to contact the residents of that first house had resulted in silence, the robbers' tactic of simply busting down the door produced a woman's screams and a man's shouting, shrill with anger and fear. She couldn't help but flinch at the sound of crashing coming from inside as the minutes passed, not just as if furniture was being upended but as if walls were being smashed and cabinets cleaned out, looking for hidden valuables.

Then the woman's screams became even more frantic before abruptly silencing, while the man's protesting bellows cut off in strangled grunts as if he was being beaten senseless. A minute or so later two robbers emerged dragging a woman in her early twenties between them. She stumbled along, hands duct taped behind her back and eyes wide with terror above a strip of duct tape covering her mouth, muffling her continued streams.

Was what Ellie thought was happening here actually happening? She felt like she was going to be sick, not just with sympathy and horror for the fate the woman faced but with fear for herself. At her side Hal shifted with glacial slowness, hand finding hers and gripping it tight in reassurance.

The woman struggled every step of the way as she was shoved to the truck in the gas station lot, her legs taped at the ankles and knees before being casually tossed inside. The men who'd taken her tromped back to the house to continue looting, passing a few of their friends who were carrying food, useful items, and valuables to pile in the front yard, presumably to be sorted.

"What are we going to do?" Ellie hissed, so frightened she barely dared to breathe the words, and wasn't sure Hal even heard.

He squeezed her hand, reply equally quiet. "We wait until they leave, then we make a dash for our car and get out of here."

"What if they stick around all day? What if they see us?" She tried to quell her rising panic as she imagined herself being taped up and tossed into the back of the truck on top of a pile of other women, facing who knew what nightmare in the clutches of these animals. "I say as soon as these guys get far enough away from the gas station, we sneak to the car and get out of here. Maybe we can free that girl and any others they kidnap and take them with us."

"You think they'll leave their bikes unguarded?" her friend whispered incredulously.

"You think we have a good hiding place here?" she shot back with equal heat.

He hesitated. "Let's see what happens," he finally said.

That was probably their best bet at the moment. Ellie fell still and silent again as the robbers finished looting the house, picked through the pile of stuff on the lawn, then began hauling a surprisingly small amount of it, mostly food and useful items, to pile in the gas station lot near the sidewalk.

Ellie wondered if they were going through all this trouble just to take enough stuff to fill up a couple trucks and whatever those motorcycles could carry. She could only assume the robbers had more trucks waiting elsewhere, maybe even some semis with empty trailers, ready to swoop in and be loaded up once the looting was done.

Other teams of robbers were returning to the station with their own armfuls of loot, along with a few girls who couldn't have been much older than their late teens who were dragged kicking and screaming to the truck to be tossed in with the first.

She and Hal both froze again as the nearby group of looters moved on to the second house, much more clearly visible now through the chain-link fence. To the point where Ellie felt like they were going to be spotted at any moment.

Although to her relief, at least there were no screams when this house was broken into; from the way the robbers cursed a blue streak as they poured into the house, she could only assume the residents had fled out the back door and hopefully to safety while these animals were occupied in the first house.

She couldn't help but think those people had the right idea. She just hoped wherever they'd gone, they managed to stay hidden.

"That took over fifteen minutes," Hal abruptly whispered. "At this rate they could be here for hours."

"Then you agree that we should try to get to the car?" Ellie hissed back. "One of the groups that came back was carrying cans of gas . . . we can grab them and go."

He paused, thinking it over. "If it looks like they're leaving the gas station unguarded then yeah, let's get out of here."

She couldn't help but feel a surge of relief at that; the sooner she escaped this nightmare, the better.

The robbers made a surprising racket ransacking the town. Along with the screams and crashing of breaking things, elsewhere in the town she heard whoops, the noise of engines revving, and even gunshots. She just hoped those last were men with their blood up shooting into the air, and those surprisingly loud *cracks* echoing through the streets weren't each some innocent person being murdered.

Although a distant part of her hoped they came from residents fighting back against the robbers, or even law enforcement arriving to stop this madness. After all, the US was one of the most well armed countries in the world, specifically for this reason. And if there was ever a time when she could cheer citizens standing up and raising weapons in defense of their homes, it was when a gang of animals were beating down their doors kidnapping their wives and daughters while the police were busy managing a crisis.

The group of robbers finished with the second house and poured towards the third, coming within a few feet of where Ellie and Hal huddled against the bushes. Ellie didn't even breathe as they flooded up the front walk, smashed through the front door, and began their search, thankfully without discovering her and her friend's hiding place in the bushes.

Although there were plenty of opportunities for that any of the dozens of times these men came tromping out to dump loot on the pile; she and Hal would practically be in their line of sight at that point. In fact, she almost wondered if they shouldn't try to find another hiding place *now*, while the robbers were still searching the house and before they carted anything out.

Ellie lost the nerve to even consider that idea moments later, when someone else's hiding place was apparently discovered.

From the lack of screaming coming from the third house, she'd assumed the residents had also fled out the back door. But after a few minutes of listening to the crashing sounds coming from inside, she suddenly heard a woman's shrill shriek split the air, as much surprise as fear. It was quickly joined by eager shouting from the searchers as they realized they'd found another victim.

Ellie's stomach churned in horror as the shrieks continued, becoming more and more frantic, before turning to something tortured that suggested something truly awful was being done to the poor woman.

Listening to that, along with the harsh laughter and taunts coming from the robbers inside, broke something inside Ellie. Before she could rethink the decision she scrambled to her feet and vaulted over the low fence, dashing along the cover of the bushes across the front yard and vaulting the fence leading to the second house.

Behind her she heard Hal curse and rush to follow her, catching up as Ellie reached the back of the second house and ducked behind it, out of view of the third house and the street. Even then she didn't allow herself to stop, although she kept her ears pricked for any shouts that suggested she or her friend had been spotted and pursuit was on the way.

There was nothing; the nightmarish noises coming from the third house continued uninterrupted, and the background of bedlam in the rest of the town remained the same.

"Are you crazy?" Hal hissed at her as she reached the far side of the second house and paused to search for a route to the first house that offered cover. "It's too early to move!"

Ellie didn't even glance at him, eyes roving the backyards in front of her as she replied. "We were right in view of anyone coming out that door, and I didn't want to sit there listening to a poor girl get gang raped until they came out and found me for my turn."

Her friend flinched, looking like he was going to throw up. "Okay yeah, maybe you had the right idea going now." He joined her searching the yards for a safe route. "Let's just take it carefully from here, okay? Rushing in a panic could get us into more trouble than it gets us out of."

She nodded grimly, wishing she had her little .22 pistol with her. When her dad had given her the gun she'd wondered if she'd actually be able to shoot someone, even to defend herself. But after what she'd just heard from inside that house, she doubted she'd even hesitate to put a hollow point bullet in any of those monsters if they came for her.

But she didn't have her gun, and even if she had she probably wouldn't have been able to hit anything farther than five feet away. Two situations she resolved to rectify if she made it out of this nightmare and ever got home; she'd learn to shoot like a pro, and she'd never let her pistol out of her sight again.

Heck, she'd even take the thing into the shower with her.

Hal abruptly motioned, then ducked low and made a dash for a nearby playhouse. Ellie bit back a curse and followed, piling behind him into the limited space between it and the trunk of a tall tree. Her friend waited only moments in its cover before continuing on, circling around the tree then dashing for a gap in a bank of rosebushes growing along the chain-link fence at the boundary of the first house.

There was barely room for one person in that small space, so Ellie waited behind the playhouse as Hal gingerly climbed the fence while trying not to get caught on any thorns. He proved unexpectedly agile, dropping into the other yard and bolting for a row of garbage cans against the back of the house. Once he safely reached them he wedged himself between two and paused, turning to look expectantly back at her.

Ellie sucked in a breath and darted for the gap, worming through the rosebushes and scrambling up the fence. She bit back a curse as thorns bit into her jeans, tugging the tough material out of their grip before any could pierce through and prick her. For a precarious moment she half crouched, half hung on the top of the fence, feeling like she was doing some bizarre yoga pose, before she caught her balance and swung her legs over to land in a crouch.

Following her friend's example, she bolted for the garbage cans and wedged herself behind one. Hal patted her shoulder in approval, then gestured for the high cinder block wall between this house and the gas station. There was a tree growing near it, carefully pruned back so it didn't overhang the gas station lot but otherwise growing strong.

Shut In

The coast still looked clear, so they rushed to the dubious cover between the trunk and the wall. Once there her friend offered her his back to step up on so she could peek over the top row of cinder blocks, supporting her weight with no apparent strain. She cautiously raised her eyes among a few branches sporting new buds until she could see.

The lot looked deserted aside from the men bringing stuff to add to the pile near the street. Ellie took a last long look then hopped back down, leaning close to whisper in Hal's ear. "If we can try to time it between robbers hauling loot, and approach from around the back of the gas station and make a beeline right for the car, we can hide behind the front of it and sneak the last distance to the doors. Then we should be free to drive off."

"In that case, given your stunt driving in LA you should be behind the wheel in case they give chase," he whispered back.

She shuddered at the mental image of speeding down I-70 with a dozen motorcycles moving to cut her off, or simply filling their sedan full of bullets until they crashed. "If we get out fast enough, hopefully they won't have time to give chase and will decide it's not worth it."

"Fingers crossed."

They made their way to the back of the first house's backyard, climbing over the wooden fence there to the yard of the house behind it. From there Ellie once again peered over the gas station's cinder block wall on Hal's back, for longer this time as she timed their next move.

First she let a few groups come with loot, trying to get a feel for how frequent they were. Then, as one finished up and started to leave, she hopped down and slapped her friend's shoulder to indicate it was time to move.

They both hopped up to grab the wall's flat top, pulling themselves over and dropping down onto the pavement of the gas station's back lot. Then they rushed behind the station, going around to the far side where robbers coming to and from the pile had a poor angle to see them, and inched along the wall until the car came into view.

Hal, leading the way, peered around enough to see the loot pile. He eased back again and held up a hand to wait, and for a few breathless minutes they clung to the brick like spiders in the middle of a white wall, hoping nobody glanced their way. Then her friend risked another look, glanced back at her and nodded, and they were off.

Ellie ran low and fast, looking at the loot pile which currently stood abandoned. In a few moments that felt like an eternity she was at the green sedan, dropping down beside Hal with her hands splayed on the dirty pavement, peering around the bumper to check the pile.

Another group had arrived, raucous as they tossed around precious items as if they were so much junk before heading off again. She tried not to listen to the awful things they were saying as they wandered out of earshot.

She glanced back at her friend and nodded, motioning it was time to go.

But before she could begin circling the front of the car to reach the driver's side door, a shout from the street made her jump and freeze, torn between ducking down again and making a beeline for the door to try to get inside, start the engine, and get away.

A flash of motion by the truck caught her attention, and she realized the shout hadn't been directed at her. She sank back down behind the front of the car and held her breath, peering underneath the bunker to see what was going on.

A man was at the back of the truck, bruised and bloody and desperately sawing at something out of view inside the bed with a kitchen knife. Ellie guessed he was a resident from the first house, and he'd followed their example of vaulting over the cinder block wall in an attempt to save his wife or girlfriend.

The truck was far more exposed than their car, however, and men with guns had appeared from seemingly nowhere to converge on the man. He dropped his knife and desperately hauled the woman from the first house, hands freed but legs still taped, out of the truck bed, spinning to bolt back towards their house with her slung over one shoulder.

Ellie bit back a scream as a hail of gunfire mowed the man down in a spray of blood. The scene was so brutal she almost couldn't believe it was real, although it had a horrific immediacy to it that no action movie could reproduce. The man dropped, his wife tumbling from his shoulder and hitting the ground hard, barely managing to catch herself before slamming her head on the pavement.

The woman hauled herself around to hold her husband, tears streaming from her eyes and not even the tape gag completely blocking her horrified scream. Then she looked up, devastation turning to terror, and tried to drag herself away with just her arms as the scrape of shoes on pavement replaced the sound of gunfire.

"Go!" Ellie hissed, deciding she'd seen enough.

She ducked around the front of the car and took a step towards the driver's side door, then froze as another gunshot was accompanied by the deafening crash of the window just in front of her shattering. She looked up to see a man pointing a gun at her, while movement at the corner of her eyes showed more men turning her way, weapons raised.

Frantic, Ellie tried to dodge three different directions in less than a second, ending up in a tangle of limbs on the ground before scrambling frantically back to her feet. By that point the men who'd come to stop the husband had moved to begin circling the sedan, weapons raised, and there was nowhere to run.

With no other option she stood there frozen, barely aware of the terrified mewling noises escaping her mouth. Hal had similarly froze on the far side of the car, his expression dominated by helpless rage and despair that he tried to hide behind fierce determination.

The robbers closed in around them, filling the air with a mixture of mocking whoops, cursing, and threats. Above them rose a louder, more authoritative voice. "Don't move! Stop! You come within ten feet of any of us and we'll use you as target dummies!"

Ellie had no intention of moving. She huddled against the car's side,

221

despair crashing down on her in a torrent as she realized her worst fear had come true. She was about to end up duct taped and tossed in the back of the truck with the other women, while Hal would be lucky to escape with no more than bruises at the hands of these monsters.

A bigger man, the one who'd first spoken to the robbers to get them started looting the town and who owned the authoritative voice, shuffled slightly closer, keeping a big handgun pointed at her chest. "Both of you, away from the car." He gestured with his weapon. "Over there."

She inched cautiously away from the vehicle, to a spot halfway between the pumps and the front of the convenience store. Hal joined her there, and she leaned against him and clutched his arm in a death grip as he held her protectively.

All of her training in conflict resolution had fled just when she needed it most, leaving her unable to think of anything to say or do. Which probably didn't matter, because she doubted there was anything she *could* do in this situation.

A couple of the robbers had caught the woman, taping her hands behind her back again and tossing her back up onto the truck bed. Her husband they casually dragged over beside the wall, leaving him there as if he was so much trash in spite of the fact that he looked to still be alive, twitching weakly as blood continued to pour from his gunshot wounds.

"What do we do with these two?" a scrawny guy with a mean look and an even meaner shotgun asked the bigger guy.

"Wait for Hutch and see what he says," Big replied. Ellie was surprised to realize he wasn't the leader of all the robbers; maybe the group that had parked in the other gas station was the main one? Or maybe this Hutch was waiting with the trucks that would be needed to haul all this loot?

It was likely the former because after just a minute or two of standing with arms raised, which felt like an eternity with half a dozen men holding them at gunpoint, a lone man walked up to the group along the sidewalk from the direction of the other gas station. From the way everyone immediately gave him their attention he had to be Hutch.

"What's the deal?" he asked Big.

His lieutenant motioned towards the sedan, then them. "Questionables. These two were trying for the car." The way he was looking at her made Ellie's skin crawl, especially after the stuff she'd heard these lowlifes say. But it was the sort of casual interest that didn't seem like it intended to go anywhere; she'd seen it before from guys checking her out at parties who never ended up approaching her, for whatever reason.

She wished these guys wouldn't approach her. Or better yet, that they'd all drop dead from sudden terminal cases of Zolos.

"No one saw them come from a house?" the leader asked.

"Nah, we caught them just before they drove off," the scrawny guy said. Hutch just grunted in response, and Scrawny eyed Ellie in a way that made her want to take a shower. "What you want to do with them? The chick needs some cleaning up and she's getting a bit long in the tooth, but I'd say she's worth taking. Pop the dude?"

Ellie stepped protectively in front of Hal, even though she knew it was a useless gesture. She wasn't sure what sickened her more, the awful things this animal was talking about doing, or the casual way he talked about them. As if there wasn't a shred of humanity in him.

The robbers' leader grunted again. "Nah, he's the sort I'm looking for to put to work." He eyed Ellie as well, a chillingly clinical act as if sizing her up for his men even though he wasn't personally interested.

"You should be careful with us, we've been exposed to Zolos," Hal abruptly said. He stayed perfectly still as he spoke, but even so a few of the robbers tensed menacingly, fingers twitchy on their triggers.

Hutch eyed him lazily. "That a fact?"

"Yeah, we were at LAX when the infected broke containment." The young man spoke with complete conviction, although his voice quavered with nerves.

223

Ellie admired the bluff, although it was a dangerous one; men who had no qualms about taking women as sex slaves wouldn't blink at shooting them both if they thought they were a danger.

Then again, if that was going to be her fate she wasn't sure being shot right now was such a horrible alternative. It was worth a try, at least.

Hutch turned to her, eyes promising dire retribution if she tried to lie. "That true?"

Ellie nodded, speaking with her own solid conviction. "I watched them break through the police cordon just a few dozen feet away. We were trapped at the doors with them trying to get out right along with us." All technically true, if presented as worse than it had really been.

The leader continued to eye her, making her skin crawl in a way that had nothing to do with how she'd felt at Scrawny's leering. Then he turned back to Hal, tone mild. "You could be telling the truth. Seem to be, if I'm any judge." He leaned back on his heels, hooking thumbs in his front pockets as he blew out through pursed lips. "Then again, you also don't seem to be freaking out at the possibility you're going to die a horrible death. So I have my doubts about whether *you* believe you've been exposed to Zolos."

"Do we want to take that chance, boss?" Big asked nervously, shifting his bulk from foot to foot but keeping his pistol aimed steadily at Hal's chest.

"*We* certainly don't," Hutch said with a slow smirk. He turned away dismissively, speaking over his shoulder as he strode off while gesturing curtly to his men to follow. "Give 'em both to the Q Team. They can take the car too if it looks worth it."

"Sure thing!" Big called after him. Most of the others left with their leader, leaving just the big guy and Scrawny behind.

Chapter Fourteen
Captive

This was a nightmare. This had to be a nightmare.

Ellie tried not to hyperventilate, but all she could see was the leer on Scrawny's face, and in her ears rang the phantom screams of that poor woman in the third house.

That would be her soon enough. She had to swallow back bile before she emptied her stomach in pure terror.

As Hutch and his men walked off Hal huddled closer to her, speaking so quietly she barely heard him. "Hold tight. The second I see a chance to get you out of this, I'm taking it."

She fought the urge to wheel on him in a panic. Much as she appreciated the sentiment, she didn't want her friend getting himself killed. "Hal!" she hissed in warning.

"Hey!" They both lurched apart fearfully as Scrawny hefted his shotgun, glaring at her. "Shut your yap, lady. We'll be giving it a workout soon enough."

Ellie shuddered in revulsion and fell silent, although she resolved that this filthy animal was wrong about that, at least: whatever punishment she suffered for it, she was going to take a bite out of anything that came within reach of her teeth.

A tense few minutes followed, at least tense for her. The two guys guarding them settled back, glancing around warily but not seeming too worried about trouble. Beyond them more robbers brought loot for the pile, while a few dragged a limp woman with torn clothes and a bruised face, bound like the others, to toss in the back of the truck.

Nathan Jones

Ellie wondered if that was the woman from the third house, and against her will dropped to her hands and knees and emptied her stomach on the asphalt.

"Well that drops you down a few points," Scrawny said sarcastically, seeming to take sick delight in her suffering. "I'd still hit it, though."

Ellie shuddered and gagged again, spitting out a last mouthful of bile. Hal dropped down beside her, pulling her hair away and patting her back soothingly. His expression was bleak, anguished, and didn't do anything to lift the despair she'd sunk down into.

No. She'd spent half a decade learning conflict resolution, even a workplace hostage negotiation class at one point. Her fate might be looking grim, but she couldn't stop trying. So she'd try to talk to these men, see if she could dig out a shred of humanity in them and try to build some rapport.

And on the plus side, if talking got her shot that might be an improvement on her circumstances.

She hauled herself to her feet with Hal's help, spitting again then wiping at her mouth with her sleeve. Then she stepped away from the puddle of her sick, mostly to keep the queasy reek of it from making her retch again, and cleared her throat. "So what's the Q Team?"

The scrawny guy waved his shotgun menacingly, calling her a few filthy names. "Anyone tell you it was suddenly okay to talk?"

"If "Q" stands for quarantine and you're putting me around people with Zolos, I've got a right to know," she insisted. "We haven't been around any infected areas this entire time, and I don't want to catch it just because you think I'm infected."

"That so?" The guy leered at her again and she felt her skin crawl. "Guess we'll know in four days, when the Q Team can be sure you're not dying of it and you're safe to be among them." His leer took a nasty turn. "Then their fun begins."

Hal made an angry noise, although he was wise enough not to say anything. Ellie swallowed as her gut roiled again, struggling to keep her voice steady. "And what exactly lets them know we're safe?"

"Dude, don't talk to the entertainment," Big growled, still warily eyeing the town around them. He'd kept his pistol at low ready the entire time, and she got the feeling of the two he was far more familiar with this kind of thing.

Scrawny waved his shotgun lazily. "What else am I going to do?" He tossed another spine-crawling look her way. "After all, if I sweet talk her now then maybe after the three weeks are up she'll be happy to see me again."

This guy had to be nuts if he actually thought that.

The thug turned back to her. "So here's the deal. We've got us, the people we're sure were never even close to Zolos, that's Hutch's team. Then we've got our guys who might've been exposed, but we can't be sure. So we stick them in isolation for 4 days to make sure they're not showing symptoms. But they could still be carrying it, so they need to stay separate from us.

"That's the Q Team, for "Quarantine" or more commonly "Questionables", and they'll stick to themselves for seventeen more days after that, the full three weeks, so we're sure they're not carrying the virus. Then they'll go through decontamination and join us with Hutch. Until then we send them after any suspicious people who aren't showing visible symptoms. They manage quarantine for those prisoners, and get first dibs on them too." He eyed her up and down again. "Lucky them."

Ellie bit her lip hard, hoping to wake up from this nightmare.

How could he act like this, without the slightest shred of kindness or even basic human decency? *Was* he even human anymore? It didn't seem possible he could become so vile in under a week, so this disease of the soul must've been present before Zolos was ever even heard of.

And now, with law enforcement putting all their efforts into protecting people from the virus, men like this were running lose. And they had her and Hal.

The minutes passed with agonizing slowness, their two guards hanging out and looking more nervous by the second. After about an hour the other robbers finished their work and began to gather on the far side of the lot again, watching as a semi rumbled up. They loaded it up, then hopped back on their bikes or into the truck.

With a roar of engines the robbers all rumbled away, the semi following, leaving Ellie and Hal alone in the parking lot with Big and Scrawny. She expected something to happen soon after that, but as more minutes passed with their two guards continuing to look bored she settled back down into her bleak despair.

"You know what I don't get?" Big said idly after a while, words directed at his buddy.

Scrawny glanced over; he'd been eyeing Ellie again in that way that made her skin crawl; she could almost see what he was imagining doing in his ugly expression. "Huh?"

The big man waved his pistol. "What's with all those scenes on TV where someone's got someone else at gunpoint and they're asking them questions, and just to lean on their prisoner a bit more they cock the hammer on their weapon to intimidate them, show they're "really serious?"

"What about it?"

The big guy displayed his gun to the other man. "That might work for revolvers, sure, but most of the time they're using guns like this for that. Semi-automatics, right? Only you notice my hammer's already cocked? It cocks when you rack the slide to chamber a round, and cocks again every time you fire a shot. That's why, y'know, they're called *semi-automatics*."

"So?"

Big looked at his buddy like he was an idiot. "So what're the geniuses on TV doing manually cocking the hammer on a semi auto? The only time the gun's even uncocked is when there's not a round in the chamber, unless of course they decided to de-cock it for some reason, which is stupid and makes the gun unusable until you cock the hammer again."

"Maybe they de-cock their pistol just so they can menace their prisoner by cocking it again," Scrawny suggested.

It was horribly surreal for Ellie to be in this waking nightmare and listening to her captors shooting the breeze about such mundane things. As if this was just another day for them, while she was facing a future too awful to contemplate.

Insane as it seemed, she almost wondered if she would've preferred it if they'd spent the time leering and talking about all the terrible things they planned to do to her. At least that would've kept what monsters they were at the forefront, rather than giving a mask of normalcy to men who could do such evil things without apparent remorse.

Big snorted. "Anyone who knows the slightest thing about guns would just think they're a moron for that. But it's either that or in a dangerous situation they're running around with an empty chamber, and uselessly cocking the hammer on a gun that won't fire until they actually chamber a round."

The scrawny guy shrugged, looking half annoyed and half amused. "How should I know, man? Maybe it's more dramatic even if it doesn't make sense, or people who make shows for a living just write it that way because everyone else does."

The big man opened his mouth, but before he could say anything the rumble of engines caught his attention, and he perked up. "About time."

"Yeah." Scrawny eyed Ellie again. "I want to get back to the hideout already. Looking at all this food I can't eat is making me hungry, and there'll be new items on the menu there."

She genuinely hoped something terrible happened to this man. To all these animals; she was just grateful that the fear of Zolos had kept them away, or they might've already done something to her.

Like that poor woman in the truck, on her way to whatever evil hideout these robbers had set up.

Although it looked as if the men in the new trucks rumbling into the gas station lot didn't share the same fears as their buddies, aside from the gloves and face masks and a few full-body suits on display as they poured out of the vehicles and approached.

Unlike Scrawny and Big, the members of the Q Team showed no qualms about walking right up to Ellie and Hal, a few holding them securely while a few more patted them down and took the car keys, their phones, their wallets, and everything else they had on them.

To Ellie's horror, the patting down didn't stop there; she whimpered through clenched teeth as the search became a rough groping, gut churning with fear and revulsion as their pawing hands abandoned even the pretense of looking for hidden items and simply roamed her body. All the while the men laughed and talked about the vile things they planned to do once she finished her four days of isolation, as if she wasn't even there.

As if she wasn't even a person.

Even the men holding her joined in the depredations, which continued as the searchers got out rolls of duct tape and began putting it to use taping her hands behind her back and her legs together at the ankles and knees, the air filled with the distinctive "thwap" noises. They also slapped a strip across her mouth, muffling her whimpers.

Ellie was sick with dread that they were going to do something right then and there. That is, something even more terrible than what they were already doing. But to her vast relief, once she and Hal were securely bound they were hauled up and dragged around to the back of their green sedan, where the trunk had been thrown open.

It didn't look big enough to hold even one of them comfortably, let alone both, but with a lot of shoving and cursing she and her friend were packed inside, on their sides facing each other. She flinched as the trunk door slammed shut above her, although she was relieved to finally be away from the groping hands.

Shut In

For now.

Interminable minutes dragged by as men shouted outside, making preparations to leave. Ellie spent the time composing herself after her mistreatment, focusing on her shuddering breaths until she'd cobbled together some semblance of composure.

By the time she'd managed it she felt the car shake as their captors climbed inside, at least a driver and passenger, and doors slammed. Then a muted vibration began as the engine rumbled to life, and with a crunch of tires nearly directly underneath her they lurched into motion.

On their way to whatever hideout these robbers were using.

Hal's solid presence next to her proved a surprising comfort, the scent of his sweat and even the hint of BO in the confined space grounding her after the horror she'd just suffered, and her terror of what was coming when she was pulled out of this trunk again.

Assuming they survived the trip. How much air was in this trunk? Did it have ventilation? It already felt stifling, and the thought of suffocation made panic claw at her fragile composure again.

Although a dark part of her mind wondered if that would be a mercy compared to what was waiting for her.

"Ellie?" Hal hissed in the darkness, making her jump in surprise.

Her friend's voice was completely clear, no hint of being muffled by the duct tape she'd seen slapped across his mouth. She tried to speak his name, but of course it just came out as a muted grunt.

"It's fine, El, it's going to be okay." He paused, then continued in an anguished tone. "What they said, the way they treated you . . ." He swore bitterly, voice thick with guilt and helpless rage. "I-I'm so sorry you had to go through that. That I couldn't stop them."

Ellie sucked in a sharp breath through her nose, then awkwardly shifted and craned her head forward until she felt her forehead brush his hair. She leaned against his head, and when he leaned in as well, comforting her as best he could in his restraints, she felt herself dissolve

231

into shuddering sobs for a minute or two.

Then she forced herself back into composure and tried to speak through the gag again, to ask how he'd got free of his.

Hal took his own shuddering breath, and his voice became calm and determined. "Right, how I'm talking. If these idiots wanted to actually keep us gagged they should've wrapped the duct tape all the way around our heads a few times. That strip over the mouth like in the movies is completely useless, since you can just lick it until it comes off."

That sounded gross, but at the same time she wanted to breathe clearly again. And talk, of course, if for no other reason than to share a few final words with her friend before . . . before whatever came next.

Ellie got busy working her tongue across the tape sealed over her lips, and sure enough she felt it begin to come free, letting her poke her tongue farther and farther under the tape until half of it peeled off, leaving her mouth free.

She sucked in her first decent breath in who knew how long, although it was more of a gasp. "Hal?" she hissed.

"Still here. It's good to hear your voice." His own showed deep concern. "Are you okay, El?"

"I'll worry about that later," Ellie replied, afraid if she tried right now to deal with what she'd just been through, with her fears for what the future held, she'd fall apart again.

She squinted through the pitch black at her companion. He was only inches away, and their knees and heads were touching, but he still felt impossibly far away with them both bound like this. Which was a shame; she could've used a familiar, comforting presence right about now to hold her and tell her things would be okay.

Even if they probably wouldn't be. "What now?" she asked, trying to make her voice steady.

Hal thought it over for a few seconds. "Two options I can see," he replied. "We could try wiggling around until we can reach each other's hands and try to tear off the duct tape. Or, if you think you're flexible enough, you can put all that yoga to work and maneuver your arms out in front of you, and I can try gnawing the duct tape off your wrists."

She gave a slightly hysterical laugh. "If we were in any other situation, I'd say you were into some weird stuff."

He laughed back, not sounding too much steadier. "I'd be much happier if we were." He fumbled slightly. "That is, um . . ."

"I get it. I'll try to get my arms in front of me, give me some space."

Her friend's knees pulled away from hers slightly, and she heard soft rustlings and then a few thumps. "That's the best I can do."

Ellie took a breath and straightened her legs into the gap he'd created. "Okay. Sorry in advance if I kick you somewhere unfortunate."

"If we were in any other situation . . ."

Well, at least they still had gallows humor.

She got to work wiggling around to try to get her bound hands around her rump, muscles burning with strain. It didn't take long to realize that, again unlike the movies, with her hands bound that high up the wrists it was a logistical impossibility to get them past, especially in the cramped confines of the trunk.

Or who knew, maybe she just had unusually short arms.

"Can't," she finally growled in frustration.

"Okay, roll over with your back towards me."

It took a lot of squirming, fumbling, and a couple awkward moments, but finally they were pressed together back-to-back with their hands touching. In spite of the urgency of the situation, Ellie couldn't help but simply grasp his hands awkwardly for a minute or so, taking comfort in his reassuring return grip.

Then with more labored, panting breaths, fumbling, cursing, and plenty of strained muscles and burning discomfort, Hal finally managed to get the end of the duct tape strip wrapped around Ellie's wrists between his fingers. He carefully tugged until he could get a better grip, then began unwinding the tape with a series of sharp jerks. Ellie winced as the tape tugged at tiny hairs on her forearm, ones she hadn't even realized she had.

Then she was free.

With a quiet hoot of triumph, she twisted around and fumbled to free his hands, then got to work on her feet. That put them in a better position than they had been, but they were still in the trunk of their car with rapist thugs in the front.

"What now?" she hissed.

"Now we get out." Hal shifted around beside her, and she heard more panting breaths and the sound of flesh sliding on metal.

"How? What're you doing?"

He replied as he worked, voice strained. "Looking for the interior emergency release latch. I heard trunk doors are supposed to have them, and I know at least some do."

That seemed like oddly specific knowledge. "This and the duct tape. You have some experience with being kidnapped?"

Her friend chuckled tersely. "Well the duct tape is just common sense. As for the trunk latch, one of my buddies got married four or so years ago. For the bachelor party we grabbed him outside his job, put a bag over his head, and tossed him in the trunk of his own car. Thought it was a pretty good joke, until he surprised us by throwing open the trunk when we reached the party place and went to get him. He jumped out at us and tackled our buddy Carl, almost beat the crap out of him."

"Your teenage years sound a lot more exciting than mine."

"Mostly because we were all idiots." Hal abruptly grunted in triumph. "There, found it. Now the question is, do we try to jump out when the car slows at an intersection, or on the other hand they must've gassed up so they could drive it to this hideout of theirs . . . do we wait until they stop, then try to jump them so we can maybe retake the car when they come for us?"

Ellie shuddered at the idea of passing up a chance to escape this nightmare, even if it offered an opportunity to keep the sedan. "Intersection. Let's just get out of here if we can."

He must've heard something in her tone, because after a brief pause he spoke, voice gentle. "Hey, El, it's going to be okay."

She grit her teeth and blinked away the unwanted burning in her eyes. "Yeah, it will." She reached out and touched his shoulder. "Because you were here. If I'd been alone . . ."

Her friend snorted sourly. "Yeah, glad they didn't just shoot me. Although I'm kind of surprised they want forced labor along with-" he stuttered to silence, shifting uncomfortably.

Ellie shuddered again. "Yeah."

The steady rumble of what had to be the car driving on the Interstate continued interminably, offering no chances for them to escape without a suicidal jump from the trunk at better than 75 miles an hour. How far away was this hideout? Was it along I-70, so they'd have no chance to escape at some turn at an intersection before they got there?

"I wish we still had our phones," she whispered.

Hal huffed out his breath, somewhere between derision and bitterness. "To call the police? If they were in any position to help, they would've done something during the two or so hours this scum spent ransacking houses and kidnapping people a stone's throw from Denver. Unless nobody in Watkins has a phone, either."

"Even if they take a while, they *have* to respond to crime on this scale," Ellie insisted. "If we had our phones the authorities could track them to this hideout, rescue us." She rested her head against the rough material of the trunk's interior. "Or at least I could call my children and talk to them. Just in case we don't get a chance to get away."

Even as she said it, a surge of guilt swept over her. Ever since the robbers had rolled in, and especially since her capture, she'd only been thinking of her own fate. But what would happen to Ricky and Tallie if she was a prisoner in some criminal hideout? Nick was in quarantine and their children needed someone to care for them.

That was why she'd been in such a rush to find gas in the first place.

Although on the subject of Nick, she couldn't help but think with some bitterness that if she hadn't insisted on him staying in KC back when he offered to come pick them up, they might've all been safely back home at this very moment. She didn't regret her decision to prioritize her children's welfare over her own, of course, but, well . . .

Considering the trouble she was in she could admit she kind of rued it. Although that firmed her resolve that more than just for herself, she needed to get out of this for the sake of her daughter and son.

Finally, after what could've been an eternity or a half hour, she felt the car slow and the rumble of its tires changed as it pulled onto an off-ramp. Ellie felt Hal tense beside her, and the soft *click* of the trunk door latch. It opened slightly, creating a crack of blinding light she had to squint against as she pushed onto her hands and knees beside him.

The door wobbled as they passed over small bumps, almost slamming closed again as her friend struggled to keep it from moving enough to alert the robbers in the car. She knew he was hoping they'd stop at the first sign off the Interstate, so they could hopefully hitchhike along it or at least follow it to the nearest city.

But to her disappointment the man behind the wheel peeled through a hard right turn, more tires squealing in the convoy they were in, and then they were cruising at high speeds again along a smaller, bumpier road.

"Did you hear any vehicles behind us?" Ellie hissed. The last thing she wanted was to jump out of the trunk in front of a truck full of Q Team and immediately have to run for her life on shaky, cramped legs. Or just get run over by them the moment she was clear of the car.

Hal cracked the trunk door a tiny bit more, pressing his eye to the blinding crack. "I think we're in the back," he hissed back.

"Can you see any clues to where we are? Where we're going?"

Another long pause. "No idea. We can figure it out once we get away."

Considering there wasn't much else to do while she waited, Ellie tried to remember whatever she could about the area around Denver. Her mind drew a blank. Were they going to be near population centers when they got out? Out in the middle of nowhere?

A few minutes later she felt a rumble in the car as it braked. Hal once again tensed. "Get ready."

Ellie nodded, and as the vehicle slowed to the point where they weren't going much faster than she could sprint, give or take, he flung open the trunk and lunged forward to crouch on the lip, sizing the jump. She joined him, biting back a frightened noise when she saw the road blurring by beneath her.

Were they going as fast as she could sprint? It looked so much faster, and she had almost no experience jumping off moving vehicles. Why would she?

Her friend twisted around to face the other way and dropped, legs flipping out from beneath him as his feet hit the pavement. He rolled in a way that made her wince in sympathy, but she couldn't give herself time to be intimidated by his poor landing.

She took the information from his fall to try to improve her own attempt, spun on the narrow ledge of metal, and tucked her arms in as she dropped towards the ground, trying to go from zero to a sprint in no time flat.

The next few instants were terrifying and painful. Ellie felt her legs flip out from beneath her in spite of her best efforts, then she was rolling across rough asphalt, a sharp jolt against her elbow sending numbness up her arm. From the way her limbs skidded on the road even through her clothes she had a feeling she'd be sporting more than a few scrapes and bruises as well, although thankfully at the moment adrenaline blocked the pain.

As she flipped wildly, gray and blue flashing across her vision, she heard the screech of brakes. She forced herself onto skinned hands and knees the moment she stopped rolling, knowing she only had moments, and looked around wildly to determine the best escape route.

The road was a narrow slash through hilly terrain, forested with evergreens and patches of aspen, scrub oak, and other trees she probably should've recognized but didn't. She didn't have much time to take in her surroundings before Hal caught her under the arm, and she found herself sprinting for the trees to the right of the road.

Behind her she heard doors slamming and angry shouting. They barely managed a handful of steps into the thicket before gunfire roared from behind, joined by the sharp whine of passing bullets and the noise of foliage shredding and impacts on the tree trunks around her. Ellie bit back a shout and forced her shaky legs to move even faster, briefly pulling ahead of Hal as they ducked branches and dodged trees to get deeper into cover.

Crashing from behind warned of pursuit, and she ducked at the roar of more shots fired, trying to make her movements erratic. Although dodging trees was doing that well enough as it was.

What followed as an interminable blur of running, tripping and slamming into things, forcing herself to keep moving as the sounds of pursuit slowly grew more and more distant. The robbers eventually gave up even taking potshots, and finally after at least five minutes of flat-out sprinting she heard them shouting in frustration somewhere far behind, calling an end to the chase.

Even then Ellie didn't stop, not taking any chances on being caught again by those animals. Close behind her Hal followed doggedly, although he was panting like a bellows, his crashing noises far louder than hers as he stumbled through the thick undergrowth.

Finally her legs gave out and she nearly crashed face-first into a tree.

Shut In

She threw out an arm, managing to rebound off the trunk, and collapsed to the ground curled around it, lungs burning as she heaved in desperate breaths. Somewhere behind her Hal gasped in relief and she heard a crash as he also let himself collapse.

Over the bellows of her own breaths, joined by the thunder of her heartbeat pounding in her ears, she listened for the sounds of anyone else moving through the forest. All she heard was her friend panting a short distance away: they were safe.

Or were they?

"Do you-" Ellie cut off with a ragged breath, swallowing down the roiling nausea of pushing past her limits, then continued determinedly. "Do you think being handled by those animals, who've probably handled a bunch of other possibly sick people, means we've got Zolos now?"

Hal coughed, hacked, and she heard him spit. "I'd like to believe we don't." She struggled to twist enough to glance at him dubiously, and he continued. "They were wearing gloves, right? And they seemed to have decent quarantine methods, so the only people carrying the virus on the Q Team would be those immune to its effects, or who got a milder form of the illness and then recovered. Considering how deadly Zolos is, there can't be many of those out there."

Replying took too much effort, so she simply rolled onto her back and continued struggling to catch her breath, luxuriating in the feel of the burning agony in her legs slowly fading to mere rubbery exhaustion.

After a few minutes her friend dragged himself to a seated position. "Well," he said, obviously struggling for an upbeat tone as he looked at the dense thicket surrounding them, "looks as if we're back on foot in the middle of nowhere."

Ellie couldn't bring herself to match his tone. "Only with literally nothing but the clothes on our backs this time."

His expression sagged. "Yeah." He forced himself to stand, injecting some determination into his tone. "Well, we know the drill. Find a road, find a sign to tell us where we are, and make for the nearest civilization."

Then what? she thought with a bleak surge of despair. *Steal another car? Run out of gas and get kidnapped and sexually assaulted by more robbers?* She wouldn't have thought that even a serious pandemic would make travel so difficult, but with no one manning the pumps gas stations might as well not have existed at all, and without them no one was going anywhere.

The few more states they had to travel might as well have been the other side of the planet.

But at the same time, she hadn't been through everything she'd been through just to give up now. Not when her children were depending on her. So bleak as things looked at the moment there was no option but to grit her teeth, gather up every scrap of determination her exhausted body had left, and keep going.

So she pushed to her feet with a weary groan. "Let's get looking, then."

Hal nodded and glanced back the way they'd come, a trail of broken branches and trampled undergrowth that even Ellie could follow in spite of her complete lack of any sort of tracking ability. "If I could make a suggestion, even though those SOBs are probably long gone let's go the opposite direction of the road they were on."

She shuddered and nodded in agreement. "That's an excellent suggestion." Without waiting for an invitation, she turned and continued blazing a trail the way they'd been running.

He let her take the lead, the thicket too dense to let them walk side by side. "Also, we should keep our eyes open for anything useful. We're going to need whatever we can find."

True enough, since they currently had literally nothing. If Ellie had thought their circumstances had been dire in Southern Utah, now they seemed completely hopeless.

Couldn't they ever catch a break? "At least we're not in the desert," she mumbled.

Hal grunted in agreement. "That'll probably double the speed we can travel right there. And hey, no pesky spare clothes and other junk to slow us down. Can you imagine wheeling your suitcase through these trees?"

Ellie couldn't bring herself to smile, but the absurd mental picture did raise her spirits slightly. "That's it, look on the bright side."

They fell silent after that, focusing on putting one foot in front of the other. And, if her friend was anything like her, trying furiously to think of any way out of this mess.

Chapter Fifteen
Making Do

"Daddy, the chili exploded in the microwave!" Tallie called through the door.

Nick cursed under his breath and hung up his phone, tossing it on his desk. "Okay, honey! Did Ricky turn it off?"

"No, he ran into his room and slammed the door! He's in trouble, isn't he?"

He did his best to keep his tone patient. "No, honey, he's doing great." *He can't be in trouble because I'm depending on him to take care of both of you out there. Besides, if anyone's at fault it's me for giving terrible directions.*

What had he gotten wrong? He'd told his son to dump the chili out of the can into a plastic bowl and microwave it, since that would be safer than using the stove. Did chili spatter a lot in a microwave? Should he have told Ricky to cover it? Had three minutes been too long to cook it?

"It won't be as bad as he thinks," he continued firmly. "There'll still be plenty of chili. Have him get the oven mitts and take the bowl out of the microwave, then wait for the stuff that splattered to cool down and wipe the microwave clean. Next time he can cover it with a paper towel or paper plate or something to keep in from making a mess."

There was a very long pause from the other side of the door. Nick knew Tallie well enough to know she'd either wandered off, gotten bored and found something to distract herself, or he'd dumped too much information on her at once and she was staring blankly at the door, trying to figure out what he wanted.

It turned out to be that last one. "I'll have Ricky come talk to you," she finally chirped.

He sighed and slumped down on his office chair, exhausted physically and mentally almost to his limit from cleaning his office and then himself. He had his own chili to look forward to, cold from the can.

For food and water Ricky had needed to push things through the cracked-open door. That meant canned food and water in any containers his son could find. Containers which would need to be more and more imaginative, since their trip to the office was all one way.

Which was actually a worry, warning that if this quarantine went on for too long Nick was going to have to either force Ricky to handle potentially contaminated containers, which he wasn't about to do, or go out and search for an alternative source of water. Maybe an external spigot on the outside of the apartment building.

He hated having to open the door even to get food and water passed in to him, since he'd gone to great efforts to seal it off from the rest of the house with duct tape and cloth bunched along the bottom. But he'd done his best to run a fan in the window, preferring to send any potential Zolos outside rather than into the rest of the apartment. That would mean chilly conditions once the sun set, but he could live with that. Especially as the days gradually grew warmer.

Days. He'd barely been in this quarantine for *hours* and he wasn't sure how he was going to manage this; the longer it went on, he was sure, the more conditions were going to feel closer to third world. He hadn't needed to relieve himself yet, but once he did he'd have to find a creative solution. Hygiene and sanitation were going to be real concerns, too.

And that was just his own issues. What were his kids going to do without him to personally help them? Ricky was smart and responsible, at least considering his age, but there were some things he might not be able to do while following instructions told to him through a door.

Where the blazes was Ellie? She should've been back sometime today, realistically hours ago. And if not, she at least should've called to let him know what was happening. She knew the dire circumstances he and the kids were in, with him in quarantine and an eight-year-old and five-year-old left to fend for themselves.

He hadn't thought to ask about her progress or timetable when he called to tell her about the attack, and his calls since then had all gone straight to voicemail. *Again.* It would've been funny if it wasn't leaving him an emotional wreck.

Unable to contact his ex-wife, he'd done the next best thing and searched online for any news that might give clues to what was delaying her. He didn't find any specific mentions of her, unsurprisingly, or any situation he could confidently suspect she might've found herself part of.

But what he did find didn't do anything for his escalating worry.

All over the country, including in the cities that lay between Ellie and returning home to them in KC, criminals seemed to have figured out the same thing that the punks who'd broken into Nick's home last night had: that people who'd put themselves into quarantine right from the start were most likely safe, and they'd conveniently plastered their houses with notices to let the world know that.

Combined with the fact that the government was fully occupied dealing with Zolos, that meant the chaos that Nick had assumed wouldn't happen because of people's fear of catching the disease was finally exploding, and in a major way.

Gangs were running rampant in cities, taking territory and snatching up whatever they wanted from people who had no way to stop them. And out in the rural areas things were, if anything, even more outrageous, with roving bands hitting isolated houses or even small towns and ransacking quarantined homes.

There was even an uproar outside of Denver, where apparently a truly monstrous group of criminals had gone around to several towns raping and even kidnapping women. In spite of the Zolos pandemic spiraling out of control and an estimated sixth of the country infected or already dead, people were going ballistic about that sort of blatant

Shut In

lawlessness in the United States of America.

Nationwide demands were pouring in for Colorado to stamp down hard on that group and anyone else who had the same idea, and if they couldn't then the Federal government should. Some of the most incensed of those calling for action were even demanding that the Air Force send in a few fighter jets and blow the entire villainous group to bits with missiles launched from high altitude. Which was insane considering the criminals had hostages, as others pointed out while demanding the Pentagon send in Special Forces teams to rescue the kidnapped women.

After which point, most didn't seem to find the idea of the group being blown to smithereens all that objectionable.

Nick couldn't believe things had gotten that bad in less than a week. The thought of Ellie out there in that chaos, potentially driving right through areas where women were being taken from their homes to face who knew what awful fate, was driving him frantic with fear. Especially when he was still a bundle of nerves after having to kill a man to defend himself in his own home.

He felt like he should be doing something, *anything*, besides just sitting uselessly in his office while the mother of his children was out there facing that danger alone. Or well, technically with some strange dude she'd decided to carpool with, which he couldn't help but feel was even worse.

But what could he do? Even if he knew where Ellie was, and even after she'd explicitly told him not to take their children out of the safety of the apartment, after potentially being exposed to Zolos if he went to pick her up he'd be running the same risk of infecting her. The only option that seemed available was to wait for her to contact him, same as he'd had to wait the last two times she'd vanished off the face of the Earth, phone going straight to voicemail.

Only this time, he couldn't help but feel like something terrible had actually happened. Maybe that was just because he was imagining the worst after spending the last hour reading articles and watching videos of the chaos exploding across the country, but he didn't think so.

Nathan Jones

The world was going insane around him, and the woman who'd been the love of his life for over ten years was out there in the middle of it.

And there was nothing. He. Could. Do.

Even if there was once again some good reason for Ellie to be incommunicado, and she was okay but simply delayed, what options did he have if she didn't make it back soon? Should he try to rig up some sort of full-body suit, and wear it full time around his kids? He wasn't sure that was even possible with the materials at hand, and even if it was could he take that risk when it meant possibly exposing Ricky and Tallie to a deadly virus?

No, better his son turn bowls of chili into volcanoes in the microwave, while he did his best to talk the boy through any problems he and his sister ran into through the door.

In the meantime, there *was* something Nick could do . . . bury the body.

It seemed like the decent thing to do. Nobody was getting back to him from the police, city office, or coroner's office, and the punk's buddy hadn't bothered to come back and claim his friend to return to whatever family he might have. With that in mind, the idea of a human being just rotting out in the open seemed inhuman, whatever the circumstances. To say nothing of any sanitation issues to do with having a corpse sitting right outside his apartment.

So he retrieved a small hand shovel and a ground tarp from the small store of camping supplies pushed to the very back of his office's closet, unused since . . . had it really been all the way back when Ellie was pregnant with Tallie, and they'd taken that vacation to Wallace State Park for Ricky's third birthday? That felt like forever ago.

Well these supplies would get some use now, if for a far less happy reason. "Ricky, Tallie!" he called through the door. "Eat your lunch! I'll be right outside, so if you really need me yell super loud and I'll hear you."

He heard a door bang against a wall as it was thrown open.

Shut In

"Outside?" Ricky called back in alarm. "What if you get sick?"

Nick grimaced. Getting covered in that punk's blood had been more of a danger than climbing down to the bottom of the fire escape ever would be, at least as long as nobody else was anywhere nearby or used it. "I'll be careful," he replied, with the confident tone of a dad who wasn't 100% sure of something but pretended to be so his kids wouldn't worry. "Don't worry, it'll be fine."

There was no reply. Nick hefted his pathetic little shovel and the tarp and lifted the fan out of the broken window, climbing out onto the fire escape.

Considering his resolve to stay in the house until the Zolos crisis was over, he sure was going out a lot.

Burying the body of his attacker turned out to be one of the most difficult things he'd ever done. And that had nothing to do with the fact that he had to dig a hole in a narrow strip of grass at the side of the building with a shovel the size of his forearm, barely better than using his bare hands. Which meant a shallow hole, and even then he was exhausted beyond belief by the time he was done; he'd gotten in terrible shape in the last six months.

No, what tore him up was the surreal fact that he'd killed a man. He'd never really even gotten into a fight in his entire life, and now he was digging a grave for someone who'd tried to murder him in his own home with a knife.

The body, which he'd carefully wrapped in the tarp while touching it as little as possible, waited nearby in silent condemnation. It was already starting to stink, making his stomach churn every time the breeze turned from that way.

Finally, he decided he'd dug deep enough to cover the body with a few inches of dirt and sod. Hopefully that plus the tarp would keep stray dogs away, and if not he could always mound the dirt higher. Kill two birds with one stone if he needed to dig a new hole anyway, maybe to use to bury waste once he finally got around to the unpleasant necessity of relieving himself without a bathroom.

Another challenge to look forward to.

Nick dragged the body into the shallow hole, hastily piled dirt back on, and found a few loose pieces of concrete and asphalt to pile on top for good measure. With the job finally done, he slumped down on the third step of the fire escape and took a few swigs from the water bottle he'd fetched from the office halfway through digging the hole.

He choked when his phone abruptly rang.

Ellie! Tossing the bottle away, he scrambled to pull the device out of his pocket. To his disappointment the number was an unfamiliar one. Still, that didn't mean it wasn't his ex-wife on another phone, so he hastened to answer it. "Hello?"

"Nicholas Statton?"

A fresh wave of disappointment surged through him, although he tried to swallow it and keep his tone steady. "Nick here."

"Mr. Statton, this is John Barnes, from the coroner's office in-"

"About the home invasion I called in?" Nick blurted, relief surging through him. It wasn't a call from Ellie, but it was still welcome. "Thank God! I just finished buryi-"

"I'm afraid that's outside of my jurisdiction," the man cut in curtly. "I'm out in Wabash County, Indiana, calling to . . ." he trailed off. "Did you just say you finished burying something?"

He felt his face flushing. "The guy came at me with a knife. We struggled for it, and I ended up stabbing him. Burying him seemed like the decent thing to do."

There was a long pause, then John cursed quietly. Not in shock, or horror at hearing of a killing, but with the sort of tired resignation of another problem dumped in his lap. "Did you report it?"

"Of course." Why else would he be asking if that's what this call was about?

Shut In

"Okay, well, I can't really help you with that. Like I said, outside my jurisdiction, sorry. Your best bet is to keep trying to contact your local authorities."

Nick sighed, sagging back to rest his head on one of the higher fire escape steps; the narrow metal bars turned out to be incredibly uncomfortable. "All right. So what's this about, Mr. Barnes?"

There was a brief pause, and when the man finally spoke it was obvious he was making an effort to change the tone of the conversation. "I'm calling because you're listed as the next of kin for one of our deceased, Mr. Statton. I regret to inform you that Fred Statton, your father according to our records, has passed away from a Zolos infection."

He stared at his phone blankly for a few seconds. Absurdly, his first thought was that now he knew where his dad had disappeared to.

With a start he realized the silence had dragged on long enough to be uncomfortable. "Oh, um, thank you for letting me know."

"Of course." John sounded a bit surprised at his response. Or lack of it, maybe. "I understand this must be sudden, and I wish I'd had time to present it more tactfully. I've got a long list to go through, and unfortunately we're too swamped to take incoming calls. Do you have any questions about his death?"

"I . . . no, nothing that can't wait until things settle down. Thank you again."

"Take care, Mr. Statton." There was a click as the call ended.

Nick set down his phone on the step beside him, staring at it even after the screen went black to save power.

His dad was dead? He barely remembered the man, hadn't seen him since he was a kid. Where a face should be was just a blur, no memory of voice or mannerisms or anything they'd ever talked about. Just a few vague recollections of shoulder rides, and one distant memory of a trip to some park on a cold day in the late fall, with bare tree limbs rattling

249

and leaves skittering across the ground.

He'd barely spared his dad a thought in over a decade, had barely missed him in his life. So why did learning of his death leave such a hollow feeling in his gut?

Maybe just regret at all the missed opportunities. The gulf of bitterness and estrangement that would never be bridged now.

Nick reached for his phone to call his mom, hesitated, then drew his hand back. He was half afraid that, even in these circumstances, her only response to learning of his dad's death would be a snarky remark. He was in no state to put up with that right now.

Some niggling part of him suggested that he should call her anyway. That he'd missed his chance to talk to his dad one last time, and if he stayed stubborn and the unthinkable happened he might miss that same chance with his mom. And with her new family, the step siblings he was barely aware of and the stepdad he did his best not to actively despise.

No, he'd save that call for some other time, if ever. Just like he probably wouldn't tell his kids their other grandpa had also passed. Same as he wasn't telling them that he and their mom couldn't get in touch with their grandma Feldman.

They were already exposed to enough fear and misery with the country falling apart around them. Enough doubt and hardship.

Speaking of which . . . with a sigh, he gathered his things and trudged up the steps to check in with them, make sure they were still doing okay with their dad trying to parent through a door, unable to physically intervene if something went wrong.

Where in the blue blazes was Ellie?

* * * * *

After about an hour of bushwhacking, Ellie and Hal finally found a road.

It was a pitted asphalt two-lane meandering towards the mountains looming to the west. Probably the same range of the Colorado Rocky Mountains they'd crossed on the way to Denver, which at least gave them some idea of where they were.

Although it wasn't as if they could've gone too far away in a half hour or so of driving. But it meant they'd gone either north or south along the mountains, rather than east away from Colorado's capitol. Which wasn't anywhere in sight, another clue to their location.

Not that they'd expected find a hilltop in this uninhabited terrain of wooded hills with a city of over half a million people sitting on the other side.

After a bit of debate they agreed they'd be more likely to find a town if they followed the road east away from the mountains, since for all they knew it just headed right up into them without ever passing more than an isolated cabin or two. Also, it meant they wouldn't have to hike uphill, and would even be going downhill more of the time.

Night fell with them still on the road, no sign of civilization so far. Not even an abandoned house or bit of rotting fence to be seen. They also hadn't seen any road signs to point them anywhere.

Even worse, at some point the road had curved from east to southeast, then almost due south running parallel to the mountains. Since they had no idea if they were north or south of Denver, that meant they could either be hiking towards it or away, with no way of knowing how far they had to go to reach anywhere that could offer them help.

All Ellie knew was that they hadn't seen any branching roads to offer an alternative, aside from a few dirt or gravel tracks that seemed to veer back towards the mountains to accommodate joyriders in 4x4s or ATVs.

Another thing that was becoming painfully obvious was that they *needed* help. Neither of them had any idea what plants were edible around here, unless of course they'd been lucky enough to stumble across a fruit tree or berry bush, which they hadn't. So foraging was out. They'd also passed more than one stream trickling down from the mountains, but without a container or any way to easily make fire they couldn't make use of that water.

At least at first, although by the time dusk rolled around and the thirst became a monster crouched on her shoulder, demanding to be sated, she wasn't sure she cared about the risk.

"You'll care when you're squirting from both ends while we're struggling to hike to find help to survive," her friend told her grimly when he caught her striding purposefully towards a narrow trickle of water, which ran towards the road and then along it for a hundred or so yards before going underneath in a culvert and continuing on southeast.

"We might not have a choice between waterborne pathogens and dying of thirst before long," she shot back, longingly eying the trickle of water.

"But we're not there yet." He took her shoulders, looking deep into her eyes. "Let's give it a bit longer, El. We might run across a spring that offers clean water, or finally find a residence or roadside rest area or something."

Ellie didn't want to spend the night thirsty. She really, really didn't want to. It was looking to be miserable enough as the air quickly turned chilly once the sun set, leaving them with no fire, no shelter, and no warm clothing or blankets.

Hal led the way back off the road and into the woods, searching in the fading light until he found a spot where the previous autumn's fallen leaves lay thick on the ground. He quickly got to work rigging up a shelter from fresh leafy branches against a fallen log, which hung suspended between the trunks of two trees a few feet off the ground.

"Where'd you learn to do that?" she asked. "Boy Scouts?"

"Survival TV shows," he replied, shaking his head wryly. Maybe with a touch of bitterness. "Scouting was just one of the many things that wasn't really a part of my childhood."

At his direction Ellie got to work gathering up fallen leaves. They could pile them atop the branches of the shelter where needed to keep out the wind, pile them in the shelter to provide soft beds and insulation from the cold ground, and pile them atop themselves to make makeshift blankets.

"Leaves," she said, staring forlornly at the damp layer of mulchy deadfall beneath the dry, crackling top layer. She was sure they were going to be maddeningly scratchy and uncomfortable, and make a racket loud enough to wake the dead with every toss and turn. Probably full of gross bugs, too. "Nature's gift to people with literally nothing else."

Her friend ignored the sarcasm. "We can also stuff them in our clothes when we head out in the morning if it's too chilly. Nature's coat, right?"

Ellie grimaced. Sleeping in a pile of leaves would be bad enough with them outside her clothes; she really didn't want to put them where they'd be directly scratching and tickling her skin. Which she supposed went back to the literally nothing else part of it.

"Are we just the unluckiest people ever?" she asked, trying not to sound whiny. Although she felt like she'd certainly be justified in it if she did.

Hal paused arranging a new branch on the shelter to turn and look at her soberly. "Maybe not the unluckiest," he said in a quiet voice. "If we hadn't gotten away from those guys this morning . . ."

He didn't finish the thought, although he didn't really need to. She shuddered and nodded her agreement, getting back to work.

Granted, if she was still a captive of the robbers she'd probably have food, water, and shelter right now. Not to mention maybe a bathroom and other basic necessities that seemed like luxuries at the moment. But the thought of the horrors she would've suffered after four days of dubious comfort was enough to remind her that there were far worse things than being exhausted, cold, hungry, and thirsty.

Not to mention probably coming down with a cold, after the stress and deprivation her body had endured ever since first being trapped in that plane on the tarmac in Hawaii.

253

They finished setting up the shelter and filling it with leaves in silence. Then they spent a few minutes shivering in the cold as they stared at the fruits of their labor. It was low, cramped, probably drafty, and crude, but at least it was better than huddling on the ground in the chilly night air.

"I could try to get a fire going?" Hal finally offered, although without much enthusiasm.

Ellie glanced at the last glimmer of light on the western horizon; setting up the shelter had taken longer than she'd expected, and it would be full dark in a matter of minutes. "I don't think we have time before the light's gone."

"Yeah." He hugged himself a bit tighter. "Sure would be nice, though."

Yeah, it really would've been. Getting colder by the second, and with nothing else to do, they wasted no time climbing inside the shelter and burrowing under the leaves, squirming around to make nests. Ellie was still shivering when she finished, but it was the feeling of climbing under a thick comforter on a cold night, knowing that in a few minutes she'd be warm.

She hoped.

After a succession of nights with poor sleep, and after the awful day she'd just had, it was no surprise that before long she felt her eyelids drooping, sinking into blissful sleep. She even felt herself finally starting to warm up, a blessed feeling in spite of the itchy discomfort of the leaves packed around her.

Hal's voice drifted through the darkness, comfortingly close in their little shelter. "How you doing?"

Ellie blinked her eyes open, staring at the black outline of stacked branches just above her head, then with a yawn let them droop closed again. "Fine. I don't think I'll freeze in here."

"Good." He paused, then continued hesitantly. "I mean about . . . this morning."

Oh. "I'd really rather not talk about it."

"Yeah, I get that." Her friend's voice was nearly a whisper, full of guilt and anguish. "It's just I've never been more terrified in my life, El. If something had happened to you, if I'd failed to keep you safe, I-" he cut off with a sharp breath before continuing shakily. "I don't know what I would've done."

Ellie reached out in the darkness, digging through leaves until her fingers found his arm. She followed it down to his hand and gripped it tight. "I do," she said quietly. "You would've found a way out for us. Exactly like you did."

He didn't reply, although he returned her grip with equal intensity.

She wasn't sure how long they lay like that in their nests of dead leaves, surrounded by the quiet rustles and chitters of night animals and soft breezes through the foliage. Letting those peaceful noises lull her after the day's traumas. All she knew was that she was still holding Hal's hand as she drifted off.

Perhaps it was that reassuring contact, or perhaps it was simply sheer exhaustion, but the nightmares about Watkins that Ellie had secretly dreaded would torment her never made an appearance.

In fact, she slept like the log the shelter was built against.

* * * * *

Early spring nights could be cold, even with a nest of leaves to keep Ellie warm.

That considered, and the fact that she'd fallen asleep holding Hal's hand, she supposed it wasn't a huge surprise when she woke in the early morning to discover that sometime in the night she'd huddled close against his back for warmth.

It felt . . . distractingly nice.

Even beyond shared body heat, she had to admit that she'd missed the feeling of someone's solid presence beside her as she slept. Of holding and being held. Nights had been surprisingly lonely since her divorce, something she hadn't expected considering how often she slept alone on business trips, or when Nick had pulled late nights working.

But no matter how good it felt, as soon as Ellie realized where she was, and more importantly who she was with, she hastily pulled away with her cheeks flaming in embarrassment. Then, even though it was still freezing outside, she hauled herself out of her nest and climbed out of the makeshift shelter to shiver in the early morning chill.

It had just been for warmth, and it wasn't even something she'd consciously decided to do. She just hoped it wouldn't make things awkward between them.

If her friend hadn't already been awake, her crashing out of the shelter pretty much did the job. Just a few seconds later he gingerly climbed out after her, hugging himself as he looked around. "Morning," he mumbled, joining her. "Walking's the best way to warm up I can think of. Anything you need to do before we get going?"

If he was aware they'd basically spent the night cuddling he showed no sign of it. Then again, it might've been because he seemed to have something else on his mind; he was shifting in place, scratching at his palms with an expression of clear discomfort on his face.

"You okay?" Ellie asked.

He grimaced. "Actually . . . not so much." His face flushed in obvious embarrassment, and he studiously looked off into the trees. "You're going to laugh at me, but, um, do you know what poison ivy looks like?"

She frowned as well. "I think that mostly grows farther east."

"Poison oak, then, or poison sumac or plants like that," he persisted, scratching at his hand again and shifting gingerly in place some more.

Ellie glanced down at his palms, realizing with shock they were covered in rashes. Along with more patches of red on the backs of the hands and around the wrists. "Holy cow. Did you accidentally brush against something?"

Hal winced and shifted again. "More like, uh, used it to wipe with yesterday."

She also winced, eyes widening in sympathetic horror. "Oh no!"

"It's not that bad," he said stoutly, although now that she was looking for it the stiff way he was standing suggested otherwise. "I can walk."

Ellie certainly hoped so, since they couldn't exactly sit around waiting to die of thirst. Although walking with a rash like that on his butt was going to be sheer torment; her heart went out to him, especially since it could've just as easily been her if she'd needed to relieve herself at any point yesterday.

"We can take it slower if you need," she said, patting his shoulder. She glanced around ruefully. "And on the way, we can be more careful to avoid touching anything."

Her friend snorted. "On the plus side, unless we find something to eat soon I probably won't have a reason to repeat this mistake." He gave the shelter they'd made a final look, half pride and half disgust, then sighed and limped back towards the road.

They'd been walking less than ten minutes before Ellie began to worry about how well Hal was going to hold up. His stride was becoming more bowlegged by the step, a constantly pained expression on his face, and his hands alternated itching furiously at his palms.

If things weren't so desperate she probably would've found his plight at least a bit funny. Not his suffering, of course, but the sheer absurdity of this situation. If it hadn't been bad enough to walk long distances hungry and tired and cold, he had the bad luck of wiping his butt with poison oak of all things!

The poor, poor guy.

Well, Ellie didn't have any cream for his rashes, or any other way to ease his discomfort, but at least she could help him not add to it. She gently caught his closest hand as he started to scratch his palm with it again, and at his questioning look said firmly. "I know it's driving you crazy, but no dermatological problem was ever solved by scratching it. In fact, it almost always makes it worse."

Her friend grit his teeth and let his hands drop to his sides. "Kinda makes you wonder why the urge is so strong, then. Epic fail for our biology."

She finally did laugh, but with him. "I'm sure there was some reason for it at some point."

They settled into an easy silence, walking quietly for a few more minutes. Ellie saw his hand twitch a few times as if moving to scratch, but was pleased to see he always caught himself. After like the fifth time he spoke up abruptly. "How about sunburns?"

"Hmm?"

"I can't think of any downside to scratching those." Hal grinned at her. "Actually, it's kind of nice to have a massive sunburn across your back, and to feel the sheer enjoyment of just scratching the heck out of it as much as you want."

"While your skin peels off like the mange?" she said dryly.

His grin widened and he shrugged. "Hey, it was going to come off anyway." He absently scratched at his palm, then jerked his hands apart with an irritated sound and shoved them into his pockets.

A few hours after sunrise the road they were on finally joined another one. Even better, it was an Interstate: I-25, headed north/south. Not only that, but there was still some traffic on it, although not much. And certainly none that showed any signs of stopping to help them.

Not that they would've had much chance of flagging down a passing vehicle, since they agreed it would be best to stay just out of sight of the Interstate as they followed it, in case those robbers made another appearance.

After a bit of debate they decided to head south, on the reasoning that if they were north of Denver then going that way would take them there, and if they were south of it then they seemed to recall there being more towns along that stretch of I-25.

Although after following the Interstate for a mile or so they found a sign that flew in the face of that assumption.

"Colorado Springs," Hal mused, staring at the name of the closest city on it. "Guess that mean's we're south of Denver, not north."

Ellie's eyes were locked on the distance, fighting the urge to cry: 17 miles. It had taken them so long last time to get to St. George, and now they had to go almost as far again if you counted yesterday's hiking? This time even more exhausted, after already going a day without food and water and no guarantee of finding any, or warm clothes or camping gear for that matter, before they reached their destination.

At least along the Interstate they had a better chance of finding a place with running water. They could drink until their stomachs burst, they could bathe and clean their clothes, and Hal could soothe the areas affected by his rash. They might even find some place selling food, although they'd have to rely on charity since the robbers had stolen their wallets.

Thirst was the most driving need, so desperate her head throbbed and her eyes were dry and blurry. But that didn't distract completely from the hollow, nauseous pain of her empty stomach.

"Can we make it 17 miles without food and water, if we need to?" she whispered.

"Food, I'd say so," Hal replied. "Water, we'd probably be in serious trouble by that point."

Ellie sighed. "Well, standing around staring at the sign isn't going to get us any closer, *or* find us water."

Her friend nodded, squared his shoulders resolutely, and hobbled down from the top of the hill they'd been following to once again walk out of view. Ellie joined him, gritting her teeth against the discomforts that had steadily become agonies. She alternated between squinting at the ground just in front of her to soothe her dry eyes and staring ahead in search of some sort of reprieve.

Anything, any break they could catch. Weren't they about due for one after everything they'd been through?

Chapter Sixteen
Surviving

Maybe it was the slightly less punishing heat and mildly more humid climate. Maybe it was the fact that Ellie wasn't lugging extra baggage now. Maybe it was her even her body having toughened up after days of hardship. Or maybe it was just the pure desperation of their situation.

Whatever it was, by some miracle in spite of the fact that they'd now gone almost thirty-six hours without food or water, now that they were on a good road again and could see the mile markers passing by slowly but steadily she'd realized they were traveling *faster* than they had been in Southern Utah.

Not much faster, but the fact that they were managing it at all was astounding.

Which wasn't to say that every step wasn't agonizing, until Ellie felt like her mind was drifting in a nightmare haze as she forced herself to put one blistered, sore foot in front of the other. She didn't remember ever being so hungry, her stomach a churning ball of acid torment eating through her middle. In fact, she was sure that she never *had* been this hungry. No voluntary fast, even ones that had technically lasted longer than this, had ever felt this painful.

But even her hunger couldn't compare to her thirst. There were no words to describe it, and even in the desert of Southern Utah her throat had never felt so parched, until she could no longer even swallow without coughing and struggling for long, terrifying seconds. Her eyelids were burning sandpaper that didn't alleviate the dryness in her eyes when she blinked. Her was skin cracked and even bleeding in places. Her mouth tasted like something had died in it days ago, and had spent all this time rotting. Her sweat-sodden clothes smelled almost as bad.

Nathan Jones

Judging by how Hal looked, Ellie was glad she didn't have a mirror.

Her friend had to be suffering everything she was, but on top of that his rashes had him in such obvious misery she just wanted to wrap her arms around him in sympathy every time she glanced his way. His steps had become more painful by the mile, until he was hobbling along as bowlegged as a cowboy after a long day in the saddle and even then regularly making stifled noises of discomfort.

As for his hands, he'd finally managed to bring himself to stop scratching them, admitting after he'd gone a while without doing so that the itching had all but disappeared once he did. Even so, before he got to that point he'd scraped his palms raw, and now handled things gingerly when he had to. Which thankfully wasn't often while walking along like they were.

In spite of their wretched state, somehow the miles dragged by with regular speed, one gritted-teeth step after another passing on without giving in to the need to stop and rest from the plodding crawl they were managing. Stopping would've meant delaying that much longer from finding water, which kept Ellie moving to the point of collapse and beyond.

Then at last, sometime in the late afternoon, their determination was rewarded when Hal lifted a trembling arm to point at a rest stop ahead.

She would've cried at the sight if her tear ducts had any moisture to spare. As it was she gave a sort of dry, choking sob and shambled forward a bit faster, stumbling so precariously that each step was a reeling dance to keep from falling on her face.

Her friend caught up and offered her a hand, although he didn't look much steadier. Normally Ellie's pride wouldn't have allowed her to accept the help, but in her current state she was relieved to throw her arm around his shoulders.

To her amazement, somehow the act of steadying her seemed to improve his balance as well. Maybe they were supporting each other.

They shambled down the off-ramp together, towards the inviting

Shut In

beacon of the dingy rest area bathroom ahead. Ellie's thirst was so all-consuming she wouldn't have thought anything could distract her, at least until she saw the single car parked in front of the building.

They'd seen more than a few cars pass by along the highway, although harsh experience had taught them not to even bother trying to flag them down; even without the danger of robbers it would've just been pointless. This car seemed in good condition, making its abandonment a mystery.

If it *was* abandoned.

Ellie nudged Hal towards the vehicle, changing direction to make for it. But about twenty feet away he balked, pulling her to a stop so abruptly they both nearly dropped flat on their faces. "You really want to check out a random car?" he asked nervously. "Even if the owner's long gone, for all we know it could be here because they had Zolos and went into a bathroom to die."

That scenario was chillingly plausible. "Is it worth the risk, to have a car that can take us home?"

Her friend hesitated. "The risk of dying trumps a whole lot of upside."

Ellie looked forlornly at the vehicle. "I don't see any water in there anyway. Let's revisit this debate once we're no longer dying of thirst."

He nodded and jerked his head towards the bathrooms. "Not from there, I'd say. People passing through here could've spread the virus all through the inside of that building, and on all the doors too. Let's poke around and see if we can find an out of the way outdoor spigot that probably wouldn't have been used."

Unless other visitors had the same idea, she thought grimly. But it was smart to diminish the risk, so she joined her friend circling the outside of the rest station.

There was no spigot to be found on the building, although they found a bank of snack and drink vending machines. Unfortunately, in spite of the fact that they'd been locked away behind thick metal mesh specifically to deter thieves, someone had gone to the effort to tear away the mesh, smash the glass, and take everything. The looters had even dug deep enough into the machines to get at the cash in them.

Even beyond the fact that they were empty, knowing that so many people had to have been around the machines, handling them, was enough for Ellie and Hal to give them a wide berth.

Undeterred by that setback, her friend expanded the search to the other outbuildings and the rest of the yard, their halting progress frequently interrupted by longing glances towards the drinking fountain sitting tantalizingly in view through the glass doors of the main building.

Finally, though, they found the access for the main valve for the sprinklers. There was a spigot poking out of the ground there, and when Ellie turned it on and a surge of icy water gurgled out they both gave a ragged cheer and shared a jubilant hug.

The spigot was so low and at such an awkward angle that it would've been impossible to get their mouths to the tantalizing stream without getting sprayed in the face, so they shivered and spluttered their way to drinking their fill with cupped hands as water splashed around them.

It was glorious.

By the time Ellie forced herself to stop gulping handfuls down, her stomach was almost uncomfortably bloated and she was torn between blissful contentment and wondering if she'd gone a bit overboard. Hal was already sprawled on the grass nearby, staring up at the sky with a somewhat glazed expression on his face.

She turned off the tap and hobbled over to collapse near him, forcing herself to take the herculean effort of taking off her shoes and socks so her feet could finally breathe. She was a bit self-conscious about how they smelled after days of walking without washing them and no clean socks to change into, but contented herself when her friend mimicked her actions that *his* smelled even worse.

Or maybe that was just perspective, and behind his carefully blank expression he was thinking she should get a biohazard sign to hang across her toes. Ellie tried to be subtle about twisting around so her feet were as far away from him as possible, and downwind to boot.

She resolved to ask Hal to step around the main building before they left so she could do her best to wash up without soap. No doubt he'd want to do the same, especially where he had his rashes.

Unfortunately, leaving seemed to be happening sooner rather than later. They hadn't found anything here so there was no reason to stick around, and even though both of them were at the end of their rope they knew they needed to keep going until they found something worth stopping for.

Or reached Colorado Springs, if they were really unlucky in their search.

Hal obligingly headed out of view, seeming glad for a chance to sprawl on the grass out in front and rest some more while Ellie took the time she needed to clean up. With no good options she decided to strip down just long enough to splash water over her filthy body, gasping at the shock of cold and rethinking her life's choices with every handful. She scrubbed as best she could with the minimum of water, unsatisfied with the end result but refusing to endure a more thorough soaking.

She was glad they'd reached the rest area when they had; any later in the day and it would've been too cold to even think of washing with this icy water.

After the nightmare she'd gone through yesterday morning, she was surprised how little it affected her to be bathing out in the open like this, even if she was mostly hidden from I-25 behind the main building. Maybe it was because aside from Hal the world just felt empty at the moment, barely any cars on the road and certainly nobody taking the risk of stopping at a *public* restroom.

Still, Ellie didn't waste any time shivering her way back into her filthy pants and shirt, although that was motivated as much by cold as any feelings of vulnerability.

Once dressed she spent another minute washing out her underwear and wringing as much water out of them as possible. She had no desire to wear them wet, since the chafing was already miserable enough, so into her pockets they went to hopefully dry by the time they stopped for the night. Although it didn't take long to rethink the choice, since it turned out going commando in dirty jeans might've been even worse.

Still, in spite of that mild discomfort Ellie was surprisingly refreshed by her efforts. She wanted Hal to be able to enjoy the same opportunity before they left, so she wasted no time heading around to let him know he could take his turn.

She found him dozing on the grass in a patch of sunlight between two trees with one tanned forearm over his eyes, expression surprisingly peaceful. It almost seemed a shame to wake him, but he'd been insistent that they needed to get going soon.

Still, she found herself hesitating to cross the distance, eyes lingering on his face, still handsome in spite of a couple days' worth of stubble. Or maybe partly *because* of it, since she found herself distracted wondering what he would look like with a full beard. Even slightly hollow cheeks thanks to deprivation and discomfort just made his features seem sharper and more chiseled.

Ellie could admit she was lucky she hadn't sent the young man packing when he asked to carpool with her. There was no telling what situation she'd be in without him, but one thing she could say for sure was that she didn't want to imagine being alone out here. The fact that he'd been with her through everything made it all bearable.

Even made it seem possible they'd actually make it home in spite of the obstacles they faced.

And when they did? The thought of parting ways so Hal could seek out his own family, possibly never seeing him again, sent an unexpected pang through her. She didn't want to have to say goodbye to him. She wanted-

With a start Ellie realized the directions her thoughts were going.

Shut In

Feeling her cheeks heating, she tore her eyes away from their wistful contemplation of his sleeping face and hurried the rest of the distance to where her friend rested, crouching to gently shake his shoulder. "Your turn."

He groaned, not so much as shifting from his comfortable position. "To splash icy water all over myself? Can't wait."

"Hey, it's not as bad as you think." *It's even worse.*

Ellie helped her friend to his feet, wincing in sympathy as he hobbled out of sight. She hoped washing would help his rashes, since there wasn't much else they could do for them.

While waiting for him she settled down on the grass for her own nap, curling up on her side with her face tucked under her arm. She wasn't sure how much time passed before she heard Hal calling.

She sat up with a groan to see him approaching from around the building, wet blond hair plastered to his head and making the hints of red in it stand out far more noticeably. "Guess it's time to move on," he said as he joined her, still shivering slightly. "That should warm us up."

"Onwards to Colorado Springs and a chance to gain and lose yet another car?" she said dryly.

He motioned towards the abandoned car. "Unless you want to try our luck with the Zolosmobile."

Ellie made a face and shook her head, quickening her step as they gave the vehicle a wide berth. Absurdly, the thoughts going through her head at that moment were about the green sedan they'd got in St. George that the robbers had stolen.

It was going to be hard to return it to its owners when it was in the hands of some group of rapist looters somewhere south of Denver. Then again, some realistic part of her had always known that her promise to return the car was just a justification; with the nation spiraling into ruin in the wake of this pandemic she probably never would've had the means to keep her promise.

Nathan Jones

The people who'd given her the car had probably realized that as well, writing it off the moment they tossed the keys out the door. That made her feel even worse, but right now she was too tired to dwell on it.

They left the rest area behind, continuing on just out of view of I-25. They only popped into sight of it long enough to make sure there were no approaching dangers, or curiosities worth a closer look.

There were none, just like there'd been nothing at the rest area. Aside from water, that was. Ellie was certainly grateful for that, but even so there'd been no food or warm clothing or blankets or any other necessities. And definitely no vehicle to take them home. Which meant that unless they got lucky in the next few hours, they could probably look forward to another miserable night in a makeshift shelter with leaves for blankets.

Well, there was always tomorrow. At the rate they were going they should reach Colorado Springs sometime in the afternoon, assuming hunger didn't slow their pace to a crawl.

And they didn't run into any more trouble.

* * * * *

"Dad, the lights aren't turning on!" Ricky called through the door, yanking Nick out of his fitful doze.

Seriously? He felt like he'd just barely managed to push aside his worries long enough to finally fall asleep, and now this? He cracked his eyes open with a groan, which swiftly became a grunt of alarm as he noticed a few things simultaneously.

First off, it was pitch black. Or at least darker than he'd ever seen it in the city; the streetlights and general glow of residences and businesses was nowhere to be seen. Secondly, the rumble of the fan he'd left running in the window had fallen silent. He still heard the honking and engine noises of cars outside, if anything even more frantic than usual, probably because the stoplights were out.

It obvious that something serious had happened. Specifically, the electricity seemed to be out.

His son, after waiting for a response and not getting one, continued in that half guilty, half whiny tone he used when he thought he was about to get in trouble for something he didn't think was his fault. "I really needed to go to the bathroom but I couldn't see, so I did my best in the dark. I-I think I got pee everywhere."

Normally that admission would've been enough to seriously irk Nick, and a punishment would be forthcoming. Or at least a scolding about why he hadn't just sat down if he couldn't see to aim. But as it was, Nick barely even gave it a second thought because there were far more pressing concerns.

The power was out. That was potentially a serious problem, and one they'd have to hurry to prepare for.

"Listen to me, Ricky," he said in his best no-nonsense tone. "There's a flashlight in the top drawer of my bedside table. Go get it so you can see, then come back. There are things you need to do, right away, or we're going to be in some trouble."

There was no reply, but he heard a few thumps as his son felt his way down the hallway towards his room. Nick hoped he didn't get lost; even in a familiar place, moving in pitch darkness was an entirely different thing than moving in even poor lighting. All those distances you thought you knew like second nature suddenly became skewed, and you found yourself smacking your shins on chairs and tables, tripping over junk on the floor.

And the confusion was only amplified when you were frightened, as Ricky surely was right now. And he wasn't wrong to be, although his motivation was a simple fear of the dark while Nick's fears were far more tangible.

He hadn't expected the pandemic to cause utilities to shut down. After all, it wasn't like an earthquake or explosion or electromagnetic pulse or anything else had destroyed actual infrastructure. He would've thought that things like electricity and water and cell phone service and internet would be critical enough that the authorities would prioritize keeping them going at all costs, to prevent the disaster from growing even worse.

But it looked as if he was wrong. Frankly, now that he really thought about it he supposed he was surprised the power had lasted this long. And with power out internet was gone too. For all he knew cell phones wouldn't be up for much longer, either.

Honestly, he should've seen it coming when he heard about truck drivers and other shipping industry personnel refusing to go out on their routes, closer to the beginning of this disaster. If they weren't willing to ship food where it was needed due to the risk of exposing themselves to Zolos, what made him think that employees at power plants, water and sewer works, and natural gas companies would? Especially as more and more people fell sick, and so couldn't have gone to work even if they'd felt it was safe.

In fact, he seemed to recall reading a story about trash starting to pile up in Kansas City, escalating sanitation concerns and giving rise to the very real fear of attracting vermin that would spread Zolos, and perhaps even less common diseases that would further exacerbate the problem. The reason for the trash pileup wasn't fear on the part of sanitation employees when it came to doing their rounds, but an actual outbreak among them that spread to most of the workforce within days.

Needless to say, the garbage trucks stopped going out after that. Nick had been having his kids toss the messiest of the garbage out the kitchen window, while he'd been collecting his own garbage at the bottom of the fire escape to bury.

Whatever the scavengers didn't get at, that is; he just hoped he wasn't drawing vermin to the apartment, now that he thought of it.

He caught hints of light around the doorframe as Ricky returned. "Dad? I got the flashlight, and the power's still out."

"Yeah, I don't think we should expect it to come back anytime soon," Nick called back. He wondered if the power plant employees had gotten sick or if they were staying home to avoid the risk. Either way, until Zolos stopped being a threat electricity was probably a thing of a past.

If he wanted to way, way indulge his hindsight, he supposed he could've purchased solar panels. Not that he would've been able to install them on the apartment roof.

"Not ever?" his son asked, sounding fearful but trying to hide it. "It's really dark, even with the flashlight."

"I know, kiddo," he replied grimly. "But you should get out the other flashlights and try to find the box of candles in the kitchen cupboard, because we'll probably need them."

"Okay."

Nick had a sudden thought. "Wait a sec!" he called anxiously. "Before that, actually as quickly as you can, you need to fill up the bathtub."

There was a long pause. "You want me to take a bath in the middle of the night? In the *dark*?" He could just imagine the look his son was giving him as he said that.

"No!" Nick said, more sharply than he'd meant to. He took a hasty breath. "Listen, Ricky, this is important. You need to fill the tub right up to the top, and you need to make sure you and Tallie don't even touch that water. You'll need to use it for drinking and flushing the toilet."

"You want us to drink from the bathtub?" Ricky sounded grossed out.

"You'll be grateful for it when there's no more water in the pipes."

There was another pause as his son mulled that over. "Why would the electricity going out make the water stop? The garbage stopping didn't."

They didn't have time for this, but his son would work quicker if he understood the urgency. "The water still works for now because it flows on water pressure. But it needs electricity to run the pumps, so if the electricity stays off the water will stop too. Probably in a few hours. We need to get as much water as we can before then."

There was no response. "Ricky, I'm going to wipe down all the empty water containers you've given me so they're clean for you to use. In the meantime you need to fill every other container you can find. Even yours and Tallie's clothes hampers, and that stack of plastic bins from the move in my bedroom closet. Then once you're done plug the sinks and fill them up, too."

"That's a ton of water," his son complained. "Do we really need that much?"

"Even more than that, probably. If we run out we'll have to go outside and find more, and any water we find might be infected by Zolos." Actually, this was the first time he'd considered that the water in the pipes might be infected, too.

Holy cow, that was a terrifying thought.

"Okay, fine, I'll fill them up," Ricky called, loud enough that a couple seconds later Nick heard Tallie crying in her room, calling for her mommy in the dark.

"Get your sister to help you!" he yelled through the door. That should calm her down by keeping her occupied. He hoped. "And be sure she knows not to touch the water in the bathtub!"

He heard the hollow sound of water running in the tub, and the murmur of his daughter's sleepy voice as Ricky impatiently explained what was going on in full big brother mode. As Nick listened to them, he wracked his brain for anything else that they needed to do sooner rather than later now that the power was out.

The food in the fridge and freezer would've been a concern, if there'd been much left. Nick hadn't deliberately set out to eat it all up fearing something like this might happen, it had just ended up being how things went. Mostly because the supplies he'd grabbed from the store were less appetizing than what he could make from the fridge.

Shut In

Now, however, he was grateful that the only things left in there were a few packs of frozen vegetables, part of an old stick of butter, condiments, and things like that. He'd have to see if he could talk Ricky and Tallie into eating that stuff before it went bad.

Nick left his kids busy storing water and pulled up the flashlight on his phone. He was about to start cleaning his empty water containers with its light, then realized that he now had no way to charge the device and the flashlight feature drained the batteries ridiculously fast.

Crap.

He might be able to figure out some way to charge it in the future, but until then he *had* to save it to communicate with Ellie, and in the most dire of emergencies so he could try to call for help from the overworked authorities. So he kept the flashlight on just long enough to dig through his camping supplies for a battery powered lantern, then turned his phone off.

The next hour was a frantic flurry of shouting instructions through the door as his kids worked to store as much water as possible. Judging by the laughter and shouting he heard from them once or twice, he had the feeling they might've been goofing off. But under the circumstances he vastly preferred that to them panicking.

As best Ricky could judge, the water pressure stayed steady during the entire time. But that might've been because it was the middle of the night, and other people might not have realized the problem and rushed to fill their own containers yet.

He had a feeling that in the morning, as everyone started to wake up and use the plumbing, the water pressure would plummet.

Speaking of which . . . "Ricky, Tallie?" he called through the door.

His daughter was too afraid to go back to her bed in the dark, so she'd curled up outside his office's door to talk to him. She'd begged him twice to let her come in so they could cuddle, nearly breaking his heart when he had to explain to the five-year-old yet again why he had to stay quarantined.

273

Nathan Jones

He heard a yawn loud enough to be audible through the door. "Ricky went back to sleep, I think," she reported.

"Well if you want to bring your blankets and pillow and sleep in the hall, you can," he told her. "But before you do, you should use the bathroom while there's still water pressure. It's going to be harder when you have to manually flush it with water."

"What?" Tallie said blankly.

He bit back a sigh. "Go potty, even if you don't think you have to. The water might be off when you wake up in the morning."

Another noisy yawn. "Okay." The faint light around the door frame faded as she took the flashlight her brother had left her down the hall. He heard the door shut, leaving him in darkness, and with a sigh felt his way over to his makeshift bed and wrapped himself in a blanket.

He knew things could be far worse, and he was glad they weren't, but even so everything looked so bleak right now it was hard not to despair. He wasn't sure how he was going to talk his kids through everything they needed to do to survive when there was no power.

How would they cook food? Did they have enough that didn't require preparation, stuff in cans or otherwise processed, that his kids could eat it cold, even if they complained? What about hygiene, and water when even the large store they'd prepared ran out?

Nick mopped sweat off his face and huddled deeper in the blankets, wondering why he'd left the window open since the fan wasn't working anymore. He hadn't gone to all that effort to repair the broken one with cardboard and duct tape just to shiver in the cold and sweat in the heat of his blanket because he couldn't be bothered to shut it.

He heard the swishing noise of cloth being dragged from outside, then the rustles as Tallie curled up in her own blanket. He could imagine her burrowing so deep in it that only a few locks of her dark brown hair showed.

"Night Daddy, love you," she murmured sleepily.

Shut In

"Night sweetie girl, love you," he said back, wiping his face again. Then he huddled into his own blankets and allowed himself to give in to exhaustion, sinking down into restless sleep again.

Chapter Seventeen
Colorado Springs

Nick felt better when he woke up.

His bedding was soaked with sweat, but the midmorning warm air coming through the window had done wonders, and he felt comfortable again. In fact, he'd slept longer than he had for a long time; exhaustion had finally caught up with him, maybe.

He climbed out of his sodden blankets, wondering if he should risk wasting water to try to clean them, and stumbled over to the door. "How's it going, kiddos?"

Tallie's voice drifted back to him, from the kitchen he thought. "We're eating chips and candy for breakfast!" He heard Ricky furiously shushing her.

Nick slapped his forehead. "Richard Berthold Statton . . ."

His son's voice came back, tone whiny. "What was I supposed to do? The microwave's not working! Neither is the stove!"

He immediately forgot about what his kids were eating. "You're not supposed to use the stove without me or your mom supervising you."

"Well what was I supposed to do?" Ricky demanded again, sounding sullen. "Mom is who knows where, and you're stuck in your office! How am I supposed to cook anything?"

"You'll just have to eat food cold, son." Nick had a sudden thought and opened the door a crack, leaning forward to sniff the air out in the hallway. "Ricky, did you leave the stove on when you discovered it doesn't work?" He didn't smell gas, but that was a real worry.

"No, I turned it off." Ricky poked his head out into the hallway, hair

276

disheveled and still wearing his pajamas.

Nick hastily yanked his head back into his office and shut the door, worried about spreading germs into the rest of the apartment. "If you really need to, you could try turning the stove on and lighting it with matches. You have to be very careful, though, and I'll need to talk you through it. But first I need you to turn the stove on again, all the way, and then sniff near it and see if you smell gas. Then turn it off right away."

"Okay." An agonizing minute or two passed before he heard his son's voice again. "I don't smell anything."

So the gas was off, too. Scrud. "You turned it off again?" he pressed. If it suddenly came back on he didn't want to blow up the entire building.

"Yeah, I turned it off," Ricky said impatiently.

"Okay, what about the water? Is there still pressure, or is it off too?"

"It's off," his son replied immediately. "Tallie couldn't wash her hands when she went potty, so I had her use some of that hand sanitizer stuff we use for road trips."

"Okay, good job. Go ahead and turn on the sink and keep it on."

"But with the stove you said-"

"If the gas turned back on we could all die if the stove is on," Nick explained patiently. "But if the water comes back on we'll want to know right away, and we will if we have the tap on."

"Oh, okay." Ricky's voice faded away as he spoke, probably back to his breakfast of junk food.

"And open a can of soup to share for breakfast!" He shouted after the eight-year-old. There was no response; he needed to have a sit down with his son about communicating, which was even more important under the current circumstances.

Sighing, Nick scrubbed a hand through his hair, still damp from sweat, and shambled over to the window, staring out at the city. It had been oddly quiet for days now, but now he actually saw people out and about. They were dressed up in masks and gloves, moving cautiously to avoid touching anything, and giving everyone around them a wide berth. Most were carrying containers of some kind, obviously searching for sources of water.

They were probably among those who'd tried to turn on the tap after waking up in the morning, only to discover the pressure was gone and they hadn't taken any precautions to have water stored for an emergency. He was glad he'd thought of it, and had pounded his head against the wall last night talking his children through getting as much water as possible.

They'd need it in the coming weeks.

Would this Zolos crisis ever end? How had the plagues of the past finally died out? Nick seriously hoped it wasn't from literally dying out, as in anyone capable of carrying the disease succumbed to it and everyone else developed an immunity. That would spell the deaths of billions of people before things settled down.

In spite of the need to preserve his phone's battery, he risked turning it on, relieved to find he still had a signal. Unfortunately, Ellie's phone was still going straight to voicemail with the box full as well. He cursed quietly to himself; his ex-wife miraculously showing up to whisk the kids away to her house would solve a lot of problems right now.

He got online, searching for any local news about the power outage, and ideally an official response about when it would be back up. There was none, which he supposed wasn't surprising, although he *did* find mentions on the city's website about the water being out. There were even instructions for how to safely draw water from the Missouri River and purify it to avoid exposure to waterborne Zolos. Including the step by step process for building a purifier using crushed charcoal and sand, then boiling that purified water as a last precaution.

All valuable instructions, which Nick resolved to write down for future reference after he turned off his phone.

Shut In

Before doing that, though, he searched for news of any breakthroughs in the effort to develop a vaccine or some other cure. There was no good news he could find there, although he saw plenty of bad news about just about everything else.

KC wasn't the only place where utilities were shutting down, and lack of water especially was forcing people to head outside, further exacerbating the spread of Zolos. The most pessimistic estimates had as much as a third of the population of the United States now infected or already dead, with that number projected to climb drastically as people ran out of resources and were forced to leave the safety of their homes in search of them.

There were plenty of those resources, since so many people dying so quickly wasn't exactly putting a strain on food supplies that would otherwise be critical at this point. The main problem was that food and other necessities were often stockpiled in warehouses somewhere, and truckers weren't available to distribute them. Federal emergency services was doing their best to gather the available resources into safe, sanitary hubs where people could go get them, but their efforts were hitting one roadblock after another as their people, more exposed to the infected than anyone else, fell ill in alarming numbers.

Including the nation's Armed Forces and law enforcement officers, stymying efforts to cut down on robbery and looting as desperate people took what they needed.

Nick felt his nose starting to run and shut off his phone so he could absently wipe it. He'd always suffered allergies in the spring and fall, and the last few days had been especially rough since he'd been keeping the window open with the fan on to hopefully blow any Zolos from the intruders outside, if they'd even been carrying it. Letting all that pollen and other junk in where it could irritate his sinuses.

He almost had a heart attack when his hand came away from his nose bloody.

For a moment he just stared at it in blank disbelief, pulse pounding in his ears. No. No no no. This couldn't be happening. This *wasn't*

279

happening. It was just a nosebleed from dry air. He got them all the time.

Even though Nick knew the symptoms of Zolos by heart at this point, he still fumbled to turn his phone back on to check the CDC website: dizziness, chills, excessive sweating-

Holy cow! His eyes darted frantically to his blankets, still damp and stinking with his sweat, then back to the screen.

-bleeding from all orifices, debilitating weakness, nausea and cramping, finally severe internal bleeding leading to death.

Nick scrambled for the small mirror from the camping supplies, which he'd been planning to use when he got around to shaving. With it he carefully checked his eyes, mouth, ears, and lower orifices. Then he did a few exploratory jumping jacks and held his gut, trying to feel any discomfort there. His stomach churned and he felt like he was going to be sick, but that was from dread, not any actual problems.

Wasn't it?

No, of course it was. He didn't and hadn't felt dizzy, he'd stopped sweating as soon as he got out from beneath the thick blankets he'd been huddling in to ward off the night's chill, and it wasn't as if he hadn't sweated under heavy blankets once it got warm before. As for chills, he'd been chilly when he climbed into bed because he'd been cold, but then he warmed up and was fine.

He just had a nosebleed, from dry air probably . . . all of his other orifices were fine. He also felt strong as a horse, no hint of weakness whatsoever. No cramping, no nausea other than from that spike of fear over whether he might be sick, which was fading as he calmed down.

Whew. He'd almost driven himself into a panic over allergies.

There! It said right on the website that by the bleeding from the orifices stage the chills and sweating would be severe, and the illness would swiftly progress to debilitating weakness and the other symptoms. He should monitor himself over the next few hours, see what was up, but most likely everything was fine.

Shut In

Grabbing some toilet paper to wad up and stuff into his nose, he headed to the door to call through instructions for what his kids needed to get done that day. Then he needed to figure out how to crap in a bucket, since he was finally reaching the point where he couldn't put the unpleasant experience off any longer. And then he'd want to think about digging another hole for waste.

Time to resign himself to living in third world conditions for the foreseeable future.

* * * * *

Ellie never thought she'd regret working so hard to keep the pounds off.

Her friends had all expressed their admiration for how quickly she'd lost the baby weight after Tallie, and kept it off as she reached the downhill stretch of her late 20s and felt her once bulletproof metabolism begin to slow.

Nick had certainly been appreciative of her efforts.

But now, limping along at what could only generously be called a walk, stomach a hollow void and mind either a vague blank or consumed by agonizing thoughts of her favorite foods, well . . .

She deeply regretted every mile ran, yoga session sweated through, and slice of cheesecake or freshly baked chocolate chip cookie or salted chocolate caramel she'd waved off.

Would she have more energy if her body had some extra pounds to burn? Would she be able to focus on moving forward in a straight line, rather than discovering she'd randomly veered off on the downhill slope of the hill beside the Interstate as she daydreamed about fried chicken sandwiches, and steak and mashed potatoes, and caesar salads, and-

Gah! Thinking of food again. It was almost impossible not to, even though she knew it just made her situation more miserable.

Hal put a supportive hand under her arm and gently led her back to a straight line. "Just a few more miles," he said, voice hoarse.

As luck would have it, while the mile markers counting down to their destination were correct, his prediction wasn't: a minute later they laboriously hobbled to the top of a low rise that gave them a view of the road ahead, to be treated to the sight of hundreds of tents and temporary structures enclosed in a high chain-link fence, sprouting up from a field stretching along their side of I-25.

A quarantine camp, built well outside the city limits of Colorado Springs.

For a moment Ellie just stood frozen, staring at the carefully laid out rows of widely spaced, small tents, and the mass of humanity on display among them. She'd never expected to be happy to see a quarantine camp, let alone eager to approach one, and ruefully thought back to the extreme lengths she'd gone to in LA to avoid going anywhere near that one.

Amazing what a week of hardship could do to a person's perspective. Then again, even if she *had* still felt that way about this camp, it wasn't as if they had much choice under the circumstances.

The moment of stunned silence was broken when Hal whooped, with surprising energy considering their hunger, thirst, and exhaustion, and whirled to pull her into a crushing hug. "This is it! We can finally get help!"

Ellie hugged him back, staring at the camp over his shoulder. Just that suddenly, all the walls of determination she'd built to keep herself moving through this ordeal collapsed, as if the sight of help only a few hundred yards away had given her permission to let herself have a moment of weakness.

She found herself shuddering with sobs as her pent up emotions flooded out, finding desperate strength of her own through her exhaustion to clutch back at him. She wasn't sure how long they stood holding each other, exulting in their ordeal finally being over, feeling some of their burden of despair lift at the sight of civilization.

It was a good moment. Incongruously, one of the best in her life in spite of the surrounding circumstances.

Ellie finally lifted her head from his shoulder, laughing a bit self-consciously as she wiped at her eyes. "Thanks," she said. "And sorry for just falling to pieces like that."

Hal laughed too, light green eyes warm. "If you hadn't, I would've. Being there to pat you on the back helped me keep it together myself." They both laughed again, easing the awkwardness of the moment, and she shifted to pull away from him.

Then he leaned down and pressed his lips to hers.

For a moment she was too shocked to respond. She should've seen that this could be where the moment they'd just shared was headed, but she honestly hadn't. To her even greater surprise, she found herself slipping back into his arms and returning the kiss with unexpected fierceness. He was a good man, and he'd been by her side steadfastly through one of the worst times of her life. And it went without saying he was good looking.

And she'd been so lonely, had missed this feeling for so long.

Then sanity reasserted itself and Ellie pulled away sharply with a gasp, taking a step back. Hal was the better part of a decade younger than her. He was barely out of his *teens*, for crying out loud! Or, well, four years out.

Still, it was ludicrous to think they'd have any hope of something serious, and in the middle of trying to survive humanity's potential extinction was a terrible time for a casual fling. Besides, all her focus needed to be on getting back to her kids. Nothing else mattered right now.

Hal was looking at her with a sinking expression, as if he could read her thoughts in whatever it was he saw on her face. He stepped back too, shaking his head. "Misread the moment, sorry."

Ellie looked away, heart still pounding from their kiss. "Not the moment, maybe, but everything else," she said gently. "This can't happen, Hal. You know that."

The young man shrugged, trying for casual but looking more like despondent. "Maybe not. I just think you're incredible, El. Brave, and determined. Beautiful. I want . . . I just think you're amazing, that's all."

The flush in her cheeks deepened at the deep sincerity in his words, but she shook her head firmly. "You're a good man, Hal. You're pretty amazing yourself. But this still can't happen."

"If that's what you really want," he whispered. His cheeks had reddened, too, and he quickly turned away towards the camp, clearing his throat and forcing briskness into his tone. "I guess we should, um, go get that help we desperately need?"

Ellie nodded and fell into step beside him, an awkward silence hanging heavy as they limped down the rise towards the camp.

There was a roadblock on the southbound side of the Interstate, a few patrol cars and a bunch of sturdy barricades. The lanes behind the roadblock for a hundred yards had become an impromptu parking lot, with hundreds of vehicles carefully parked in the two outer lanes with the center lane open, so any of them could leave at any time if needed.

That was an encouraging sight, she hoped.

A car full of people passed them as they approached, pulling to a stop at the roadblock and waiting patiently. A few seconds later a policeman in a full hazmat suit emerged from one of the patrol cars to go and talk to the driver, adjusting the strap of some heavy military style rifle slung over one shoulder as he walked.

"Well, this should give us some idea of whether or not we should start running," Hal said out of the corner of his mouth as they continued forward more cautiously. His tone was strained, obviously still smarting from her rejection.

Ellie snorted. "You think the cop guarding a government quarantine camp is going to just up and start shooting at an innocent family?"

"Probably not." He shrugged. "Still, crazy as things have gotten it doesn't hurt to be cautious."

True. She'd never expected to be kidnapped and groped by a gang of robbers in some sleepy little town in the United States of America, so it was obvious the world she knew was dying as fast as the people who lived there.

The policeman didn't suddenly go nuts on the family in the car, of course. After a few minutes, when Ellie and Hal were almost within earshot of whatever conversation he was having with the driver, he abruptly stepped back and waved the car forward.

Another officer in a hazmat suit emerged from a patrol car to guide the new arrivals to a parking space. Then, while keeping a cautious distance, he watched as the family gathered their things before guiding them on towards a pavilion near the camp's entrance, where a few people in the bright yellow hazmat suits of relief workers waited.

The policeman at the roadblock had shot Ellie and Hal a few glances as they approached, and now instead of heading back to his car he waved at them to keep coming, thankfully leaving his big rifle slung over his shoulder where it was.

Although he called out long before they got anywhere near him, tone friendly but firm. "Welcome to the Colorado Springs Quarantine Camp! We have a specific protocol for new arrivals, so I'm going to need to ask you to stop at that distance while I ask you a few questions."

They obligingly stopped, although Hal raised his voice with some urgency. "Before we get started, Officer, we need to report that we were attacked and kidnapped by a gang of robbers two days ago. We barely managed to escape."

The officer straightened, expression darkening inside the slightly cloudy faceplate of his hazmat suit and tone becoming sharp. "Was this somewhere east of Denver?"

Her friend nodded. "In Watkins."

The other man cursed and shook his head grimly. "We're aware of this group. They've been operating in Denver for years, and used the chaos as an opportunity to step up their activities. We're dealing with it."

"Dealing with it?" Ellie burst out. "There's over thirty men out there attacking small towns, raping women and taking them as sex slaves! They put their hands all over me, and would've done worse if we hadn't escaped! Even in a disaster like this, how is that not top priority in the United States of America?"

The policeman grit his teeth in clear frustration. "It is, ma'am, I assure you. Law enforcement is stretched to the limit dealing with relief efforts, and the detachment of Armed Forces assigned to Colorado to assist us was struck by a Zolos outbreak. Half are sick or in quarantine, and the other half are barely enough to handle the big cities. But we're moving against this group soon, and we're going to help all the people they've taken, you have my word."

Hal nodded at that, apparently satisfied. "That's a relief to hear, um . . ."

"Officer Merrill," the man growled.

Ellie decided to take a cue from her friend and stop trying to rile the man whose help they desperately needed. "It *is* good to hear," she said. "I'm Ellie, this is Hal."

Merrill nodded, somewhere between polite and curt. Or maybe that was just the baggy hood of his suit making the movement seem exaggerated. "Where you folks from?"

"Kansas City," Hal replied. "We were driving there from LA, trying to get home to our families. If we can get some help here, maybe a chance to contact them to let them know we're okay, we'll be out of your hair as quickly as possible."

The officer hesitated, expression becoming weary. Like he was expecting more outbursts from them. He also absently reached up to grip the strap of his rifle. "I'm sorry, sir, ma'am. As a matter of public safety, we need to hold you in quarantine until we're certain you're not carrying the Zolos virus."

Shut In

Ellie felt her heart sink; had they avoided the quarantine camp in LA just to end up in this one? Even if it was a step up from starving and dying of thirst out in the middle of nowhere, that didn't mean she wanted to be stuck here when her children needed her.

"How long will that take?" Hal demanded.

Merrill looked away. "Twenty-one days."

"Three *weeks*?" Ellie demanded, so shocked she didn't care if the question came out as more of a screech. "Why? You'll know whether or not we have the virus after just a few days, when we should be showing symptoms."

The policeman shook his head. "I'm afraid it's not that simple. You could be among the rare few who were exposed but don't get sick from it, or only suffered mild symptoms before recovering. You'd still be contagious, though, and we have to make absolutely sure you're safe before we can allow you to continue on."

She shook her own head adamantly. "I can't wait three weeks! My ex-husband might be infected with Zolos, and he's the only one who can care for my kids. Right now I've got an eight-year-old caring for a five-year-old all on his own. I *need* to get to them."

Hal put a sympathetic hand on her arm. Or maybe a cautionary one; Merrill's eyes had hardened in firm resignation, and he was fiddling with the strap of that big scary rifle of his. "That's not an option, I'm afraid. We have a mandate to detain all travelers to prevent the further possible spread of Zolos."

"But we haven't been in physical contact with anyone else since this all began," Ellie said in a voice of quiet desperation. "It's just been us two for over a week."

The officer gave her a funny look and glanced at Hal, and she felt her face flushing when she realized the conclusion about their relationship he must be reaching from that. But at the moment she had far bigger concerns than whether some policeman in Colorado thought she was a cougar.

In any case Merrill just shook his head, finally looking deeply apologetic. "I'm sorry, ma'am, but we just can't take that chance. You'll have to go in the camp."

She eyed the nearest thing to hide behind, wondering if she could make it there before the man shot her. Wondering if she was really willing to go that far, disobey the proper authorities and risk hers and Hal's lives.

After all, Nick had things in hand. And how likely was it that some random thug who'd been breaking into the homes of people in self-imposed quarantine was actually carrying the virus? A day or two more and her ex-husband could be confident he hadn't exhibited any symptoms of the disease. He'd be able to risk going back out around Tallie and Ricky, if he really needed to.

Only . . . back when he'd offered to bring the kids and come pick her up in Utah, Ellie had adamantly insisted he not take *any* chances where they were concerned. Was she ready to go back on that now?

Merrill saw her eyeing a nearby bush and reluctantly unslung his rifle, although he kept it pointed at the ground. "Ma'am, please don't force me to do something I'll have to live with. I *will* follow orders, for the safety of the people of Colorado."

Hal patted her arm soothingly and leaned towards her, lowering his voice to an urgent whisper. "We're dying of hunger and thirst, El. I know this has to be tearing you apart, but what options do we really have? Wait three weeks and hope for the best, or get shot on some road two states away from home while resisting arrest by a lawful authority?"

Ellie thought a bit bitterly that he'd thought it was sexy when she'd jumped the median to avoid that roadblock in LA, which was pretty much the same thing. But she couldn't deny he had a point. She stared beyond the policeman at the rows of widely spaced tents, feeling a surge of numb despair.

Three weeks. Her children could be gone by then. Her mom could be gone. Not to mention Hal's mom and siblings and other loved ones he was trying so hard to get home to.

There was a more selfish consideration, though. "What if someone else in there is carrying Zolos?" she asked. "You want us to expose ourselves "for the safety of the people of Colorado?"

Merrill ignored her sarcastic tone. "Well like you told your boyfriend, you'll be kept separate for five days to ensure you don't show symptoms. From that point you can join the general population, and mingle with the others or keep to yourselves to your heart's content."

Hal flushed. "We're not together," he protested sheepishly. Although his tone suggested it wasn't his preferred arrangement.

"I really don't care, sir." Merrill used his rifle to wave them away from the Interstate, towards the front of the camp where the aid workers were processing the new arrivals from the car. "Please come with me. Out in front, if you would."

Hal gently urged Ellie in that direction, and with her shoulders slumping in defeat she went. She felt like she was failing her children with every step, though.

The policeman who'd been escorting the family had already gone back to the cars, but Merrill stayed hovering warily nearby while they waited for the other new arrivals to be processed. She and Hal stayed far from the couple and their three kids, waiting as the relief workers talked to them for a few minutes.

Ellie had been able to slightly forget her agony of bodily discomforts with the excitement of reaching the camp and talking to Merrill, then the unpleasant confrontation with him. But in spite of her frantic worry for Tallie and Ricky, during a wait that seemed to last forever those discomforts all came rushing back, so insistent she slumped to the ground in misery.

It took everything she had not to curl up in a ball and whimper; there was probably food a stone's throw from here, and water too. Having to suffer when relief was so near, after going without for so long, was pure torment. Especially when she felt like a traitor to her family for doing so.

Finally the relief workers finished with the family and one led them into the camp, past two wary looking guards in hazmat suits with batons, pepper spray, and stun guns on their belts. The remaining worker called them over, having them stop the same distance of twenty feet that she'd kept the family to.

"Boy, you two look like you've had a real time of it," she said, giving them a sympathetic smile through the clear plastic faceplate on her suit's hood. She reached under the table and pulled out two water bottles, fresh out of a cooler and beaded with water droplets. "Here, they're safe," she assured them as she tossed the bottles underhand one after the other.

Ellie was pretty sure she'd found her new best friend as she desperately wrenched off the cap and chugged the entire bottle in one breathless rush.

The relief worker neatly laid two clipboards out in front of her, then began working through a long list of questions for them. It was nothing particularly daunting, somewhere between filling out paperwork for a visit to the doctor's office and going through customs while traveling outside the country. Hal also seemed to have no problem working through the bureaucratic tangle, probably used to it from traveling to visit his dad.

While Ellie was fine answering every question posed to her, she also had some of her own. "Are you going to be able to feed this many people for three weeks?" she asked, looking through the fence at all the people among the sprawling tents. She *really* didn't like the idea of being trapped in some quarantine camp when it ran out of food.

The relief worker, who'd eventually introduced herself as Cathy, gave a weary snort. "Actually, that's the fun-" she cut off, sounding embarrassed. "I was going to say the funny thing, but that really wouldn't be appropriate under the circumstances." The woman slumped down on her chair with a sigh, staring off into the distance. "No, Ms. Feldman, food won't be a problem."

Shut In

Ellie exchanged glances with Hal, and they both stayed quiet waiting for the relief worker to elaborate. After an uncomfortable silence Cathy gave a start, realizing what they wanted, and reluctantly continued. "In any other situation, if the nation suddenly ground to a halt like this we'd be experiencing critical shortages in weeks, if not sooner. Especially in population centers. But with the, well, all the people we've lost to Zolos, there's plenty of everything left for the survivors."

She sagged a bit farther down on her seat, expression bleak. "In fact, if things continue as they are we won't have to worry about running out of ready resources for years. They'll go bad before we can use them all. Not to mention the livestock and wild game populations, and agriculture that maintains itself with minimal care needed, like orchards and vineyards."

Hal gave the camp a dubious look. "I don't see any orchards or cow pastures around here."

Cathy snorted again. "True, we need to send trucks out for supplies from the nearest FETF stockpiles, or wherever else they can find them. The drivers have a risky job, and not all of them return. Probably due more to desertion than sickness, though." She shook her head, straightening briskly. "But to make a long story short, you guys will be just fine in the camp. You'll eat like kings, have all the necessities you need, and we run power for a projector so you can watch movies every night. It'll be fun."

Ellie didn't see how anything that kept her from her children for the better part of a month could possibly be fun, crappy movie nights or no. But she didn't put up a fuss as the woman continued to ask questions and jotted down their information.

"Is there some way I can contact my family?" she asked during a lull as the relief worker took a bit longer writing the answer to a more detailed question. "I left them in a bit of an emergency when my phone was taken from me."

Cathy gave her a sympathetic look; over the course of filling out the paperwork they'd told her about the attack in Watkins. "Cell phone

291

service is getting patchy in places, but we have a couple satellite phones available for use by residents once a day. It's hands off, you have one of us punch in the number while you stand in the clean zone, and you can shout the conversation across the tent."

That sounded annoying, but Ellie supposed beggars couldn't be choosers. "Can I use it soon?"

"The moment we get you processed," the suited woman assured her.

After a few more questions they were finally led towards the entrance to the camp. "You'll notice we have a lot of one-man tents," Cathy said, waving at the endless rows of temporary shelters, "as well as a lot of two or three person tents, and relatively fewer cabin tents big enough for families and almost no proper barrack tents to hold large numbers of people, like we'd usually use for relief efforts in a camp like this."

Ellie had already noticed that the tents were ludicrously widely spaced, to the point where the camp sprawled three or four times as big as it needed to be and had to be a nightmare for efficiency. "Is all the space so that so people can say separated?"

The relief worker nodded. "We're doing whatever we can to keep people from coming into physical contact by any means possible. Along with having your own isolated tents, we have the people who prepare the food do so in hazmat suits, fully sterilized at regular intervals, and then more people deliver the food directly to the residents so they don't have to gather in public areas like mess tents to eat."

"That must take crippling amounts of man hours," Hal pointed out.

"It would, if we weren't using residents to do the jobs," Cathy agreed. That provided a very interesting avenue to explore, but before Ellie could jump on it the woman continued with brisk determination. "Latrines completely circle the camp, as well as some bisecting it. Each section of camp uses a specific one, and people are encouraged to wipe down every surface they touch before and after use.

"Social interaction is allowed and even encouraged, but unless you've specifically been in contact with a person before entering the camp we strongly urge you to keep a distance of at least six feet, better yet ten, at all times as you socialize."

The suited woman had been leading them to a fenced-in and well guarded section near the front that, well . . . Ellie couldn't think of any generous way to put it but that it was filled with cages of chain-link fencing. They were completely closed off by plastic sheeting, clear on top to let in light and along the front with an optional privacy curtain, and opaque along the other three sides. They were so carefully sealed, in fact, that each one needed a filtered vent for air circulation.

The vast majority looked small enough to barely accommodate one person, with only a relative few big enough for couples or families. Inside the cages were hard, plastic-covered cots sitting on trampled grass, with no sign of toilets or even buckets for the people inside to use to relieve themselves; they must've had some other accommodation. Maybe separate latrines.

Most of the cages were full of despondent people, slumped on their hard cots or sprawled across them motionless, napping or simply in a stupor of boredom. More than a few were using the limited space to do what exercising they could, while others were talking to neighbors through the plastic walls.

"These are the isolation cells," Cathy said, tone apologetic when she caught their expressions. "I'd like to paint them in the best light, but they're basically exactly what they look like. A necessary evil to reduce the risk of infection for the residents in the camp at large."

"Reduce," Hal repeated. "Which is why even after keeping us in cages for a while, you still have all those other policies in place to prevent contact with other people or anything they've touched."

The woman nodded, shoulders slumping wearily. "We keep everyone with obvious Zolos symptoms who miraculously survive and get better in the cages for the entire duration, of course. But even if people show no symptoms after five days, they might still be carriers. As I'm sure you know, roughly one in ten people survive the virus. A fraction of those are highly resistant or even immune and exhibit little to no symptoms at all, but remain carriers."

She grimaced "And then you might also find truly selfish and despicable sorts among those who got sick but survived, who are now recovered and come to the camp but lie and say they were never exposed so they can avoid having to stay in the isolation cells for weeks. Or, who knows, maybe they just want to get everyone sick because they're monsters. Anyway, just one carrier let in among the residents would be catastrophic. We can't afford to let our guard down in the slightest until someone's gone three weeks, when we can be sure they're no longer contagious."

Ellie hadn't considered all of that. Feeling sick, she thought of Hutch's vaunted Q Team and the poor people they'd taken. His stupid quarantine procedure would get them all infected with Zolos, and while she had zero sympathy for the robbers, she hated to think that a bunch of innocent people stolen from their homes now faced even more terrible circumstances because of those animals.

The other woman's expression showed a hint of wry derision as she continued. "Unless of course the CDC is able to wade through their gigantic backlog, and we can begin testing people for Zolos en masse. As it is, we'd be waiting way longer than three weeks to get results back anyway, so what's the point?"

She hadn't been aware there was a test for Zolos, although realistically why wouldn't there be? It sure would be nice, since it meant she'd be able to get out sooner to help her kids. "Is the test accurate?"

"It has been so far." Cathy's expression briefly clouded through her hood's faceplate, likely imagining what sort of catastrophe awaited if it failed even once, before she shook herself and forced a smile. "But like I said, doesn't make much difference to us at the moment. Maybe sometime in the future you'll have the option of being tested, get out of the camp a bit sooner to get back to your kids."

The relief worker led them to an empty row of cages, made with different plastic and slightly different chain link fence sections, as if they'd been made at a different time than the others. "Here's your home for the next five days," she said, bright tone incongruous with the note of apology that remained in it. She paused, shifting awkwardly as she looked between them. "Which just leaves the question of what living arrangement you want. I know you've been traveling together, but I'm still obligated to offer you individual isolation cells. Especially since you're of different genders."

Ellie exchanged a wry glance with Hal. She'd traveled safely with him for a week without the slightest issue, and she trusted him completely. On top of that, the prospect of spending five days alone in what amounted to a plastic cage sounded awful.

On the other hand, the fact that he'd just kissed her made things a bit awkward between them. Not enough to make her go for an individual cell, though. "I think we're good sharing an enclosure," she said firmly.

Hal nodded, looking relieved; he obviously didn't like the prospect of being alone any more than she did. "Yeah, we're good."

"Okay then." The woman motioned to their right. "This cell here is your new home for the next five days. It's technically a three-person one, but the number of incoming residents has slowed drastically in the last few days, and I figure you could use the extra space."

"Thank you," Ellie said. The cage looked incredibly cramped and uncomfortable, but considering the conditions she'd been living in the last few nights it might as well have been a luxury suite.

"Once you're settled in I'll issue you blankets, clean warm clothing, and toiletries," Cathy continued. "They'll be yours for the duration of your stay in the camp." She unzipped a plastic door that opened onto a chain-link door on the cage, putting a key in one of those circle padlocks to open it. She only had the one key, so Ellie had to assume all the cages used the same lock for convenience.

The woman stepped aside to let them go in and take a look around. Ellie had strong reservations about that, like the cage was a trap waiting to snap shut on her, so she procrastinated at the doorway. "What's the camp's routine like?"

The relief worker motioned vaguely at the rows of tents. "Not much to say. Meals are delivered out somewhere between six to eight in the morning, eleven to one for lunch, and five to seven in the afternoon. We run a movie on a big screen with a projector every night at sundown."

Ellie waited, but nothing more was forthcoming. "That's it?"

The woman frowned, looking uncertain; Hal also seemed to confused as to what she was getting at. "Stay out of trouble, obviously," she replied.

"So you don't have anything to occupy the pris-camp residents?" Ellie pressed.

She knew from personal experience how potentially volatile confined, bored people could be. And the kerfuffles she'd seen had been things like conferences with a lecturer canceling at the last minute, or people waiting for mass transportation that was running late. She didn't even want to imagine the powder keg represented by a bunch of residents locked in a quarantine camp, with people dying all around them, including loved ones, and them possibly next. Then on top of all that overwhelming pressure of just sitting around with nothing to do but think about the mess they were in.

That was how riots started, or a rash of increasingly serious misbehavior. Either of which would necessitate severe crackdowns that would see them all stripped of autonomy and treated like prisoners in truth.

Cathy didn't seem to see the problem. In fact, if anything she was impatient with the line of questioning. "There are camp chores, of course. A lot of those, and volunteers can earn extra rations and things like phone and internet privileges. But with so many idle hands sitting around, jobs tend to get snapped up quickly. And if people bring in things like books or games they're welcome to make use of them. Otherwise the rule is don't cause problems, and you'll be fine."

Ellie wasn't worried about herself or Hal, she was worried about everyone else. But she supposed she should probably see the situation in the camp herself before deciding whether she should try to talk to the people in charge about potentially defusing a powder keg.

Besides, she was sure they weren't stupid and were keeping tabs on the problem.

"Do you need to use the latrine before you go in?" the relief worker asked. "Otherwise you get a chance once an hour, a separate set of latrines that are thoroughly sterilized between each use to a level we simply can't manage for all of them, only the highest risk ones for the isolation cells."

Hal glanced at her and shrugged, and she shrugged back; after days of starvation and thirst, even after drinking a bottle of water she was fine for the moment. "I think we're good," she said. "But what about the phone call? During my last call with my ex-husband he told me he might be infected, so he was going into quarantine in his office and leaving my eight-year-old son to care for his five-year-old daughter on his own."

Cathy's expression was suitably horrified at that. "Oh honey, I'm so sorry." She hesitated. "I think I can get you in for an emergency call in that case." She glanced at Hal. "And you, hon?"

He hesitated. "My family was in an exposed apartment complex. They were fine last I spoke to them, but . . ."

"But I'm sure you want to know for sure." She turned away from the open cage. "Okay, let's head to the phones. Then after that you'll probably want to eat, even if it's between mealtimes."

Ellie bit back a longing groan at that. "Thank you, Cathy," she said quietly, voice fervent with sincerity. "Thank you so much."

The woman shifted in obvious embarrassment. "We do what we can," she mumbled.

At one end of the cages, still in the fenced-in isolation area, were a few clusters of tents near a row of porta-potties where a dozen or so relief workers and guards in hazmat suits busily managed residents let out of their cages.

Ellie and Hal gave the potentially infected people a wide berth, with Cathy picking them a route that would keep them well away as she guided them to one of the tents. She led the way in, tying back the entry flaps so they wouldn't accidentally brush them as they followed.

Within the tent was a single phone, enclosed in a plastic box. "Don't touch anything in here," the relief worker said, motioning for them to stand on a plastic tarp near the entrance, still beaded with droplets and reeking of bleach. As they complied she moved to the phone and hovered her hand over the number pad. "I'm afraid I can't offer you privacy under the circumstances. What's the number?"

Ellie told her, and the woman briskly punched it in. But to her dismay, the phone's speaker immediately made the noise of a call going to voicemail, followed by the beginning of Nick's familiar, professional message.

Cathy gestured, a silent question about whether she wanted to leave a message. Ellie nodded, and they all waited tensely for the beep. "Nick, this is Ellie," she called across the distance. "I'm not sure what's going on with you, hope you're okay, but I'm just calling to let you know I'm in a quarantine camp outside of Colorado Springs. I had no choice but to stay, and they won't let me go until I've waited out the whole three weeks to make sure I'm not a Zolos carrier."

She took a deep breath. "I'll try to call you when I can, but I lost my phone so you won't be able to call me. I'm sorry I won't be able to come back to help you with the kids. Keep them safe, and let them know I love them."

The relief worker hung up. "Try again?"

Ellie nodded and gave her the number again. It once again went immediately to voicemail. As Cathy hung up Ellie stood staring at the phone with dread churning in her gut, barely aware of the woman getting the number of Hal's family so he could make his call.

There could be any number of reasons why Nick's phone was off, even something as simple as that he'd forgotten to charge it. But that didn't stop her mind from immediately jumping to the worst possibilities.

What if friends of the criminal her ex-husband had killed had come back? What if Nick had been infected by Zolos during that attack, and it had somehow managed to infect their children? What if the building had caught fire and forced them to flee into a disease-ridden city?

What if what if what if.

The call connected, and a woman's sharp voice answered. "Hello?"

"Mom, it's me!" Hal called across the tent, voice thick with relief. "Are you all right?"

"I'm fine," she replied, not much warmth to her tone. "We made it to your apartment and we've been surviving, mostly." She sniffed. "You didn't leave us much to work with, though."

Wow, her friend hadn't been lying about their relationship being strained. The young man flushed. "You know I empty the fridge and freezer before visiting Dad."

"So once again that useless waste of space makes things harder for me." Hal visibly tensed, looking about to heatedly protest, but before he could his mom continued. "Well you'll need to find us more when you get back. Nonperishable stuff, too, because the power's out in the whole city."

"Wait, what?" Ellie burst in, not caring if she was interrupting. "The power's out?"

There was a pregnant pause. "Who is that?"

"My friend Ellie," Hal said, shooting her an apologetic look. "We've been traveling together."

His mom made an incredulous sound. "So while your brothers and sister are starving, you took your sweet time getting back so you could shack up with some skank?"

Ellie felt her cheeks catch fire, overcome by a surge of embarrassment and anger she hadn't felt so strongly since high school. By the phone Cathy shifted awkwardly.

"Mom!" Hal said sharply, then hastily continued before she could get a word in edgewise. "I'm stuck in a quarantine camp for three weeks. I'll be back when I can. Don't go outside unless you absolutely have to."

"Three week-" she began in a furious tone, but Hal was already nodding to the relief worker to hang up. She wasted no time doing so.

"Sorry," he told Ellie, looking at the ground. "I guess now you see how she is."

She supposed she did; she had to admit part of her had wondered if Hal's relationship with his mom was a mark against him, but it seemed more reasonable now. She patted his arm. "Now we know the power's off in KC."

He looked relieved at her letting him off the hook about her mom's outrageous insult. "That might be why you couldn't get ahold of your ex," he said. "He probably turned off his phone to save the battery." He frowned. "I should've told Mom to do the same."

With some effort, Ellie resisted the urge to say she wouldn't be too heartbroken if that woman's phone died and Hal wasn't able to talk to her anymore.

Cathy cleared her throat. "Sorry, but we should get you guys to your enclosure."

Nodding, Ellie joined her friend as they followed the relief worker out of the tent, then down the rows of cages to their prison for the next five days.

Hold it together, Nick. It's only three weeks . . . you've got this.

He'd better, since there was no other option.

Chapter Eighteen
Separated

". . . let them know I love them." *Click.*

Nick turned off his phone then sat staring at it in the growing dark, a hollow feeling in his gut. Ellie wasn't coming. She'd been his last fleeting hope of caring for the kids while he was trapped in quarantine, and now he didn't know what he was going to do.

What *could* he do? Just assume he didn't have Zolos because he hadn't shown any symptoms, and hope for the best? With the lives of his children at stake? He was almost done with the four days when he'd expect to get sick, and like his scare at the school and store on that first day, he'd done his time with no reason to believe he was carrying the virus.

Then again that was probably what the third of the country who were dead or dying, as well as the seventh or so of the world's population, had thought. Look at how that had turned out for them.

What was he going to do?

Nick closed his eyes, took a steadying breath, then climbed out of his office chair and shambled over to the door. "Kids!" he called firmly. "I just got a message from your mom!"

Their rush to the other side of the door was so enthusiastic that he heard them even barefoot on the carpet. "Did you call her back?" Ricky shouted. "Is she on the phone?"

It was physically painful to have to disappoint them. "She told me she's staying at a camp. They're going to take care of her and keep her safe, but she has to stay there for three weeks."

"A quarantine camp?" Ricky asked anxiously. "Is she sick?" Tallie started to cry.

"No, she's fine!" Nick tried not to shout. "They're just keeping her there to make sure she doesn't get sick, okay?"

His son wasn't done with the uncomfortable questions. "Mom was going to come and take care of us. What do we do now?"

"We'll have to work even harder to take care of ourselves," Nick replied. "Let's talk about what else we need to do now that we know she's not coming for a while."

"What if I can't?" Ricky whined. "I can barely do all the stuff you try to tell me to do right now." He started crying, and because he was Tallie started up again too.

"You can," he assured his son. "You're doing great."

"No I'm not!" Moments later he heard a bedroom door slam.

Nick bit back a curse and leaned his forehead against the door. While he was sitting like that, struggling to deal with his mounting frustration and hopelessness, he heard Tallie's tiny voice, still full of tears. "Daddy, I know you're being cor-cor and teened right now, but can you take a break and spend some time with me? I'm lonely and Ricky always tells me to go away when I want to cuddle."

His heart broke at the pain in his daughter's voice. "You know I can't, sweetie. But how about you get your blanket and pillow and come lie down by the door, and we can talk for a bit."

"They're already here," she said morosely. She sniffled. "I want Mommy to come back."

"I know, Tallie," he said quietly, swallowing a lump in his throat. "Me too. But she'll be gone for another three weeks, and there's nothing we can do about it."

* * * * *

Being locked in a cage for the foreseeable future . . . wasn't as bad as

Shut In

Ellie had expected.

Sure, before long she knew she'd be climbing the chain link walls and ceiling, or even trying to outright gnaw through them, if not from desperation to get back to her children then out of sheer boredom. But that hadn't hit yet.

What *had* hit was the relief, guilty as it was considering her need to get home, of not having to hike until she dropped from exhaustion. Not having to go hungry or thirsty or freeze or sunburn. Of being able to catch up on much needed sleep, even on an uncomfortable cot, and let her dead muscles rest and begin to heal.

Cathy made sure they got a meal within half an hour of being locked in, brought around by a camp worker in a hazmat suit. It was soup, watery and not particularly filling, and definitely nothing any half decent cook would put their name to, and packets of crackers that probably didn't add much nutritional value. Although they did provide some much needed salt for the bland soup.

It was simultaneously the least enjoyable meal Ellie had ever eaten, and the most delicious. She supposed there was something to the saying that hunger was the best spice.

Along with the food they were each provided a two-liter jug of water, fresh from some tap but not overly chlorinated or filled with other junk like some tap water she'd tasted while traveling. To be honest it was better than what she drank at home, which was something.

Once her belly was full for the first time in she couldn't remember how long, exhaustion hit her like a lead blanket, pulling her down onto her cot with a groan of relief. She rolled herself into the thin, scratchy blanket they'd provided and allowed herself to drift off, mumbling a sleepy "good night" to Hal even though it was still the middle of the day.

Ellie started awake to the sound of a cage door clanging shut. It turned out to be hers, Hal coming back escorted by a relief worker in a yellow hazmat suit. "Bathroom break," he said as she blinked the sleep from her eyes and sat up. The sun was significantly lower in the sky, so she must've been out like a light for hours.

The relief worker paused in closing the door. "You need to go while I'm here?" he asked, voice muffled by his hood. "Next chance is in an hour, and until then if you have an, ah, emergency in your cell, you'll have to clean it up yourself."

As it turned out, her bladder was uncomfortably full, and there was sort of a queasy feeling in her lower gut that suggested the bad soup she'd eaten earlier was in a hurry to work its way through her. "Yeah," she mumbled, pushing to her feet and reaching for her shoes. "I probably should."

As it turned out, a simple trip to the bathroom was a major hassle under quarantine procedures. At the bank of porta-potties she was directed to a dispenser for gloves, and once she had them on the relief worker gave her a container of chemical wipes. "Clean every surface you might possibly touch, before and after you do your business," he said in a bored voice. "Then when you're done clean the outside of the wipe container too."

On the plus side, the porta-potty was surprisingly modern, constantly ventilated and with an airtight flushing mechanism so there was barely even any odor. Presumably measures to keep airborne Zolos from spreading. Instructions on the back wall outlined steps for flushing, mainly closing the lid to prevent spray during flushing and then as the flushing mechanism was automatically sanitized.

Ellie probably went overboard wiping down every conceivable surface, even those that were supposed to be sanitized by the flushing mechanism. But after all, she was in a *quarantine* camp using toilets reserved for those most likely to be carrying Zolos, so maybe not.

It took forever, and she was half surprised the aid worker waiting outside didn't start pounding on the door to ask if she'd fallen in. Then she discovered that the diet of gas station snack foods she'd subsisted on for the last week, then days of starvation, hadn't done much to help her stay regular. She eventually gave up, confident she could hold out for at least an hour if she had to, then began the laborious process of wiping down every surface again.

A lazy, selfish part of her wanted to make a token effort and get out of there. After all, she was confident she wasn't carrying Zolos. But since that was the reason she'd been instructed to wipe the place down *before* using it, since she probably wasn't the only one who felt that way, her sense of personal responsibility wouldn't let her take any half measures that might affect others.

After all, Ellie couldn't be completely sure she was safe. And what if the next person to use this porta-potty was having a bathroom emergency and didn't have time to properly wipe the place down? She needed to faithfully follow the instructions for before *and* after use, because it only took two people making a mistake to turn one Zolos case into two, maybe even more.

And even the best people made mistakes. Helping people in the workplace deal with that reality with patience and supportiveness had been a major part of her job.

So she spent just as long readying it for the next user, then wiped down the outside of the wet wipes container. Job done, she gratefully ducked outside and discovered that the reason the relief worker had been so patient was because he'd just wandered off. One of the guards watching the porta-potties took her back to her cage, using his universal key to open the lock and let her inside. She was barely through before he slammed the door behind her and clicked the lock shut.

"Hey, you were way faster than me," Hal said lightly as she kicked off her shoes. He was lounging on his cot, apparently twiddling his thumbs with nothing else to do.

"Really? Then you must've taken forever," she shot back wryly as she settled onto her own cot. She was wide awake now, but it wasn't as if there was anything else to do.

Luckily, during their time together her friend had proven interesting and entertaining, so talking to him was a great way to pass the time. He had a way of sneaking wry humor into their conversations, so one second she'd be focused on the topic and the next she'd find herself laughing her head off.

Maybe it was because it was on both their minds, but they talked a lot about their families, Ellie's children and Hal's brothers and sister. Todd was the oldest of those, a couple years older than Ricky, then Linny, or Caroline, had just turned seven. The youngest, Denny, was about Tallie's age, and actually sounded like he had a lot of the same quirks as Ellie's daughter.

Whatever relationship her friend might have with his mom, he genuinely cared about his siblings. It was obvious in the smile he wore pretty much the entire time he talked about them, the amusing and heartwarming stories about the time he'd been able to spend with them.

He seemed equally charmed by Ellie's stories about Ricky and Tallie, and joked that they should arrange a playdate for the kids when they got back to KC. "It sounds like they'd get along great," he concluded.

That put a bit of a damper on the conversation for her, the indirect reminder that they were three weeks away from getting home to their loved ones. And then only if they could somehow arrange transportation once they finally got out of the quarantine camp.

Thankfully, before the mood could turn gloomy a camp worker came around with dinner.

Ellie could only conclude that the camp had small meals for lunch and probably breakfast, but made up for it with a good solid dinner. They were given two frozen hamburgers each, not large but big enough, heated piping hot in foil wrappers. They were also each given an apple, a carrot, and a bottle of soda. There were even candy bars for dessert.

"We should save what food we can in case of an emergency," Hal said, suiting his words by tucking his soda and candy into the duffel bag the relief worker had provided for the spare change of clothes, blanket, and toiletries she'd provided him.

Ellie was famished, but she heartily agreed with the idea. Days of starving had driven home the firm resolution that she never wanted to be in that situation again if she could avoid it, and anyway on the way into the camp she'd been wondering how stable the mood here was. If a riot or Zolos breakout caused the relief workers to stop providing food, or even forced them to flee the camp entirely, it would be good to have extra supplies.

Ditto with the spare clothes and blankets and water bottles they'd been given; having to walk away from the faucet in that rest area, with no way to store any of that water for the trip, had driven home once again just how incredibly useful even something as simple as a water bottle was.

As the sun set and darkness fell, loudspeakers across the camp announced that the nightly movie would be starting soon. It was projected onto a big white cloth on the western end of the camp, pretty much as far away from the cages as possible. Which became readily apparent as the screen flickered to life, the images on it joined by faint, tinny sounds she could barely make out.

Ellie patted her cot, which had the best view of the screen, in a silent invitation for Hal to come sit by her. The part of her that didn't want him to get the wrong idea warred with the part of her that had wanted to hold his hand in their little leafy burrow, and lost.

Besides, with the sun down it was starting to get chilly, and she knew from inadvertently cuddling with her friend that he was practically a human hot water bottle.

Hal settled down at the far end of the cot, giving her plenty of space. She was actually a bit disappointed by how much, then annoyed for feeling that. "Well, at least the clear plastic on our cage faces the projector screen, we can watch the movie from jail," he said wryly. "Too bad it doesn't have subtitles."

"I can pick out a word here and there," Ellie said, trying to be optimistic. He chuckled, and they fell silent and watched.

At least for a few minutes. Then the young man shifted slightly, cleared his throat, and glanced at her out of the corner of his eye. "Hey, um, I wanted to talk about what happened earlier."

It wasn't a stretch to guess what he was talking about, and Ellie tensed slightly; if he couldn't take the hint this was going to be an awkward movie. An awkward five days, even.

Especially since part of her was secretly glad he wasn't giving up so easily. She shoved that part down. "I thought we left things pretty clear."

He looked calm but determined. "You did. But-"

"No buts," she cut in sharply. "I didn't change my mind in a few hours. Whatever I might feel, it doesn't solve all the complications that come from such a large age difference."

"So you feel something?" Hal said quickly. When she fumbled for an answer he gave her a hopeful smile; she'd be lying if she claimed to be unaffected by it, protests dying on her lips as he continued. "Then maybe there is something to talk about. I've spent my entire life overcoming problems. I don't see any as insurmountable, especially if it's something I really feel strongly about." His voice became more intense in a way that made her heart pound. "Or someone."

Ellie couldn't bring herself to meet his gaze. Because she wanted to, and she wanted to see what might happen if she did for long enough. Instead she pushed to her feet. "Then let's focus on the not-insurmountable problem of getting home. That's what we need to be worrying about right now."

"Three weeks of forced confinement has sort of taken the urgency out of that," he murmured patiently. He remained seated, looking up at her with those piercing green eyes of his. "El, you know I care about you. If you can honestly tell me you don't feel the same then that'll be the end of it, and I can resign myself to that."

He paused for an agonizing few seconds, then continued quietly. "Can you honestly tell me that?"

Ellie couldn't hold his gaze and looked away. "This is a terrible time for this."

Shut In

"Will there ever be a better time with the world falling apart around us?" She had no answer for that, so he continued with deep feeling. "You're the most amazing woman I've ever met. I've never known anyone more determined, more intelligent and resourceful, more courageous . . ."

He paused, solemn eyes holding hers as if she was the only person in the world. As if nothing, not the end of society or the quarantine camp they were in or anything else, mattered in that moment but her. It made her heart pound even harder. "More beautiful," he continued softly, with deep feeling. "After all we've been through together, Eleanor Feldman, I can't imagine loving anyone else."

Love? She felt her face heating. "Hal," she said, making her voice as gentle as she could, "we barely even know each other. And you're-"

"Younger than you," he finished wryly. "That doesn't change what I feel." He reached forward, hesitated, then took her hand and held it lightly. Giving her a chance to pull away again if she wanted.

She surprised herself by not doing so.

That seemed to embolden Hal a bit. "I'm not blind to the obstacles. The age difference means we've experienced entirely different things in our lives, have different perspectives and priorities. And you have children, and a complicated relationship with your ex. And people would probably judge us for being together. If things were normal our relationship might be pretty much doomed from the start."

He gently squeezed her hand, sending a thrill through her, and his voice gained intensity. "But things aren't normal, Ellie. We can't be sure we'll even be alive next week, and even if we are the world might never be the same again. I barely cared about busybodies judging me when society still functioned, why worry about what people might think when the world of last week hardly even exists anymore? I don't want to die knowing I had a chance to be with you and didn't take it."

Ellie reluctantly took her hand back. "I don't want to die knowing I failed my kids, Hal," she said quietly. "You're right, we do have different priorities."

He looked away, disappointed. "You know I'm with you every step of the way in finding your family, no matter what you decide about us."

"What about when I find them?" she pressed. "What if we *did* have a relationship? Are you ready to have two young children in your life, maybe even take on a parental role if our relationship got to that point?"

Hal gave her a strained smile. "Hey, I do pretty good with kids. I just got finished telling you all about my brothers and sister, remember? I'm already involved in raising them, at least as much as my mom lets me. And from what you've told me about Ricky and Tallie, they sound pretty amazing."

Ellie looked away. "I need some time to think about this, okay? For me, a relationship isn't just some impulsive fling to jump into on a whim. It can't be. If it's not serious, if it doesn't have a future, then it doesn't matter how much I might want it. It can't happen."

"It's not a whim for me, Ellie," he said with pure conviction. "I've never been more serious about anything in my life."

She had to force herself not to make a snarky quip about that not saying much given his age; it wouldn't be fair to him. "If that's true, then give me the space I need to make a decision."

She'd meant that figuratively, but Hal made it symbolic and retreated to his own cot, although he shot her a wry smile. "I can live with that. Although it would've been nice to cuddle during this soundless movie."

Oh boy, was he not wrong about that. Especially when facing the prospect of being isolated for days in this little plastic cage; having the comfort of being held by someone she trusted, someone she could even admit she had feelings for, would mean so much.

To avoid giving into the temptation as much as to get him to drop the subject, Ellie latched onto something else he'd said. "Well, why don't we supply the dialogue ourselves? Some of the funnest movies I've ever watched have been with friends making up outrageous lines."

Shut In

Hal perked up, showing boyish enthusiasm for the idea, and allowed himself to be distracted from more serious topics.

The rest of the movie was spent pleasantly, with more smiles and even laughter than she'd expected, given the situation. Once the ending credits finished and the screen turned off, her friend quietly wished her goodnight before wrapping up in his blanket facing away from her. Ellie appreciated him giving her the space she'd asked for, but was surprised to find she also regretted the distance.

Was she seriously considering this?

Her friends would tease her for being a cougar, assuming they were still alive and well. They'd tell her this was some crazy impulsive rebound relationship after the divorce, and she was making a huge mistake she'd regret.

But Hal hadn't been wrong, that what they'd experienced together had created a bond she'd rarely felt before. She liked him, she trusted him, and, if she was being honest with herself, she was more than a little attracted to him.

If he really was sincere, and if he was mature enough to take a relationship seriously, then what exactly was stopping them? Her own dad had been almost a decade older than her mom, although the situation wasn't at all the same for multiple reasons, including that they'd gotten married and had her when they were both older.

Still . . .

Still, Ellie had always been a firm believer that when emotions were involved it was wise to avoid making a decision, let alone taking action, until she'd slept on the issue and had time to consider it more carefully. That wasn't always possible, but where it was she did the best she could to abide by that resolution for minor choices, and doubly so for important life decisions.

Like this.

So she curled up in her blanket and turned to face away from Hal, towards the chain links and opaque plastic of the cage wall. She was uncomfortably aware that they were both facing away from each other, when she was having trouble avoiding admitting to herself that she'd rather be facing the other way and looking at him.

Heck, she'd rather be holding him. Ellie closed her eyes, struggling to push her roiling emotions down, and tried to let her exhaustion pull her once again into sleep.

And, hopefully, in the morning a better understanding of how she felt about her friend, and what she wanted in their relationship.

* * * * *

"Tallie! No! What are you doing? NATALIE ELEANOR STATTON!"

Nick lurched out of bed at the sound of Ricky's furious shouting, swiftly followed by Tallie's familiar, piercing "you're being mean and it's not fair!" wail.

He was still only half awake, stumbling towards his office door, when the furious pounding began from the other side. "Dad!" his son yelled. "Tallie was playing in the tub!"

"I wasn't playing!" Tallie interrupted her air raid siren yelling long enough to shout. Her crying swiftly drew closer as she joined Ricky outside. "I-I had an accident because I couldn't see in the dark, so I needed to take a bath."

"Dad told us not to go in the tub," her brother scolded her. "Even if you have an accident!"

She sniffled miserably. "I didn't *want* to, the water's really cold and it splashed everywhere when I got in."

"I *know*! That's why you're not supposed to get in there!"

Actually, they weren't supposed to touch the water to avoid contaminating it. But that ship had obviously sailed. Nick sighed; he supposed he shouldn't be surprised. It was optimistic to expect two little kids to be responsible about something like this.

"Hey, hey!" he called, interrupting their argument. "It's okay, we'll just use that water for flushing the toilet. Just don't get any of the other water dirty, because we need it for drinking and if it's dirty we'll get sick."

Tallie sniffled some more. "I'm cold. I'm going to bed."

"Okay good night, sweetie, love you," Nick told her. There was no answer. He didn't hear Ricky, either.

With a sigh, he settled down beside the door with his back to the wall, head in his hands. It hadn't taken long for the novelty of camping out in the apartment with no power to fade for his kids. They were obviously struggling, and to be fair so was Nick; being confined in his office was proving to be even worse than he'd expected, and he'd assumed it was going to be pretty miserable.

Everything about it was less than ideal, far closer to third world conditions than he'd ever been before. Even, ironically, on actual camping trips.

He could live with the tepid, stale water, the cold food eaten straight from the can, and sleeping on a few cushions dragged in from the den's couch. He could even live with having to relieve himself into a bucket and then go outside to dispose of it, leaving the increasingly filthy container outside on the fire escape the rest of the time.

Nick honestly wasn't sure his best efforts were doing enough when it came to hygiene and basic living conditions, because at some point in the last day or so the apartment had started to reek, and it was getting worse and worse. He didn't know if it was because of the waste he'd dumped into the open hole outside in lieu of burying it when it got full, or if there were dead people in other neighboring apartments, or if it was solely the dead body he'd buried near the bottom of the fire escape, but whatever was causing it Ricky and Tallie had complained that the apartment was starting to smell really bad.

Even the office, which he kept constantly aired out, got a hint of that reek.

He'd told his children to endure the stink rather than opening their windows and potentially exposing themselves to the virus. He wasn't sure if that was necessary, or even the right move, but he'd go with caution where he could. Then again, if the stink was coming from people dead from Zolos in other apartments, then maybe getting fresh air from outside was the best option.

He didn't know. Every option seemed to have its problems, and his mind was so wound down from stress and worry that he was pretty sure he wasn't thinking completely straight.

"Dad?"

Nick jumped at the tiny voice coming from right outside the door. "Ricky?" He hadn't realized his son was still there. Especially since the boy usually shouted through the thin barrier as if he was on the other side of a football field. "Is something wrong?"

"Something?" He heard strained laughter. Or maybe it was sobbing. "Everything's wrong! It's dark, and it's so cold I have to wear my coat and socks at night, and we're almost out of food we don't need to cook . . . how am I supposed to cook all those bags of rice and beans you got at the store? I wouldn't know how even if we did still have the stove."

"I-" he trailed off helplessly; he'd have trouble solving that problem even if he was there with his kids. "We'll figure something out," he finished lamely.

"Everything takes forever when you have to tell me what to do through the door," Ricky continued. "And I usually get it wrong anyway! And Tallie won't do what I tell her to, and she's driving me crazy because she's bored, and I-" he cut off with a hiccup. "I can't do this, Dad."

He sounded so forlorn. Nick put a hand on the door, wishing he could hold his son. "Sure you can, kiddo. I know things seem hard right now, but you're doing great."

Shut In

"No, I'm not!" The shout was so loud and sudden it made him jump, the boy's moroseness turning to sullen fury in an instant. "I can't take care of Tallie, I can't take care of myself, you're just sitting in your office shouting at me all the time instead of helping, and now Mom's not coming!"

"Ricky . . ." Nick trailed off helplessly.

His son's fury was gone as quickly as it appeared, and he began sniffling in pure misery. "I'm scared, Dad. We're trapped in here, and we don't have electricity or running water or anything, and Zolos is everywhere. Are we going to die?"

"No!" he snapped. "Don't even think like that, Richard Statton. We'll get through this." There was no response. The silence hung heavy as Nick agonized, then he took a deep breath and spoke firmly. "Listen, the four days to see if I have any symptoms of Zolos are almost over, and I'm feeling fine. Just hold out a little bit longer, and once we're sure I'm not sick I-" he cut off to steel himself, hoping he was making the right decision, then continued determinedly, "I'll come out and take care of things, okay?"

It wasn't what he wanted, and Ellie would probably kill him for taking the risk, but what choice did he have? The kids couldn't take care of themselves, and their mom couldn't come to help them for weeks. There was no one else who could do the job, no one he could ask. So it had to be him.

Ricky took a shuddering breath. "Really?" he asked in a tiny, hopeful voice. "Is-is it safe?"

I sure hope so. "If I don't have any symptoms, it'll be safe," he promised solemnly. "Just keep things together and take care of your sister for another day, and tomorrow night I'll come out and take over for you."

His son sniffled one last time. "Okay."

Nick rapped lightly on the door. "Why don't you get some sleep, buddy. We'll talk in the morning."

Nathan Jones

"All right. Love you, Dad."

"Love you, son."

Once Ricky was gone Nick crawled back over to his own makeshift bed, climbing under the covers. But while he'd advised his son to sleep, he wasn't able to take that advice himself. He was far too worried about the future, second-guessing every decision he'd made since that phone call from the elementary school had woken him up from his nap a week ago and this nightmare had begun.

Especially the promise he'd just made Ricky. He hoped he'd made the right choice, but honestly what else could he do?

Giving up on sleep, and needing something to keep him going before he let his despair swamp him, Nick risked turning on his phone to see if Ellie had managed to get another message to him. But although he'd been prepared for the very probable disappointment of there being none, what he wasn't prepared for was that his phone had no signal at all.

Coverage was down in this area. Temporarily? Under these circumstances probably not.

It was just one thing after another, wasn't it? He cursed quietly to himself and banged his head back against the door, then winced and listened to see if he'd woken up his kids. If so, neither of them voiced a complaint.

So he was trapped here, completely cut off from the world, his children unable to care for themselves without him. Did he have any choice but to wait out his last day to see if he showed symptoms, then risk going out to take care of them?

How had he ended up in this nightmare? Had it really been just over a week since things had been normal? When his world had been falling apart around him because of his divorce and financial troubles, and he'd thought things couldn't possibly get any worse?

Nick didn't want to tempt fate by wondering what else could happen.

Epilogue
Big Decisions

After a day in the cage, Ellie was seriously contemplating the value of leaving out some food in a hypothetical 72-hour kit in favor of a cheap paperback.

Any paperback, even a freaking dictionary. In fact, as boredom gripped her in its claws until she wanted to scream, she actually amused herself by trying to figure out what item would prove most entertaining for the longest period of time for the smallest size and weight.

She even dragged Hal into the mental exercise. It beat the awkward silence that had dominated the morning, although it didn't take long to conclude that a simple deck of cards offered the most variety of ways to entertain yourself. That or a self-charging phone or tablet loaded with all their favorite books, songs, and videos, although to Ellie that felt a bit like cheating.

Although since it was possible to have something like that, even the self-charging part probably, she wondered if that wouldn't be a surprisingly useful thing to have prepared. In hindsight, unfortunately.

Besides keeping them entertained trying to figure out the best way to be entertained, it kept Ellie distracted from thinking about her cellmate. Because now that she'd allowed herself to entertain the possibility of actually having a relationship with Hal, she was letting herself notice all the things she'd grown to like about him. The things she'd done her best to ignore when confronted by all the obstacles to being with him, and more importantly because she needed to focus all her energy on getting home.

But now that she literally had all the time in the world and nothing to do with it but fret about her children, it made a pleasant distraction to sneak glances at her friend and quietly admire his broad shoulders, his chiseled jaw and high cheekbones. The solid muscles not even the ill-fitting sack of the camp coveralls issued by the relief worker could hide.

The warmth in his clear green eyes, and the burning intensity that filled them when he looked at her, making her heart pound in spite of herself.

But it was more than that. Ellie thought of the quiet strength with which he'd supported her throughout this ordeal. The warmth and understanding he'd shown when she'd opened up about herself on cold nights in the wilderness, about her past and her fears for her loved ones. The trust and vulnerability he'd shown when he'd done the same. The way his solemn focus on serious issues could unexpectedly shift into understated wit that made her laugh no matter how grim the situation.

The remembered feeling of being snuggled up against his broad, warm back, nose full of his scent, and realizing how much she'd longed to stay there instead of fleeing the crude shelter they'd made. To have him turn around and wrap his arms around her and-

Holy cow, she wasn't just falling in love with him, she was apparently already well on her way. How long had these feelings been simmering in the background while she focused on survival and her family?

Logically, Ellie still acknowledged the obstacles to them being together. But the more she looked at it, the less those obstacles seemed to matter. The more she wanted to throw herself into his arms and hold him and be held, to feel his lips on hers again.

And on a more pragmatic note, five days trapped in a cage with a boyfriend sounded far more appealing than five days of them both moping about not being able to act on feelings they obviously shared.

That thought, the realization of just how easy it would be to pull closed the privacy plastic over the front of the cage and just go to town, grounded her back to reality again. Ellie took a deep breath. "Hal."

Her friend immediately perked up, guessing from her tone what she wanted to talk about. "I'm here."

That was either a really "duh" thing to say, or an incredibly insightful one. She decided to give him the benefit of the doubt. "Thank you for giving me the space to think through, um, what we talked about last night."

Hal nodded solemnly. "Have you?"

Instead of answering directly, she gazed out beyond the camp at the majestic Colorado Rockies rising in the near distance and took a breath, giving herself time to build up to it before finally turning back to him. "What would you say if I told you I don't believe in sex before marriage?"

He blinked, looking slightly crestfallen. "I, um, you don't?"

Actually, Ellie had never made a big deal about that before; she'd been with Nick for over a year before they even discussed getting married. In fact, easily half the reason they'd decided to tie the knot had been because she was pregnant with Ricky and they'd agreed it was time.

But for this specific circumstance, with Hal and given their situation and the messed up world around them, she thought it was a sensible resolution. If for no other reason than to gauge his true commitment to her.

Not to mention it also gave her a chance to confirm that her own feelings were genuine, and this wasn't some impulsive fling or rebound relationship. After all, she'd only known Hal for a bit more than a week.

Holy cow, was that all it had been? Eight days? Ellie felt like they'd been through a lifetime of ups and downs, admittedly mostly downs, together. It amazed her to think that the young man she'd assumed was a teenager, who'd wheedled his way into hitching a ride home to Kansas City, would come to mean so much to her.

"What would you say to that?" she repeated, gently but firmly.

Hal was slow to answer, genuinely considering the question. "I think it feels right," he finally said. "If this is something serious for us, let's take it seriously."

Ellie felt an unexpected flood of relief. As well as, if she was being honest, a bit of disappointment; looked as if she was in for more lonely nights in the quarantine camp. Still, mostly what she felt was a warm sort of happiness at his answer. It had been nearly perfect. "In that case yes, Hal. I do . . . have feelings for you."

Her friend, or she supposed she should start thinking of him as her boyfriend now, a thought that sent a thrill through her, beamed as if she'd just confessed her undying love. He started to take a step forward, then paused and cleared his throat. "How, um, do you feel about kissing before marriage?"

She just laughed in reply, and he grinned wider and finished stepping close so he could gently cup the back of her head, leaning down to press his lips to hers.

Ellie melted against him, sinking into the thrill of not only the heat of the kiss, of being with this remarkable man who by some stroke of good fortune she'd found herself with, but of allowing herself to let go of her reservations and sink fully into the moment. She didn't know what the future might hold but it felt good, felt amazing, to not have to face it alone.

* * * * *

It was late night when the timer counted down to the end of Nick's fourth day since being exposed to that thug who'd broken into his home.

In spite of that, Ricky and Tallie had resolved to stay up for it, as determined as if they were ringing in the New Year rather than greeting their dad from his office exile. Although the prospect of being able to see his children again certainly felt like a holiday.

They talked through the door into the night, Nick frequently responding to his children's demands to know what time it was. He used his laptop for it, since without internet he judged that even if right now, here in KC, his phone didn't have a signal, preserving its batteries was more vital to survival.

Hah, keeping his phone charged for survival. That was a phrase he never thought he'd use, aside from maybe ironically.

Just as if it was New Years, they actually counted down the final ten seconds to when he judged the attack had taken place. Tallie actually cheered when they reached zero. Of course, their excitement hit a bit of a damper when Nick insisted on doing a thorough inspection of himself for symptoms. Which was more challenging than he'd expected in the light of a flashlight. It also didn't help that his kids were constantly egging him on to hurry up as he tried to be thorough.

Finally, though, he announced that he didn't see any symptoms. As his kids cheered again he used some hand sanitizer to do a last wipe down of his skin, then changed into the clean clothes Ricky had tossed through the door for him.

Then, taking a breath, he unlocked and pulled open the door all the way, for the first time in what felt like an eternity.

Tallie immediately burst out of the nest of blankets she'd made in the hallway next to Ricky's makeshift bed, squealing in joy as Nick knelt and held his arms open for her. But just before his daughter threw her little arms around his neck, a horrible thought struck him.

What if he was infected after all? What if he was just resistant or immune to the disease and that's why he hadn't shown any symptoms, but he was still infectious? A carrier, or whatever it was called.

Was that even possible with Zolos? None of the news reports and videos he'd watched had mentioned anything like that, and it didn't seem likely he'd be immune to a virus nobody had ever seen before that wasn't like any known deadly strains.

Before he could second guess his decision yet again and act on the risk, it was too late: Tallie was in his arms and peppering his face with relieved kisses. Even though it was wonderful to hold his daughter again after he'd been so desperate to be there for her these past few days, comfort her obvious loneliness and fear, he couldn't ignore considerations of safety.

If something happened to his little girl because of it . . .

Nick gently but firmly pushed her away. It might be too late, same as when he'd hastily cleaned himself after getting that thug's blood all over him, but he had to mitigate the damage if there really was still a risk. It hurt to hold her back when she was crying for joy and hugging him with all her might, struggling to keep her arms wrapped around his neck. In fact, it felt like cutting off a limb.

But he did it.

And when he noticed that Ricky was hanging back, cautious, he was glad he had; his son had more common sense in the moment. "See your brother keeping back in case of Zolos?" he asked gently into Tallie's hurt look. "That's what you were doing, right Ricky?" His son nodded, looking guilty but not sorry, and Nick nodded back.

On the one hand it hurt him on a deep, irrational level to be so openly shunned by his son. But at the same time he was happy about it; that was the caution he should've insisted on from Tallie, as well. "Good. Keep it up for the next little while, okay? You too, Tallie. And since I was too late to warn you away, you should probably keep your distance from your brother, too."

His daughter's devastated expression tore at his heart. "But why, Daddy? You're not sick."

"I know, sweetie. But sometimes people can not be sick but still get other people sick."

"So anyone can get me sick?" She started to cry. "That means I can't cuddle with you *or* Ricky!"

Nick had to fight the overwhelming urge to sweep Tallie up in his arms and hug her tight. "Just for the next few days. Just in case."

"It's always just in case," she pouted. "This is even worse than when you were in the office with the door locked."

Shut In

She wasn't wrong. Yet in spite of this new precaution, he felt like he wasn't doing enough. Or the right thing. Like when he'd stupidly let his daughter hug him in the first place, putting his own selfish need to hold her in his arms over her safety.

At the same time, he could admit that locking himself back into his office wasn't an option. Ricky looked haggard and exhausted, practically crying with relief that his ordeal was over. The poor kid had barely managed to take care of himself and his sister while Nick was in forced seclusion, even with him calling through the door and talking the eight-year-old through the stuff he didn't know how to do. But he'd obviously been pushed beyond his limit.

"Hey, at least we get to see each other now," Nick said, offering the most cheerful, confident smile he could manage as he wearily pushed to his feet and shooed his children back a safe distance. He wasn't sure how much good it would even do, but maybe he could find gloves and wash his hands frequently, as well as everything he touched, and keep his room off limits.

For the moment, though, he was out. Best make good use of that. "Come on. Let's take a look at the apartment, get things sorted out and a hot meal cooked, maybe heat some water to wash up if you're still not ready to go to bed."

He'd been considering the best way to cook food going forward, and had settled on lighting a small fire out on the fire escape landing; the irony wasn't lost on him. Along with the camping supplies they had a small portable grill, and while there was only half a bag of old charcoal briquettes with it, he figured he could scrounge firewood.

Even if he had to break apart furniture or start tearing out wooden fixtures. Or, for that matter, go out in search of anything he could burn that wouldn't be missed in the surrounding area.

The apartment wasn't the disaster he'd feared, while listening to his kids go about their lives with only the most indirect supervision. Sure, the kitchen had dirty dishes, paper plates, and plastic utensils scattered everywhere and the garbage can was overflowing. And the den was

323

strewn with toys, dirty clothes, bedding, and empty junk food wrappers.

Although it amused Nick to notice that, while his kids were usually prone to spill their snacks everywhere and leave him to clean it up, with convenient food getting harder to find in the apartment they'd apparently been very careful to find every last morsel they'd dropped.

Hey, he could stretch the ten second rule to a week or two. Zolos tended to make other worries seem far more inconsequential.

He should've expected getting a home cooked meal made on an outdoor grill would come with its share of challenges. Not to mention taking forever. Within ten minutes of starting Ricky and Tallie both zonked out, curled up in their blankets in the hallway.

Nick decided he'd let them sleep and store what he cooked to serve in the morning. They probably weren't sleeping as well as they should with everything that had happened, either. Especially Ricky, who'd had to carry so much on his little shoulders.

He got water boiling for rice, then stood staring grimly out at the dark skyline of Kansas City. He didn't want to think about how many people were left out there, or what they were going through; it took all his energy just to focus on his own family.

In a way, he envied Ellie stuck in that quarantine camp. He almost wondered if he shouldn't take the kids out to the one outside the city. Then again, if he felt worried about being around his kids after being exposed to a single stranger who might be carrying Zolos, how much worse would it be in a camp where they specifically gathered infected people?

No, for better or for worse he was back with his children, in this apartment; he'd just have to hope for the best. But he knew he wouldn't be sleeping for the next few nights, until he was sure Ricky and Tallie weren't showing any symptoms.

Or for the rest of his life, unable to forgive himself, if they did.

Shut In

End of Shut In.

Ellie's and Nick's story continues in Going Out,

Book Two of the Isolation series.